PRAISE FOR
NEW YORK TIMES BESTSELLING AUTHOR
JULIET BLACKWELL
AND THE WITCHCRAFT MYSTERIES

"A smashingly fabulous tale."
— *New York Times* bestselling author Victoria Laurie

"It's a fun story, with romance possibilities with a couple of hunky men, terrific vintage clothing, and the enchanting Oscar. But there is so much more to this book. It has serious depth."   — *The Herald News* (MA)

"Blackwell has another winner . . . a great entry in a really great series."   —RT Book Reviews

"I believe this is the best of this series I've read. . . . Juliet Blackwell is a master . . . but truly, reading the entire series is a pleasure."   —Fresh Fiction

"[Blackwell] continues to blend magic, mystery, and romance in this sixth novel that shines with good humor and a great plot."   —Kings River Life Magazine

"This series gets better and better with each book. . . . A good mystery that quickly became a page-turner."
—Dru's Book Musings

"An enticing, engrossing read, a mystery that's hard to put down, and wickedly fun."   —MyShelf.com

continued . . .

"Sparkles with Blackwell's outstanding storytelling skills."
—Lesa's Book Critiques

"Funny and thoughtful . . . an easy read with an enjoyable heroine and a touch of witchy intuition."
—The Mystery Reader

"A wonderful paranormal amateur sleuth tale. . . . Fans will enjoy Lily's magical mystery tour of San Francisco."
—Genre Go Round Reviews

"An excellent blend of mystery, paranormal, and light humor."
—The Romance Readers Connection

BEWITCHED AND BETROTHED

A Witchcraft Mystery

Juliet Blackwell

BERKLEY PRIME CRIME
New York

BERKLEY PRIME CRIME
Published by Berkley
An imprint of Penguin Random House LLC
1745 Broadway, New York, NY 10019

ISBN: 9780451490612

First Edition: June 2019

Printed in the United States of America
1 3 5 7 9 10 8 6 4 2

Cover art by Victor Rivas/Shannon Associates

Chapter 1

A salty, heavy shroud of fog obscures the night.

Frigid waters close over my head. Sparks of silvery moonlight dance on the surface of the bay, calling to me. I flail and kick, struggling to lift myself, to breathe sweet air, my arms and legs numb with cold and exhaustion. The cheerful lights of San Francisco peek through the fog, tantalizingly far away; the island behind me is closer, but gleams and pulsates in the light of the full moon like a living, malevolent thing. The Golden Gate is the third point on the triangle, and I am in the center.

A foghorn sounds in a mournful cry.

Strong currents wrap around my legs, tugging at my feet, pulling me toward the Golden Gate and out to the vast Pacific Ocean. Lost at sea. Lost forever.

I can't go on.

I fear drowning, but remind myself: *Witches don't sink.*

At least *I* don't. I had been in the bay once before and popped up like a cork. But . . . what about now?

Icy fingers grip my ankles, drawing me down. The water closes over my head again, and I try to scream.

"Mistress!"

I struggle toward the surface. Fighting, flailing. I have to.

I *have* to.

"Mistress!" a gravelly voice called again. "Are you all right? Why are you all wet?"

I opened my eyes. I was in my own home, in my own bed. Safe.

Oscar, my ersatz witch's familiar—a shape-shifting cross between a gargoyle and a goblin—perched on my brass bedstead, leaning over to peer at me. His fearsome face was upside down and his breath smelled vaguely of cheese.

Soaked and shivering, I let out a shaky sigh. I wasn't sweaty from fear, but *dripping* wet—and smelling of brine—as though I had, indeed, just emerged from the San Francisco Bay.

"I had a nightmare," I said.

"Yeah, no kiddin'. That's one heck of a nightmare if you're manifesting in your sleep. Were you swimming or something?" Oscar waved a handful of travel brochures under my nose. "Hey, check these out. I think we should go to Barcelona first, maybe."

"Oscar, I can*not* discuss my honeymoon plans with you at the moment." My brain felt fuzzy. I sat up and glanced at my antique clock on the bedside table. Its hands glowed a mellow, comforting green that cut through the darkness. City lights sifted through my lace curtains, but even raucous Haight Street was hushed at three o'clock in the morning.

"But it's the witching hour," Oscar whined.

"Ideal for spellcasting, not for making travel plans."

Oscar cocked his head. "What better time is there?"

"In the morning. After coffee. When normal people are awake."

"But we're not 'normal people'—like we'd even *want* to be, *heh!*" He chuckled, a raspy sound reminiscent of a rusty saw.

I'm Lily Ivory, a natural-born witch from West Texas who wandered the globe for years, searching for a safe place to settle down. On the advice of a parrot named Barnabas, whom I had met in a bar in Hong Kong, I had come to San Francisco—specifically, to Haight Street— where a witch like me could fit in.

I love it here. For the first time in my life I have friends, a community, a *home*.

If only the beautiful City by the Bay weren't so chock-full of murder and mayhem.

Oscar was right, I thought, plucking the soggy night-gown away from my skin. It was unusual to manifest during a dream, to bring a physical object—in this case, water from the bay—from the realm of slumber into the waking world.

I shivered again.

"Just saying, we're both awake right now," Oscar continued. "And not for nothing, but you might want to dry off and maybe put a towel down before you ruin your mattress."

Throwing back the covers, I hopped out of bed and headed to the bathroom to take a shower. Washing away the waters of the bay with lemon verbena soap, I lingered under the hot spray until warmth settled down deep in my core.

I emerged from the bathroom to find that Oscar had gone. He had left the travel brochures fanned out in a semicircle atop my comforter, and on the nightstand was a steaming mug of chamomile tea. He had also managed to dry the bed, somehow, and to make it up with fresh sheets.

Oscar might not be a typical (read: obedient) witch's familiar, but he definitely had his moments. Not to mention he had saved my life on more than one occasion.

I sat on the side of the bed, sipped the tea, and picked up a brochure with a glossy photo of Barcelona's famous Sagrada Família. The next brochure featured the Eiffel Tower, and the last the Voto Nacional de Quito, in Ecuador.

I had promised Oscar he could tag along on my honeymoon so that we could search for his mother, a creature suffering under a curse that transformed her into a gargoyle. The problem was he had no idea where she might be, only that "gargoyles live a *long* time." I reminded myself to discuss this with my fiancé, Sailor, so that we could come up with a targeted approach before Oscar whipped up an entire world tour for us. Recently it had been difficult for Sailor and me to find the time—and the peace of mind—to talk about much of anything, much less gargoyle-guided tours.

I yawned. Speaking of honeymoons, I had a bucketload of decisions to make before the wedding, and more than a few wrinkles to iron out. My grandmother's eccentric coven had recently arrived in town; I was about to be married to a beautiful but secretive man—an attachment to whom, I had been warned, might weaken my powers. Oscar kept disappearing to search for his mother even though he was supposed to be helping secure the perfect venue for my upcoming wedding, and recently I had come to realize that instead of one guiding spirit, I had *two*, and they weren't getting along, which was messing with my magic. And finally, my beloved adopted city of San Francisco was facing a frustratingly nonspecific existential threat that primarily involved a cupcake lady named Renee.

I took another sip of tea. I also still needed to find just the right vintage bridesmaid dresses for my friends Bronwyn and Maya. Under any other circumstance I would have said "Wear what you like!" but the style editor for the *San Francisco Chronicle* was planning to do a feature on our antique bridal wardrobe, which would be great publicity for my vintage clothing store, Aunt Cora's Closet.

I may be a witch and a soon-to-be bride, but I'm also a small-business owner vying for customers on increasingly competitive Haight Street. I needed the exposure.

I also needed some rest.

Grabbing an *in fidem venire praesidii* amulet off the dresser mirror, I held it in my right hand and walked the perimeter of the bedroom in a clockwise direction, chanting:

I have done my day's work,
I am entitled to sweet sleep.
I am drawing a line on this carpet,
over which you cannot pass.
Powers of protection, powers who clear,
remove all those who don't belong here.

As I lay back down and switched off the light, waiting for sleep to take me, I couldn't shake the sensation of the waters closing over my head.

It wasn't like me to have a nightmare. Much less a *manifesting* nightmare.

It was enough to worry a weary witch like me.

Chapter 2

The next morning Aunt Cora's Closet was bursting at the seams with witches.

Fourteen elderly women—an entire West Texas co-ven, plus my mother—crowded the aisles of my shop, searching for glittery garments to rival the silver bugle bead jacket my grandmother Graciela had nabbed from my inventory a few days ago.

"The sparklier, the better," said Agatha, pawing through a rack of '80s-era, padded-shoulder flapper-revival tops.

"I want one exactly like Graciela's, except in blue," said Kay, her thick tortoiseshell glasses magnifying her rheumy eyes to a comical extent as she tilted her head back to examine a royal blue sequined jacket through the bottom of her bifocals. Her beaded glasses chain clicked. "Blue brings out my eyes."

"No two vintage items are the same, that's what makes them so special," MariaGracia said, then added in a loud whisper: *"If you want that silver one you can win it from Graciela on pagan poker night."*

My mother, Maggie, was flipping listlessly through a rack of 1950s sundresses, listening to the goings-on with a slightly bewildered expression. Not only was my mother not part of the coven, she had only very recently come to approve of magic at all. I couldn't imagine what the long road trip from Texas had been like for her, given her boisterous, opinionated travel companions.

"This one's nice," said Winona, holding up a bolero jacket encrusted with gemlike rhinestones known as crystal chatons. Their facets reflected the late-morning light streaming in through the store's street-front display windows. "It's purple, that's my color."

"That's not purple, it's *eggplant*," said Caroline in an imperious tone, tucking her subtly highlighted blond hair behind one ear as she studied a full-length silk charmeuse evening gown.

"Purple, eggplant, what's the difference?" Winona shrugged.

"And *that*, my dear, is why you've never mastered color magic," quipped Caroline.

"Well, at least I can work with a pendulum without breaking a black mirror," muttered Winona, slipping some cheesy crackers to Oscar, who was currently in his public guise as my pet Vietnamese miniature pot-bellied pig.

The thirteen coven members were women of a certain age: Darlene, Winona, Betty, Caroline, Iris, Kay, MariaGracia, Nan, Pepper, Rosa, Viv, Agatha, and, of course, my grandmother Graciela. They represented all sizes and colors and temperaments; sort of a witchy United Nations drawn from the far-flung corners of our dusty West Texas county. I had grown up with and around these powerful, stubborn, quirky witches and was overjoyed to have them with me now.

I *needed* them with me now, given everything I was facing in San Francisco.

Even if they were helping themselves to some of my best sparkly inventory, for which I would not, of course, allow them to pay.

"My mom—Lucille—can add a little bling to just about anything, if that's what you're after," offered Maya. "Her shop's right next door; you could get things altered, or even custom-made. All the glitter you could ask for."

A chorus of "oohs" and "aahs" greeted this suggestion.

Graciela, secretly delighted that her discovery of the silver bugle bead jacket had caused such a sensation, was investigating a rack of gauzy negligees, muttering racy comments. She spoke in a spicy mixture of Spanish and English that I was unwilling to translate for my coworkers.

Bronwyn and Maya were helping to rehang items, but were mostly, with good-natured fascination, observing the chaos on the shop floor.

The coven had been hitting the touristy highlights when they stopped in for jackets to ward off the summer chill. Nan and Iris already had donned garish sweatshirts purchased from the ubiquitous street vendors that catered to the tourists who flocked to town, ready to enjoy all this city had to offer but ill-equipped for its microclimate. People often equated "California" with "warm," only to discover that San Francisco had little in common with Los Angeles or San Diego. Here, a day might start out chilly and damp, soar to eighty degrees by lunchtime, then plummet into the fifties with the arrival of a thick blanket of afternoon fog. Locals learned to dress in layers.

I yawned. I'm usually not bothered much by lack of

sleep, but the memory of last night's dream troubled me. Could it have been a prophetic vision, or simply random snippets of worry and anxiety forming themselves into a story line? Or was someone—or som*ething*—harassing me by sending mares to disrupt my rest? I considered consulting the coven about it, but decided to wait for a more appropriate moment.

As I fiddled with the antique engagement ring on my finger and watched the druzy stone glitter under the shop lights, I hoped that whatever the nightmare signaled wouldn't interfere with my upcoming wedding.

Me. *Betrothed.* I still couldn't quite believe it.

At last, their hands clutching purple Aunt Cora's Closet bags filled with new-to-them clothes, the coven— and my mother—clambered back aboard the ancient yellow school bus to resume their tour of the city. Wendy, Bronwyn's coven sister and a San Francisco native, had offered to be their tour guide on the condition that she pilot the old bus. Impressed but concerned that Agatha had managed to drive them all the way from Texas, Wendy had suggested tactfully that, since San Francisco's famously steep hills were a bit of a challenge for even the most skilled chauffeur, it might be best for a local—and, as Wendy pointed out quietly to me, someone with 20/20 vision—to be behind the wheel.

"I'll see you all tonight. I'm bringing the pizza," I said.

The coven was staying with my friend Calypso Cafaro, a botanical expert with a big old farmhouse near Bolinas, up the coast. Since Calypso had filled her home with air beds and cots for a drawn-out witchy slumber party, the least I could do was to provide the occasional dinner. Calypso's farm was where the hand-fasting would be held in a mere two weeks, assuming

Oscar was able to broker an agreement with the woods spirits. This could be tricky, because I had received their help once in the recent past but had neglected to properly repay the favor.

So there was that.

"Make sure there's a vegetarian option?" Viv said, hanging out one of the windows of the old school bus. She was watching her cholesterol, but was very fond of cheese.

"Got it right here," I said, patting a pad of paper with thirteen special requests. The coven members were nothing if not opinionated. Some were vehemently anti-anchovy, others all-veggie, still others pro-pepperoni ("A meat lover's version would be delightful!"). I wondered if I should try to fit all their requests onto half a dozen pies or save myself time and trouble, and just order thirteen individual pizzas. "I'll bring some snacks as well."

"Oooh, garlicky knots?" someone called out; I couldn't tell who.

"Garlicky knots." I nodded, jotting it down. "Anything else?"

"With dipping sauce!" Rosa said.

"Knots and dipping sauce. Got it."

Seeing where this conversation was going, Bronwyn intervened to bring it to an end. "Now, won't that just be lovely! Have a wonderful tour, ladies. Tomorrow, I'll bring the makings for margaritas! Bye-bye!"

Wendy closed the door, threw the bus in gear, and roared off in a cloud of diesel exhaust, carefully navigating the crowded streets of the Haight. Bronwyn and I waved until the bus disappeared, then turned to each other.

"Phew!" Bronwyn said.

"You can say that again," I said with a smile.

"Phew!"

Bronwyn was nothing if not obliging.

A lovely, ample, fifty-something Wiccan, Bronwyn had been enjoying the opportunity to discuss the healing properties of botanical teas and tonics with Graciela's coven—not to mention grilling them about details of my misspent youth. Still, she and I had businesses to run. Bronwyn had special-order herbal infusions to mix, and I—well, I had laundry to do.

Every garment that came into my store first had to be inspected and cleaned. As much as I disliked doing laundry per se, I adored sifting through the new acquisitions. Finding inventory was a perennial challenge in my line of work, so I made frequent visits to estate sales and garage sales, as well as the Bay Area's many charitable thrift stores and flea markets. Maya scoured the attics, basements, and closets of the people she met through her long-term pet project interviewing and recording the stories of elderly Bay Area residents. And sometimes the inventory came to me: As my shop gained a reputation and had become better known, I began fielding calls from those helping their elderly aunts, mothers, and grandmothers clean out their closets.

Currently, half a dozen Hefty bags filled with Maya's latest acquisitions awaited me in the workroom at the back of the store, which was separated from the shop floor by a thick brocade curtain. I was eager to see what new treasures she had discovered. Opening one sack, I ran my hands along a cool satin aqua-colored poodle skirt from the mid-'50s, then brought out a 1960s lace cocktail-length gown with a pinch waist. Both items went into the hand-wash pile. Very few true vintage items could be run through the jumbo-sized washing machine that crowded the back room.

Maya joined me, a cup of steaming chai tea in her

hand. Maya was in her early twenties but seemed much older and wiser than a lot of people twice her age. She wore no makeup or jewelry, but her black hair was twisted into shoulder-length locks and decorated with beads and a single streak of bright blue.

"Lily," Maya said, "I wanted to ask you about something. I found a . . . well, a special item."

"I sure hope it's spangly, because the aunties snapped up most of our glittery goods," I replied as she lifted one of the Hefty bags onto the workroom table, a jade green Formica dinette set from the 1960s, and began searching through the bag.

"I wouldn't say it's spangly, exactly. Here it is."

Maya held up a man's long-sleeved blue chambray shirt. It was faded and old, and not at all attractive. Definitely no sparkles.

But that's not what bothered me. Even from across the workroom I felt its vibrations: a low, malevolent hum. My eyes fell on a series of numbers stamped in black ink over the chest pocket: *258.*

That was one nasty shirt.

Chapter 3

"What is *that*?" I asked her.

"I think it's a genuine piece of history," said Maya, restrained excitement showing in her dark eyes. "I already talked to Carlos's cousin Elena, who works on Alcatraz as a National Park Service ranger. We think it might be part of an inmate's uniform from the old prison."

Carlos Romero was a San Francisco homicide inspector who had become a good friend over the course of several police investigations. I had met his cousin Elena a few months ago, at Carlos's birthday party. When she heard I'd never been to Alcatraz, she'd encouraged me to come for a visit and promised me a personal tour. I had demurred; I had no desire to visit a penitentiary bound to be full of angry ghosts and mournful spirits. Not to mention bad vibrations.

"A . . . *real* inmate's uniform?" I asked. "Are you sure?"

Along with selling gaudy sweatshirts, the city's

sidewalk vendors peddled a vast array of Alcatraz-themed items, such as T-shirts emblazoned with *Alcatraz Swim Team* or gangster Al Capone's mug shot. Black-and-white-striped infant onesies seemed a bit macabre to me, but then I've never had my finger on the pulse of popular culture.

"I'm not certain, but I think it might be," said Maya.

"Didn't the prisoners wear black-and-white stripes, like in the movies?" asked Bronwyn, who had taken a break from straightening the racks and putting away the garments the coven had tried on and rejected.

"That's what I thought, too!" said Maya. "But apparently not, they wore jeans and blue chambray shirts like this one."

"Jeans? How stylish," Bronwyn said.

"You'd think so, but not really," Maya said. "Before the rebellious youth of the 1950s made them cool, jeans were considered working-class clothing: sturdy and inexpensive, worn by farmers, construction workers, miners panning for gold . . ."

"And prisoners?" I asked.

"Yep. I did a little research online last night. If the shirt *is* real, then the number over the pocket means it belonged to a prisoner who escaped from Alcatraz in 1937."

"I didn't realize anyone actually escaped from the Rock," Bronwyn said. "I thought that was the point of putting a federal penitentiary on an island in the middle of the bay—it was considered escape-proof."

"I can see how being stuck on an island would slow an escaped prisoner down, since you can't just walk away," I said. "But Alcatraz Island is only, what, a mile offshore? Isn't there an annual swim contest from there—called 'Escape from Alcatraz,' as a matter of fact?"

"Yes, but those are highly trained athletes competing in a triathlon," Maya said. "Keep in mind that not everyone knows how to swim, especially not in the past, when swimming pools were few and far between. Plus, the currents in San Francisco Bay are very dangerous— even good swimmers can get caught and swept out to sea."

Once again, the memory of last night's nightmare washed over me. *Currents tugging at my legs, pulling me toward the Golden Gate.*

"But you're suggesting someone *did* escape?" I asked.

"Apparently that's still up for debate." Maya consulted her notebook. "Let's see: A total of thirty-six prisoners were involved in escape attempts. Most were foiled while still on the island, six inmates were shot and killed in the attempts, and five prisoners made it into the water but were never seen again. Since their bodies were never found, the authorities concluded they were swept out to sea and drowned; but because there's no proof of *that*, either, it's possible some actually made it to land. Over the years, there have been supposed sightings of the escaped prisoners reported in South America.

"The number 258 on the pocket was Ray Perry's inmate identification number," continued Maya. "In 1937 he slipped into the water, never to be seen again."

"Where did you find this shirt?" I asked Maya. I hadn't gone near the thing, repelled by its vibrations. But now I stroked my medicine bag to center myself and held out my hands for the shirt.

"It was in Mrs. Archer's attic, along with these other items," Maya said, gesturing to the contents of the Hefty bag and passing the shirt to me.

"What do you think, Lily?" Bronwyn asked, sounding intrigued but concerned. "Does it feel like it could belong to an escaped prisoner?"

"It's . . ." I held the chambray shirt close. The cotton fabric was soft with age, but its vibrations were pure malice. I sensed despair, rage, a bleak nothingness. "I'm pretty sure it's . . . genuine."

I held it out, away from my core, and the three of us stared at it.

"Did Mrs. Archer say anything about it?" I asked.

Maya shook her head, the beads in her braided locks making a pleasant clacking sound. "She said it was there when she moved in, thirty years ago, in a bunch of boxes left behind by the previous homeowner. There were old photographs and that sort of thing up there, too."

"What was this Ray Perry in prison for?" asked Bronwyn.

"Kidnapping and bank robbery," Maya said.

At least it wasn't murder, I thought, then reflected on how bizarre my life had become that I was afraid the spirit of a murderer might be lurking in the vintage items that passed through my hands.

"What do you think, Lily? Pretty interesting, isn't it?" Maya asked.

"It's fascinating, Maya, I agree. But we can't sell this. It could be dangerous to whoever wore it."

"Dangerous how?" Bronwyn asked.

"The vibrations are . . . off."

"I guess that would make sense," Maya said. Unlike Bronwyn and me, Maya wasn't sure what to make of magic, and had a natural tendency toward skepticism. But she'd been around me enough to know that I was tapped into something she didn't understand, and she respected it. "Perry was a federal prisoner, after all, and if this really was his shirt, it's possible he survived a desperate swim in the cold waters of the bay. I imagine that experience would leave behind some bad juju."

"Some very bad juju," I said, retrieving a copper Sri Yantra talisman from my collection in the shop's glass display case. "Wear this for a few days, please, Maya, just in case. You've been handling the shirt, and it's better to be safe than sorry."

"Be glad to. I've been admiring this necklace for days," murmured Maya, studying the charm. "What is it supposed to do?"

"It's for good luck and protection," I explained. "The nine interlocking triangles form a total of forty-three smaller triangles. I'm . . . feeling triangles lately." Recently, triangles and the number three had been coming to mind. In a way, that was no surprise: Three is a sacred number in many faiths and belief systems. But the moment I spoke, I realized something: Either I was intuiting more than ever before, or I was paying more attention to my insights. Maybe all that witchy training was finally paying off.

"Cool," said Maya, slipping the amulet over her head and patting the copper sphere against her chest.

"What about you, Lily?" Bronwyn said, looking worried. "Shouldn't you wear one, too?"

"I've got my medicine bag and guiding spirits, and my witch's intuition and what-all. I'll be fine."

"Okay, so what do we do now?" Maya asked, nodding at the shirt.

"I think . . . maybe I should burn it. I'll have to give that some thought."

"*What?* You can't burn it, Lily," Maya protested. "It's a piece of history."

"It's horrifying."

"Horrifying, but historic."

I wasn't convinced.

"Besides," continued Maya, "I wasn't suggesting selling it. I've already spoken with Elena Romero about it, remember? She's coming by the shop in an hour. She wants the shirt for the park service's museum—assuming it's genuine, that is."

Oh, it's genuine, I thought.

"That might be a problem, Maya," Bronwyn said. "Lily thinks the shirt is dangerous."

"Well, we can't just *burn* it," Maya said. "What would I tell Elena?"

"Could you cleanse it of its evil vibrations, Lily? Or bind them, perhaps?" suggested Bronwyn.

I blew out a breath. "All right, let me think. . . . I suppose if I restrained the vibrations with a binding spell, and Elena immediately put it under glass in the museum, it would be safe enough. It's not as though she's going to wear it, after all. Right? I'll talk to her about it."

"Good," said Maya. "I know it's creepy, but it's also fascinating. Like Alcatraz itself. You really should go visit it one day, Lily."

The frigid bay waters, closing over my head.

I took the shirt upstairs to my apartment over the store, and performed a hasty binding spell over it, using a small vial of saltwater from the bay to cleanse it. I was familiar with those waters; they had once cleansed me.

But cleansing required harnessing the salts of the bay and concentrating them within a serenity spell. In last night's dream, the bay waters weren't cleansing as much as threatening.

Once again, I shivered at the memory. My nightmare and today's appearance of the inmate's shirt from Alcatraz could be a simple coincidence. Except that I had learned the hard way that events in my life were rarely coincidental and almost never simple.

I shook it off. This was no time to allow my mind to wander. Spellcasting was all about focusing one's intent.

From the living room bookshelf I retrieved a smooth stone I had found in the Ruby River in Montana, and extracted a rusty, square-headed nail from my medicine bag. I had picked up the nail in an old silver mining ghost town in New Mexico, the site of a terrible mining tragedy that killed twenty-two men.

I cast a quick salt circle, then set the nail upon the stone and struck it thrice with an iron hammer while intoning a spell in Latin. Finally, I scored the stone three times with the point of the rusty nail and returned the nail to my medicine bag.

Later I would cast the stone into the bay, completing the circle, but for now I braided and knotted yard-lengths of orange, blue, and black yarn, focusing my intent while chanting:

By knot of one, my spell's begun.
By knot of two, the wish comes true.
By knot of three, so mote it be.
By knot of four, this charm is a door.
By knot of five, my intent comes alive.
By knot of six, the enchantment I fix.
By knot of seven, the strength of eleven.
By knot of eight, I cast this fate.
By knot of nine, what's dreamt is mine.

I wrapped the prisoner's shirt in brown paper and tied the whole thing with the braided strings. The shirt's vibrations were still bleak, but that was to be expected. It was no longer dangerous—as long as no one put it on. It was too easy to forget the effect clothing can have upon a person; to change into a new set of clothes can, indeed, change the wearer, if only very subtly. Everyone is different, of course, and some need a touch of darkness in their clothes to highlight the sunshine in their lives.

But not this shirt. Not #258. This shirt was too much of a burden for even the strongest among us to bear.

Chapter 4

Satisfied the evil had been contained, I carried the wrapped shirt downstairs and left it atop the washer in the workroom. Out on the shop floor, I found Elena Romero and a man, both of them wearing National Park Service uniforms, chatting with Maya and Bronwyn.

Elena was a plump, attractive woman in her late twenties. She shared Carlos's dramatic features, but her eyes revealed a free-spirited openness that Carlos, a hardened homicide inspector, almost never displayed.

"Lily!" she said, giving me a hug. "It's been too long."

"Indeed it has," I said. "I'm so glad you came by."

"Allow me to introduce my friend and colleague, Forrest Caruthers," Elena said.

Forrest appeared to be in his forties; tall and lanky, he was a crusty cowboy type. "Nice to meet you. And before you say it, yes, it is ironic that a park ranger is named Forrest. My mother must have been prophetic.

On the other hand, she wanted me to be a doctor, so there you go."

I smiled. "It's nice to meet you. You both look so official in your uniforms!"

"It's pretty spiffy, isn't it?" Elena said, pirouetting. The National Park Service uniform consisted of army-green pants, a gray button-up short-sleeved shirt, a green wool jacket, and a broad straw hat with a brown leather band stamped *USNPS* and embellished with a metallic gold acorn.

"There's only one problem." Elena took off her hat, revealing an indentation encircling her thick, dark locks. "Hat hair!"

Forrest doffed his own, but his sandy hair was sparse. "I don't know what she's talking about. I don't have that problem, personally."

We laughed.

"You'd both best keep your hats on, then," said Maya. "You look too official for anyone to poke fun."

"Makes me feel like Dudley Do-Right, in a good way," Elena said, putting the hat back on and gazing around the shop floor at our bounty of inventory. "I keep meaning to drop by and do a little shopping, but I rarely find myself in this neighborhood. Still, if you told me you had a pig I might have made a special trip."

Oscar snorted and preened, rubbing up against her legs.

"Thank you so much for coming in," said Maya. "I could have brought the shirt to you, if that was easier."

"No problem," said Elena. "Forrest and I were in the area today, anyway, and while we're here we're distributing these flyers—we're bringing some to the Golden Gate Park office, and are asking merchants if they'd be willing to help out. Would it be okay to place a flyer in your shop window, Lily? It's for a good cause."

The robin's-egg blue and milk chocolate brown poster was done up in a retro Art Deco style and advertised the "Alcatraz Festival of Felons!" a full day—and night—of events on the island. Tickets were expensive: $250 per person, with an additional charge of $50 for those wishing to camp out for the night "in genuine Alcatraz cellblocks."

I couldn't help but wonder: Was a creepy old federal penitentiary the best venue to hold a charitable fundraiser? But then I reminded myself for the thousandth time: I didn't exactly march to the same drummer as my compatriots.

"It's coming up soon, but there are still some tickets left so we're trying to get the word out. Kyle Cheney is organizing it," Elena said.

"I'd say his assistant, Seth, is doing the actual organizing," said Forrest. "But Mr. Cheney is the creative force behind it."

"Wait—do you mean *the* Kyle Cheney?" asked Bronwyn. "The one who made a fortune in the computer industry, back in the 1990s?"

"The very one," said Elena. "He's pledged to match ticket sales and donations, dollar for dollar. Half the festival's proceeds will go to the city's historic renovation fund, and half to support the city's homeless."

"I hear he personally funded that homeless shelter in the Tenderloin that was going to shut down," said Bronwyn. "He seems like a good guy."

Forrest nodded. "Mr. Cheney's surprisingly down-to-earth. When he approached us with the idea for the festival, he said, and I quote: 'It seems rude to just sit on all this money.'"

"Well, we can't match Kyle Cheney's level of generosity, but Aunt Cora's Closet could contribute something," I offered. "A coupon, maybe, or a chance to win a dress of one's choice? Something along those lines?"

"I'll bet my mom would donate free alterations," suggested Maya. "Good cause, and good publicity."

"That's so nice of you!" Elena replied. "You should contact Mr. Cheney's assistant, Seth. Mr. Cheney's a little hard to get in touch with, and besides Seth's the one in charge of donations. His number's on the poster."

As I went to tape the poster in the front shop window, I scanned the list of the festival's many sponsors. One name stood out: Renee Baker's Cupcakes.

Maybe Renee was just doing her part as a member of San Francisco's business community. Or perhaps she was simply being civic-minded, like I was. Or perhaps her intentions were nefarious. Whatever her motives, Renee was no simple cupcake baker, and it was high time that I checked in on her. The last time I had seen Renee she was being treated by paramedics for a head injury sustained during an attempted coup by her underling. She was probably feeling better by now . . . and unless I missed my guess, she would be up to her old tricks, which involved establishing something called the *coincidentia oppositorum,* which was a male-female alliance that would make a play for the magical soul of San Francisco. Last I knew, she was looking for her male counterpart. This wasn't an easy role to fill: It had to be someone magical and evil enough to buy into her ambitions, but simultaneously trustworthy enough not to betray her.

I fervently hoped she hadn't found him yet. That would be . . . bad.

It struck me that I should probably get a handle on

Renee before even thinking about planning my honeymoon. I added *Visit Renee the Shady Cupcake Lady, ASAP* to my mental to-do list.

Suddenly I felt a slight pitching under my feet, my senses swam, and I heard a low rumble. The old Victorian building creaked around us.

"What in tarnation was *that*?" I asked.

"Just a little temblor," said Bronwyn. "We had one last night, too, did you feel it? Around three a.m., I think."

"A little temblor? As in an *earthquake*?" I'd lived in the City by the Bay for a while now, but this was my first experience with an earthquake. The others smiled, trying not to laugh at my reaction, and I could not understand how they could be so blasé.

"It's just a little one, Lily," Maya said.

"You'll get used to it, dear," Bronwyn confirmed.

"That's nothing," Forrest said. "You should've felt the Loma Prieta quake, the one that took down sections of the freeway and some buildings. Killed a number of poor souls."

The others nodded.

"I was taught the small ones are a good sign, because they release some of the pressure along the San Andreas Fault," Forrest continued. "But now I hear seismologists don't think that's true after all. I guess we don't really know all that much about earthquakes, when it comes right down to it."

As I thought that over, the jaded locals, unfazed by the idea that the earth could shake and bring down buildings, continued their conversation.

"Kyle Cheney's a real history buff," Elena was saying. "And he's gotten to know some of the docents and curators out on the island. Also, get this: During the festival, after the sun sets, there's going to be a ghost tour of the island led by a paranormal investigator named Charles Gosnold."

"Oh!" said Bronwyn. "I know Charles! We haven't chatted in ages. He must be doing well for himself, if he's running in Kyle Cheney's circle. Good for him!"

Maya and I exchanged a glance. She knew that in private I referred to Gosnold as "Charles the Charlatan." In my view he was a hack, full of puffery and nonsense, the kind of paranormal "investigator" who gave those of us who were actually connected to the world beyond a bad name—or at the very least tagged us as slapdash, New Age "woo-woo" crackpots. But Bronwyn had a much bigger heart than I, with a soft spot for oddballs.

Which, now that I thought of it, might explain why she had taken the likes of *me* under her wing.

"So, is it true? Is Alcatraz haunted?" Bronwyn asked Elena. "I did the night tour once, and I swear I saw something . . ."

Oscar snorted loudly, which brought a chuckle from Elena, who leaned over to give him a good scratch behind the ears. When she straightened, he trotted over to lie down on his purple silk pillow, a gift from Bronwyn.

"Who can say? A lot of people report hearing the clanging of cell doors or whispers and cries, that sort of thing. But it's hardly surprising in a building of that nature, a prison built to house inmates too notorious or too dangerous to be held elsewhere, like Al Capone and Machine Gun Kelly, or the Birdman of Alcatraz. . . ." Elena shrugged. "It's only natural that people would think the island was cursed. To me, what's most surprising is that Alcatraz looms so large in our imaginations, considering it operated as a maximum-security prison for only twenty-nine years."

"Is that right?" Bronwyn said, surprised.

"From 1933 to 1963," Forrest confirmed.

"Why was it closed down?" I asked.

"It became too expensive to operate. Alcatraz is called 'the Rock' for good reason—it's pretty much a barren rock," Elena explained. "All water, food, supplies—*everything* needed to support life and to run a prison had to be ferried over by boat, no mean feat. Keep in mind the warden as well as the guards and their families also lived on the island, so there was a lot of demand."

"But if Alcatraz was only open for so short a time," I said, "why is it so famous?"

A thoughtful look on her face, Elena turned to Forrest. "What do you think, Forrest?"

"There's something about that island that's intriguing—the desperation of the inmates so close to San Francisco and the Golden Gate Bridge yet at the same time so very far away. The inherent romance of an isolated isle, maybe. And it's had more than one incarnation: It was established as a military fort and prison in the nineteenth century, complete with dank underground cells referred to as 'the Spanish dungeon.' The Federal Bureau of Prisons built the penitentiary on the foundation of the old fort, leaving the basement untouched."

"So the Spanish dungeon's still intact?" I asked.

"Sure is. It's creepy down there. The paranormal folks like to say the only place more haunted than the dungeon is the hospital wing."

"Great places for ghosts," Bronwyn murmured, sounding hopeful.

We fell silent for a moment, contemplating the lonely island out in the bay. Complete with a dungeon and, apparently, a haunted hospital wing.

"It's certainly ripe with rumors of ghosts," said Elena. "But the official NPS line is that no, there are no errant spirits wandering Alcatraz. So, anyway, Forrest and I could go on all day about the history of the island, but why don't we save that for when you all come to take a tour?"

"Yeah," said Forrest, checking his watch. "I hate to say it, but we should be moving on."

"Maya, would you get the shirt, please? It's in the workroom, on the washing machine." I turned to Elena and Forrest and took a deep breath. "I know this is going to sound strange, but I have to tell you there's something a little *wrong* with that shirt. Elena, has Carlos mentioned anything about my, um . . ." I trailed off, trying to think how to phrase it.

"About your 'special talents'?"

"I guess you could call them that." I used to play my cards very close to my chest, but I was learning to be more open about myself—and my "special talents."

Elena nodded. "He's told me a little. I get it. We have a beloved aunt who has quite a knack for reading cards, believes in things like amulets, and shops at *botánicas*. A lot of the family is Catholic, so it leads to some tense holiday dinners, but when it comes right down to it, it makes as much sense to me as anything else. And our *tía* gets it right more often than not."

I had known Carlos for a while now—we met not long after I'd opened Aunt Cora's Closet—and though we had been inching toward a real friendship, I still knew very little about his private life. He wasn't what you'd call a big talker, into self-disclosure. I knew—at a profound level—that Carlos was a good, decent man. I knew that another cousin of his had been married to an old boyfriend of mine, Max, and that she had died by her own hand. And I knew that he was remarkably open to my "special talents," as Elena had phrased it, though he was careful not to gain a reputation as the SFPD's "woo-woo guy." But that was about all.

"That's good to hear," I said. "Because I'd like you to keep an open mind with what I'm about to tell you."

"Deal." She inclined her head in agreement.

I glanced at Forrest, who smiled. "I'm just along for the ride."

Maya returned and set the brown paper bundle on the counter in front of us.

"I'm going to unwrap this so you can view the shirt," I said. "But then I'll tie it up again because it's important to bind the shirt's vibrations. They're seriously negative."

"Negative how?" Elena asked.

"I don't know their source—I don't have that kind of sight. It might be the result of the inmate who wore the shirt, or his experiences in prison, or it might be something else, entirely unconnected to Alcatraz. But I do know they're there. The shirt should be safe enough if you or someone else wants to inspect it, but then put it on display behind glass. Maybe tuck the knotted braid of strings in the pocket?"

"Okaaay. . . ." Elena said, frowning.

"And whatever you do, do *not* put it on."

"Why would we put it on?" Forrest asked, puzzled.

"I'm not saying you would, and I hope it wouldn't even occur to you or to anybody else. I'm just saying . . . wearing the shirt could be dangerous. According to Maya's research, it may have belonged to a prisoner named Ray Perry. Do you know anything about him?"

"He wasn't a serial killer or anything like that," said Elena. "But Perry was one tough customer, like most of the inmates at Alcatraz."

"If I recall correctly, Perry was a prisoner early on,

in the thirties, when prison officials enforced the rule of silence," said Forrest.

"That sounds ominous," Bronwyn said. "What was the rule of silence?"

"In the prison's early years, inmates weren't allowed to speak with each other except during mealtimes and when out in the yard; the rest of the time they had to be silent. The inmates hated the rule of silence, and there were claims that it drove some prisoners mad."

Bronwyn gasped. "I think I saw something about that in an old Clint Eastwood movie. A man cut his own fingers off!"

"That's from *Escape from Alcatraz*, which was based on the escape of Fred Brooks and the Albright brothers, Jim and Cole, but was largely fictional," Forrest said smoothly, in what sounded like a practiced speech he had no doubt delivered hundreds of times to those touring the island. "Much of the mystique of Alcatraz came from the fact that Warden Johnston purposefully kept the public in the dark as to what life was like out on what came to be known as the 'Devil's Island.'"

"It was a good movie, though," said Bronwyn.

Elena smiled. "It really was. *Birdman of Alcatraz* was a good movie, too, and almost entirely a work of fiction."

"A rule of silence seems pretty extreme, doesn't it?" asked Maya.

"As I said, several inmates were supposedly driven mad by it," said Forrest. "Whether or not that's true, I can't say. However, it is known that the psychological impact of imprisonment is often more difficult to cope with than the physical challenges. Even the notorious gangster Al Capone confided to the warden that Alcatraz had broken him."

"And on that note . . ." I unwrapped and untied the shirt and spread it on the counter.

Elena and Forrest moved in to take a closer look.

"What do you think?" Maya leaned forward. "Could it be genuine?"

"I'm no textile expert," said Elena, studying the chambray closely. "But this certainly looks like the shirts in the museum's collection. And 258 was Ray Perry's inmate identification number. This is an amazing find, Maya. If we can authenticate it as genuine, we'll be sure to give you credit on the display."

"Mrs. Emmy Lou Archer had it in her attic," said Maya. "She deserves the recognition. All I did was open an old box."

"But you recognized what it was," said Elena. "This is *amazing*."

I didn't find the shirt amazing so much as profoundly disturbing, but was happy that Maya and Elena and Forrest were able to appreciate the garment's historical importance without attaching fear and loathing to it. *What would it be like to go through the world without feeling threatening vibrations?* I wondered. Not for the first time, I reflected, having supernatural powers was a double-edged sword.

"Does the discovery of this shirt prove that Ray Perry survived his escape from Alcatraz?" asked Bronwyn.

"I don't know that it proves anything, really," said Elena. "First, we have to establish that it is, indeed, genuine and that it belonged to Ray Perry. And even if we can authenticate that, it doesn't necessarily mean Perry survived the escape. Maybe he took it off during the attempt, and it washed up on the shore. Maybe he left it in his cell and it was included with his personal effects and given to his family. Plus there's the fact that

I never thought he would have been able to escape on his own."

"How do you mean?"

"I don't know how anyone could have escaped from Alcatraz without some assistance. There were rumors that some of the guards were on the take; maybe Perry got close to one of them and was able to persuade him to help."

"But that's pure speculation," Forrest added. "We spend all day, every day, out on Alcatraz; the theories abound."

"I'll bet they do." I retied the braided strings around the shirt, wrapped it in the brown paper, and handed it to Elena.

"Remember—nobody puts this shirt on," I said. "*Nobody*."

Elena nodded. "Display purposes only. Roger that."

"I'll walk you out," Maya said to Elena and Forrest, then turned to me and Bronwyn. "Anyone up for a coffee or chai? My treat."

"I don't pay you nearly enough to treat us," I said, grabbing a twenty-dollar bill from the petty cash box. "Drinks are on Aunt Cora's."

"Even better," Maya said with a smile. She tucked the bill into her pocket and escorted the national park rangers out of the shop. They chatted about the history of Alcatraz as Maya closed the shop door behind them, the bell tinkling.

As I picked up the royal blue beaded top that had been too big for Agatha, my hands froze on the hanger.

Was it my imagination, or did the familiar tinkle of the bell over the door sound a little . . . off?

Shrill. Alarming.

Oscar snorted awake, leapt up from his silk pillow, and ran to the back room.

I dropped the sparkly top and turned to look out the front window.

From outside, there was the high-pitched peal of tires upon pavement.

A woman screamed.

Was that *Maya*?

Chapter 5

"*Call 911*," I yelled to Bronwyn as I ran to the door.

"What's going on?" Bronwyn asked, picking up the phone and dialing. "What do I tell them?"

"I don't know yet," I said, my voice breathless. "But it's trouble."

Halfway down the block, a crowd had gathered. Bright blue and brown Festival of Felons flyers were strewn about the street and the sidewalk, fluttering in the breeze. I pushed my way through the bystanders to find Conrad—a "gutter punk" friend—with his arms wrapped around Maya.

Forrest looked frantic, a cell phone to his ear.

Elena was nowhere in sight.

"Yes, we've got the plate number," Forrest said into the phone, and recited the string of numbers and letters to the dispatcher on the other end of the line.

"Maya, are you all right?" I asked, putting my own arms around her. "What happened? Where's Elena?"

Maya had tears in her eyes; her voice was shaky.

"Th—they took her! A white van pulled up at the curb, a man in a ski mask jumped out and grabbed Elena. It all happened so fast . . ."

"Someone *kidnapped* Elena?" I clarified, glancing at Forrest, who appeared helpless and miserable. I could smell waves of guilt coming off him.

"I didn't even see it," he said, the phone still to his ear. "I was in the dry cleaner's, asking them to put up a poster . . . I heard the commotion, but I didn't see it. I didn't even . . ."

"*Dude,*" Conrad said in a hushed tone. Several of his friends—young people who lived in the park and scrounged to get by—milled about, helping to pick up the scattered posters. I recognized a few of the self-described "gutter punks" who had helped clean up after Aunt Cora's Closet was vandalized, but in general I had a hard time telling them apart. One was tall and redheaded, another was short and dark. There were several facial piercings and tattoos among them, but by and large they were of average height with lanky hair that ranged from dishwater blond to dull brown to dusty black. They were all painfully thin, and most appeared under the influence.

"Did any of you see what happened?" I demanded.

They shook their heads, and the redhead handed me a messy bunch of posters he had gathered. "That's . . . whack, dude."

"Totally whack," agreed a young woman. "Sorry."

Maya let out a long, shuddering breath.

I was still trying to wrap my head around what just happened. Elena Romero—the sweet, smart National Park Service ranger we had been chatting with moments ago—had been snatched off bustling Haight Street in broad daylight?

Who would do such a thing? And why?

I looked up and down the street.

Bright colors caught my attention. Lying in the gutter was the braided string I had used to bind the Alcatraz inmate's shirt.

Carefully knotted threads in orange, blue, and black.

The first police officers to arrive interviewed Maya, Forrest, Conrad, and a dozen other bystanders, all of whom reported the same thing: A white van screeched up to the curb, a man in a ski mask jumped out and grabbed Elena, and the van roared off. A second man had been driving but nobody had gotten a look at his face. That was about it.

Forrest kept shaking his head. "I should have done something, I should have—"

"It all happened so fast," said Maya. "Even if you'd been right here, no one could have done anything. *I* certainly didn't react in time to help."

"But I'm . . ." I imagined Forrest was going to point out that he was a big, hearty man while Maya's slight build was only an inch over five feet, but he trailed off with a shrug. "I just wish I had been there. Look, I think—Elena's a federal employee, so this might be a matter for the FBI. I'm going to go talk with some people, see if I can marshal some federal resources, if you're all right here."

"We'll be fine, Forrest, thank you," Bronwyn said. "Please let us know as soon as you hear anything."

"I will." He hesitated, shifting his weight on his big booted feet as though wanting to say something further, then simply nodded again and loped down the sidewalk.

Conrad, Bronwyn, Maya, and I returned to Aunt Cora's Closet and huddled in the workroom, trying to comfort each other and waiting to see if the police needed to ask us any more questions. The brocade curtain remained open so that we could hear the sounds of the police radios squawking, see the commotion and the red lights flashing out on the street.

This wasn't a homicide—I *prayed* it wasn't a homicide—but I was pretty sure Carlos Romero, SFPD homicide inspector, would arrive soon to try to figure out what had happened to his cousin.

"Why would anyone kidnap dear Elena?" asked Bronwyn, pouring each of us a mug of her new tea blend, "Summer Blush," a fragrant mix of hibiscus, lemongrass, and a few secret ingredients. I passed around a plate of chocolate-chip-and-butterscotch cookies I had managed to keep hidden from Oscar since last night—a new record.

Conrad added three heaping teaspoons of sugar to his mug and helped himself to several cookies. After years spent avoiding reality by using drugs, Conrad had decided to get sober, joined a twelve-step program, and asked for my magical assistance. Where I used to have to coax him to eat, he was now hungry all the time and had developed a mean sugar habit. Now I worried about his diet, but it was better than worrying about what drugs he was taking.

"*Dude.* Maybe she's secretly an heiress to a great fortune," Conrad suggested.

Maya looked incredulous. "Do wealthy heiresses typically work for the National Park Service?"

"Seems like a stretch, sure," said Conrad, munching on a cookie. "But what other reason could there be?"

"A disgruntled ex-husband or boyfriend?" suggested Bronwyn, her soft chocolate brown eyes shadowed with worry.

"Maybe," said Maya, her voice sounding strangely hollow. "But the kidnapping was so *organized*—there was the guy driving, in addition to the guy who jumped out. Wouldn't a psycho boyfriend just wait in the bushes outside her apartment or something? Why go to the trouble of recruiting an assistant and kidnapping her off the street in broad daylight, with dozens of potential witnesses? Lily, did you sense anything?"

"No, I'm so sorry. I had a premonition just after you left the shop, but it didn't tell me anything except that something terrible had happened."

"Could there be some sort of political connection?" Bronwyn suggested.

"These are National Park Service officers," said Maya. "Who could they anger?"

Bronwyn nodded, conceding the point, and sipped her tea.

"I wonder whether there's a connection to that inmate shirt," I said, glancing at the braided strings I was still holding. I had tried to give them to the police officers, but they hadn't been interested. I would try again with Carlos, though part of me wanted to keep the braid so I could see if my fiancé, Sailor, or his cousin Patience—both talented psychics—might be able to pick up anything from it.

"The shirt? Why?" asked Maya. "How?"

"There was something hinky about it."

"Are you saying the shirt itself attracted the violence, somehow?" Bronwyn asked.

I had thought it impossible for Maya to look any bleaker until another wave of worry passed over her features.

"Not as such, no," I said. "I mean, that wouldn't make any sense, would it? Why would a criminal be lying in wait on the off chance someone left the shop with a genuine Alcatraz inmate's shirt? And how would a criminal even know what was in the bundle?"

The bell over the front door tinkled, and Carlos Romero strode in. He was a good-looking man with romantic, dark features. Not much taller than I, Carlos exuded confidence and a don't-mess-with-me attitude, no doubt honed from his years working big-city homicide. He wore his usual uniform: khaki pants topped by a hip-length black leather jacket.

He looked as bleak as the rest of us, but with a frantic edge I had never noted in him before. He declined our offers of tea and cookies, placed a chair directly in front of Maya, leaned toward her, and in a gentle but stern voice, asked her to tell him everything, one more time.

Unfortunately, there wasn't much to tell.

"Have you traced the license plate number?" asked Maya.

"The van was reported stolen a few days ago," said Carlos. "And it was just found illegally parked not far from Pier 39. No sign of the perps. Forensics is on the scene, and there are uniforms canvassing for witnesses, but it's such a busy area, with so many people coming and going, that it's probably a long shot."

"And . . . Elena?" I asked.

He shook his head. "What else can you tell me, Maya? Anything at all."

"I'm so sorry, Carlos. It all happened so quickly, seconds after we walked out of the store. None of it makes any sense."

"Does anyone have a personal grudge against Elena?" I asked. "A boyfriend, maybe?"

"Not likely. Elena's married to a woman, Bethany. She and Elena's sister are tracking down friends, making up a list of her former romantic involvements, that kind of thing. But nothing so far. Bethany's going crazy."

"Of course she is, poor dear," Bronwyn said.

"You'd been corresponding with Elena, correct?" Carlos said to Maya. "Could I see the texts?"

"Of course." She handed him her phone, and Carlos scrolled through the messages. "That's all of it. We spoke on the phone once, but otherwise we texted."

"How did you two come to be in touch?" Carlos asked.

"I went on that Alcatraz tour with her a while back, remember?" Maya said. "So I thought of her when I stumbled across an old inmate's shirt."

"Lily, anything you can tell me that no one else may realize?" Carlos asked, handing Maya's phone back to her. "According to those texts, Elena and Forrest were here to pick up the shirt. Was that all?"

I nodded and held up the braided strings. "This was left in the street. I used it to bind the shirt."

"Which means what, exactly?" Carlos asked.

"The vibrations were pretty dark—"

"Wouldn't you expect that from something a prisoner wore?" Carlos interrupted. "Life in prison is no picnic."

"Yes, but—this was something more. There was . . . an edge to it. I know that seems vague, but the vibrations were distinctive, like nothing I've felt before. I assumed it was because the shirt belonged to an escaped prisoner, who was presumed drowned in the bay."

Carlos raised an eyebrow. "If he drowned in the bay, then how did someone get ahold of the shirt?"

"That I can't tell you."

"Okay, next question: If the shirt is dangerous, why did you give it to Elena?"

"I did a binding spell," I protested. "I was a little nervous about letting Elena have it, but she promised to put it on display under glass right away, which I thought would be safe. It wasn't as though she was planning on *wearing* it."

Carlos blew out a breath and ran his hand through his near-black hair. "All right. But you're saying these strings, the binding thingie, was torn off the shirt?"

"I found it in the street."

"It must have been ripped off in the tussle," said Maya. "But there wouldn't be any fingerprints or DNA—the guy was wearing gloves."

Carlos took the strings and studied them. "Forensics wouldn't be able to pick up fingerprints from this, anyway."

"If you don't think it's useful as evidence, I'd like to have it back," I said. "I'm hoping Sailor, or his cousin, will be able to 'read' something from it."

Carlos paused, then gave an almost imperceptible nod. "Fine. You keep it for now, see what it can tell you. Since Elena's a federal employee, Forrest thinks the FBI will get involved, which means they'll probably be talking to you as well. In the meantime, if any of you think of anything else, anything at all, call me immediately, day or night. And Lily—you might think about installing some security cameras. I know San Francisco doesn't always feel like it, but this is a big city, after all."

He strode toward the front door.

"Carlos, wait!" I called out, hurrying to join him at the door. I grabbed a Raven mystical stone from the display counter and pressed it into his hand. "Do me a favor? Keep this in your pocket."

His dark eyes settled on the shiny stone.

"Raven, huh?"

"To open the mental paths in your mind, for clarity and wisdom, and for general good health." I was blushing by the time I finished running down Raven's list of attributes. Carlos was remarkably open to my magic, but he had his feet firmly planted in the "real," logical world.

He nodded and pocketed the charm. "I'll take any help I can get. Thank you."

The door swung closed behind him. I turned to find Bronwyn, Conrad, and Maya watching me, as though hoping for direction. If only I knew what to suggest.

Oscar snorted.

"I'm going upstairs, to see if I can learn anything from this binding braid," I said. "Y'all okay down here? Or if you want to take the rest of the day off, Maya, it's totally fine. In fact, maybe we should close the shop for the rest of the day."

"I'd rather stay," said Maya. "It's . . . I'd rather be here. With people. My mom's on her way, too. She had a fitting across town but one of the women in her shop called her to let her know what happened."

"We'll be fine," said Bronwyn, her hand on Maya's shoulder. "We've got tea and cookies, good friends and vintage clothes. What more could we need?"

Conrad helped himself to another cookie, and added: "*Dude*."

There wasn't much else to say.

I mounted the stairs to my apartment, Oscar trotting along behind me, his piggy hooves tapping loudly on the wooden risers. At the landing outside my door he transformed. When we're among other people, Oscar assumes the form of a Vietnamese potbellied pig, but when it's just us—or us and Sailor or Selena—he's his natural self, a gobgoyle, for lack of a better word. He reached to my waist at full height, with batlike ears, a longish snout, oversized hands, and big, bottle glass green eyes. He used to have wings, but a while back I had been forced to destroy them in order to save him. I still felt guilty about that.

Oscar had entered my life as my witch's familiar, but had become more like a partner or a sidekick. Goodness knows he almost never did what I told him to do, which was a stellar quality in most witches' familiars.

"Anything?" I asked him the moment we stepped inside our home and I had closed the door.

Oscar shook his head and walked toward the kitchen. "I tell ya, the world these days. What are you gonna do? It's like Carlos said, San Francisco isn't as friendly as a critter might expect."

"That's it? You think this was just a random act of urban violence?"

"Course not. I'm betting it's related to that creepy prison shirt."

"I was afraid of that, too. But here's the thing: The kidnapping was obviously planned. Why would someone steal a van and wait outside my shop on the off chance that Elena would be leaving with the shirt? And for that matter, how did the kidnapper know about the shirt? *I* didn't even know about it until this morning."

He shrugged and started scrounging in the snack cupboard.

"We out of potato chips?" he asked. "Better add that to the shopping list. It's a kitchen staple, you know. Not to mention Cheez Doodles. And Tater Tots."

"Oscar, please—this is a big deal. If the kidnappers just wanted the shirt, why wouldn't they have simply snatched the bundle out of her hands? Let Elena go, or leave her in the van, once they had it?"

"Plus, why would they leave the van in the touristy part of town?" Oscar pondered. "Lotta people coulda seen them. Me, I woulda gone down by the docks, someplace quiet, if I wanted to dump a body."

"A *body*?" Fear ran through me, a shock hot and cold at the same time. "*No*."

I said this last almost like a prayer, a mantra, as though I could change reality with magical thinking. But I knew only too well that wasn't true. Absent-mindedly, I toyed with an appliquéd oven mitt my mother had sewn; it was old and stained, and one edge was slightly charred from an incident with a noodle casserole and a cranky old oven in Madagascar. But for years it had been the one tangible item that connected me to Maggie, and it still felt comforting in my hands.

Oscar had settled on a bag of salted peanuts, which he was crunching loudly and chewing with his mouth open, spilling peanut shells on the floor.

"Oscar, do you know something, or are you just speculating?"

"Sorry," he said with a casual shrug that negated his apology. "I always forget how attached you get to cowans. And you don't even know this woman, hardly."

"I don't have to know her well to care about what happened to her. Besides, she's Carlos's cousin, so I'd be in on this no matter what."

He shrugged again. "What time are we going to Calypso's house? I have a hankering for some pizza."

"It's not even noon."

"Helloooo? Lunchtime?"

"Fix yourself a sandwich," I said, distracted.

Oscar was right about one thing: Pier 39 was among the busiest tourist areas in all of San Francisco, with hundreds of people milling about at all hours. How would the kidnappers get a struggling woman out of a van without being seen? Had they somehow incapacitated her? And if they had, wouldn't carrying an unconscious woman raise suspicions?

Worry clawed at my belly. I kept thinking about that shirt.

"Mistress, lookee here: More ideas for your honeymoon!" Oscar thrust another handful of glossy brochures at me. One was for New Zealand, with a striking image of snow-capped mountains on the cover; another was for Beijing, featuring the Forbidden City.

"*Heh*. 'Forbidden,'" Oscar snickered. "Yeah, *right*. Why would you call a place 'forbidden'? Doesn't that just make you *itch* to go there?"

"Oscar, honestly? I appreciate the thought, but this isn't a good time. A woman's life may be in danger."

"So go to Alcatraz already, mistress, and figure it out," he said. "*Duh*."

"What do you mean—how would a trip to Alcatraz help right now?"

Oscar heaved a sigh. "The kidnappers left the stolen van near Pier 39, correct?"

"Correct."

"The ferry to Alcatraz leaves not far from there, at Pier 33, correct?"

"Correct."

He made a rolling motion with one oversized hand, as though waiting for a witchy nitwit to catch up. "And Elena's a National Park Service ranger at *Alcatraz*? Who was carrying an old inmate's shirt from when Alcatraz was a prison . . . ?"

"You think the kidnappers took both Elena and the shirt to Alcatraz? But why? She would have headed back there, anyway. Why steal a van and kidnap her here on Haight Street when they could have just taken the ferry to the island and waited for her to arrive?"

"Yeah, huh, good point," he said, perusing a Mandarin language textbook. "You got me there. All I have to say to you is *bǎi nián hǎo hé*."

"Meaning?"

"'May you have a harmonious union that lasts one hundred years.'"

"What?"

"It's a blessing for your wedding."

"Oh. Um. Thanks."

"There's another one in here wishing you the arrival of a son as soon as possible, but I thought that might be taking it a little far."

Now a different sort of anxiety struck me, deep in my belly.

Sailor and I still needed to Talk—with a capital *T*.

"But hey, mistress, this is the sort of thing you're good at. Maybe you should go to Alcatraz and figure this out so we can move on to important things, like making honeymoon plans."

Oscar was right again: This *was* the sort of thing I was good at. At least in a flailing, roundabout kind of way that merged magic with luck and tenacity. "Never give up" had been the unofficial motto of my childhood. "*Nunca te rindas*, Lily," Graciela would say whenever I became frustrated because a spell was not working. "You think life is easy? You will see. *No te rindas, nunca*."

This was my role, whether I wanted it or not. And these days, at least, I wasn't alone. I had a lot of magical help: Sailor, Patience, Aidan, Hervé, and now my grandmother's coven.

Elena Romero was in danger, and the source of that danger might very well be supernatural.

If I truly was San Francisco's resident witch detective, I had best get on with it.

Chapter 6

Visiting Alcatraz Island wasn't as simple as I thought it would be. As Oscar had said, the Red and White Fleet ferry launched from Pier 33, true, but because the National Park Service could accommodate only so many visitors at once on the relatively small island, ferry reservations were required. The man in the ticket booth informed me that the first available booking was in two months.

"Two *months*?" I asked.

"It's summertime," he repeated. "Alcatraz is one of the most popular attractions in the entire national park system."

"And there's no other way to visit the island?"

"Not legally."

I blinked.

"I'm saying, Alcatraz isn't that far off shore. Some people try taking a boat or an inflatable raft to get to the island. I wouldn't recommend it, though—as I said, it's against the law and most are picked up by the Coast

Guard. Assuming they even make it that far and aren't swept out to sea through the Golden Gate."

The currents tugging at my legs, pulling me toward the open sea . . .

I thanked him for his time and ceded my spot in line to a large family visiting from Iowa, who had been smart enough to reserve their tickets for the tour months earlier.

Now what?

"Young lady, here's an interesting thing about this area." An older man with a bushy white mustache called me over to his folding table covered with brochures and maps. He wore a khaki vest with a huge *Alcatraz: Just Ask Me!* lanyard around his neck. A half-completed *New York Times* crossword sat in front of him, testimony to how few people took him up on the lanyard's offer. "Did you know that the Golden Gate refers to the opening, not to the bridge itself?"

"How do you mean?"

"The Golden Gate is the mouth of the bay, where the ocean and the bay waters meet. The bridge was built across it in 1933, and took its name. Ever since, people say 'Golden Gate' like it refers only to the bridge. But it doesn't."

"That is interesting," I said.

"Didn't make reservations for the ferry, huh?"

I shook my head.

"Lots of people make that mistake. Too bad, Alcatraz is worth a look-see."

"You volunteer there?"

"I do. Ever since the wife passed, got to keep myself busy. Fact is, I used to be a guard at the prison."

"You were? When was that?"

"In 1962, right before it closed for good."

"You don't look that old," I said, before I realized

that was a rude thing to say. I sometimes had trouble with the social graces.

"I like to keep fit. Look good for my age, though, right?" He chuckled and curled his arm in the air, flexing his muscle. "Anyway, I was just a kid back then, fresh out of school. Name's Ralph Gordon, nice to meet you."

"You, too," I said, picking up a brochure with a map of Alcatraz Island on the cover. I tried to think of something I could ask the former guard that would be relevant to Elena's disappearance, but my mind was a blank. Ray Perry had escaped decades before Gordon arrived on the island.

I glanced up at a huge version of the poster Elena and Forrest had asked me to put up in the window of Aunt Cora's Closet, touting Kyle Cheney's Festival of Felons. It was coming up soon, on the night of the full moon.

I supposed I could buy a ticket for the creepy penal party, but it was still five days off. That did me no good. More important, it did Elena no good.

"Oh, sorry, I'm Lily Ivory," I said when I realized the former guard was waiting for me to reply.

"Go ahead and take that map, then, Lily Ivory, and if you have any questions, just ask. If I'm not here, I'm out on the island in the museum." He turned his attention back to his crossword puzzle. "Now, if only I knew a twelve-letter word for 'fetch, or double.'"

"Doppelganger."

"Excuse me?"

"It's a twelve-letter word for 'fetch, or double.'"

"Oh! Thanks!"

So much for a trip to Alcatraz. Now what?

While I was in the neighborhood, I decided to check in with Aidan Rhodes, who had an office at the wax museum. Aidan was a sort of witchy godfather to the magical community in the Bay Area. I didn't entirely trust him, but we were allies in fighting whatever peril San Francisco was facing. In addition, we had been working together to train Selena, a teenager with more power than she—or the grandmother who was raising her—knew what to do with. I had found the whole process enlightening; nothing like teaching someone else how to do something to master it thoroughly oneself.

And Aidan often *knew* things. Such as, perhaps, why a national park ranger had been kidnapped off Haight Street in broad daylight.

But first, I had one more thing to do to complete the binding spell I had cast upon the inmate's shirt this morning. I walked to the edge of the dock, brought the smooth river rock out of my backpack, thanked it for helping to contain whatever evil might have been in the inmate's shirt, and dropped it into the dark, unfathomable waters of the bay.

It probably wouldn't help Elena at this point, but if the kidnappers had wanted the shirt for its inherent malevolence, this would help to thwart their intentions.

It was a beautiful afternoon, sunny and breezy, so I decided to get a little exercise and walk to the wax museum. As I passed the historic old pier buildings, heading toward the raucous tourist mecca that is Pier 39, I took in the lively scene. Mounds of glossy seals lounged and barked on the old docks, entertaining humans with their antics. Seagulls cawed and played tug-of-war over discarded French fries. Street performers and jewelry vendors studded the sidewalks, selling souvenirs of all kinds. Eateries and food carts hawked fresh seafood and luscious clam chowder served in sourdough bread bowls. The air was filled with the distinctive aroma of fresh crabs cooking in huge vats of boiling water, mingled with the tang of salt off the bay.

Crowds jostled me as I made my way along the sidewalk, but I didn't mind. I enjoy tourists. They give off a bright, green-apple scent, and retain a refreshing openness to the new things they are seeing and experiencing. Even when they limp back to the sanctuary of their hotel rooms at the end of a long day of sightseeing, their auras are mellow.

As I approached the wax museum, I spied the man I was planning to marry. *Sailor*.

The sight of him made my heart skip a beat, the breath catch in my throat. He was tall and dark haired, his broad shoulders encased in a heavy motorcycle jacket. Sailor was often brooding, sometimes sullen, and occasionally downright cantankerous. But when he smiled . . . well, let's just say he held my heart in his hands.

I stopped short when I realized Sailor was with a statuesque auburn-haired woman who looked like a model in her chic dress and jacket. They spoke for a few moments, then he leaned down and kissed her on the cheek before she walked away.

Jealousy, bitter and acrid, surged through me. Who was *that*?

I trusted Sailor . . . but still. Whoever the woman was, she appeared elegant and refined—not at all like me. And why didn't I know her, or *any* of Sailor's friends, for that matter? As far as I knew, he had declined to invite anyone other than his closest relatives to our upcoming handfasting.

Sailor turned and saw me. Guilt flashed across his strong features, replaced almost immediately by a crooked smile.

"Lily! Fancy meeting you here," he said, giving me a kiss and hug. He smelled subtly of cigarettes, a scent I loved even though I knew I shouldn't. Sailor had quit smoking a while ago but as soon as he began working with Aidan again, he had started back up. He smoked only one or two cigarettes a day, but I worried it would easily ratchet up. Nicotine addiction was a bear.

"Who was that woman?" I asked, gesturing with my head to the woman who had disappeared around the corner.

"A client," he said.

"Is that right?"

He studied my face, and said: "Tell me what's wrong,"

"You're not supposed to read my mind, remember?"

"I don't have to be a mind reader to know when something's bothering my fiancée." My heart skipped a beat at the word. "'That woman,' as you call her, is an old acquaintance who wanted to meet Aidan. She's nobody important, Lily. Surely that's not what's bothering you?"

Yes—though I wouldn't admit it. "No, it's not that. A cousin of Carlos's, Elena Romero, was kidnapped this morning by two men in a white van, right in front of the store."

He frowned. "I don't like the sound of that."

"It gets worse," I said. "She had just left Aunt Cora's Closet with a shirt that might have belonged to an escaped prisoner from Alcatraz."

"An original item, not a souvenir?"

"We think so. The vibrations it gave off were quite bleak."

"Why did you give it to her?"

Guilt surged up in me. *I never should have let Elena take the shirt.*

"I cast a binding spell over it, and it had been partially cleansed by the waters of the bay. . . ." I trailed off. "Elena promised to put it in a display case, behind glass. I—I thought it would be all right to let her leave with it."

Sailor reached out and drew me into his arms.

"Sorry," he whispered into my hair. "Of course you wouldn't have let her take it if you didn't think it was safe."

"Still, you're right, it's my fault."

"It's not your fault that there are madmen on the streets, Lily. You're not in control of all the evil in this city, at least not yet." He pulled back and searched my face, cocking his head. "You sure you're all right?"

"I'm just tired. I was visited by a nightmare last night."

"I'm sorry I wasn't there to wake you." His voice was husky as he brushed his fingers along my cheek.

"Anyway," I said, taking the binding strings from my woven backpack and holding them out to him. "Would you try to read this for me?"

"It's a binding braid?"

I nodded. "It was torn off the shirt when the kidnappers grabbed Elena. I wonder if you might be able pick up anything? Or . . . maybe Patience could?"

"If you want to ask Patience, she's upstairs, meeting with Aidan right now."

"Really? What's she talking to Aidan about?"

"Is that any of our business, my nosy witch?"

"No, of course not. Sorry. I mean, I wondered . . . whether it had anything to do with what happened to Elena."

"Why would it?"

"No reason."

"I'm sure Patience would agree to read for you—for a price—though these days we're about equally talented at reading inanimate objects."

Working with Aidan had boosted Sailor's psychic abilities, a fact over which he felt torn. The two men didn't much care for each other, so theirs was a complex relationship, but at least Sailor had returned to Aidan's employ on a more equal footing than previously. Aidan's powers had been diminishing in recent months, while Sailor's had grown. Both men were important to me—Sailor romantically, Aidan professionally—so it thrilled me to imagine them getting along, working together against the threat San Francisco was facing.

"I didn't know that," I said. "That's great."

"She's still better at reading the crystal ball, though, and at divination in general." He glanced around, then led the way into a small alley between brick buildings. "Sorry, this isn't ideal, but it will have to do."

An alleyway off a busy street wasn't the best place for a psychic reading, but a powerful practitioner like Sailor would make it work. The point was to focus one's intent. Witches like me got into the right mental and spiritual place by chanting and brewing; my grandmother's coven piggybacked on one another's power. Sailor had the ability to tap into the psychic plane that we were all part of, whether we knew it or not.

He held the braid in both hands, closed his eyes, and tilted his head back. After a long moment, he lowered his head and opened his eyes.

"Lily."

"Yes?"

"Not you—you know how I see things in floral symbols? I see a lily."

"What kind of lily?"

"The kind common to funerals: shaped like a cone, with white on the outside and an orange stamen."

"A calla lily?"

"Yes, that's the one."

"They may be associated with death and funerals here, but in Mexico calla lilies are considered a party flower, a sign of spring and renewal."

"Well, there you go: Interpreting symbols is dicey. I'm thinking funerals, you're thinking good times and renewal."

I blew out a breath. "Given that someone was just kidnapped in broad daylight, and we're dealing with a cursed prisoner's shirt, I fear your interpretation might be more apt."

He raised an eyebrow, but remained silent.

"Selena's been drawing calla lilies lately," I said. Selena liked to draw, and tended to go on binges, sketching the same thing over and over again. I had assumed these were a reference to myself because before I met Selena she had been drawing lilies as a portent of my coming into her life. Or at least that's what her *abuela* thought, and I wasn't one to go up against the knowledge of grandmothers. "So, that's it? A calla lily? No vision of a woman held in a cell somewhere specific or anything useful like that?"

"Sorry. I might be able to see more if I go into a full trance at home. Okay if I take the braided strings with me?"

I nodded. "Yes, thanks. I'll take any help I can get."

He gazed at me for a long moment. "What else?"

"I . . . well, Aidan said something a while ago. . . ."

"Oh, great, can't wait to hear what *Aidan* thinks."

"Oscar said something as well."

"This is getting better all the time."

"I mean . . . maybe this isn't the best time, but I feel like we need to find the time and space to talk before the handfasting. I know we moved up the date so that Graciela's coven could be here, but we've both been running around so much we haven't really . . . talked."

"Spit it out, Lily. You're having doubts?" Sailor's face was grim, his eyes, usually so warm, now seemed icy. He shrugged. "It's not a problem. This is all going too fast. We'll postpone the handfasting."

"What? That's *not* what I'm saying, Sailor, not at all. I'm just thinking there are some things we need to talk about, to make sure we're on the same page."

His eyes remained on me for a long, unreadable moment. Finally he seemed to relax, ever so slightly.

"Why don't I bring a bottle of wine to your place tonight, and we'll talk about everything on that intriguing mind of yours?"

Happiness surged through me. But then I remembered. "I'd love to, but I can't tonight. I'm supposed to go to Calypso's. I'm in charge of pizza."

"And I'm not invited." It was a statement, not a question.

"Not this time. It's a coven thing." In view of what had happened to Elena, I had considered canceling tonight's trip to Calypso's, but what could I do in this moment that the SFPD couldn't? Besides, the coven might be able to help in some way. "Tomorrow night?"

"Tomorrow I've got a family gathering at Renna's house."

Sailor—and his cousin Patience—were members of a large, extended Rom family with some extraordinary psychic abilities. Aidan had made it clear that we needed Sailor's Rom on our side in the upcoming supernatural battle that loomed over San Francisco. Unfortunately, most of the family members I'd met so far weren't exactly wild about me. Still, they were essential, if somewhat prickly, allies.

"I can't skip it," continued Sailor. "Not with things ratcheting up the way they have been. Aidan tells me the cupcake lady has been garnering allies."

"I wasn't certain Renee was still a factor. Last time I saw her she was a little worse for wear." Not long ago, Renee-the-cupcake-lady had cast a befuddling spell over me through a tasty meat pie, but wound up with a concussion at the hand of her own minion. I tried not to take pleasure in anyone's misfortune, but couldn't help relishing the memory of Renee's humiliation. Especially since she had threatened my protégée, Selena.

"According to Aidan she's back, with a vengeance," Sailor said. "And more careful about the people working for her, I would imagine."

"So, when do you think we could talk about . . . things?" I felt a fluttery sensation of not-quite-panic at the base of my throat. Aidan's warning that Sailor and I hardly knew each other clawed at me. Even though the handfasting might not be legal—Bronwyn was still waiting for her certification to be able to officially marry us—in many ways being bound together in front of my family and friends would feel more permanent and serious than any piece of paper from city hall.

A muscle worked in Sailor's jaw as anger settled over his features. "Why don't you just come out and ask me what you're worried about?"

"Children," I blurted out.

"Beg pardon?"

"How do you feel about children?"

"I . . . like them. Some of them, anyway. Others, not so much. I'm not wild about sticky hands."

"No, I mean—do you want to have children? With me, I mean."

"As opposed to having children with someone else?"

"Sailor, I'm serious."

One corner of his mouth hitched up, then the smile spread. "That's what's bothering you? Lily, you're going to drive me to an early grave. Here I thought you were going to tell me that you had gotten cold feet and wanted to call the whole thing off." He shook his head and let out a relieved sigh. "That's it, I'm reconsidering my promise not to read your mind. Otherwise, my heart might not make it."

"You better *not*," I said, returning his smile and tapping my temple. "Right here's a no-go zone."

He glanced at his watch. "So sorry, princess, but I really do have to run. Look. We'll talk about this later, I promise."

"No—I need an answer now, Sailor. It's important to me."

Sailor paused, and his voice was gruff. "Why on earth would you think I wouldn't want to have children with you? Just the idea of a baby Lily knocks my socks off."

"Or a baby Sailor."

"Lord help us both."

I smiled.

He kissed me. "We'll find time to discuss this more, Lily, I promise."

"Soon?"

"Soon."

We shared a smile, and I watched as he walked away.

Chapter 7

I cast a friendly greeting over my shoulder as I sailed past the wax museum ticket booth. The young, heavily made-up woman within, Clarinda, looked up from her dog-eared paperback only long enough to scowl at me and shout that I needed to buy a ticket. I ignored her. I was there to see Aidan, not view the exhibits.

Clarinda didn't care about such niceties. Besides, she didn't like me.

Neither did Noctemus, Aidan's familiar. The beautiful long-haired white cat was perched on a ledge over his office door, and hissed the moment she saw me.

"Always good to see you, too, Noctemus," I said. "Is your master in?"

"Now you're talking to cats?" The sardonic voice of Patience Blix, Sailor's cousin, came from behind me.

"She started it," I said, hoping I didn't sound defensive.

Though we had become sort-of friends and colleagues recently while working together to prove Sailor had not committed a murder, I still felt awkward when faced with Patience's overt beauty and brash confidence. She made a living as a psychic and dressed like a sexy Halloween version of a Rom seer, with a long gauzy skirt that fell to her slim ankles, ringed with little gold bells that tinkled as she walked; a peasant blouse pulled down to reveal her broad, smooth shoulders; plenty of gold-coin necklaces; and bangles on her slim arms. Abundant black hair cascading down her back like Snow White's didn't help my confidence, either.

I glanced down at my outfit: a wide-skirted sundress from the early '60s topped by a turquoise cardigan, and tangerine-colored Keds. The Keds had become my footwear of choice to match with any vintage outfit. One never knew when running from a demon or murderer might be required.

I was content with my own style, but still. Patience was . . . well, she was *Patience*.

"Aidan had to leave," Patience said. At my lack of response, she added: "I presume you're here to see him? Not a fan of the Chamber of Horrors, I'm guessing."

"Not exactly, no." The wax museum made me nervous, all those life-sized poppets standing around, as if waiting to spring to life at the hand of a powerful practitioner. But as uncomfortable as the sports and historical figures made me, the Chamber of Horrors crew was something else entirely. I shivered, then imagined what it would be like to be a simple tourist who didn't associate such things with reality. "You?"

She shook her head. "I've got enough horror in my life. What did you want to talk to Aidan about?"

I almost snapped "none of your business" before realizing Patience could help.

"A friend—Carlos Romero's cousin—was kidnapped today. Snatched off the street in front of my store, by a couple of guys in a white van. The van was found abandoned down by the Alcatraz landing pier, but no sign of Elena."

A slight frown marred Patience's otherwise smooth brow. "That sounds traumatic."

"It was, actually. Thanks."

"I meant for your friend, princess, not you."

"Why does everyone call me 'princess' lately?" I asked

She gave me an ironic half smile. "You might want to ponder that."

"Anyway, I was hoping to ask if you could read for me. Maybe you could see something that would help."

She leaned against the doorframe and Noctemus, purring loudly, jumped into her arms. Apparently the feline didn't hold Patience in the same disdain as she did little old me.

"Last time you asked me to read for you, it didn't go well," Patience said dryly. "You still owe me a mirror, by the way."

"Things have changed," I said, hoping I was telling the truth. The last time Patience tried I hadn't been very cooperative, and my uncontrolled energy had made a bit of a mess of things. Since that encounter I had been training with Aidan, and studying on my own, and had a much tighter rein on my magical abilities. Or so I hoped.

Patience arched one brow. "Is that right? Well, in that case I'm game if you are. Is this woman a good friend of yours? If not, I'll need something of hers to try to get a reading. I can't just conjure a connection out of thin air."

"Sailor has a binding braid that she touched. Would that work?"

"I doubt it. Something personal would be better—a

sweater or a piece of jewelry, something she's worn recently."

"I'll ask Carlos to find something of hers for you to read from."

She nodded. "Do that, and I'll try. But I need a favor in return."

"What is it?"

Patience glanced around. The museum was quiet today, with a middle-aged couple admiring the sculpture of Barbra Streisand, and a picture-perfect young family—parents and two kids, a boy and a girl—lingering by the entrance to the Chamber of Horrors, daring one another to go in. The door to Aidan's office was under a glamour spell, so most visitors didn't realize it was there, and since Patience and I were in front of it we were rendered invisible, or at least unnoticeable, as though within a cocooning spell.

Still, Patience dropped her voice and whispered: "I'm afraid . . . I'm not sure, but I think my aunt Renna needs help."

"What's going on?"

She hesitated. "What do you know about demons?"

"To stay away from them. Why?"

"I . . . listen, I don't want to say too much. Renna read for a client, and ever since then . . . well, I'd rather you just came to see her, to tell me what you think."

"Are you saying Renna is involved with a *demon*?"

She stared at me but didn't reply.

"I'm not Renna's favorite person," I warned.

"So what? You're not my favorite person, either, but we make do."

I laughed. Coming from Patience, that was a compliment.

She continued. "Here's the deal, my little witch: I

read for you and in return you meet with Renna and tell me what you think."

"Deal, my little psychic," I said. "And just so you know: I would have been happy to help regardless. But I just saw Sailor—why didn't he say anything about it?"

Her expression hardened. "You tell me."

"What does that mean?"

"I suspect Sailor doesn't want you involved. He's very protective of you."

"Sailor doesn't need to protect me from anything," I said, irked. "Quite the opposite."

Her only answer was to shrug and languidly stroke Noctemus, who rubbed her head against Patience's arm. Still, the agitation in Patience's big, kohl-lined eyes belied her true frame of mind.

"I'll talk to him about it," I said, adding this to the long list of things my intended and I needed to clarify before our wedding. "Oh, I wanted to ask you one more thing."

"But of course," Patience said, in a mocking tone. "Please, tell me what else I can possibly do for you. I live but to serve."

"I've always admired that quality in you."

"I'll just bet you do."

"I was wondering . . . I know it's sort of last minute, and it's probably a lot to ask, but it occurred to me . . ."

"Spit it out, princess."

"Would you stand up with me at my handfasting?"

She straightened, and Noctemus jumped to the floor. "Ex*cuse* me?"

"Would you be one of my bridesmaids? Maya and Selena already agreed, but Bronwyn's busy officiating, and I thought . . . well, three is better than two, what with the threefold rule and the three points of a triangle and all that. I've got triangles on the brain lately. And . . . after what we went through together for Sailor I would like you at my side. Standing. With me."

It would have been worth posing the question if only for the frozen look on her face. I had never seen Patience at a loss for words. She stood with her mouth slightly agape.

But then the haughty demeanor overtook her again, and she hiked one eyebrow as her eyes tracked a couple strolling by us, arm in arm, oblivious to our presence.

"Would I have to wear one of those noxious taffeta prom dresses you're always pawning off on unsuspecting souls?"

I smiled. "Well, we're all wearing vintage—Susan Rogers from the *Chronicle* is going to do a photo shoot. But you are welcome to choose any outfit you like from the store. Want to come by tomorrow afternoon and look through our inventory? Maya's still searching for the right ensemble, and Selena's coming over at two so we thought we'd make an event of it. A little vintage-dress therapy."

Again, an unsure look came over her face, and I fought the impulse to give Patience a quick hug. *What do you suppose she'd make of that?*

I smiled at the thought.

"What are you laughing at?" Patience demanded. "Is this some sort of twisted practical joke?"

"Of course not," I said, realizing with a start that Patience might be just as insecure as the next person, when it came right down to it. Growing up with psychic abilities was probably no picnic, just as growing up a witch in a small town had been traumatic. "I'm sorry; I'm smiling because you look so shocked. To tell you the truth, I sort of surprised myself, but now I'm in love with the idea. Be my bridesmaid? Please say yes."

She blew out a breath. "Does this mean I have to arrange a bachelorette party, or something? If you think I'm going to chaperone you and Maya and Bronwyn to some cheesy male strip show, you're out of your mind."

"That won't be necessary," I said with a smile. "Reading for me would be more than enough."

"I don't give toasts, either."

"No toasting required."

"All right, then. Your bridesmaid, huh? What the hell. This should prove interesting." Patience glanced at the watch hanging from a gold chain around her neck. "Gotta go—I'm already late for an appointment and am jammed up all afternoon. Want to come over tonight?"

"I have a thing with my grandmother's coven tonight." As much as I was worried about Elena and hated to put the reading off, it couldn't be rushed. For Patience to "see," she needed her crystal ball and other accoutrements, and we both needed sufficient peace and concentration to divine together. "And I'll need to get in touch with Carlos about getting something personal of Elena's. Can we meet tomorrow?"

Patience glanced at the calendar on her iPhone. "I could come over to your shop in the afternoon. I could look for a dress, and then you could draw a circle, make divining easier. And after we'll go see Renna. Agreed?"

I nodded. "Sounds like a plan."

I watched Patience saunter toward the top of the stairs and wondered at this latest turn of events. Who would have thought I would ever consider Patience Blix a friend? This was why Bronwyn was forever coaching me not to make assumptions about people, I supposed.

Speaking of whom, Bronwyn was going to be thrilled at this development. She had a bit of hero worship for

Patience, as did Selena. Maya was the only one who seemed immune to the psychic's Gypsy charms—at least so far.

I was about to slip a note under Aidan's door when Noctemus started rubbing against my legs in a friendly gesture—or perhaps she was simply being passive-aggressive, since I'm pretty sure she knew I was allergic to cats.

I sneezed.

Noctemus stared at the doorknob, as though willing me to open it. Was this an invitation?

Half expecting the cat to change her mind and take a swipe at me, I slowly reached out one hand to the knob. Surprised to find it unlocked, I turned it and pushed the door ajar. Noctemus slipped into the dimly lit room.

"Aidan? Hello? Anybody home?"

Aidan's office was decorated in what I privately thought of as Barbary Coast Bordello: lots of deep red velvet upholstery and drapes with gold tassels, dark wood furniture, a thick Oriental rug, amber wall sconces, a beautiful stained-glass Tiffany lamp brightening up one corner. One entire wall was covered from floor to ceiling in wood bookcases, chock-full of arcane occult reference books.

Noctemus purred softly and stalked over to deposit a few long white hairs on the ruby velvet drapes.

Just in case, I peeked into Aidan's special octagon room, a small closet-sized space built to open other-worldly portals and maximize magical power. The only other time Noctemus had invited me into Aidan's private lair was when she decided that I needed to know a piece of Aidan's secret: Terrible burn scars marred half of his face and body.

But no Aidan this time.

Ensconced in one niche of the octagon room was my lachrymatory—a tiny bottle that held the salt residue of tears I had shed many years ago. Those salts were the magical equivalent of a nuclear bomb; Renee-the-cupcake-lady would quite literally kill to get her hands on them. Aidan had protected it with an Etruscan funerary curse that no one—not even I—knew how to safely release without his help. The lachrymatory appeared to be untouched.

I felt bad about intruding into Aidan's sanctuary, but Noctemus was acting so out of character that I wondered if she was trying to tell me something. Maybe I should wait a few minutes, see if he turned up.

I needed to use the telephone, in any case. That would be a reasonable excuse for my being here, should Aidan stride in and demand to know what I was doing in his inner sanctum. *You didn't lock the door and the cat invited me in* seemed like a feeble excuse for trespassing.

I called Carlos, who told me there was nothing new to report.

"Has anyone thought to search Alcatraz?" I suggested.

"Why would the kidnappers have taken her out there? Do you know something?"

"No, but they abandoned the van not far from where the Alcatraz ferry launches, and Elena's a ranger on the island, and the shirt was from Alcatraz. . . ."

"Hard to imagine they would have taken a kidnapped woman on a crowded public ferry."

"They could have had their own boat tied up somewhere in the vicinity, right?"

"And piloted out to the island in broad daylight without being seen? Seems like a long shot." Carlos sighed, and I pictured him running his hand through his hair. "Hell, it's as good a place to look as any, I suppose. At this point I'm willing to try anything. I'll put a call into the feds, and alert the park police on the island, ask them to take a look around. They'll be happy to do something to help find one of their own. Have you had any luck with those strings you found?"

"Not yet, but Sailor's going to work on them some more." As we spoke I glanced around Aidan's office. Unlike me, Aidan kept his witchy paraphernalia out in the open: a black scrying mirror on the wall, a globe made of inlaid stone, a crystal ball perched on an elaborate filigreed silver base. "Also, Patience is going to try a reading, but she needs something personal that belonged to Elena. A favorite sweater or a piece of jewelry, something she's worn recently."

"I can get that for you. Need it tonight?"

"Tomorrow afternoon will be fine. Bring it by the store anytime." I paused and my eyes fell on a couple of large leather-bound tomes pushed to one side of the large desk. The one on top was about female entities that followed their victims around in never-ending vengeance, such as the Vila and the Furies.

"We'll find her, Carlos. I'm sure of it."

"Let's make it quick. For all our sakes."

We hung up, and I slid the book over toward me, fascinated by this glimpse into Aidan's research. Renna once had told me that Sailor was being followed—and tormented—by a *vila*. Could Aidan be using it to control Sailor, somehow? Though we were professional allies, I could never quite figure out whether Aidan was friend or foe. And he was no fan of Sailor, or vice versa.

Then I studied the other volume, which was a grimoire—a spell book—from the fifteenth or sixteenth century, entitled the *Lesser Key of Solomon*, or *Clavicula Salomonis Regis*. I flipped through the subsection titled *Ars Goetia*, which was a catalog of demons. There were hundreds—maybe thousands—of the critters, an entire hierarchy of princes and archdukes and lesser demons, all categorized by terrified monks in the Middle Ages. The demons' characteristics and talents had been painstakingly noted, a seemingly endless variety. Some had wings, others rode horses, still other crawled like snakes. Depictions showed numerous eyes or half a dozen arms or legs, bodies that were often hybrids of human and animal. Demons were primordial, as ancient as the earth.

In the past, certain demons were seen as potential helpers. Students, artists, and professionals sometimes called on demons for assistance, as if they were little genies. It could work, as long as you were able to maintain control over them. But that was no mean feat.

I had met a few demons in my time, and battled a couple. Mostly, I tried to steer clear. I was a witch, but I was no fool.

I looked up to find Noctemus staring at me, her wide blue eyes—so reminiscent of her master's—twinkling in the low light of the amber sconces.

"Is this what you wanted me to find? Aidan's looking into demons? Why?" I thought about what Patience had told me about her aunt Renna. Surely Renna was too smart a practitioner to have become enthralled to a demon. But if her defenses were down, for some reason . . . I shivered at the possibility. Someone as knowing as Renna would lend a lot of power to a demon intent on ill.

Noctemus's only reply was to blink her big eyes. In this respect, Oscar definitely had an advantage, familiarwise. I would take his sometimes annoying garrulousness over subtle, inarticulate blinks.

"Ow!"

Noctemus had leapt on me and dug her claws into my arm deep enough for blood to bead up along the scratches. The unpredictable feline then sat on the other side of the desk, out of arm's length, and preened. I swore under my breath and dabbed at the wound with a handkerchief, but a drop of blood fell onto the page of the grimoire before I could catch it.

I heard something, a whisper, but couldn't tell whether it was coming from outside the office or from within: *blood magic.*

I blew out a breath. I did *not* enjoy blood magic, though I often used a drop of my own blood in my brews. Still, there was no denying its power.

I just wished I knew who—or what—was suggesting it.

Chapter 8

Every time I returned to Aunt Cora's Closet, with its aroma of freshly laundered clothing and the sachets of herbs I hung on the rods, and my friends Bronwyn and Maya and Conrad, warm and welcoming, who watched over the store while I gallivanted around town . . . I reminded myself to count my blessings. My life was wildly complex, true, but it was a gift.

Almost always.

"Lily, I have some bad news," said Bronwyn after I stashed my things.

"What happened? Is it Elena?" I said, bracing myself.

"No, no, nothing like that. In fact, it seems silly to bring it up at a time like this, but I still haven't received my certification for the wedding, so I made a phone call to see what the holdup was. It's in the works but it may not arrive in time for the handfasting. I don't know that I can marry you legally."

I laughed, and Bronwyn looked relieved. "It's not a problem, honest. Sailor and I can do the legal marriage at city hall anytime. The handfasting in front of my friends and family is what matters to me. You're still up for that, right?"

"Just try to stop me," Bronwyn said with a warm smile.

It was nearly closing time, so Bronwyn and Maya busied themselves straightening up the aisles, folding scarves, and rehanging merchandise while I went through the day's receipts. Paperwork was my least favorite part of running a business, but there was no avoiding it. Even for a witch.

We chatted about the wedding as we went about our tasks, laughing over some of the wilder ideas for party favors. I proposed we put together simple herbal sachets, Bronwyn suggested tiny homemade jars of jam—which sounded delicious but an awful lot of work—and Maya, who could be surprisingly traditional when it came to social customs, was in favor of baskets filled with colorful Jordan almonds with *Sailor and Lily* inscribed in sugar.

As worried as we were about Elena, the homey interlude was healing and helped to ground us. I felt as though I should be doing more to find Carlos's cousin, but so far I hadn't come up with a way that I could help the investigation on my own.

Receipts counted and logged, clothes rehung and shop floor swept, and wedding favors still undecided, we hugged each other good night. Bronwyn and Maya headed home, and I climbed the stairs to my apartment.

"Don't forget, we're supposed to bring pizza *and* garlic knots *and* snacks to Calypso's tonight," said Oscar, following me around the apartment so closely that when I stopped he plowed into the back of my legs.

"Ow!" I said.

He didn't miss a beat, just shook his big head and

kept talking. "And the grandmas are gonna make *dessert*! Spice cake! 'Member?"

"How could I forget?" I said. "Don't fret, I called in the food order an hour ago. Let me just splash some water on my face, grab a few things, and we'll get going."

I sat on the edge of my bed and dialed Sailor's number. We didn't usually talk by phone, and I knew he was busy tonight, but I wanted to know what he thought about Renna—and more important, why he hadn't mentioned it to me. I got his voice mail. I listened to his strong voice inviting me to leave a message, but then hung up. He would probably know I called, anyway.

Something was going on with him. Whether it was witchy intuition or just regular old people intuition, I just *knew* it.

I blew out a breath, brushed my hair and used an elastic to tie it in a ponytail, then went back into the kitchen. I took my old red leather Book of Shadows off a high shelf and packed it into my bag, along with a sack of gorse blossoms and a loaf of fresh-baked sourdough bread as offerings for the fairies. Oscar was negotiating with them on my behalf so Sailor and I could have our handfasting in a redwood fairy circle. He had a meeting set up for tonight.

"Time for pizza?" Oscar looked up at me, an eager expression on his face.

"Time for pizza."

"Hey, mistress, could we stop to check out the gargoyles in the Romanesque portal of the old Masonic Temple at Van Ness and Market?"

"The pizzas will get cold, Oscar."

"Calypso can reheat them. Just a quick stop, please, mistress."

I opened my mouth to ask why he hadn't already

checked out all the local gargoyles, but caught myself. I *knew* why. Oscar was nervous that he would actually find his mother, and wanted a friend at his side, just in case. He would do the same for me.

I understood. I had more than my fair share of parental issues, myself, and had only recently been reunited with my own mother. The reunion had gone well—much better than I'd ever allowed myself to hope or imagine—but our relationship was still a far sight away from what one might call "easy."

I picked up eight pizzas—lots with half-and-half toppings to accommodate the many different tastes—and garlicky knots with dipping sauce, as well as an assortment of appetizers, at Escape from New York. The car filled with the tantalizing scents of freshly baked dough and tomato sauce, cheese and veggies and pepperoni, and I realized I would spend the entire trip to Bolinas reminding Oscar to keep his snout out of the boxes. Since I'm no novice when it comes to Oscar's antics I had bought him his very own box of cheesy sticks to munch on as we drove. Still.

We stopped at the Masonic Temple, which was at one of the city's busier intersections. With no parking spot in sight, I edged over at a red curb in front of a fire hydrant.

"The Romanesque-style arch is inspired by cathedrals in France," Oscar said as we checked out the buff, lionlike creatures holding up part of the portal. "But they're not really gargoyles, now that I look at them. And that there's King Solomon, in a canopy of sculpted angels."

"You've been doing your research."

"Yup."

"Why is there a statue of King Solomon?"

"It's a Freemason thing," said Oscar. "Did you know

that there's a truncated pyramid shape formed by connecting Market and Mission, along Montgomery Street, with the base formed by Van Ness? The Transamerica Pyramid building sits at its capstone."

"Why?"

"Why not?"

"I mean, is it just a coincidence or were the streets laid out that way on purpose?"

"I guess that's the question. The truncated pyramid is a prominent Freemason symbol, and it's also on the seal of the United States."

"I thought that was an eagle."

"It's on the other side."

"Oh. Like on the dollar bill?"

He nodded. "And you know how cowans feel about their money. Whooo-eee," he said, imitating me. "*Heh.*"

"But . . . is it supposed to *do* anything? Offer protection of some sort? From what I know about pyramid power, it's meant to play on magnetic forces. But that requires an actual three-dimensional pyramid, not just a triangular design."

Oscar shrugged. "Maybe it's just a coincidence."

"Maybe." I thought back to the *Lesser Key of Solomon* and the *Ars Goetia.* A "Solomon's Triangle" was used to capture demons . . . unless of course the demon turned tables on the conjurer.

"Look what else I found on the Web," Oscar said, and started to read: "*The term 'gargoyle,' in the strictest sense, refers to carved figures meant to be used as rainspouts, particularly popular in Europe during the Middle Ages—whereas chimeras are figures that may or may not serve as rainspouts. Here in San Francisco, there are examples of metal gargoyles situated on the flèche atop Grace Cathedral; others are visible at the entrance of the Russ Building downtown; still others are perched upon the brick walls of San Francisco General Hospital.* Wanna go to Grace Cathedral?"

"Wait, your mother is a chimera, then?"

"Well, since you asked: *'Chimera' refers to any imaginary beast used as decoration, while 'gargoyle' refers to carved grotesques used as architectural features to carry rainwater away from the roofs of buildings. From the French word for 'throat,'* gorge. *Also see* gargle. Gargle. Heh. Gargle's a funny word." Chuckling, Oscar repeated: "Gargle gargle gargle . . ."

Goblin humor.

"But I don't like the way they say 'grotesque,'" he continued. "That's kinda mean, isn't it? If you ask me, *they're* the grotesque ones."

"I think it's intended in the architectural sense, as in something complex and inventive, which isn't insulting. So, to be clear: Is your mother a gargoyle or a chimera?"

"I never saw her spout rainwater through her throat, if that's what you mean. Yeah, so maybe I meant 'gargoyle' in a sort of generic sense."

"That opens things up a bit," I said, thinking to myself that if Oscar had to search the world for a chimera, he was going to be one well-traveled gobgoyle. As would I, of course, since I had promised to help him look. "Anyway, we don't have time to track down every gargoyle—or chimera—in San Francisco just at the moment. I've got a lot to do."

"You *always* have a lot to do," he grumbled. "Chasing after murderers and whatnot. And it's worse now with that girl witch."

"Selena?" Selena and Oscar had what can best be described as a sibling-type relationship: competitive and sniping, and very occasionally close.

"Yeah. It's like I've always said: 'If it's not one thing, it's Selena.'"

I smiled and started the engine. "You did *not* always say that."

"I should have."

"I'm sorry if I've been preoccupied lately, Oscar," I said as we drove through busy downtown avenues, heading for the Golden Gate Bridge. "You're right, there's a lot going on and I haven't given you the attention you deserve."

"Thank you, mistress," Oscar replied, his growl filled with emotion.

"You're welcome. Hey, you know what?"

"What?" Oscar bounced up and down on the car seat excitedly, good humor restored.

"I was thinking: You know where it seems like there should be gargoyles, but there aren't?"

"Where?"

"San Quentin prison," I said. "I went there once, and the facade is castellated, like a castle, but there are no gargoyles."

"What's with you and the penal system lately?" He hiked his skinny shoulders and shivered. "Prisons give me the willies. You wouldn't catch the likes of Oscar out on Alcatraz, I'll tell you that much."

"Is there something about Alcatraz in particular that you don't like?"

He shrugged. "I'm just saying, I'd rather avoid the place."

"I know what you mean." I couldn't stop thinking about Elena. Had her assailants taken her to Alcatraz, and if so, why?

Besides my worry for Elena, I was out of sorts. This was a time in my life that I was supposed to be concentrating on finding the perfect bridesmaid dresses for Maya and Bronwyn and Selena—and now Patience!— and fretting about fripperies, such as party favors and guest lists, not worrying about evil shirts and a kidnapping. Also, something was up with Sailor, I was certain of it. I adored him and had in no way changed my mind about the handfasting, but we really did need to carve out the time—and mental space—to clarify a few things between us before the big day.

"Let's talk about something else," I suggested as we passed over the Golden Gate Bridge. To our left, the sun was just beginning to set, casting spectacular pink and tangerine streaks over the ocean.

I glanced to our right, and my eyes fell on Alcatraz. The Rock. The lonely, miserable island in the bay.

"Okay," said Oscar, munching on his cheese sticks. "So, I've been thinking: Should I be a flower pig or a ring bearer?"

"Bronwyn's grandchildren are going to be the flower children, remember?"

"I could do it better than *them*."

"Because tossing flower petals requires advanced skill?"

"See? I told you. You're in a bad mood lately."

I stewed for a moment. "You're right. I'm a little jumpy, and a lot preoccupied. Among my worries is that you still haven't negotiated a settlement with the woods folk so we can use the fairy circle for the handfasting. Will you be able to get it done tonight, do you think?"

"Those guys are pretty touchy. Negotiations are ongoing, is all I can say."

"I brought the fairy money and the bread."

"You know, you could always get married at the Slovenian Hall or something. Doesn't have to be in the fairy circle. Plenty of people get married indoors."

"I can't get married at the Slovenian Hall."

"'Cause you're not Slovenian? I can smooth it over, no worries. I know a guy."

"It's not that. I'm sure it's a lovely place, but . . . this is a *handfasting*. And I'm a *witch*. I need the blessing of the woods spirits. I can feel it in my gut."

"Are you sure that's a premonition? Maybe you're just hungry. Hey, maybe we should open one of the pizzas!" Oscar said, and reached for a pizza box.

"Don't you dare."

Grudgingly, he put it back.

"Cheesy stick?" Oscar offered.

I shook my head. "Thanks, but no. Seriously, Oscar, I'm trusting my gut on this one. The fairy circle, in the redwoods. That's the only place that will do."

Oscar muttered under his breath.

"Sorry?"

"I said: Are you sure it's the *location* that's worrying you?"

"What else would it be?"

"Cold feet?"

"Why would I have cold feet?" I asked, a tad stridently.

Oscar widened his eyes and looked away, as if to say, *Sheesh, told you so.*

"I do *not* have cold feet," I insisted. "I'm just . . . I have a lot to do to pull this whole thing off, and it's hard finding the time to get it done. That's all. And for right now, tonight, I'd like you to finish the negotiations with the fairy folk so I can concentrate on using Graciela's coven to help focus my intent and figure out what the heck's going on with my guiding spirit."

"Ssss."

"Why are you hissing at me?"

"I wasn't hissing."

"Yes, you were."

"It was a sibilant *s*."

"A what, now?"

"Guiding spirit*sss*. With an *s*. English Grammar 101, mistress."

I stroked my medicine bag and reminded myself to breathe. "Well, thank you for the refresher."

Oscar continued, "Two spirits, that's your problem, right?"

"Right."

"Lotsa people would think it was cool. You know, the pairing of opposites. Light and dark, sun and shadow, yin and yang, up and down, east and west, north and south . . ."

"A witch and a gobgoyle?"

"*Heh*," Oscar cackled. "Good one."

"Thing is, though, I don't need two guiding spirits. I was fine with just the one, thank you very much."

"I'm not sure that's up to you, mistress. All due respect."

By now we were driving along the winding redwood-flanked roads to Bolinas. Calypso Cafaro lived in a big old farmhouse tucked into a clearing in the forest. She lived alone but did not seem lonely; in fact, everything about Calypso seemed balanced and serene. Her home was full of books and herbs and comfy, overstuffed furniture. Wind chimes, glass orbs, and napping cats graced the broad front porch. She kept chickens and doves, and had a relationship to plants that went beyond the pale.

Hers was a life that a part of me envied: living independently in such an enchanted realm, free to practice magic and beliefs without censure or limits. But I had chosen a different path: I was going to be united with a wonderful and complicated man and—whether I wanted it or not—would remain enmeshed in San Francisco's supernatural power struggle.

Oh, also, I had a few crimes to solve.

Elena's image appeared in my mind again: her easy smile, her hat hair, her spiffy National Park Service uniform. Where *was* she? What could have happened to her?

I edged my Mustang through the overgrown hedges that crowded the long driveway to Calypso's house, wincing as their branches scratched the car's cherry red finish. The hedges, like many of Calypso's plants, were enchanted and closed behind us, screening Calypso's magical domain from the outside world. Leading up to the big yellow farmhouse was a path lined with rose trees, and a bounty of bushes that were flowering out of season. Behind the house was a glass-paned greenhouse and an extensive vegetable garden.

A calico cat lazed on the wraparound porch.

"This place always reminds me of a picture out of a calendar," said Oscar, with a rare note of awe.

"I couldn't agree more," I said. "Complete with the redwood fairy circle, the perfect place for a handfasting. So, are you coming in or do you want to take a couple of slices of pizza and go chat with the woods folk directly?"

"Sheesh. Anybody ever tell you that you have a one-track mind, mistress?"

"These negotiations seem to take a lot of time, so I thought you might want to make the most of this opportunity."

"I told you, time works different in the fairy world."

"All the more reason to get started. Here are the gorse blossoms and fresh-baked bread to sweeten the deal." I handed him the burlap bag. Woods folk were tricky, and easily insulted. I had to trust in my gobgoyle emissary.

Said emissary was at the moment picking at his talons and debating which pizzas to try, which wasn't exactly filling me with confidence.

Finally Oscar settled on one slice each of the cheesy cheese, the veggie, and the potato pesto pies. We both avoided the pepperoni; pork products were off the menu now that Oscar took the form of a pig a good portion of the time. I promised he could have the leftovers—and dessert—when he was done, and after polishing off the pizza slices he scampered off to the woods with the burlap bag full of gifts.

As I gathered the pizza boxes and bags of food from the car, Calypso joined me, a thick gray braid resting on one shoulder, a blousy chartreuse linen shirt over flowered leggings, her bare feet covered in henna designs and her toenails painted a bright red. An ankle bracelet tinkled as she came over to help me.

"*Lily*. How lovely." We embraced.

"How's it been going with the grandmas?" I asked. "Everything all right?"

"I'm having the time of my life! They are absolute fonts of knowledge—though they do bicker a bit, don't they?"

"Only when they disagree. Which is often."

Calypso laughed. "Still, I'm learning scads, so much so that my hand's beginning to cramp from writing everything down."

"One of them could probably whip up a salve for that with the ingredients in your greenhouse and garden."

"Kay's already on it," Calypso said, her eyes falling to my forearm as I handed her the pizza boxes. Noctemus's scratches were inflamed and angry-looking. "Looks like you need a salve, yourself."

"I love cats, but they don't always love me," I explained.

I followed her up the steps to the front porch and into the cool front hall. The house had the detailed craftsmanship and woodwork characteristic of homes built in the 1920s. The wainscoting was painted a creamy white, and built-in bookcases and cabinets abounded. Calypso ushered me into the large kitchen, chock-full of herbs hanging in bundles from the wooden beams, mason jars filled with a wide variety of fungi and seeds, pods and moss.

Rosa, Viv, and MariaGracia sat around the old wooden farmhouse table, sorting through pieces of paper and index cards and writing things down in a massive leather-bound book that looked a lot like my own Book of Shadows.

"Lily! We're exchanging recipes," said Viv.

These "recipes" were not for casseroles but for spells, as well as healing salves and plasters, tonics and teas. Years ago, the coven had made the same kind of contributions to my own Book of Shadows, and I hoped to gather more while they were here.

I kissed them all as they exclaimed over how fabulous Calypso was and what a great time they were having.

I found my mother, Maggie, in the dining room, putting the finishing touches on my wedding trousseau.

It was still hard to believe that my mother had come for my handfasting, much less that she had arrived bearing such marvelous presents. In addition to the trousseau, she had given me her wedding gown so I had the perfect dress to wear for the handfasting. My mother and I had a fraught history: Maggie was a small-town Texas beauty queen who, when I began exhibiting my special witchy talents, had become frightened of her own child and sent me to live with Graciela. For a long time we had little contact. But in the past few years my mother had come to regret what she had done. For my part, I had matured and though I still felt hurt by her choices, I had begun to feel empathy for the scared woman who had made them, and we'd begun a rapprochement.

Most astoundingly, after a lifetime of wanting nothing to do with the supernatural, or with me, my mother had asked Graciela to coach her in knot magic so that she could make me a trousseau. Maggie was talented with a needle, but knot magic was something else entirely. A pile of tangled strings on the table gave silent testimony to her lack of skill.

"Lily!" My mother stood and held out her arms, and we hugged. Then she sank back down in her chair and sighed. "I fear I'm terrible at this knot magic, and yet I can't seem to stop trying."

"You know what they say," I said. "Once you go magic, you never go back."

She smiled. "Is that what they say?"

"Something like that," I said with a laugh. "How's everything been going?"

"Very well, considering. Calypso gave me my own room, so I have a little privacy. Graciela's friends are wonderful, but . . ."

"It's nice to have a little time to yourself."

"Exactly."

We chatted for a few minutes, then I asked, "Where's Graciela, do you know?"

My mother directed me to the greenhouse, where I found my grandmother consulting with Darlene, Pepper, and Iris. They were skilled garden witches, with a deep connection to plants, roots, seeds, and botanicals of all kinds.

"Good thing you're here, *m'ija*," said Graciela. "Look at this."

She gestured to some lady's mantle, whose cuplike leaves held a portion of silvery morning dew, as though offering a tiny fairy a drink.

"A 'wine cup,' right?" I was no slouch at botanicals, myself. "What's wrong with that?"

"It's not morning," explained Darlene. "And we're inside a greenhouse. So where did the dew come from?"

"Plants seem to operate by different rules in Calypso's garden," I said. "You've probably noticed that her bushes and trees bloom out of season."

Iris shook her head and held up another plant with delicate fernlike leaves and diminutive pink-petaled flowers.

"Herb Robert, right?" I ventured.

"Also known as red robin," said Rosa. I looked up to find that nearly the entire coven had joined us, crowding into the jammed greenhouse.

"Or crow's foot," said Viv.

"I always called it squinter-pip," said Caroline.

"Storksbill," said Agatha.

"Stinking Bob," said Betty.

"Or . . . death come quickly," said Iris in a hushed tone.

Chapter 9

"I can't say I like the sound of that last one," I said. "What is it supposed to indicate?"

"Could be a lot of things," said Pepper, gesturing toward a large container of a plant with glossy green leaves and little white flowers hanging along a slender stalk. "But in conjunction with the wine cups and the Solomon's tears . . ."

I hadn't noticed the Solomon's tears when I walked in. *There had been an awful lot of Solomon in my life, lately*, I thought as Graciela finished Pepper's sentence:

". . . it could be an indication of the prophecy."

"This is the prophecy that claims I was drawn to San Francisco to undertake a supernatural showdown of some sort," I clarified.

She stuck out her chin and nodded.

"A wine cup is for the fairy folk, isn't it?" I asked. "What do they have to do with the prophecy?"

"Good question," murmured Winona. "There's something amiss in the fairy world. The woods folk are all atwitter."

"And look," said Graciela, "Those *alcatraces* are blooming out of season as well."

"*Alcatraces*?" I asked as my eyes fell on conical white flowers with orange stamens.

"Calla lilies," Nan translated.

"They're called *alcatraces*? As in Alcatraz?" I asked. "Like the island?"

"I always thought Alcatraz meant 'pelican,'" said Viv.

"Me, too," said MariaGracia.

"It can also mean a kind of seabird," said Caroline. "Many words have multiple meanings."

"Okay . . ." I said, pondering my nightmare, and Sailor's vision, and Selena's drawings. "So what's wrong with herb Robert and Solomon's tears? They're both medicinal plants."

"As you well know, medicine can be poison if applied inappropriately," said Graciela. "*Y lo que me preocupa*—what's bothering me—is the way they're intertwined. Also, Calypso says that was a flat of pansies. She never planted the Solomon's tears here."

"You're right, that's weird," I conceded.

The wisewomen all nodded.

"Are we sure this is even directed toward me?"

"You, or, you know, *el otro*," said Graciela.

"*El otro*, the 'other one' refers to my supposed brother, right?"

Not long ago I had learned that my father (might have) had another child, a boy. Which meant I had a half brother out in the world. Somewhere. Whether he would be an ally or a foe was the real question.

"We think so," said Graciela. "Can't be sure, of course. Rosa will read for you later, see what she can."

Again with the reading. I didn't enjoy being read for. I was accustomed to holding my metaphysical cards to my chest, even within a trusted coven. It occurred to me that the last person who had read for me was Sailor's aunt Renna.

Speaking of whom . . .

"The prophecy and shape-shifting pansies aside," I said. "I need to ask you all something serious. Two things, actually. A friend of mine was kidnapped. And I think . . . it's possible I might have to go up against a demon soon."

There were several sharp intakes of breaths.

"Are they connected? The kidnapping and the demon activity?" asked Graciela.

"I don't think so . . . I have no indication that they are. And the demon stuff might be something else entirely," I said. "I haven't met with the person afflicted yet. But apparently the last time I was involved in something like this I didn't protect myself adequately, so I'm trying to be smart. Not rush in, and all that." I explained to them what Patience feared, and how powerful a practitioner Renna was.

There was a lot of head-shaking, glasses-cleaning, *tsk*ing and mumbling, which continued for so long that I started to get worried. If none of these thirteen wise-women knew how to approach a demon, who did?

Finally, Kay ventured: "A MoonWish spell."

"Yes, a MoonWish spell would be best," murmured Nan.

"It will take several days," continued Kay. "Use a jar of clover honey with the comb still in it for the first day's sacrifice."

"It will take *five* days." Viv was very into number magic. "Use charms for the five senses, and draw the five points on a pentagram."

"Oh! That's perfect, five days from now will be the full moon," said Iris.

"The dark moon would be better for demon binding," said Betty, "but full is second best."

"You'll need genuine sulfur to charge the sigil," said MariaGracia. "Charcoal incense dipped in oils will not do."

"But I don't want to *charge* anyone's sigil," I protested. "I want to get rid of it altogether."

More murmuring and shaking of heads.

Graciela explained, "Demons are elemental and eternal, *m'ija, tu sabes.* You should know that. There's no getting rid of them. A demon is never truly banished; he can be called anywhere, anytime."

"First you'll have to summon him in order to control him," said Pepper.

"Don't forget the hexing incense," said Rosa.

"Or frankincense," suggested Agatha.

Suddenly all thirteen women were full of advice, which they started calling out indiscriminately.

"Bring a scrying mirror."

"And a Solomon's Triangle, of course. Anointed with olive oil and myrrh."

"Use a black candle separation spell in addition to the banishing spell."

"A full MoonWish spell should be cast, and I'd say separation and binding rather than banishing."

"Viv's right, take the full five days and pay close attention to how quickly the candles burn, and the dripping of the wax."

"Blood energy is best," Graciela said. "In fact, a blood sacrifice for the final night of the spell."

That stopped the discussion, as the women exchanged glances. The cat scratches on my arm throbbed.

"You know, Solomon's tears are also called Solomon's

seal," said Darlene in a muted tone. "They should be used to create the Solomon's Triangle, to bind the fellow. Lily should harvest them by the light of the moon . . ."

". . . and dress them with her blood," Graciela emphasized.

"And that will keep her soul tethered while she goes up against a *demon*?" asked my mother, Maggie, in a shaky voice.

She was standing in the doorway, as though reluctant to enter. I hadn't realized she had joined us, and I wondered how much she had heard.

Graciela nodded, and the others followed suit, though their affirmation seemed rather anemic.

"Probably," said Graciela.

"It should," said Darlene.

"We think so," said MariaGracia.

We all fell silent for a long moment.

"But first, *tengo hambre*," Graciela said. "How about that pizza?"

One of the things I loved about my grandmother—which also drove me crazy, in equal measure—was how she could talk about blood magic and going up against a demon (and "probably" triumphing) one moment, and pizza the next. Graciela had a thing or two to teach me about putting things in perspective and, like most witches I knew, rarely missed a meal.

Food was not only sustenance, it was a magical transformation of ingredients through mixing and stirring, heat and love, a way to ingest life from the earth, and to enjoy in fellowship.

We gathered around Calypso's huge dining room table. Mullein leaves, also known as hag's taper, had been dipped in fat and lit like candles; they cast a warm, embracing glow. In the center of the table were items representing the four elements: berries, leaves, and stones for earth; feathers and flower petals for air; ash and candles for fire; and seashells and driftwood for water. Bright ceramic plates had been laid out, flanked by brass goblets and colorful woven napkins.

"I never use this room for anything but crafts anymore," Calypso said, holding up her cell phone to take a picture. "This is wonderful. Everybody say 'cheese'!"

"No!" cried Caroline, Viv, and Rosa, hiding their faces.

"Don't mind them. They're *supersticiosas*," said Graciela with a dismissive wave of her hand. "Superstitious."

"No photos, Calypso," I said. "It's a thing for some witches."

"I'm so sorry," said Calypso. "How silly of me. I didn't even think . . ."

According to Calypso, she "used to be" a witch. I was not sure how she had pulled that off; I always thought once a witch, always a witch. Calypso had helped to heal Aidan when he first arrived, gravely injured, in San Francisco, and for a brief time the two had ruled the Bay Area magical community together. When it came to plants, Calypso was without peer, but she was even more lacking in standard occult training than I was. It would never occur to me to take someone's photo without first asking their permission, in case they feared for their soul.

"Now, just never you mind them, Calypso," said Iris. "Betty and I *love* to have our picture taken, don't we, Betty?"

"That's because we're what's called 'photogenic,' unlike *some* people I could mention. I want a photo of me in my new jacket!" said Betty, pulling on a rainbow-colored explosion of a waistcoat. Betty was a petite woman, who, with her cotton-top hair and bright red–rimmed glasses on a chain, looked as if she had been sent from central casting to play the role of an "eccentric little old lady."

Darlene posed with Iris and Betty, and Calypso captured their image on her smartphone, with the wonderfully witchy display behind them. Then we stood around the table, holding hands, and Graciela led a prayer of thanks that I remembered from childhood:

Grain and plant, milk and meat,
upon the table plates are heap'd.
Earthly bounty, gifts of life
sustenance and strength are rife.
We thank the mother and honor her seat.
May her heart forever beat.

We sat down to pizza and pitchers of lavender lemonade, which some of the women spiked with vodka. I imbibed a tad, nervous about the prospect of being read for after dinner.

The meal was long and leisurely, the conversation lively, but I couldn't join in fully—in vodka or conversation—without worrying about what my grandmother had said, and what lay in store. Plus my concern over Elena's fate and my own looming wedding.

At the moment, I was one big ball of nerves.

Dessert was Calypso's freshly made mint and melon ice, and an assortment of iced spice cakes the grandmas had baked. Oscar still hadn't shown up, so I made sure to set aside a piggy bag of baked goods; I would never hear the end of it if he missed out on cake. Calypso brewed a pot of sweet-and-spicy tea from various fruit peels, pink peppercorns, and fresh herbs, and I made a mental note to ask if she would be willing to share her recipe with Bronwyn tomorrow. Some of us were fiends for coffee; Bronwyn was a tea fanatic. She could make a fortune selling a tea like this.

I was still pondering whether I could dissuade the coven from reading for me when Pepper nabbed the delicate porcelain cup I had been drinking from and passed it down to Rosa on the other end of the table. Each woman held on to it in her hands for a moment, singing a soft chant before passing it on. When the cup finally landed in front of Rosa, she made a great show of turning it upside down onto her saucer, turning it thrice. The porcelain made a scraping *scritch* with each turn.

I held my breath, and waited.

At that moment I spotted the mandragora I had made—a kind of house elf carved from the root of the mandrake bush—sitting on a nearby shelf, a piece of pizza in his lap. Calypso had named him Finall. He didn't move yet seemed to meet my gaze, intelligence in his eyes, as though he understood.

Meanwhile, the gaggle of women was watching Rosa, who had to borrow Calypso's reading glasses. They were too small for her and sat perched on her prominent beak like a bird on a tree branch.

She hummed and nodded, then spoke.

"She's blocked by the struggle of the duality. There are two spirits, the Ashen Witch and the other."

Until very recently whenever I brewed, my guiding spirit would appear, her amorphous face showing itself in the plume of steam rising above my cauldron. For the longest time I had not known who she was, but have since learned that she was a magical woman called the Ashen Witch, who had walked this earth a long time ago.

I then went up against a creature named Deliverance Corydon—the Ashen Witch's nemesis—and apparently had not adequately protected myself, because a part of Deliverance had taken up residence somewhere within me, and the two spirits were fighting.

"That does it, then," announced Graciela. "We'll need to perform the sundering/fastening ceremony on the full moon. Lily, you are excused."

"But wait—can you see anything about my friend Elena? She's the one who was kidnapped."

Rosa shook her head. "Sorry, dear, it doesn't work like that."

"But—," I began.

"We need to confer, *m'ija,* as a coven," said Graciela. "*Solas.* In private."

I felt a little annoyed, but reminded myself that I was not, in fact, a member of their coven. Far from it. I might have friends, colleagues, even a familiar. But when it came to witchcraft, I was a solo act.

"We must be properly prepared," continued Graciela. "Besides, Lily will need the time to carry out the separation spell before attempting any kind of demonic exorcism. Also, we're going to the Japanese garden and the de Young Museum tomorrow; we've got tickets for the new Pre-Raphaelite show; and the day after that we're going to the Exploratorium."

"But . . ." I protested, feeling like a whiny little girl. Was I regressing in the company of my mother, grandmother, and magical aunties? "A friend of mine was kidnapped today, and another friend might be troubled by a demon. Couldn't y'all do the touristy things at a later date?"

"We've never been to San Francisco, dear," said Winona.

"I wanna see Chinatown," said MariaGracia, and

others chimed in with their requests. Lunch at a dim sum restaurant met with widespread approval.

"Is there anything y'all could do tonight to help Lily?" my mother persisted. "I don't want her to have to wait until the full moon."

I looked at her with a rush of gratitude. It was the first time I could remember Maggie standing up for me.

"We could draw down the moon," suggested Pepper.

"We could certainly do that," said Caroline. "We'll stand together, link our strength with yours. It might help."

"It *will* help," said Agatha.

Drawing down the moon with an experienced coven was a special event for someone like me. Bronwyn's coven had cast with me before and lent me their strength, which had been wonderful. But Graciela's coven was in a different league entirely. If Bronwyn's coven was a top-ranked college football team, Graciela's coven was the Super Bowl champ. There was no comparison.

Calypso and my mother waited on the porch swing while the coven and I convened in the meadow behind the house. The evening was fresh, the trees and flowers scenting the air with their fragrance. The sky was clear, a waxing gibbous moon glowing overhead. Crickets and frogs chirped, and an occasional bat dived and swooped by.

The coven came together with the well-choreographed movements of thirteen women who had known one another and worshipped together for decades. They chanted softly in unison; I couldn't make out the words but I felt their intent. It was loving, warm, and strong. I could feel myself letting go, letting down my guard as we shared the chalice, calling to the Lord and the Lady of the forest, to the great mother, to the moon. The walls I had built to shield myself—to prevent others from understanding my magic, from knowing I was a witch, an outcast, a weirdo to be culled from the herd—began to tremble. Slowly at first, then faster, the barriers I had so carefully erected between me and the rest of the world started to tumble.

Safe. The word reverberated through me.

Was this what it felt like, I wondered? To relax, to feel at ease, to be free of constantly second-guessing oneself? To allow others to judge, yet not run in fear of being rejected?

I soaked in the warm, strong hum. The profound sense of humor. The wisdom of the aged, and the light that had fallen on generations of strong women.

Together, we drew down the moon.

Afterward, a contented, silvery silence enveloped us like a cloak.

"It's going to take more than that for you to triumph, *m'ija,*" said Graciela, breaking the spell with her usual matter-of-factness. "But it's a start."

When it was time to go home, I couldn't find Oscar anywhere. I called and called, but there was no response.

"I'm sure he's fine, dear," said Calypso, walking me to my car and handing me a bag containing leftovers for Oscar along with a decorative blue mason jar of local clover honey, complete with honeycomb. "These things take time. He's welcome to spend the night here when he comes out of the woods, but as you know, he'll probably make his own way home."

Oscar remained in his piggy guise around Calypso, but she knew he was a shape-shifter. She was the one who had told me about his hidden wings, which enabled me to rescue him when he'd gone missing before.

His last disappearance had terrified me. But in all likelihood, Calypso was right—Oscar was just hanging out with the fairies. How many times had he told me that time passed differently in the fairy realm, so that a few minutes there might be an hour aboveground? Oscar would return on his own time, and in his own way.

He'd *better* return. I needed him, I loved him, and had no reserves left to cope with missing him.

Driving home alone, I was in a definite funk. Despite the profound magical contentment from drawing down the moon with the coven, I felt angst in the pit of my stomach resurface as I brooded about my upcoming nuptials, Elena, Renna—and now Oscar. Oh, and I mustn't forget to add Renee-the-cupcake-lady to the mix.

As soon as I got home I would start the clock on the five-day MoonWish spell. I had been relatively green the last time I'd tried to go up against a demon, which was why I was now in a predicament, with two guiding spirits warring within me.

As I drove south across the Golden Gate Bridge I couldn't keep from looking over at Alcatraz and the placid waters of the bay, remembering last night's mare. Would it visit me again tonight?

Most of the city seemed to be asleep as I passed through the Presidio, skirted Golden Gate Park, and continued along the Panhandle. I parked my car in the driveway I rented around the corner from my store, off Haight Street, which was still lively with folks pouring out of bars.

As I approached Aunt Cora's Closet, I spied a man lingering in my doorway, hat in hands.

My heart pounded. *Carlos.* I hurried to join him.

"Is . . . did you find Elena?" I asked.

He shook his head and glowered at an inebriated group of young people across the street, stumbling along and laughing loudly. "Could we talk inside?"

"Of course."

I let us in, and Carlos declined my offer of tea or something stronger as we took our seats at the jade green linoleum table in the workroom. Only then did I realize that the hat in his hands had a band with a shiny acorn on it: It was part of a National Park Service uniform.

"It's Elena's spare. Bethany said she wore it just a few days ago."

"This is helpful, Carlos. Patience is coming by tomorrow, so I'll see if she can pick anything up from it. In the meantime, have you found anything?"

"Still no sign of Elena. But there was a body found out on Alcatraz."

"Who is it? Is it related to Elena's kidnapping?"

Carlos gazed at me intently. "Have you told me everything you know, Lily?"

"Of course. What's wrong?"

"Why did you suggest we search Alcatraz?"

"Well . . . Just because of the timing, with the prisoner's shirt turning up, and then Elena's connection to Alcatraz, and where the van was dumped."

"That's all? Nothing occult, a premonition or anything along those lines?"

I shook my head. "Nothing specific. I did have a nightmare. I was swimming in the bay—or floating, really, I don't actually know how to swim—anyway, I was trying not to drown, and I could see San Francisco in the distance. A dark island was close behind me. It scared me."

Silence reigned for a beat. "That's it?"

"Well, Selena's been drawing calla lilies, and Sailor saw one, too, and my grandmother told me 'alcatraz' means 'calla lily' in Spanish."

"I thought 'alcatraz' meant a 'gannet.'"

"What's a gannet?"

"A seabird of some kind."

"I also heard it meant 'pelican.'"

"Sorry to be rude, but who gives a damn what it means?"

I wasn't the only one in a bad mood lately.

"I have no idea, Carlos. You asked me whether I'd had any sort of premonition, and while I don't usually dream premonitions, I don't usually have nightmares, either. So I thought they might be connected. As you know, I rely on intuition more than hard-and-fast facts."

He inclined his head as though ceding my point.

"Can you tell me who was killed?" I asked again.

"The medical examiner is still working on an official identification, and the crime scene's being processed. I'm only discussing this with you because it looks like he was killed in a ritual of some sort."

"What kind of ritual?"

"That's what I'm hoping you could tell us. I just have to figure out how to get you out there to look at it. Since the crime scene is on Alcatraz, it's a federal case; I have no jurisdiction."

"Then what can you tell me about it?"

"I haven't seen it yet. But Forrest said it looked 'satanic.'"

"By which he means . . . ?"

"It's anybody's guess. You know how it is—a few candles, some herbs. Could be unrelated, could be nothing. These days, if there's anything even slightly out of the ordinary, somebody thinks it's satanic. But . . ." He hesitated. "Apparently most of the blood was drained from the victim."

"That's not good," I said.

"That's why I'd like your input. I'm going to see if the FBI will allow us to go out and take a look. You'll come, won't you?"

"I will." The idea of setting foot on that island scared me more and more, but was also looking increasingly essential. "Too bad you don't have an ID on the body. That might tell us something."

"Like I said, there's no official ID." He paused, as though debating whether to say more. "But the preliminary fingerprint results suggest that he's a man named Cole Albright, aged eighty-seven."

"Cole Albright? Wait, isn't that the name of a man who supposedly escaped from Alcatraz, back in the early 1960s?"

"The very one."

"He was presumed drowned."

"Apparently word of his demise was exaggerated."

"But if he escaped, why would he go *back* to Alcatraz, especially after all these years?"

"Excellent question. And that's not the weirdest part."

"I'm afraid to ask."

"The man was wearing a light blue, long-sleeved shirt that appears to have been part of a prisoner's uniform."

"He was wearing his original prison uniform?"

Carlos shook his head. "Not according to the prison logs. This shirt was stamped with the number 258. It belonged to a man named Ray Perry. Escaped from Alcatraz and presumed drowned in 1937."

My heart dropped. The shirt with disturbing vibrations, whose binding strings had been ripped off and dropped in the gutter. The shirt I had last seen when I wrapped it up and handed it to Elena.

The cursed shirt.

Chapter 10

"So what we have so far," said Carlos, "is one kidnapping and one murder. You think the murder of Albright might be a ritual of some kind?"

"I really can't tell you anything without taking a look at the scene."

"Like I said, it's an FBI matter. Let me make a few phone calls, see if I can call in some favors, let them know we might have some local information that would help with the case."

"I tried to go to Alcatraz earlier today. Did you know you have to wait for months to get tickets?"

"Why did you try to go?"

"To poke around."

"Uh-huh. No 'poking around' Alcatraz without informing me, understand? Don't even think about hiring a boat or something equally foolish."

"You're the second man who's told me that today. Do I look like the kind of woman who would so easily break the law?"

"Truthfully? I think you would move heaven and earth to protect an innocent from harm," Carlos said softly. "Which I happen to admire about you, actually, except for one thing: That's *my* job. I have a badge and everything."

"Can't argue with that."

"But since I'm under no illusions that you'll do as I say, let me just say this: Be careful, look before you leap, and if at all possible don't go in without backup. That's me."

I nodded. "One more thing? I know this is a strange question, but I feel like I have to ask it."

"Go ahead."

"I barely know Elena. She wouldn't . . . you don't think she would be involved in this somehow, do you?"

"Involved how?"

"This sort of thing, the occult, good and bad, can be very . . . seductive. Sometimes people get in over their heads . . . Elena might not have understood what she was doing, or the risk she was running, and found herself caught up in something she couldn't control."

He shook his head. "No way, Lily. Elena's about the most grounded, honest, straightforward person I know. Do you know how hard it was for her to come out to her mother, to tell her she was in love with a woman? But she didn't pull any punches, said she had to lead an authentic life. Also, she's a pretty devout Catholic, goes to church every Sunday, and tries to live her faith every day. Now, I've been a cop long enough to know that you can never be certain about what's in somebody else's heart, so I'll just say this: Nothing in Elena's life points toward what you're suggesting."

"Good. I figured. I'm just trying to take everything into consideration, the way my friend the homicide detective told me to do, a long time ago."

He gave me a ghost of a smile and stood.

"Well, I'm headed back to the office. I want to look into the recent whereabouts of one Cole Albright."

"At this hour?"

"You know what they say. No sleep for the wicked."

I let myself into my apartment above the store, and a shape popped out of the kitchen.

"Mistress!"

"Oscar! You scared the dickens out of me!"

"What's a dickens?"

"I have no idea, actually. How did you get home?"

"How do you mean?" he asked.

"Never mind," I said, wondering why I bothered to ask such things since he never answered me. "How did things go with the woods folk? Graciela's coven said they were agitated."

"They were a little outta sorts, but you never can tell with those guys. They're touchy, I tell you what. Lucky Oscar's on the job."

As I started to pull together the ingredients to begin the five-day MoonWish spell, Oscar chatted nonstop about his underworld meeting, which apparently included some scrumptious snacks.

"Wait—you ate something?" I paused, holding the ancient pestle above the mortar Graciela had given me when I left home. I had filled the stone bowl with a variety of dried herbs and seeds known for their protective properties. "I thought that if you ate fairy food you couldn't ever leave their realm. Isn't that part of the folklore?"

He cackled. "You crack me up! Where'd you read that, in a book of fairy tales?"

"Maybe. Or . . . I think Aidan might have mentioned it once."

He waved a hand. "What Aidan doesn't know about the woods folk is a *lot*. That's why he always left this sort of thing up to yours truly. The fairies aren't really as scary as they're cracked up to be. You wear your clothes inside out, maybe ring a few bells, bring some bread, you're golden. Well, except . . ."

"What?"

"Don't start dancing with them."

"Why is that?"

"Because you'll never be able to stop and will dance yourself to death."

"Okay, thanks. Safety first."

"Anyway, it turns out they do have a favor to ask of you."

"They do? That's progress! What is it?"

"Get rid of Alcatraz."

"I'm sorry?"

"They would like you to get rid of Alcatraz."

"You mean get rid of the curse, or the ghosts, or something?"

He tilted his head. "Nah, pretty sure they want you to get rid of the place."

"It's an island."

"More like a big rock, really. Anyway, they're not unreasonable. You don't have to get rid of it entirely, or anything."

"Well, that's a relief."

"Just sink it. Let it be an underwater rock."

"Oscar, are you serious? How in the world am I supposed to accomplish something like that?"

He shrugged. "Did you get potato chips?"

"No, I haven't made it to the store yet. I've been a little busy."

Oscar let out a long-suffering sigh.

"But," I said as I took a well-wrapped bundle out of

my bag, "I did bring you cake. And pizza crusts. You could dip them in ranch dressing; there's some in the fridge."

"Who would leave behind *pizza* crusts?" Oscar asked, incredulous, as he ripped open the package.

"Rosa and Viv only like the 'soft parts,' and Caroline is watching her figure and said she didn't need all those carbs."

Oscar munched on the crusts, shaking his head at the mysterious ways of humans. The idea of sinking Alcatraz left him unfazed, but someone walking away from pizza crusts was beyond his reckoning.

"Oscar, I don't understand. Why don't the woods folk like Alcatraz?"

"There's something off about it. Always has been, but it's worse lately. The only ones who like it are the birds. It's 'for the birds,' get it?"

"Funny."

"Ooooh, spice cake with cream cheese frosting. My favorite." Oscar crammed two of the little cakes in his mouth at once.

"So let me get this straight: In exchange for allowing me to hold my handfasting in the redwood fairy circle, the woods folk want me to get rid of Alcatraz Island. Is that what you're telling me?"

Oscar nodded.

"I know weddings can be costly, but doesn't that seem a little steep?"

"The Slovenian Hall's looking better all the time, am I right?"

"How am I supposed to sink an entire island? It's one of the most popular attractions in the whole National Park System, so I'm pretty sure folks would notice if it went missing. Getting rid of it would probably be illegal, among other things."

Oscar cackled.

I heard the sound of Sailor's boots on the stairs. *Good*. I needed advice.

I ran to the door. It swung open, and Sailor strode in: tired and rumpled, and sexy as all get-out.

"Sailor! I'm so glad you're here. I need to talk to y—"

"Lord, I've needed you today," he growled.

He grabbed me, pushed me up against the wall, and kissed me. I kissed him back, and all questions and concerns fled my mind.

So much for talking.

Chapter 11

At least I wasn't accosted by nightmares.

I slipped out of bed at three a.m., trying not to awaken Sailor. Pausing by the bed, I took a moment to savor the scene: His dark hair was rumpled, blue-black stubble shadowed his chin and cheeks, his olive skin was striking against the pure white sheets. There was something about seeing such a big, strong man looking cozy and vulnerable; it always made me wonder what he must have been like as a child. What his own children would be like.

I sighed, contentedly. Then I got to work.

Three in the morning was the witching hour; the perfect time to spellcast.

I consulted my Book of Shadows and finished gathering the supplies the coven had suggested. I used precious frankincense and myrrh oils to "dress" a thick black candle, massaging it while I intoned a charm. Using a mixture of salts and herbs, I drew the five points of the star, concentrating on what they represented: the east, west, north, south, and the sky. The two arms, two legs, and head of our human bodies. The five senses of taste, touch, hearing, sight, and smell. I carved symbols of protection, clarity, and control into the wax of a thick black candle, and then placed it at the heart of the pentacle.

Then I set about brewing in my iron cauldron. Oscar perched atop a kitchen cabinet, hunkered over gargoylelike, watching and lending his aid. Whenever he was nearby, the portals opened more easily for me, allowing the connections to other ages, other planes to slip through. Even now, I didn't know exactly how it worked, but there was no denying that it did.

And yet, even after I cut a tiny *x* in my palm with my athame and added a drop of my own blood to the cauldron, my guardian spirit—the Ashen Witch—refused to appear in the cloud of steam bursting above the brew. Apparently she was still struggling with the traces of Deliverance Corydon within me. This was why I needed Graciela's coven's help.

This, and possibly fighting off demonic forces influencing Renna. Oh, and I was expected to destroy Alcatraz. *What in the world? Why would the fairy folk want me to destroy Al—*

I cut myself off. I couldn't allow myself to go down that rabbit hole. I needed to concentrate. Right here and now the only thing that mattered was lighting the candle, focusing my intent, and starting the five-day countdown toward the full moon.

Chanting, I closed my eyes and subsumed myself to the long line of ancestral power that had led, over the centuries, to me and to this moment. I set out Calypso's beautiful mason jar filled with local clover honey—including the honeycomb—as today's offering, as per the coven's instructions.

Finally, I lit the candle. It sparked loudly and blew a huge torchlike flame that nearly struck the ceiling before settling down.

"So mote it be."

My cuckoo clock chimed six thirty. I had lost track of time, which often happens when I cast. No sense in going back to bed now; instead, I started making breakfast and Conrad's morning brew, a concoction I'd come up with to shore up his strength in his fight for sobriety. Oscar had long since gone to sleep, but bounced out of his cubby over the refrigerator at seven, lured by the tantalizing aromas of biscuits and coffee.

"I'm famished," said Oscar, reaching for the honey.

"Not that one," I said, handing him another jar. "That's for a sacrifice."

"Who you castin' against?"

"A, um . . . demon. Maybe. Hopefully not, but . . . maybe."

His bottle glass green eyes grew huge.

I put the finishing touches on the brew for Conrad and left it to simmer on the stove while I brought Sailor a cup of coffee in bed. He was a grumpy fellow before his morning caffeine.

"Where've you been?" he asked, his voice rough with sleep. "I missed you."

"I've been brewing."

"For me?" asked Sailor.

"After a fashion." I smiled and set a fresh cup of Kona in front of him, spilling a few drops on my coverlet in my zeal. "After all, coffee is an everyday brew, a magical concoction that acknowledges all the elements: beans from the earth, the water, the aroma and steam in the air, and the fire that transforms it all."

"Don't forget the everlasting gratitude of the extremely appreciative man who drinks it."

I smiled and perched on the side of the bed.

A wary look came into his eyes, and he scooted back to sit up against the headboard. "Are you sure this is the best time for our 'talk'? I was thinking in the evening, over wine . . ."

"I agree. I don't think either of us is in the right frame of mind at the moment, and I've got to cleanse the shop before opening, and you probably have to run off to do . . . whatever it is that you do. Which, now that I think of it, might be one of those things we talk about when we do, you know . . ."

"Talk."

"Exactly."

He took a sip of his coffee and let out a sigh. "All right then, my little witch, what is it you want to talk about while we're not talking, then?"

"For one, Patience asked me to meet with your aunt Renna."

He swore under his breath.

"Why didn't you ask me yourself?" I asked him. "If there's something I can do to help your family . . ."

"Listen to me, Lily. I don't want you going anywhere near Renna, do you hear me?"

"Of course I hear you. I'm sure half of Haight Street hears you."

"Please," he said in a gentler tone.

"Why? What's going on? I might be able to help."

He didn't answer. He kept his eyes on his coffee, but I could see the muscle in his jaw flexing.

"Patience said there might be some sort of demon-y . . . something?" I ventured.

"Listen. Renna has some rather sketchy clients. She'll read for *anyone*, if they meet her price. Based on what little she's told me, and what her husband, Eric, knows, it seems a couple of guys came to see her for help locating something specific. Renna performed a discovery reading, and it's possible there were some inadvertent connections made through the tarot, and things went haywire."

"Are you saying she's possessed?"

He paused, inclined his head, and then said: "No, I don't think it's anything so extreme. But she's been having trouble sleeping and is highly agitated and quick to anger. With a heightened libido, according to Eric. He was enjoying that aspect of things until he noticed she was not being herself."

"Could she have summoned something?"

"Renna's an experienced practitioner who knows how to take the proper precautions. I can't imagine she would be so foolish."

"It's happened to the best of us. In any case, I think Patience is right: Looks like I need to meet with Renna."

Sailor swung his legs over the side of the bed and stood, every movement agitated. He scooped his jeans off the floor and started to pull them on. I watched; despite his bad mood, I enjoyed studying his naked torso, the movement of the muscles.

"I don't want you going anywhere near Renna." He gestured with his hand. "I'm serious, Lily."

"I believe you're serious," I said. "What I can't believe is that you think you have the right to tell me what to do or not do. I have to do what I think is right. Besides, I already promised Patience I'd help."

"I didn't realize you two were such buddies."

"We got a little closer when we were working together to get you out of the slammer. In fact, I asked her to be a bridesmaid."

"You *what*?" He threw his head back as though searching the ceiling for an answer to my behavior. "It didn't occur to you to run that by me?"

"Not really, no. And speaking of which, who is going stand up with you at the handfasting?"

"I thought we weren't having this talk yet. If we are, I need a refill on the coffee, and fast. Maybe add a shot of bourbon."

Because talking is that tough? I thought, but did not say. I smelled the minty but slightly rank aroma of Conrad's brew, which signaled it was ready. It wouldn't keep. "No, you're right, I need to start my day, and so do you."

"Let me handle Patience. I'm going to see her tonight. I'll tell her you can't assess Renna."

"You'll do no such thing, Sailor. I promised her I would go, and it's your aunt we're talking about. I want to help."

"This might all be a moot point, anyway. The family's gathering tonight, and we might be able to fix whatever's ailing her."

"And if not?"

He took a deep breath, and I could see the muscle work in his bewhiskered jaw. "You and I aren't demonologists, Lily. Do you remember what happened when you went up against Deliverance Corydon? Correct me if I'm wrong, but aren't you still dealing with *that* legacy?"

"Graciela's coven is going to help. In fact—"

"I don't want you risking yourself again, Lily. The first time I met you was over the demon at the School of Fine Arts, remember? How many times do you think you're going to be able to face something like that and walk away? Once you've met a demon—much less battled one—they never forget you. Remember what happened with your father—it could happen to you, too."

"I'm casting a five-day spell to prepare, and I'm stronger and smarter than I was when I dealt with the demon at the School of Fine Arts."

He snorted.

"I don't need you to protect me, Sailor."

"All evidence to the contrary."

"Honestly, Sailor. We can't have that kind of relationship. I need your support, not your . . ." I searched for the word. "Your controllingness."

"That's not a word."

"It is now. Anyway, I promised Patience, and I consulted with the grandmas, and I've started a MoonWish spell. And Carlos is going to take me out to Alcatraz to look at what might be a ritual killing of some sort, and I'm thinking all of this might be connected to Elena's kidnapping, somehow, and I'm going to have to figure it out."

Sailor sank back down to sit on the edge of the bed, leaned his elbows on his knees, and cradled his head in his hands. Finally, rubbing his hands over his face, he looked up and shook his head.

He spoke in a quiet, carefully restrained voice. "Lily, do you ever think about things like this before just leaping in?"

"You're a fine one to talk," I said, anger surging through me. "Besides, has it occurred to you that if you and I always stopped to think about being careful, you and I would never have ended up together?"

Our eyes held for a long moment.

"I—I have some brew on the stove," I said, moving toward the door. I felt bad about snapping at him, but the very idea of Sailor telling me what to do rankled. Still, Oscar was right, my patience was in limited supply lately. "I have to get it before it scalds."

Out in the kitchen, Oscar avoided my eyes and moved slowly, pretending he hadn't heard our argument, chewing his biscuits carefully, the deep red of the raspberry jam on his jowls looking disconcertingly like blood.

I used pot holders to remove the heavy cauldron from the stove, and poured the brew into a mason jar to cool.

"What's the brew for?" Sailor asked as he joined us in the kitchen, his jacket and boots already on.

"For Conrad," I said. "To help with detox. I told you he was sober."

"For how long?"

"Not long. But he's trying, and it's a struggle. I'm hoping this will help."

He looked at me a long moment. "I'm sure it will. Just knowing he's got you on his side will help."

"Thanks. Are you going already? No breakfast?"

"I wish I could. I'm sorry to rush, but I have to go to my place to change before meeting a client at nine."

I wrapped up a couple of buttered biscuits and handed them to him. "Take these with you, at least."

"Thanks." He tucked them in his large jacket pocket.

We stared at each other for another long moment.

"I should go, then," he said, gesturing to one of Selena's drawings on my refrigerator. It was a calla lily sprouting from a seed. "Oh, by the way, that drawing? That's the lily I saw when I held that binding braid you gave me."

I nodded. It made sense. Selena was intuiting the same thing that I was. We were all obsessed with *alcatraces*—and Alcatraz—at the moment.

"I'll walk you out," I said as he moved toward the door.

"No need," he said, pausing with his hand on the knob. "You get yourself some breakfast and relax before work. How about . . . tomorrow night? Are you free?"

I nodded. "Sure. Tomorrow night."

"We'll talk. For real."

He kissed my forehead and left, his boots beating a thunderous tattoo on the wooden stairs.

I collapsed in a kitchen chair and put my head on the table. Oscar reached out one oversized mitt of a hand and awkwardly caressed my hair.

"Tell you what," he said. "Imma book the Slovenian Hall, just in case. They have a liberal cancellation policy."

Chapter 12

I jumped up and hurried to the window, indulging a superstitious faith that if I watched from the window when Sailor left, it would keep him safe.

He stopped to speak with Conrad, who was sitting on the curb in front of the store. I couldn't hear what was said, but the two men talked for a few moments, then Conrad stood, and they shook hands. Sailor strode across the street to his motorcycle. He threw one leg over the seat of the bike then glanced up at the window.

I fought the impulse to hide, as though I were doing something wrong. Instead, I waved. He smiled, waved back, pulled on his helmet, and roared off.

It was hardly our first fight, but it made me sad. Especially since I was already so worried about the hand-fasting.

I prepared three biscuits with eggs, cheese, and roasted poblano peppers, grabbed the jar of brew, and went downstairs to join Conrad outside on the curb.

"So, what were you and Sailor chatting about?" I asked oh-so-casually as I passed him the plate and brew.

"Thanks, Lily, this looks awesome." Conrad took a huge bite, making *mmmm*ing sounds. "Sailor congratulated me on getting sober, said he knew it wouldn't be easy but he didn't have to be a psychic to know that I was strong enough to make it all the way. Helluva nice guy."

I smiled. Sailor was many things, but "helluva nice guy" was not a common description.

"Also, get this: He asked me to stand up with him at your wedding."

"He what?"

"I guess he didn't have a best man yet. Imagine *me* being someone's best man. He must be a little hard up for friends if *I'm* his best option—no offense."

I reached out and squeezed his hand. "Not at all, Conrad. I think you'll make a wonderful best man. It means you'll support us, and our union. You'll do a great job at that."

"*Dude*," Conrad said. He looked miserable. Not high, but miserable. Ill. "You know, one of the problems with getting sober is that all the problems you got high to forget are still there, waiting for you. Worse than before."

I nodded, not sure what to say. Substance addiction wasn't my particular burden to bear, but I had seen its effects often enough to know how easily it could destroy lives. My brew helped with the fever and shakes, the flulike symptoms that came with detox, but didn't have much effect on the actual addiction. As much as I wished I could force Conrad to stay sober with my magic, it wouldn't last. Fundamental change had to come from within, from the Con's heart.

"I tried calling my mom," he said.

"Is that right?" I asked, careful to keep my tone neutral. "How did that go?"

"She hung up on me."

"Oh, Con, I'm so sorry. That's wretched."

He smiled. "I like the way you talk, Lily. Always have, but even more so now that I'm sober. Oh, hey, I sound like it's all about me and my problems, right? Is there any word on that poor lady who was kidnapped?"

"Not yet."

"Dude."

I lingered while Conrad finished his breakfast, enjoying the feeling of soft morning sunshine on my cheeks. Summer mornings in San Francisco were typically foggy and gray, so the sunny weather was a nice change. Haight Street was mellow at this time of day, with a handful of shopkeepers sweeping the sidewalks outside their establishments, a few folks rushing to work, to-go coffee cups in hand.

"You know, I noticed the poster in your window," said Conrad as he wiped his mouth with the napkin and set down the plate. "That dude's a good guy."

"Who? Kyle Cheney?"

He nodded. "He's helped us gutter punks a lot, funds some shelters, soup kitchens, things like that. He's helped finance some small local businesses, too.

"Coupla dudes I know actually got jobs with him."

"Really? What kinds of jobs?"

"Co-Opp Industries, is what it's called."

"It's a cooperative?"

"Nah. It's like, security, I think? Which is kind of funny, since usually it's the security guys running us gutter punks out of places."

"A job's a job, I guess."

"Sounds like quite the party out on Alcatraz, right?"

Conrad said, then hung his head, deflated. "Not that I party anymore. This sobriety thing is a drag."

I refrained from pointing out that it had been only a few days. "One day at a time. Isn't that what they say?"

He nodded. "One crappy day at a time."

Maya arrived, chai latte in hand. After greeting Conrad, she turned to me: "Anything new?"

I shook my head. "Not that I've heard."

We went into the shop and I performed my daily cleansing and protection spell while Maya started sorting through the remaining items from the Hefty bags.

"I feel responsible," said Maya, her voice tight. "You told me that shirt was dangerous. I should have believed you. I never should have let Elena leave with it."

"Maya, we have no reason to believe the shirt was the reason this happened. And even if it was, it is most certainly *not* your fault."

"I read more about Alcatraz online last night when I couldn't sleep. Do you know that there were a bunch of Hopi from New Mexico held in a military prison on Alcatraz, long before the federal penitentiary opened? Some people say their ghosts still linger."

"Were they executed there?"

"I don't think so. Can ghosts remain anyway?"

"I'm really not sure. We might run that one past Charles Gosnold. I'm willing to bet he'd have an opinion."

She gave me a reluctant smile. "Ghosts or not, Mark Twain said the island was 'as cold as winter, even in the summer months.'"

"What can you tell me about Cole Albright?"

"He and his brother and one other prisoner made papier-mâché heads—complete with human hair they got from the barbershop—and put them in their beds to fool the guards. Then they crawled out through the ventilation grilles, which they had pulled out and broadened by hacking away at the crumbling concrete. They managed to float away one night on a raft made out of raincoats, shrouded by thick fog."

"And they were presumed drowned?"

"Yes, but because the raft was found, but the bodies weren't, some people think they got away. There were a few supposed sightings of them in South America. And a few years ago a letter was delivered to the FBI, signed by one of the escapees, in which he said he would turn himself in, in return for health care because he had cancer."

"Did they think the letter was genuine?"

"It doesn't look like it, at least not in the official story online. But who knows?" Maya said, shaking her head. "I'm going crazy. I thought about calling in sick, but sitting around at home would be worse. And classes are out until next month so I don't even have homework to distract me."

"That reminds me, have you been to the School of Fine Arts lately?"

"Not for a couple of weeks. Why?"

"Did anything seem amiss to you last time you were there? Any rampant arguing, wild love affairs, that sort of thing?"

She cocked her head. "I thought you put an end to all that."

"I think I did. I was just wondering." What with the woods folk agitated, and the goings-on out on Alcatraz, I was starting to wonder if there might be some sort of generalized gathering of malicious spirits. Or something.

Sailor was right. We needed a demonologist on this paranormal team.

Bronwyn arrived at Aunt Cora's Closet with a bag of bagels and Charles Gosnold in tow. Charles was tall and rather pear shaped, his well-padded shoulders shoved into an ill-fitting jacket. Charles wasn't a bad person, I reminded myself. But when it came to the paranormal he was "all hat and no cattle," as folks would say back in my hometown of Jarod, Texas.

"Aren't you amazed that Charles has been asked by none other than Kyle Cheney to lead the ghost tours for the Festival of Felons?" Bronwyn asked, holding up her coffee mug in salute. "To Charles!"

"Is that still on?" I asked. "The Festival of Felons, I mean."

"Why wouldn't it be?" Charles asked.

"I heard . . . never mind. Just wondered. Congratulations, Charles. That's really . . . quite an honor. Kyle Cheney, huh?"

"He called and asked me personally," Charles said, puffing out his chest.

"Charles is going to make commemorative T-shirts!" gushed Bronwyn.

"Indeed I *am*. Alcatraz ghost tour T-shirts to commemorate the occasion. I'm thinking bright blue. The spirits are fond of blue." Charles jumped back as Oscar came over to him and snorted. "Oh! That pig is sort of an ugly little thing, isn't he?"

"He can *hear* you, Charles," Bronwyn admonished him. "And besides, he's not *ugly*, he's *beautiful*. He's our beautiful itty-bitty Oscaroo."

I glanced at Maya, who was looking decidedly glum.

I turned to Bronwyn and asked: "Bronwyn, would you be okay looking after Aunt Cora's Closet today? With Oscar's company, of course."

"I'd be happy to. It's quite a social day for me: Charles and I are going to catch up over bagels, and Susan's coming by later to set up the photo shoot for the paper. And I imagine Duke will be in later as well."

Duke was a retired fisherman and "Bronwyn's fella," as he liked to call himself. He often hung out with us at Aunt Cora's Closet, his outdoorsy mien adding a nice note to the atmosphere and making the shop more welcoming to men.

As Gosnold launched into a long-winded—and loud—tale about his latest ghostly encounter, I said in a low voice to Maya: "I might just have a cure for what ails you."

"No offense, Lily, but I'm really not up for a spell. That brew you whipped up for the Con smells a little . . . pungent."

"I was thinking more like action. Let's try to figure this out."

"Where would we even start?"

"How about with the woman who sold you the shirt?"

Mrs. Archer's house was on 19th Street off Geary, not far from the Russian neighborhood I had visited with Patience not long ago. It was a nondescript stucco structure that shared its walls with its neighbors, as the town houses tended to do in this area. There was a garage at street level, so we climbed a flight of steps to the entrance on the second floor.

Mrs. Archer—"call me Emmy Lou"—met us at the door. "That's a nice van you've got there. Good for your line of work, I'll bet. I like the color."

Worn, vaguely gray wall-to-wall carpet smelled of stale cigarette smoke and many generations of cats, and Emmy Lou wore a wig of glossy black hair that highlighted her strong features. Her eyes were slightly cloudy with age, and her hands soft as velvet.

Not long ago I'd been fooled by a sweet-seeming old woman, so I tried to keep up my guard, but it was tough around Emmy Lou Archer.

"I was born up in Plainfield, New Jersey, one of six children. My father moved the family here to Richmond to work in the shipyards during World War Two. But then he dropped dead from a heart attack when I was eight—ate red meat, butter, and fried foods every day; folks didn't know from cholesterol back then—so my mother became a genuine Rosie the Riveter, can you imagine?" We had all taken seats in the living room, whose worn upholstered furniture had been spruced up with tatted doilies. "She worked sixteen hours a day building ships for the war effort. We grew up with a sense of responsibility to give back, that we did. So as soon as I was of age, I went into the navy myself."

"Mrs. Archer received a Good Conduct Medal," Maya said.

"That's impressive," I said.

"I served in an entertainment troupe, singing and dancing; then went on to work in a photography lab, a few other jobs here and there. But I don't mind telling you, I did a mean tap dance back in the day."

"Shirley Temple, eat your heart out," said Maya with a warm smile.

Emmy Lou laughed, a deep rumble. "I feel bad for the folks who gave their lives, and their health—physical and mental—for their country, when all I did was dance and develop photos, that sort of thing. But lucky for me we weren't in combat at the time, and keeping morale high is an important job as well." She sat forward in her chair. "Maya, help yourself and your friend here to some cookies. My friends from church brought them over. And there's some Nescafé if you want coffee."

"Thanks. Would you like a cup?" asked Maya, moving into the kitchen. I watched her go, admiring the ease with which she interacted with the elderly. They all seemed to want to mother her, which amused me since Maya was one of those rare young people who seemed very much on top of things.

"How long have you lived here?" I asked Emmy Lou.

"My late husband and I bought this place with our retirement savings," she said, stroking an orange tabby that jumped into her lap. "Been nearly thirty years now. It belonged to a friend of my late husband's cousin. He left a pile of stuff here . . . that was part of the deal, why we got the place so cheap."

"What was his name?"

"Oh, I . . . don't really remember. He had a Polish last name, that's all I recall. After he got sick he just didn't want to be bothered packing things up."

"That's why there were boxes left in the attic," Maya called out from the kitchen.

Emmy Lou nodded. "We cleaned up most of the house, but never got around to those boxes. I always meant to look through them, but they're out of sight up there in the attic. . . . Take it from me, girls: Time slips away before you know it."

"That's good advice," I said.

Maya returned with a small plate of homemade snickerdoodles and two small mugs of coffee. I took one from her.

"So you have no idea how the former owner might have come by the inmate's shirt from Alcatraz?" I asked Emmy Lou.

"I'm sorry, I really don't know."

"And you don't remember his name, other than that it was Polish?"

Emmy Lou cast a slightly distressed look toward Maya, and I caught myself. I was getting better with age and practice, but my intensity had a way of putting people on edge.

"We're sorry to be so pushy, Mrs. Archer," said Maya. "It's just important that we try to figure this out. It's hard to say whether it might be involved, but a woman was kidnapped yesterday, so we're following up on any lead we can think of."

"Kidnapped?" Her dark eyes widened in alarm. "Why, that's dreadful!"

"It is," said Maya. "And it's unlikely the clothes from the attic boxes are involved, but we'd like to be sure."

After a long pause, Emmy Lou said: "Well, I can't imagine how those old things would be involved in a kidnapping, but I've lived long enough to know all kinds of things can happen. I can't remember the previous owner's name, but I could probably find it. It must be on the deed of sale for the house, right?"

"If it's not too much trouble, we'd appreciate it," Maya said, her tone gentle. "I'd be happy to help you look."

"In the meantime, would it be all right if I went up into the attic?" I asked. "I know it's an imposition, but it would really mean a lot to me."

She nodded. "If you want to, have at it. I'll warn you, though: I haven't been up there in years. Even when I was younger, I didn't like to go up there. It's always given me the creeps. Maya can tell you what a state it's in."

"I guarantee you, I've seen worse," I said. "Dusty attics are an occupational hazard, right, Maya?"

"You can say that again. I'll show you the way."

"If you find anything valuable, like an old painting, bring it on down. I could use the cash," Emmy Lou called out after us.

The attic was accessed through a small hatch in the ceiling of the upstairs hallway. Maya pulled the string down, unfolded the wooden stairs, and we climbed up, switching on the light at the very top.

"I swept this place out when I finished looking through everything," said Maya. "The boxes over here seem to hold family mementos: Christmas ornaments, photographs, children's artwork, that sort of thing."

I looked around the small attic space. The ceiling was low, and we had to hunch over to avoid hitting our heads on the sloping eaves. Emmy Lou had been right: There was nothing much to see.

"Where was the box with the prison shirt, do you know?" I asked.

She shook her head. "I don't really remember. I peeked into all the boxes up here and took the ones with clothing in them downstairs to look through more carefully. Carrying a box down those stairs took a lot of concentration."

"Next time you should ask me to come with you."

"In case I find another cursed shirt?"

"No, so I can help you with the lifting and carrying. We could have handed the boxes to each other."

She shrugged.

"Maya, it occurs to me that you and I have something in common: We're both independent to a fault at times. There's no sin in asking for help, you know. I'm coming to learn that. But it's still hard sometimes."

Maya smiled. "Right you are, boss. Anyway, there were a bunch of boxes stacked over in that general area. . . ." She gestured toward the far side of the attic.

I scuttled over, closed my eyes, and tried to "feel." I'm a terrible necromancer, but I often feel the presence of ghosts. It was a physical sensation, like an army of ants marching up and down my back, or whispers of breath on my cheeks. Was it possible Ray Perry had hidden out in this attic? And if so, would I be able to feel something that would lead me to him? Seemed unlikely, but I would give it a try.

Feeling self-conscious, I said: "Would you mind leaving, Maya? I'll be able to concentrate better by myself."

"You're sure?" She looked skeptical.

I nodded. "I won't be long. Seriously. This is what I do, remember?"

"Okay, but if you need me just shout. I'll go see if I can help Mrs. Archer locate those house papers," Maya said, and disappeared down the access stairs.

I sat on the dusty wood floor, cross-legged the way I'd seen Sailor do dozens of times. I stroked my medicine bag, closed my eyes, and *bam*.

Standing in front of me was the image of a man in a blue chambray shirt. Number 258.

Chapter 13

He was clear as day. Like a life-sized black-and-white photograph, right in front of me.

I squeaked and jumped to my feet. I never see ghosts. I *can't* see ghosts . . . or could I? What was going *on*?

I stroked my medicine bag, closed my eyes, and reached for calm.

When I opened my eyes, the image was still there. It wasn't what I would have expected from a ghost—he wasn't misty or wavering in any way. But then, I'd never actually *seen* a spirit, so I wasn't sure what they looked like.

"H-hello?" I tried.

He just stood there, not interacting, almost like a hologram, and his eyes were empty, devoid of humanness. Was this what necromancers saw? From the outside it had never appeared to be like this, but then I had never asked the necromancers I knew—Sailor or my friend Hervé, or Patience for that matter—to describe precisely what they saw, or how.

Maybe something else was going on. I thought about what Aidan had told me, which Graciela's coven had confirmed at last night's reading. If I now had two guiding spirits, the Ashen Witch and Deliverance Corydon, then wouldn't my magic and my abilities change? Could Deliverance Corydon, as much as it pained me to admit, be lending me new skills, such as necromancy?

Or was I getting ahead of myself?

"Is there something you want to tell me?" I tried again. When there was no response after a minute, I asked: "Is this where you . . . are?"

It had been on the tip of my tongue to ask if this was where he *lived*, but somehow that seemed rude to demand of a dead person.

Again, no response. I tried a few other questions: "Are you Ray Perry? Did you escape from Alcatraz?"

Suddenly a calla lily appeared in his hand. He held it out to me, looking for all the world as if he were asking me out on a date.

My fear had subsided, replaced by frustration. My talents appeared to be broadening, but what was the point of being able to "see" someone if I still couldn't communicate with them?

Downstairs, I heard the doorbell ring, followed by muffled voices. I tried to maintain my concentration, but my eyes searched the attic, trying to figure out what my next move should be.

My gaze fell on a box labeled FAMILY PHOTOS. They probably belonged to Emmy Lou, but was it possible they had been left here by the previous homeowner? The man with the Polish name?

Feeling like a snoop but motivated by my worry for Elena, I folded back one cardboard flap.

Inside were numerous old photos taken in and around the house. The colored snapshots had faded to shades of yellow and blue, the clothing styles indicating the photos had been taken in the 1970s. Emmy Lou and her husband had bought the house in 1990. That settled it: I was going to assume these belonged to the former owner.

I dug through the box and found an old framed black-and-white picture of a man in a guard uniform, standing in front of Cellblock D. I couldn't be sure, but I was going to guess this was Alcatraz Island. The name over his pocket was impossible to read, but it was long and started with a *P*.

"Can you tell me anything at all?" I said to the ghost, or the apparition, or whatever it was. I held the photo out to him. "Are you connected with this man? Was he your guard?"

Suddenly the apparition flew at me, his finger in front of his mouth as though he were miming "*shhhh*," like the crotchety old librarian in my hometown elementary school. I fell back on my butt, but the apparition disappeared as quickly as he had flown toward me.

"Last chance," I said, trying to still my heart. "You have anything for me? Want to tell me something?"

After several more minutes of nothing—no sound, no more apparition—I turned off the light and brought the box of old photos with me as I climbed back down the stair ladder, closed the hatch, and joined Maya and Emmy Lou in the living room.

"I hope you don't mind," I said as I set the box on the coffee table. "I noticed this up in the attic; are these your family photos?"

Emmy Lou leaned forward and took a peek.

"Oh, no, those must have belonged to the former owner. If you're interested in them, please help yourselves. He didn't have any family to take his things, and if no interested parties have crawled out of the wood-work in all these years, I'm pretty sure it's all up for grabs. It's a help to me to clean things out."

"Thank you. I noticed one photo in particular," I said, handing her the framed picture of the guard. "Was this the man who sold you the house?"

"It might have been. But it was thirty years ago; I barely remember meeting him when we signed the papers. A lawyer handled the sale."

"Oh, Lily, we did find the name of the former owner," said Maya, holding out a sales agreement for the house, dated 1991. "But I have no idea how to pronounce it."

I read: "'Ned Przybyszewski'." I couldn't read the name on the guard's uniform, but it was long and started with a *P*. It would match. So what did that tell me?

My eyes fell on a large pink bakery box. It was from Renee Baker's cupcake shop.

"Where did that come from?" I demanded, an edge to my voice.

"It was just delivered!" said Emmy Lou. "A thank-you present from a very nice man who came to the house the other day, the morning after you were here, Maya. I have no idea why he would thank me, though; I told him I had already sold all my old clothes to you."

"Who was it?"

"A young man in a van like yours, but it was white, with no name on the side."

"Did he leave a card, or a number, any way of getting in touch with him?" I asked.

"His last name was Jones, and he left a number. It's somewhere around here. . . ." She trailed off as she pawed through a pile of correspondence, coupons, and newspaper advertisements on a small side table by her chair. Finally she extracted a piece of scrap paper.

"Here it is. I told him not to bother; I couldn't offer him anything because Maya had already taken all those old clothes to your store. But he said, 'Just in case.'"

I asked to use her phone and dialed the number. A recorded voice stated it had been disconnected.

"How did he know you had clothes to give away?" Maya asked.

"You know, it didn't occur to me to ask," said Emmy Lou. "But he was a very nice man. Still, I'm not supposed to eat sugar. Why don't you girls take those cupcakes home with you? I have a hard enough time resisting the snickerdoodles."

"Thank you," I said. "That would be great. Could you describe the man who came looking for clothes?"

"Well, let's see. . . . He was young, thin, white, in his twenties, I would say. He had brown hair; I didn't really notice his eyes. Really nothing remarkable, though he was very polite." She beamed at Maya. "Good to know the next generation is so well mannered, like Maya here."

Had this mystery man somehow found out that Emmy Lou Archer had an inmate's shirt from Alcatraz in her attic? That seemed far-fetched. On the other hand, it seemed even more unlikely that another vintage clothing dealer—with a nonworking phone number—just happened to come by immediately after Maya had left.

"So, Mrs. Archer—," I began.

"Emmy Lou, please."

"Emmy Lou, then," I said with a smile. I leaned toward her and cast a quick comforting spell to appease any nervousness my social awkwardness might have engendered. "Could you tell us anything else about the shirt, or the former owner of the house, or Alcatraz, maybe? He never mentioned being a guard out there?"

She shook her head. "I'm sorry, as I said, I didn't

really deal with him. My husband took care of most of the paperwork; I don't think our paths crossed more than once or twice. And I know people love to talk about Alcatraz, but I've never gone there. People say that place is cursed, that's what I hear."

"Any federal prison is going to seem a bit bleak, I would guess," said Maya.

"True, but one of my church friends, Norma, was part Miwok Indian. She said her grandmother always told her the island was cursed. That's why there were never any native villages out there, even way back when."

"Also because there's no source of freshwater," Maya said quietly.

"Well, now, it's true that Norma had a lot of different beliefs. When we bought this place, as a matter of fact, she refused to come in until we'd taken a bundle of leaves and waved smoke here and there."

"A smudge bundle?" Maya asked.

She nodded. "Yeah, that sounds right. Norma said there was something off about the former owner, and maybe there was. How do you get to be that man's age with no friends or family?"

"Did you smudge up in the attic?" I asked.

She looked surprised by the question. "No, as a matter of fact, I don't think we did. You think maybe that's why I never liked it up there? Norma said there was bad juju."

"Norma sounds like an interesting woman. Might I meet her?"

"I'm afraid she passed away a couple of years ago."

I couldn't think of anything else to ask, and Emmy Lou mentioned needing a nap, so we thanked her for her time and left with a box of old photos, and a box of potentially ensorcelled cupcakes.

Back in the van, I asked Maya: "So who do you suppose I should talk to about a Native American curse on the island of Alcatraz?"

"That's a tough one," Maya said. "Sounds like the plot of a bad teenage slasher movie to me. You know, a prison built on top of an ancient Indian burial ground, everyone but the blond female lead falls victim to a curse and dies in a horrific manner. Sounds more than a little . . . I don't know, ethnocentric? Not to mention cheesy."

"Good point. I still want to check it out, though."

"Fair enough." Maya consulted her phone. "Let's see. . . . This looks promising: There's a Professor Guzmán at Laney College in Oakland, who's Chochenyo Ohlone."

"Chochenyo?"

Maya shrugged, still fiddling with her phone. "I'm afraid I'm woefully ignorant about the native peoples from this area, but according to this site, a number of tribes were grouped under the name of 'Ohlone,' which is a Miwok word meaning 'people of the west.' The Chochenyo were basically the East Bay folks. And the Ohlone had sovereignty over the island of Alcatraz. Anyway, there's an office phone number here. Looks like Dr. Guzmán teaches anthropology, so I'll bet he could tell you a thing or two. Want me to call him?"

"That would be great, thanks."

Maya discovered Guzmán had office hours the next day, and made an appointment for noon tomorrow.

Then she sat back, watching the houses go by, a touch of defeat in the slant of her shoulders. "So what now? Back to the shop? There's always laundry to do."

"Honestly, Maya, it would be fine if you wanted to take a couple of days off. Bronwyn and I can handle the store, and if not, it's not the end of the world if we need to close early or open late."

"I'd rather keep busy," she said with a shake of her head. She fiddled with her phone for another moment, then shut it off. "Lily, do you think the man who came to Mrs. Archer's asking for clothes was the one who took Elena?"

"That would be my guess."

"How would he have learned about the shirt?"

"I wish I knew. Listen, would you mind making a quick detour before going back to Aunt Cora's Closet?"

"I'm at your disposal," said Maya. "More clothes?"

"More cupcakes. Maybe we could get some clues as to what's going on by talking with Renee."

I headed to Renee Baker's cupcake shop.

A large handwritten sign in Renee's window, on butter yellow paper and decorated with tulips, declared: CLOSED FOR REMODELING, BACK IN A JIFFY!

"Strange that they're closed for business, yet still have baked goods on their shelves," said Maya. "Also, they just delivered a box of cupcakes to Mrs. Archer."

"Strange, indeed."

The building next door used to be occupied by a vintage clothing store. There was paper up in the windows, and another big sign, this one professionally printed: PARDON OUR DUST! RENEE'S IS EXPANDING! . . . JOIN US ON ALCATRAZ FOR THE FESTIVAL OF FELONS!

Below this was a photo of Renee standing beside a veritable tower of intricately decorated cupcakes. She was a plump, middle-aged woman with an easy smile and a maternal, unassuming air. It was always hard to believe she posed any kind of sinister, supernatural threat to the city.

"Wow, Renee must be doing well if she's expanding. Most of us can barely afford to pay rent on a living space, much less a cupcake shop," said Maya. "It's strange to see that old vintage clothes store gone, isn't it? Sad."

I nodded. We were both thinking of the former owner of the store that previously occupied the space; Maya and I had stumbled upon her, gravely ill, a while ago. She hadn't made it.

"So, what is it with you and the cupcake lady?" Maya asked as we returned to the car and headed back to Aunt Cora's Closet. "She wound up with a concussion last time you two got together."

"That wasn't *my* fault," I said, my voice scaling up. "Renee deals with some scary folks."

"Don't take this the wrong way, but so do you."

"That's true. But somehow I doubt that either you or Bronwyn is going to betray me and then knock me over the head in an attempt to gain control over the magical community in San Francisco."

"Well, I'm not going to *now*," she teased. "But seriously, *that's* what's up with Renee?"

I nodded.

"You're telling me she's . . . like you? A magical person?"

"Magical, yes. But not like me in any other way, I hope."

"I wondered why you were in such a state about her. You really should take your own advice, you know, and ask for help from time to time."

"Funny, I feel like I ask for help *all* the time," I said, as much to myself as to Maya. "But I get what you're saying. I think . . . I've kept you and Bronwyn in the dark about certain things. Mostly I didn't want to worry you, or put you in danger."

"So Renee-the-cupcake-lady is dangerous?"

"Very much so, yes. She traffics in way more than sugar."

"Well, darn it. It's getting so a person can't even indulge in a bit of frosting without worrying."

I smiled and gave her a quick squeeze. "There are always Snickers bars. Oscar swears by them."

"Oscar's not what I would call discriminating when it comes to food."

"True enough."

I parked in the driveway around the corner from Aunt Cora's Closet, dropped the pink box of cupcakes in a Dumpster, and headed for the store. As we walked along the sidewalk, I spotted posters featuring Elena's smiling face, with MISSING! printed in large letters. My heart sank at the sight of her, and at the thought of what she—and her loved ones—were going through. The posters reminded me of the flyers my friends had put up when Oscar disappeared not too long ago. They hadn't helped me to find him—in fact, I had known where he was, I just couldn't figure out how to get him back—but they had filled me with warmth, knowing that the community was rallying around me.

At times like this, when facing ghosts and demons and killers, it was important to be reminded that there was a lot of good in this world. Most people were caring and decent, as a matter of fact; ready to go out of their way to help a stranger.

"I'm going to take these things upstairs," I said. "I'll be right back."

Given what Emmy Lou Archer had said about smudging the house, it made sense to draw a protective circle around this box of photos. Just in case.

But first, I turned my attention to Elena's hat. Despite Carlos's protestations, I still wondered whether Elena could somehow be involved. I knew firsthand how seductive the promises of magical powers could be. And if my inkling was right, that her disappearance might be connected to something more, something demonic, well . . . a person didn't have to be evil or corrupt to fall under a demon's thrall, just vulnerable in some way.

And down deep, we were all vulnerable in one way or another.

I held the hat to my chest, but all I felt were positive, upbeat vibrations. Open and caring, easygoing. Like Elena herself, apparently. Or perhaps this reflected the old her, before being exposed to temptation.

I realized I was at the stage of the investigation where I suspected everyone, and not for the first time imagined how hard it must be to work in law enforcement and not become overwhelmed by fear and suspicion of everyone, always.

"We'll wait and see what Patience can read, if anything," I muttered to myself as I put the hat aside.

Next I flipped through the old photographs in the cardboard box. There were lots of snapshots that appeared to be from the '50s and '60s, and a handful of older, sepia-toned portraits.

But at the bottom of the box was a bundle wrapped in a stained, light blue cloth, tied up with twine in a thick knot.

As I tried to undo the knot, I felt something: the hum of magic. This was no simple tangle of strings.

Deciding it was better to be safe than sorry, I got up and drew a salt circle, placing protective stones at the five points of the pentacle and lighting candles on the four directional points. While doing so I chanted softly in a mixture of Spanish, Nahuatl, and English, as Graciela had taught me as a young girl:

"Yehwah-tzin, I ask for protection, que me salvaguarde y me esconde, con vigilencia, en esto y siempre. In toptli,

in petlacalli; in estli, in yollohtli. I light the candles, reconozco su poder, su potencia. Se les ruego. Así sea, y se hará, so mote it be."

Then I examined the knot more closely. It was clumsily tied, reminding me of the magical knots my mother was trying to make at Calypso's house. These were unevenly spaced, and the power was muted. An amateur's work.

I chanted while I untied it, easily defeating the original spell. I laid the cloth open to reveal a stack of black-and-white photos of prisoners and prison guards, as well as photos of cellblocks and what looked like tunnels. These were similar to the archival pictures Maya had shown me on the Internet, chronicling life on Alcatraz. Why would they be hidden away and guarded by magic?

Suddenly I realized what was bothering me wasn't the knotted twine, but the cloth the photos had been wrapped in.

Unless I missed my guess, the scrap of fabric was the heavy, blue chambray of an inmate's shirt.

And the dark stains?

Blood.

When I returned downstairs to the shop, I found Selena sitting cross-legged on the floor, shining coins and little *milagros,* Mexican charms of body parts that were used to ask for cures. She wore faded jeans, no makeup, and her black hair hung down her back in a long braid. The teenager had a special sort of metal magic, and as she polished metal, she infused the items with a tiny whisper of her magic. Lately the challenge had been to find enough for her to work on. I bought up old silverware at estate and garage sales whenever possible, but when Bronwyn remembered the old coins—pennies, francs, pesetas, and the like—that she'd been collecting in tall glass jars for years, it was a bonanza.

"Hi, Selena," I said. "Ready for a little vintage clothes therapy?"

She didn't look up.

"Selena? I said hello."

"Hi, whatever," she finally said, her voice sullen, and she refused to make eye contact. Selena was working on her social skills and rarely greeted anyone unprompted. Her attitude strained my patience, but I tried to remember how strange I had been at her age, as an awkward young witch with great power, and reached down deep for empathy.

"Selena," I tried again. "I wanted to ask you: Why have you been drawing these pictures?"

I held out one of her calla lily drawings. She glanced up but did not respond, instead starting in on polishing a new batch of coins.

"It looks like a calla lily sprouting from a seed," I prompted.

"That's not a *seed*," said Selena.

"Sorry. What is it, then?"

"An island."

"Which island?"

She shook her head.

"What made you think about drawing it?"

"I draw what I see. It's not weird. Maya says a lot of artists get images in their minds. I can't help it."

"I understand, Selena. You're not in any kind of trouble, I'm just trying to understand. I saw a calla lily in a . . . sort of a vision. And Sailor saw one, too. So I'm trying to figure out if it's significant that you're drawing these."

"Didn't Selena draw lilies when she first got to know you, Lily?" asked Bronwyn. "Perhaps it's as simple as that."

Selena remained on the floor, carefully attending to one coin after the other. She used ketchup as a non-toxic tarnish remover, and her white cotton rag was stained a bright red.

Blood sacrifice.

The way Carlos had described the homicide scene on Alcatraz, it sounded like the elderly victim might well have been used—or possibly even volunteered—as a blood sacrifice. Blood sacrifice was often connected to demonic conjuring. . . . But who would have done such a thing, and why?

I felt a slight rumble underfoot and heard a crack and groan as the building's old timbers settled.

"Whoops, another temblor!" sang Bronwyn. "What do you think, two-point-eight?"

"More like a three, or three-point-two," said Maya, already tapping on the computer to look up the seismic count of this latest tremor.

"I can*not* get used to y'all being so infuriatingly *calm* about the earth moving under your feet," I said, my heart pounding. "Doesn't that freak you out?"

"The big ones are scary," Bronwyn conceded.

"You can say that again," said Maya. "But I grew up with tremors, Lily, so I guess they don't faze me much. Especially the soft, rolling ones. I don't like the ones that slam you with a sudden jolt."

"It seems unnatural to me," I muttered. "Anyway, Maya, while you've got the computer open, could you look up Ned Przybyszewski?"

"The guy who used to own Mrs. Archer's house? Spell it for me?"

I did, and she tapped it in.

"Let's see. . . . Interesting."

"What?"

"That name's not as rare as one might imagine.

Przybyszewski is one of the most common Polish names. Who knew?"

"Do you see anyone by that name connected with Alcatraz?"

She nodded. "According to this website, a Ned Przybyszewski was a prison guard there from 1935 to '63. Almost thirty years."

"Is there a photo?"

"Nothing posted online. But I'll bet one of the docents at Alcatraz would be able to find one. Want me to call Forrest Caruthers?"

"No, no thank you. They've got enough on their hands at the moment." I realized I hadn't shared the news of Cole Albright's murder with my friends. In part it was my habit to keep things to myself, but I also didn't want to further worry Maya about what might have happened to Elena. Because if Albright had been butchered . . .

"How about a photo of Ray Perry?"

"Yeah," said Maya. "I remember seeing his mug shot when I was doing research. I'll find it. . . ."

"Thanks. And the Albright brothers as well, if you can."

"Leave me out of this," Bronwyn said, busily mixing custom concoctions behind the counter of her herbal stand. "I have serious issues with the entire penal system."

"But you told me you signed up to go on Charles Gosnold's ghost hunt during the Festival of Felons," said Maya.

"Yes, well, that's different. That's about spirits, not the penal system."

Maya chuckled.

"Bronwyn, I wish you wouldn't go," I said. Presuming Cheney's festival was still going on as planned, I didn't want my friends on that cursed rock. I didn't want *anyone* out there, but especially my loved ones. "Surely there are nicer ghosts you could visit here on the mainland?"

"But I've already paid for it. And I'll be with Charles! What could go wrong?"

I opened my mouth to tell her about what had happened to Albright last night, but hesitated. Carlos had told me about the crime only because of the occult connection. If it wasn't in the news yet . . .

"Here he is," said Maya, interrupting my thoughts. She turned the computer so I could look at the screen. "Raymond—Ray—Perry's mug shot."

Ray Perry had heavy-lidded, rather romantic eyes, full lips, and held his chin high at a stubborn angle. No doubt about it. This was the man I had seen in Emmy Lou Archer's attic.

Chapter 14

"He looks so young," I said.

"He was younger than I am now," said Maya. "Perry was only twenty-four when he disappeared, so he must have been convicted in his early twenties. It says here he lived a life of crime: He shot an officer in Tulsa, Oklahoma, when he was just fourteen, and stabbed a cellmate to death in what he claimed was self-defense. He was an escape artist who freed himself from manacles and sawed through bars. A reporter at the time called him an 'eellike little man' who escaped once in a laundry bag, was sent to prison for kidnapping a businessman, and tried to escape in a trash can."

"I suppose that's why he was sent to Alcatraz," I said. "So he couldn't escape."

"Sounds like a punk to me," said Maya. "You know what they say: If you want to put an end to about ninety percent of crime, lock up all the men from the ages of fifteen to forty."

Bronwyn gaped at her, "*Maya!* You sound so . . . punitive."

Maya smiled and continued typing on the keyboard. "I'm not saying we *should* do it. I'm simply saying it would solve a lot of problems. Oh, Lily, here are mug shots of the Albright brothers."

"I've got to say that Cole Albright is rather nice-looking," said Bronwyn, whose curiosity had overcome her scruples. She had joined us at the computer.

"He was a brutal criminal, Bronwyn," said Maya.

"I don't know the man, but according to that photo, he's a historical hottie."

Maya smiled. "And here are photos of the fake heads the Albrights put in their beds when they escaped."

The papier-mâché heads were painted on only one side—presumably the unpainted side was hidden by the pillow—and had human hair glued to their crowns.

"They look sort of macabre, don't they?" I asked.

"Maybe they haven't aged well," Bronwyn said with a chuckle. "Or maybe they were bewitched to seem alive."

"You're right, the only way those heads would fool anyone is if the guards didn't look too closely," said Maya. "Which they probably didn't. No one would have been looking for fake heads. And then the men slipped out of their cells through the entrance to the ventilation shaft, which they had been widening bit by bit, probably for years."

"How did they manage that?" asked Bronwyn.

"They say that's one of the problems with Alcatraz: Over time the fog and salt from the bay rusts the iron rebar and crumbles the concrete. Anyway, the prisoners had been planning the escape for a year or more, leaving their cells at night to work on a raft made out of rubber raincoats. On the night of their escape they inflated it with a concertina, an accordionlike instrument."

"Gutsy," I said. "I'll give them that."

Maya nodded. "And amazingly smart. Someone had given them the tidal charts so they would know when to leave and minimize their chances of being swept out to sea. An oar and the flotilla made of raincoats was found near Angel Island, which is why some people believe they made it to shore."

"Imagine what they could have amounted to if they'd applied that sort of initiative and determination outside of prison, in the civilian world," Bronwyn said, shaking her head. "It was a brilliant plan of escape; what a waste."

"Maybe they did survive and went on to lead exemplary lives," said Maya with a smile. "You never know."

"So Przybyszewski"—I stumbled over his name— "was a guard when both Ray Perry and the Albright brothers escaped?"

"Yeah, I guess the dates would fit," said Maya. "Whether he was on duty both times, I can't say from this. Why?"

"I don't know," I said. "Just trying to find connections."

The bell over the door rang and Patience strode in, a small rolling suitcase trailing along behind her.

"Greetings, all and . . ." She glanced around the store. "Sundry."

"Hi, Patience," I said, then turned to Maya, Bronwyn, and Selena. "I forgot to tell you: Our wedding party has been expanded by one. Patience is going to be my third bridesmaid."

"Cool," said Selena in a shy voice.

"Super," Maya said dryly.

"Oh! Isn't that just lovely!" gushed Bronwyn. "Have you picked out a dress yet, dear?"

"That's why I'm here," said Patience. "And after, we can do that reading for you, Lily. I've got my stuff with me. Selena, be a sport and put this in the back for me, will you?"

Selena jumped up and hurried to do Patience's bidding, sullenness gone.

It figures, I thought, rather sullen myself.

"I haven't found the perfect outfit yet, either," said Bronwyn, excited as a schoolgirl. "Let's shop together!"

"Oh, goody," Patience said. No one but me—and perhaps Maya—seemed to detect the sarcasm dripping from her words, so I bit my tongue.

The next half hour was pure bliss. Maya cranked up a playlist of 1920s music, and she, Bronwyn, and Patience started trying on the outfits I picked out for them, and Selena ran back and forth with the garments, fully embracing this most feminine of pastimes.

Everything Patience tried on looked fabulous on her, and if I had been in a pettier frame of mind I would have assumed she was doing it just to make me feel bad. Which was silly, of course, because she was a natural beauty. Her womanly curves were especially stunning in the formfitting cocktail dresses from the late '30s and early '40s, a fashion era in which an hourglass figure was especially sought after.

Carlos walked in just as Patience flung the dressing room curtain open between fittings and emerged clad only in a corset and a slip.

He froze. Their gaze met and held. Patience thrust one hip out, put a hand on her waist, and raised one eyebrow.

Carlos cleared his throat. "Sorry to intrude," he said after a beat. "Should I come back another time . . . ?"

"No, no, of course not," I said, coming around from behind the horseshoe counter and standing in front of Patience, trying to wave her back into the dressing room. "We were just trying on dresses. Aunt Cora's Closet can feel a bit like being at home, hanging out with friends, walking around in one's altogethers, you know how it is. . . ."

Patience let out a peal of laughter and, at long last, stepped back into the dressing nook and drew the curtain closed.

"Try this one, Patience," said Selena, cradling an emerald green floor-length 1930s gown and ducking into the dressing nook.

"So what can I do for you, Carlos? Patience hasn't been able to read for me yet . . ." I said, suddenly embarrassed that he should find us trying on dresses instead of searching for clues to Elena's whereabouts. Carlos looked tired, with dark bags under his eyes. I imagined he hadn't slept much.

"It's not a problem," said Carlos. "I wanted to talk to you about the crime scene on Alcatraz."

"*Crime scene?*" Maya asked, ashen. "Tell me it's not Elena."

"No, sorry. I thought Lily might have mentioned it. The victim was an elderly Caucasian male."

Patience stepped out of the dressing room, this time wearing the green dress Selena had selected.

Silence descended. Patience had gathered her usually wild black hair into a smooth twist at the back of her neck, and in the elegant gown looked as if she were one of the brighter stars of Hollywood's Golden Age. The dress was sleeveless and mostly backless, exposing

as much skin as possible without, somehow, looking ris-
qué. The silky emerald green fabric alternately hugged
her body and flowed, reminiscent of a Grecian goddess.
The gown's deep V neck featured scrolled beading that
evoked a butterfly in both pattern and shape on the
bodice, before wending its way down and around the
mesh overlay.

"Oh, my," murmured Bronwyn, placing the tunic
she'd been considering back on the rack. "I guess I'd
better step it up."

"I know what you mean," said Maya, who had tried
on a crushed velvet tea-length dress that looked cute,
but nothing in Patience's league. "Wow."

Carlos said: "Nice outfit. So, is it Halloween every
day around here?"

"Well, now, that depends," Patience drawled, and I
wondered if she was imitating my accent. "If I knocked
on your door, big guy, would there be candy?"

Carlos was hard to read—he had that carefully
bland expression common to experienced cops—but I
was pretty sure he was shocked, and intrigued. Perhaps
not in that order.

"I, um," I stammered. "I can't remember, have you
two met?"

"We have now," Carlos said.

"Carlos, this is Patience Blix, Sailor's cousin. Patience, this is Homicide Inspector Carlos Romero of the
San Francisco Police Department." It's possible I placed
a little extra emphasis on the "*Police* Department."

"Charmed, Inspector."

"Ms. Blix."

They stared at each other, their gazes locked.

Finally, Carlos turned to me. "Hate to ruin your afternoon of dress-up, Lily, but I need you to come out
to the island with me to check out the scene, let us

know if any of your acquaintances or colleagues might have been involved."

"Now?"

"Now."

"*Stop*," said Patience. She came over and took Carlos by the hand. "You're the cousin of the missing woman."

He nodded.

"Don't go out there, to Alcatraz," Patience said. She turned to me. "Seriously, Lily. I have a very bad feeling about this."

Carlos patted the gun in his chest holster. "I appreciate the thought, Ms. Blix, but I'm prepared."

"I appreciate the confidence, Inspector Romero," she replied tartly. "But not for this, you aren't."

"You should listen to Patience," I said as Carlos marched me to his car. "She knows what she's doing and she doesn't kid around with stuff like this."

Heeding Patience's warning, I had packed supplies in my backpack and bag: my Hand of Glory, which is a rather macabre sort of candlestick capable of lighting up the darkest room; several protective amulets; a mason jar of all-purpose protective brew; various salts and crystals to be used in casting. Given Patience's warning, the dream I'd had, Elena's kidnapping, and now a ritualized murder, I thought it was wise to be prepared. Also, I had tucked my engagement ring away in my jewelry box for safekeeping; I couldn't bear to think of losing it at a crime scene, ritualistic murder or not.

"Are you suggesting I not do my job—which also may well have something to do with my cousin's disappearance—because a woman dressed up like a raven-haired Mae West tells me she has a 'bad feeling'?"

Yes, that's exactly what I'm suggesting.

"I'm saying you need to take her advice into consideration because she's a talented psychic, and you're too good a detective not to take advantage of all available resources. Patience might be reacting to the same sort of 'curse' that I felt was related to the prison shirt. Or it could be something else."

"She's that good, huh?"

"She's better than good."

"Hope she doesn't read minds," he said softly as we climbed into his car.

"She's a knockout, right?" I smiled. "Don't worry— you're pretty well guarded. It's common to cops and veterans, people who've seen a lot of trauma."

"Are *you* a mind reader?"

"Oh, no, not at all. But I can sense auras. I get a feeling for . . . people. Sometimes. I try not to, actually, since I've been fooled more than once. And just so you know, according to Sailor most psychics don't go around reading people's minds without their permission."

"Well, I suppose that's something. . . ."

"So you managed to get us permission to go to Alcatraz, eh?" I said as Carlos drove us to a dock near Pier 33, Alcatraz Landing. "I guess being a homicide inspector has its perks."

"An officer's going to pilot us over," he said, his usually inscrutable dark eyes shadowed with worry.

"Are the ferries still running?"

"Yes, the island is still open to tourists. The scene of the crime is off-limits, of course, but it's not on the tourist track, anyway. The dungeon is considered too architecturally unstable to be open to the general public."

The small police craft was piloted by a big, mostly silent man named Riggs, who nodded politely as I clumsily stepped off the dock and into the boat, but otherwise kept his pale eyes on the water.

It was a beautiful, breezy day. The water was almost turquoise, a rarity for the bay, which was more typically a grayish-green. Sailboats glided past us, tilting rakishly in the wind. The views were breathtaking: the soaring Golden Gate Bridge, radiant in the sunshine; the charming fishing village turned artsy town of Sausalito north of the bridge; the skyscrapers and picturesque hills of the city. I couldn't help but wonder what it must have felt like for prisoners making this same journey, knowing it would be a very long time—if ever—before such sights would be within reach for them. Knowing they were relegated to the Rock while one of the most vibrant, beautiful cities in the world beckoned from just over a mile away.

Glancing back at the San Francisco piers, it really didn't seem all that far a distance to swim. But the escapees had set out at night, in thick fog, and the bay waters were cold, rarely getting above the midfifties Fahrenheit. And as Maya had mentioned, the prisoners weren't top-notch athletes, trained to swim against strong currents.

Still. Ray Perry was a young man and apparently resourceful. And his body had never been found. Is it possible he had succeeded where others had failed?

Not without help, I remembered Elena saying.

I stroked my medicine bag and reminded myself to stay grounded, trying not to dwell on my nightmare, on the sensation of floating, of nearly drowning, in the icy bay waters.

"Did you find out anything about Albright?" I asked, to distract myself.

"Only what you probably already know: He and his brother were convicted of bank robbery and spent time in Leavenworth and Atlanta penitentiaries, but after repeated escape attempts were shipped out to Alcatraz.

After the escape there were some alleged sightings in their home state, and in South America. Some diehards claim they've been living in Brazil this whole time under an assumed name. The FBI received a letter a few years ago, allegedly written by Albright, requesting medical care in exchange for turning himself in, but they didn't deem it credible."

"That's it? No other rumors?"

"I actually called down to the province where the Albrights were alleged to have been living in Brazil. The FBI had been in touch before me, of course, so the local police department was familiar with the case. The man I spoke to claimed that the Americans there couldn't have been the Albrights, because they seemed too young. At least, I think that's what he said; Portuguese and Spanish aren't totally mutually intelligible. I may have missed something."

The trip to the island took only ten minutes, though Riggs had to approach the island slowly and carefully from a northern angle due to the strong currents.

As the boat edged up to the dock, I studied the cream-colored buildings streaked in black and gray, the ruins of old employee housing, the guard tower. I could feel malevolence and dread reaching out from the island: Something was stirring, dark and twisted.

As though the island itself were pulsating. Alive. Powerful.

This was the island the woods folk wanted me to make disappear. I got it now.

"I can't believe people pay for the privilege to come here," I said in a low voice, to no one in particular.

"Believe it. And they pay a lot," said Riggs. The boat banged against the moorings, jostling us as he tied on to the deck. "The behind-the-scenes tour costs around a hundred bucks."

"And here you get to go for free," said Carlos, handing me my bag and backpack. "Don't say I never gave you anything."

"Yeah, thanks a lot," I said, then chanted a quick protective charm under my breath.

Upon setting one foot on the Rock I felt the vibrations through the soles of my feet: a deep, malevolent hum, like an evil bass. *This should be interesting.*

Forrest Caruthers met us at the dock.

"Good to see you, Forrest," I said, trying to ignore the island's humming. The wind buffeted us, seagulls cawing loudly overhead.

"Carlos said you might be able to pick up on something, somehow?" His cowboy face was sketched with worry. "Gotta say, it sounds a little crazy to me, but at this point we're willing to try anything. If this murder is connected to Elena's kidnapping . . ."

"Do we know they're connected?" I asked, glancing at Carlos. It seemed likely, but Carlos wasn't the type to make assumptions without proof.

Carlos shook his head. "Nothing solid. Yet. Like I said, this is a federal case. They're allowing us to help, but we might not be privy to everything they've got."

Three men approached, one of whom was Charles Gosnold.

"Hello, Lily," said Charles. "Just getting prepared for our upcoming event!"

"Allow me to introduce you," Forrest said to Carlos and me. "We were just finishing up a meeting. Inspector Romero and Lily Ivory, this is Kyle Cheney and his assistant, Seth. Or have you all met?"

"I'm Kyle, Kyle Cheney," said a pasty man with bright blue–rimmed glasses that appeared far too trendy for him, as though someone else had picked them out. He reached out clumsily and shook our hands with an overeager enthusiasm. Cheney was clearly one of those supersmart guys lacking in social graces; I could relate. Maya had told me that he had invented some sort of highly lucrative bit of technology as a high school student and went on to found a hugely profitable computer company. I didn't keep up with technology, but even I knew that Kyle Cheney was the Bay Area's version of Bill Gates.

"And this is my assistant, Seth Barbagelata."

With glistening, dark gold hair, light blue eyes, and the beautiful, androgynous face of one of Michelangelo's angels, Seth would give Aidan a run for his money in the ethereal-good-looks department, I thought.

"Nice to meet you," Seth said in a warm tone, holding eye contact. Clearly, he was the public face of Cheney's company, the charming one, good with people.

"Believe it or not, Seth's—great-uncle, was it?" Kyle asked, and Seth nodded. "Seth's great-uncle was a guard out here on Alcatraz."

"Is that right?" I asked. "He must have some fascinating stories."

"He was here in the '30s, when the federal penitentiary first opened, and lived with his family in one of the guard houses. I never met him, but my father's elderly cousin remembers playing here, as a little girl. The kids loved it; they took a boat into the city every day to go to school, and during the holidays went Christmas caroling around the island. They called it 'a small town with a big jail.'"

"Seth came up with the idea of the Festival of Felons, and he's the point person for putting together this shindig," said Kyle, pushing his glasses farther up his nose. "Although now it seems sort of . . . I don't know, maybe in bad taste, considering what just happened. A man *murdered*." He shook his head. "I keep thinking maybe we should call the whole thing off, or at least postpone it."

"There's no need to cancel—," Gosnold began.

"I hope you won't," Forrest interrupted, an anxious note in his voice. "I know it's an unfortunate situation but the festival is for a very good cause, after all. The event will raise needed funds for the upkeep of historical buildings. We've gotten a lot of great publicity, and I'm afraid if we reschedule, we'll lose that momentum. Also, it's only a few days away now."

"You see?" Seth nudged his boss. "That's what I said. You're just gun-shy."

"I worry about how we're perceived. Can't be too careful these days." Kyle Cheney met my eyes, as if eager for me to concur.

"Even before this recent event, well," Forrest said, with a duck of his head, "Alcatraz is no stranger to tragedy. In a strange way, it's sort of fitting."

"It seems almost hard to believe, doesn't it?" Kyle said. "With all these birds, and the spectacular view, it's easy to convince yourself you're on some pretty isle, not a former prison colony. . . . But I'm sorry. Here I am, chatting away, and I haven't let you get a word in edgewise. Seth and I were just leaving, in any case."

"It's nice to meet you," I said. "I own a vintage clothing store on Haight Street, and we'd love to offer a donation for the fund-raiser. Maybe raffle off a dress, or something?"

"That would be wonderful! Our target audience would love the opportunity to win a vintage dress from your store," Seth said, handing me his card. "It's too late to include your sponsorship on the poster, I'm afraid, but I'd be happy to put you on the festival's website. It'll be great publicity for your business, and all donations are tax deductible. Win-win! Please contact me by phone or e-mail anytime, and we'll get the ball rolling."

"Thank you, I will. And Seth, I wonder: Would any of your relatives who lived on Alcatraz be willing to speak with me?"

"Oh, you mean my dad's cousin? She died a few years ago, I'm afraid."

"I'm sorry to hear that. Did she happen to pass on any stories, mementos, photos, anything like that?"

The ferry tooted its horn, indicating a five-minute warning.

"We'd better catch the ferry. Call me, and we'll get together," Seth said. "I don't know what I can tell you, but I'd be happy to chat."

Seth, Kyle, and Charles bid us good-bye and walked down the dock to board the tourist ferry returning to Pier 33. I watched them leave, fighting the compulsion to run after them and jump on the craft as well. I didn't have to see any more of the island to know that I'd seen enough.

"This way, folks," Forrest said as he led the way up a steep road from the dock. "I'm glad you're wearing sensible footwear."

Today's Keds were turquoise, matching my vintage A-line floral print sundress, with wide pockets and a square collar. Lately I needed bright colors to brighten my mood. Over this I wore a rose-colored cardigan and my cocoa brown wool car coat, because I was by now no stranger to San Francisco's cool weather, especially near the water.

"The birds have taken over much of the island, as you can see. All sorts of gulls, cormorants, and egrets make the Rock their home." Forrest pointed down the hill behind us, seemingly unable to refrain from being a tour guide. "The Agave Trail goes around the southern tip of the island, passing through a protected bird sanctuary. It's a nice walk; there are some pretty native plantings and incredible views of San Francisco and the Golden Gate Bridge."

We passed through a large gate, to my mind reminiscent of a castle drawbridge. It led to the administrative buildings and the cellblocks.

"And the graffiti?" I asked, gesturing to large red letters on a UNITED STATES PENITENTIARY sign that warned boats to remain at least two hundred yards offshore. The letters read: INDIANS WELCOME, and INDIAN LAND. Another set of letters changed the UNITED STATES PROPERTY to UNITED INDIAN PROPERTY. A gray water tower held more red letters, these spelling out PEACE AND FREEDOM/WELCOME/HOME OF THE FREE/INDIAN LAND.

"There was a takeover in 1969, after the penitentiary had closed and Alcatraz was basically abandoned," said Forrest. "A group of Native Americans arrived and claimed the island as part of their 'Indian land.'"

"I heard some local tribes consider the island cursed," I said.

He nodded. "The Ohlone used to collect eggs here occasionally, but they never lived on the island. I heard they marooned people out here if they were guilty of misdeeds."

"They left them here to die?"

"Oh, no, of course not. There was food—plenty of birds' eggs—and fish, they could capture rainwater, dew in the morning, that sort of thing. Or maybe they were left with water, not sure, actually. The point is, the people who lived in this area didn't deem the island worth inhabiting, and many said there were bad spirits here, or something along those lines."

"So then why return in the '60s?"

"The people who came then weren't Ohlone. The leaders were drawn from lots of different tribes. It was an effort to bring attention to the needs, and the past treatment, of Native Americans. It worked pretty well for a while, and the cause attracted some celebrity attention. But eventually . . ." He trailed off, shaking his head. "A little girl died in an accident, and fires broke out. Things fell apart, as ideals sometimes do."

"It's interesting that you left up the graffiti," I mentioned.

He nodded. "The National Park Service believes that the takeover was a significant part of the island's history. People should know about it, just like they should know about the penitentiary, and the native birds, and the original fortress, the Hopi and the Civil War prisoners, the arming of the island to guard the bay. The NPS consider ourselves to be stewards of history, we're not here to pass judgment."

"That's admirable."

"And as chaotic and 'unlawful' as the takeover was, it brought attention to sorely needed reforms with regard to US policy toward indigenous peoples, and spurred on some policy improvements under President Nixon. Sometimes it takes a little lawbreaking to bring about change."

"Just not murder," said Carlos.

"That's true enough," said Forrest.

He pointed out the charred ruins of the warden's house and the officers' club, and then led us into the main cellblock. Inside, huge windows let in lots of natural light but the peeling mint green walls were marred by sections of failing stucco and mold. Everything felt cold, unnaturally so, and I remembered Maya citing Mark Twain's quote about how cold Alcatraz always seemed, even in summer. I buttoned up my coat for warmth, and safety.

Forrest led us through the dining hall, the library, and pointed out the parade grounds, the laundry area, and the isolation rooms in Cellblock D, also known as "the hole." The prisoners' cells themselves were small rooms containing a toilet, a sink, a small ventilation grate, a desk attached to the wall, and a cot. That was it.

Everywhere we turned, dozens of tourists milled about. There were families and couples, groups of teenagers. A few scruffy-looking young people reminded me of Conrad's gutter punk friends, making me think back to that terrible moment on Haight Street, when I first learned Elena had been taken. Most were sporting headphones and listening intently to recordings describing the history of what they were seeing, spinning tales of Alcatraz's most famous inhabitants: Al Capone, Machine Gun Kelly, and the Birdman.

I wondered whether the headphones kept them from hearing sinister, otherworldly sounds I kept picking up on: Unintelligible whispering, the clanging of cell doors, the mournful notes of a harmonica.

Someone sobbing, calling out for help.

In one large, open room were larger-than-life posters of those who used to live on the island: the prisoners, the wardens, and the guards and their families. The most interesting were the photos of little girls with dolls and boys playing baseball—the children of the guards—against the backdrop of razor wire–topped fences. There were snapshots of young people using a bowling alley and sipping milkshakes at a soda fountain in a bizarre juxtaposition of 1950s normality within the notorious federal prison.

I froze in front of a life-sized black-and-white photo of Ray Perry, prisoner number 258.

This was the vision I'd seen in Emmy Lou Archer's attic. Not Perry's mug shot, but this full-length photo. In a plexiglass display beside it were some of his personal effects, including a stack of unopened letters addressed to a woman in Oklahoma.

"Can you tell me about this prisoner, Ray Perry?" I asked Forrest.

"Oh, yeah," Forrest said. "That shirt you found supposedly belonged to him. The numbers were handed out as the men arrived on the island; so Ray Perry was the two-hundred-and-fifty-eighth man to arrive."

"Lily Ivory!" a man's voice called out. I turned to see the fellow with the bushy white mustache, Ralph Gordon, whom I had met at Pier 33 yesterday. "You made it over after all. Good for you."

Forrest introduced Carlos and explained that we were on "official business" due to the "commotion" in the cellar.

"Oh, I heard about that. Terrible thing."

"I have a question," I said, gesturing to Ray Perry's display. "Why weren't the letters Perry wrote sent to Oklahoma?"

"That's anybody's guess," Gordon said. "They were only recently discovered by an archivist working here at the museum. We thought they looked good in the display like that."

"And no one ever opened them?" I asked.

"Isn't it a federal offense to open someone else's mail?" Forrest said, glancing at Carlos as if looking for backup.

"Not if they're prisoners, it's not. Besides, he's long since deceased. Anyway, it's good to meet you, Ralph. And this private tour's great and all, Forrest," said Carlos. "But we're here to look at a crime scene, remember?"

Forrest gestured with his head. "You're just like Elena, you know that? Impatient. We in the NPS are proud of what we've done here."

"It's a very well-executed exhibit," I said. "But I think Carlos is right; we need to get down to business. That's what we're here for, after all."

"This little lady is here to see the crime scene?" Ralph Gordon asked the two men flanking me.

"I am, yes," I answered for myself

"Well, I'll be danged," he said. "Good luck with that."

Forrest seemed to be delaying our descent into the bowels of Alcatraz as long as possible. But after another moment of hesitation, he nodded.

"This way."

Forrest led the way down a narrow set of concrete steps, opened a locked metal door, and waved us into the dungeon.

Chapter 15

Dungeons, it turns out, are often described as cold, dark, and dank for good reason. I shivered as we descended to the windowless tunnels of the nineteenth-century cellar beneath Alcatraz, the darkness broken only by occasional pools of anemic light from sporadic lightbulbs overhead. The concrete under our feet was slick and damp, with water puddling in the corners, and the air held a distinct musty odor. Old brick walls and arched ceilings had been whitewashed at some point, but now were coated in layers of grime and decorated with cobwebs. Small rooms flanked the corridor; Forrest used his flashlight to point them out. Not all the rooms were cells for holding prisoners, he explained; several had been used to store weapons and supplies.

"Like I said, this part of the building dates back to the Civil War, and some portions may be even older," Forrest said as we proceeded down the corridor. Our footsteps rang out on the concrete floors. "The Spanish built a military fort and put a bunch of cannons out here, just in case, I guess."

"Hence the name, the Spanish dungeon?" Carlos said.

"Exactly. It was originally part of a three-point triangle to defend the bay. On the San Francisco side of the Golden Gate was Fort Point, on the Marin side there was Lime Point, and Alcatraz formed the third point. Kyle Cheney has been instrumental in restoring some of those buildings as well. He's a godsend."

"I didn't realize concrete was invented so long ago," I said.

Forrest nodded. "Oh, sure. It dates back to the Romans, actually. But reinforced concrete—held up by rebar—was introduced to the US building trades in 1849."

"Wait, you're saying Alcatraz was used as a fort during the Civil War?" I glanced at Carlos. I was no historical scholar, true, but I had never heard of California being involved militarily in that struggle. "Was there fighting in San Francisco during the Civil War?"

"No," said Forrest. "But they were prepared, just in case. Remember, San Francisco was an incredibly strategic port, with gold and other valuable minerals shipped down the inland rivers and through San Pablo Bay. California was an important resource for the Union. Also, they held some prisoners of war down here."

"How recently was this area used?" I asked. "Once the federal prison was built, they had other cells for punishment, right?"

Forrest nodded. "They used this area occasionally, especially in the early years. No doubt it was considered the ultimate threat. According to the stories, they would make the prisoner strip first, put him down in here, then throw his clothes to him."

"Why?" I asked.

"To dehumanize him, I suppose. Carlos might know more about that sort of thing than I," said Forrest. "A big part of punishment within a prison, as far as I can tell, is psychological."

"Ever since we outlawed beatings," muttered Carlos.

Forrest opened another door, revealing a barred gate within. He pointed the beam of his flashlight into the cell, and something scurried away, disappearing into a crack in the walls.

"Once the doors were closed it was pitch-black in there. The only sounds would have been the rats scuttling along, or the guard passing by on rounds. Maybe water dripping from the cisterns. That was about it. . . . If there was another prisoner, there might be some singing or crying, but they weren't allowed to communicate because of the rule of silence."

"No beds, or anything like that?"

He shook his head. "The prisoners slept on the floor, or sat against the wall. They survived on bread and water; maybe some soup every few days. Not an easy road."

"I guess not."

"If the guards wanted to punish the prisoners even more, they would throw cold water on them, which was called putting him 'on the water.' They say a lot of men went crazy down here."

"Is that true?" Carlos asked.

"Can't say for sure. But that's what folks said."

"Do you smell cigarettes?" I asked.

Carlos sniffed, then shook his head.

"Not likely," Forrest said. "No smoking in the national park system. Federal law."

"Maybe it's residue from the past," Carlos said. "The smell of smoke can linger a long time, especially when there's not much ventilation."

"They say . . . sometimes the guards would smoke to taunt the prisoners." Forrest kept his eyes on me, puzzled. "A lot of times the ghost hunter people say they smell cigarette smoke down here."

I nodded. The apparition of Ray Perry in Emmy Lou Archer's attic was the first time I'd seen a ghost with my eyes, but I had certainly caught scent of them before.

"How long did the prison use these cells?" I asked.

"In the early 1940s the director of the Bureau of Prisons decided the dungeons were cruel and unusual, so from then on, disciplinary cases were sent to the hole instead. That's up on D-Block, right over our heads."

Forrest paused in front of another iron door, this one crossed by bright yellow crime scene tape. "Okay, so, here's where we found the victim. I must warn you: It's pretty gruesome. The body was removed but there's still . . . you know."

"We know," said Carlos. He looked at me. "You ready?"

I stroked my medicine bundle and nodded.

The clanking of the iron door reverberated off the brick walls. I walked in first, with Carlos close behind me.

The metallic, shiny scent of blood filled the space, mingling with the dank mustiness of the closed-off cell and the acrid aroma of despair.

I'd seen many homicide scenes since moving to San Francisco, but this one was particularly gruesome. Smears of dark blood, long since dried, stained the concrete. Salts, herbs, and incense had been kicked and crushed underfoot by whoever had collected the body, so it was hard to tell how they had originally been laid out. Chalk marks peeked out from under the smeared blood.

"You ask me, that's some satanic shi—s'cuse me," said Forrest. "Some satanic stuff, there."

"Is that a pentacle?" Carlos asked me, pointing to the chalk marks.

"It could be . . . or it could be a Baphomet. It depends on how the body was oriented within it." A pentacle is a five-pointed star that stands on two points. Despite its popular association with evil, the pentacle is an ancient sign of protection; I used it often in my own spellcasting. The Baphomet used the same star but rotated it so that the primary point faced down, and it incorporated the symbol of a horned goat's head. The Baphomet wasn't exclusive to negative magic, but its presence did raise questions. "I wish I could have seen this before everything was disturbed, with all the blood and everything. I assume photos were taken?"

Forrest stared at me, aghast.

"It's her process," Carlos told Forrest. "Don't let the vintage dress fool you: This ain't her first rodeo."

"The, uh, FBI took photos; you'd have to ask them. Listen, if it's all the same to you, I'll wait outside," said Forrest. "Take your time. This is too creepy for me."

I barely registered his words. Carefully, I walked around the gruesome tableau, holding my hands out at my sides, palms down, feeling the vibrations. They pulsed in rhythm to the throbbing bass of the island.

I understood why a casual observer would conclude what had happened here was a satanic ritual, but in my experience, Satanists were more about the drama and the playacting than they were genuinely devoted to the dark lord. They loved the shock value. And looking more closely, I recognized a broken Solomon's Triangle and the remnants of sulfur. This didn't strike me as satanic as much as demonic.

This had been a deliberate effort to conjure a demon.

And not just any demon. Not one of the other thousands of demons cataloged by those industrious monks so long ago, or by the Tibetans or the Aztecs or by the scholars from any of the other cultures who had written down their various names and signs and characteristics. No, I was almost sure . . . *this* was a demon I had met before.

He wasn't here *now*, thank the goddess. But even so, I could feel his vibrations, his seductiveness reaching out to me.

Sitri.

I knew Sitri, and he knew me. He was the twelfth spirit, named a Great Prince in the hierarchy laid out in the *Ars Goetia*. He commanded legions of underlings.

I could be wrong, I reminded myself. It might be another, similar, demon. There were so many to keep track of.

Still, Sailor's words rang in my head: *Once you've met a demon, they never forget you.* Even with my guard up and my medicine bag humming at my waist, I was glad I had begun the MoonWish spell. I invoked a vision of that black candle burning in my apartment, helping to ground me, to keep me firmly tethered to this world.

Last time I had encountered Sitri was in a closet at the San Francisco School of Fine Arts, which just goes to show a witch can't let her guard down, even when poking her nose into caches of old clothes in closets. That was where I first met Sailor, as a matter of fact.

At the time I thought I had closed—and sealed— Sitri's portal. But I had been fooling myself; it's never as easy as that. Demons are indifferent to the designs of humans and are not easily put to rest. Other portals can be opened, and demons can be summoned or conjured almost by accident.

And this, I thought as I looked at the remnants of the scene laid before me, was no accident.

"Carlos, do you think you could get copies of the FBI's photos, or at least a list of what was taken into evidence?" I asked.

"One step ahead of you." Carlos reached into his jacket pocket and handed me an envelope of photos.

The body had been oriented within the pentacle in the shape of a Baphomet. The elderly man had sparse, white hair, but the broad plains of his face were still rugged-looking and smooth. He was ashen from lack of blood, but even so I would have pegged him for his midsixties, not mideighties. I thought of Bronwyn's comment that Cole Albright was a "historical hottie"—he had, indeed, been an attractive young man, and he had been a good-looking old man as well.

Hard to imagine what he had gone through in his last moments.

Tiny yellow A-frame evidence markers stood by bunches of herbs and salts and marked dozens of blood spatters on the brick walls and floor. In addition to a few metal bowls—which I imagined had been used in the conjuring ritual to capture the victim's blood—were three diminutive glass bottles, slender and graceful in design.

Lachrymatories. Victorian-era bottles that captured the tears of the bereaved. The tears evaporated, leaving only the salts of grief behind. Powerful salts. Renee-the-cupcake-lady had been collecting lachrymatories with a fervor that had led to violence. She wasn't the only one who might have such a collection, but I needed to track her down, somehow, and speak with her. Soon.

"Forensics has come and gone, yes?" I asked Carlos. "Could I set up a few things?"

"Like what?"

"I'd like to put out some candles, and . . . maybe a ring of salt?"

"No, sorry. Forensics went over this place with a fine-tooth comb, but you never know who else might need to analyze the scene. We can't introduce anything new."

"I understand," I said, frustrated. Especially now that the Ashen Witch wasn't showing up on a predictable basis, I yearned for the familiar support of my salts and herbs and candles. They would help me to get into the right frame of mind for something like this.

Too bad I couldn't have figured out a way to bring Oscar along. He was the best at helping me to open the portals.

The thought of telling Carlos I wanted my pet pig made me smile.

Carlos frowned. "Something funny? Albright was no Boy Scout, but he didn't deserve . . ." He gestured to the bloodstains. "This."

Chastened, I said: "I would never laugh at a homicide scene, Carlos, you know that. I was thinking about my pig."

"Why don't you concentrate on the crime scene?" Carlos snapped. "You'll have plenty of time later to play with your pet pig."

Was he just out of sorts, frustrated by his inability to find his cousin? Testy from a lack of sleep? Not that I would blame him. But could it be more? Demons had a way of stirring up emotions, sparking arguments even among otherwise uninvolved bystanders. It was something about their energy spilling out and ratcheting up insecurities and anger—and they enjoyed the mayhem they inspired, of course.

Fine. I didn't need my magical effects; I was strong enough to do this.

I began chanting, enhancing my powers by piggybacking on the potency of the already spilled blood. It shimmered around me, almost palpable, thrumming to the pulse of the island, of the human heart, of the primordial depths. I heard more ghostly sounds: cell doors clanging shut, fervent whispers and murmurings echoing off the brick walls.

The image of Ray Perry appeared, once again a frustratingly silent holograph clutching that dang lily. Was it for me?

What in blue blazes went on here? I asked him without saying a word.

He put his finger to his lips, as he had in the attic, as though miming "*shhhhh.*"

Talk to me.

His lips parted as though to speak, but he said nothing. Instead, his mouth opened, wider and wider, until it became a gaping black void, emitting ravens, spiders, flies, all manner of horrid, scuttling things.

I felt a blast of rampant anger and pure lust, encased in a violent energy.

Ssssso nice to sssseeeeee you, Lily Ivory.

There was a commotion in the hall, and I came out of my semitrance to the sound of angry men's voices. Carlos had drawn his weapon, but before he could move, the iron door to the cell slammed and the lock clanged shut, plunging us into complete darkness.

"What the *hell*?" Carlos said, banging on the door and yelling.

I pulled my Hand of Glory out of my backpack and illuminated the cell.

"What is *that*?" Carlos demanded, staring at the hand.

"It's useful, that's what it is," I said.

Carlos checked his phone, moving it about and holding it high, then low. "No service. *Dammit*."

As we gazed at each other, I felt a mounting lust begin to overtake me. I'd always thought Carlos was an attractive man, but I'd never felt this. Not this.

"Do you smell smoke?" I asked, sniffing the air.

"Again with the cigarettes?" Looking relaxed now, Carlos smiled, a warm, sensual intensity in his eyes. He lifted a hand to my hair, cupped my head in his palm. "A cigarette comes after, not before, don't you know that, *querida*?"

This isn't real, I told myself. *This isn't us*. Sitri inspires anger, but he also inspires lust.

The scent of smoke grew stronger. From far away came the distant shrieking of a fire alarm. The dungeon was made of brick and stone, which would not burn. But that wouldn't stop the flames of a demon.

My mind raced. My magic is real and it is powerful, but it is a brew-alone-in-my-kitchen kind of magic, not a throw-down-with-a-demon-in-a-firefight kind.

"We have to get out of here, Carlos," I said. "You hear me?"

"What's the rush?" Carlos said, his voice uncharacteristically deep. "We have time."

I tried the door—no luck. "Help me, please, Carlos."

"Playing coy, my lady?"

"Just get your keister over here, Inspector, and help me try this door."

Grumbling, he joined me and together we heaved. The door didn't budge.

My medicine bundle throbbed and hummed in warning. I needed to heed the voice in my head, sounding in my heart. We needed to *run*.

I put my hands on Carlos's shoulders and looked him straight in the eye. "Listen to me, Carlos. What you're feeling right now isn't real. Do you still have that Raven stone I gave you?"

"Yeah . . . as a matter of fact, I could have sworn it was vibrating earlier."

"Take it out and hold it in your palm for a moment. I'll explain it all later but at the moment we have to get out of here, okay?"

Carlos pouted. "Are you sure?"

"Positive."

"Whatever my lady wants," he said, taking the stone out and palming it. "But how do you suggest we leave? Magic?"

"There," I said, pointing to the rusty ventilation grate. "Do you have something sharp, like a pocket knife?"

Carlos handed me a Swiss army knife. I flipped open a blade and began gouging at the crumbling concrete around the grate until it loosened enough for Carlos and me together to yank it out of the wall. Carlos took the knife from me and started jabbing furiously at the edges of the hole, hacking away at the concrete until the opening looked almost large enough to crawl through.

"Let's go," I said.

"I don't think I can fit in there," Carlos said. "Let me make it a little larger."

"No time," I replied, hearing voices in the hallway, approaching. Whoever it was, the humming from my medicine bag told me they meant us harm. I held out my Hand of Glory, which promised to open locked doors. Maybe it would help with the opening as well. "Follow me."

"Why don't we just spend a little time here, together?"

"Carlos—" I stopped and abruptly changed tactics, hoping to motivate him to get a move on. "Come with me now, and I'll make it worth your while," I purred.

He gave me a smoldering look. "In that case, after you."

With regret, I shed my wool coat and left it behind, but thrust my woven backpack through the hole first, then squeezed through the small hole myself. My skirt caught on the rough edges, and jagged bits of mortar scratched my arms, reopening the cat's claw marks. My blood smeared on the sides of the ventilation shaft, and suddenly the passage seemed to open up not just for me, but for Carlos behind me.

The shaft stank with the rancid, sickening sweetness of death. But at least it wasn't full of smoke. At least not yet.

"Can you put the grate back, in case they check the cell?" I whispered.

Carlos had anticipated me and was already pulling the grate to cover the hole, propping it up with chunks of broken concrete. Still, it wouldn't take anyone long to figure out where we had gone as there was no other way to escape the cell.

I stashed my Hand of Glory in the backpack so no one would see its illumination, plunging the passageway into inky darkness.

We crawled farther down the ventilation shaft, feeling our way. It was pitch-dark but the only other option—to go back to the cell—was *not* an option. As we inched along, I heard whispers and could feel unsettled spirits fluttering by, pulling at my hair and skirts. I should have worn my jeans on today of all days.

After several minutes, we came to a slightly wider section and paused to rest. I pulled out the Hand of

Glory, and we looked around, peering behind us, then up ahead. Nothing showed in any direction. I used a string and hung the Hand of Glory around my neck, to keep my hands free. Carlos took my backpack and pushed it along in front of him, taking the lead as we progressed down the tight shaft.

"Lily? I don't know what came over me back there," whispered Carlos. "I am so sorry, and embarrassed. I hope you know that I care for you, both personally and professionally, but I would never cross a line. . . . Except that I did, and I am mortified. Please accept my apology."

"I get it, Carlos. It wasn't you, trust me. It was . . . it was the effect of something external to both of us. I felt the same way, and I'm set to marry Sailor, for land's sakes."

"Well, you should put that dang Hand down because I'm pretty sure my face is bright red with embarrassment."

"Pretty sure mine matches yours." I felt Carlos relax a little.

"So, onward and upward?"

We continued along through the tight shaft, climbing now, the cold stone walls threatening at any moment to close in on us. I'm no claustrophobe, but this was bad. It felt . . . *wrong*. The haunting sensation of ghosts surrounding us sure as shootin' didn't help matters.

"This is horrifying," Carlos voiced my own thoughts as we climbed. "It feels . . . unnatural. Is this the sort of thing you experience all the time?"

"Sort of. I mean, not every day, but yes, it can be challenging."

"You have my sympathies."

"There's an upside," I said. "I mean, at the moment it's hard to imagine such a thing, but there really is an upside."

Just then, Carlos pulled back, with an "*Ahhh!*"

"What is it?"

"A skeleton."

"A *skeleton*?"

Carlos turned back to me. "A human skeleton. Let's . . . leave that for the moment."

He managed to crawl around it, then I did the same. Whoever it was had been here for quite some time. The bones were covered in cobwebs, grime, and shreds of rotted cloth, like a quality Halloween decoration.

As the passageway snaked around a bend, we heard a distant crying.

"Do you hear that?" Carlos asked. "The ghost of a prisoner?"

"Maybe. But . . . it sounds female, doesn't it?"

A spirit—or a spider?—reached out from the wall, trying to grab my ankle. I batted it away, mumbling a charm.

"I see something up ahead," Carlos said.

"A patch of light?"

"More like a patch of not dark."

I heard a grunting, then some kicking and thudding, then a loud clang as a grate fell to the stone floor.

"That should do it." Carlos squeezed through the hole into what looked like a small storage room, then turned and helped me out of the shaft. "This way," he whispered as we headed out the open doorway into the smoky corridor.

Coughing, we ran away from the worst of the smoke. Turning a corner, we saw a bundle of clothes on the ground in front of a barred cell door. Gray and green.

A National Park Service uniform.

"Wait, Carlos—"

Heedless, Carlos rushed to grab the iron bar locking the cell. He wrenched it upward and flung open the door. Inside, shivering in the corner, clad only in her bra and underwear, was a woman.

Elena.

She was handcuffed to the cell's ventilation grate, armed with a stick she had found who knows where. In the shadowy darkness illuminated only by my Hand of Glory, she didn't seem to recognize us and lashed out, poking at Carlos as he approached, scratching him.

"*Go away!*" she screamed. "Leave me *alone*! Leave me alone. . . ." She dissolved into tears.

"*Elena?*" Carlos said in a fierce whisper. "It's Carlos. I'm here with Lily. It's *Carlos*, Elena. You're okay. We'll get you out."

"Do you have a handcuff key on you?" I asked Carlos.

"Never leave home without it," he replied. As the cuffs slid off Elena's wrists, she collapsed against him. He quickly stripped off his shirt and wrapped her in it.

Elena coughed as the cell began to fill with smoke.

"Now what?" I asked Carlos in a low voice. "The smoke's getting bad in the hallway. Even assuming the bad guys aren't waiting for us out there, I'm not sure how far we would get."

"I agree," he said grimly. "That leaves one other way."

I looked at the ventilation shaft. I really did not want to go back in there, but didn't see how we had a choice. I nodded.

Carlos opened his Swiss army knife and once again pried the rusted old grate out and began enlarging the hole in the wall.

I closed my eyes and cast over it, mumbling. The concrete gave way.

"Why don't I go first?" I said. "Elena can follow me and you follow her, help her along. This isn't going to be easy."

"Tell me something I don't know," he replied.

I squatted next to Elena, who sat huddled against the cell wall. Her hair was dirty and matted, streaked with what looked like blood and mud, though it was hard to tell in the dim light.

"Elena?" I said, hugging her and helping her to stand. "We have to go. You can do this. Carlos and I are here." I slipped an amulet around her neck to lend her strength, tried to cast a comforting spell over her, and led her to the ventilation shaft.

"We've got you," Carlos said, his voice low and fervent. "You're okay. We're okay. We're going to get out of here."

"Through there?" she asked, peering into the hole.

"Onward and upward!" I said with a cheer I didn't feel. "It'll be tight, but we'll make it. Carlos and I are old pros at this."

"You betcha," Carlos said. "Lily will go first, then you follow her. I'll be right behind you, okay?"

"What if we get trapped?"

"We won't," I said confidently, hoping it was true. The smoke from the hallway was intensifying. "Ready?"

Once again I crawled into the prison's old ventilation shaft, this time intentionally smearing traces of my blood on the inside walls. The passageway opened wider. At Carlos's urging, Elena climbed in behind me, and Carlos followed her.

I began crawling, heading up a sloped shaft, away from the cursed dungeon. It was slow going but we kept up a steady pace, hoping to outrun the smoke and fire.

It's amazing how fast one can move through tight spaces with a flame at one's feet. Literally.

I heard Elena breathing behind me, Carlos talking to her softly, encouraging her to go on. As we continued to climb, the air became slightly fresher. I reached a juncture and halted, unsure which way to go.

"Up," Carlos said.

"You sure?"

"Always up."

We continued up, inching our way to fresh air, to freedom. Or so I hoped. At long last I saw blessed sunlight pooling up ahead, and hurried toward it. A broad vertical shaft was topped by a very large metal grate. Carlos boosted me up to a shallow shelf right below the grate, then I reached down for Elena as he helped her up to me. Finally he climbed up to join us.

Carlos and I did everything we could to lift the grate, gouging at the concrete and pushing with all our might, but it was much larger and heavier than those in the cells below and would not be so easily defeated. We were trapped.

Still, we gathered around, our fingers clutching at the old metal, breathing deeply as the bay breezes poured in.

At least we had fresh air.

"Try your phone now," I said.

One arm still wrapped around Elena, Carlos sighed with relief when the call went through. It took a few minutes for him to explain just where we were, and why the rescuers should bring some hardware to undo the ventilation grate, but he hung up smiling.

"The good guys are on their way. It'll be a few minutes."

"I don't know about you, but I'm tuckered out," I

said. We all inched down to sit on the damp concrete
ledge. Elena leaned against Carlos and closed her eyes.

"How's she doing?" I asked quietly.

"Breathing's okay." He touched her cheek gently,
but she did not respond. Concerned, he lifted her eye-
lids and checked her pupils. "She might have been
drugged."

"Let me try," I said, and laid hands on her. "Poor
thing must be exhausted. I think she's just asleep."

"That's probably for the best, all things considered,"
he said, grim. "Help's on its way. Shouldn't be long now."

Carlos fell silent. I assumed he—like I—was imag-
ining what Elena might have gone through.

"So, quite a day, wouldn't you say?" I asked to
lighten the mood. "Definitely one for the books."

"Can't say I've had a day quite like it. Can't say I'd
care to have another."

"I suppose all's well that ends well."

Carlos opened his mouth as though to speak, but
hesitated. "Lily, about earlier . . . Again, I'm so very
sorry. I don't know what came over me."

"A demon, that's what came over you."

He looked aghast. "You're saying I was *possessed*?
By a demon?"

"No, no. That's not what I meant. Demons have a
way of influencing humans, bringing out the worst in
our nature."

"So then there's a demon here? You saw him . . .
or it?"

"Not exactly. Demons don't have to be physically
present to affect things. I *felt* him. Or the memory of
him being called, more like."

"So that really was a ritualistic killing?"

"I can't be sure, but I think so. Do you remember

what happened at the School of Fine Arts a while back?"

Carlos looked at me from the side of his eyes. "Are people jumping out of windows again?"

"No. Nothing like that. At least, not that I know of."

"You're not exactly reassuring me here." He looked up through the grate, as though willing the rescue to arrive, already. "Last time he was confined to the school, wasn't he?"

"There are historical reasons for him to be there, but he's not bound to the building. He's not a ghost. If someone opened a portal somewhere else—"

"Like on Alcatraz?"

I nodded.

"Why on earth would someone summon a demon?"

"Lots of reasons. Wealth, fame, success . . . or, believe it or not, sometimes more innocuous reasons. If it's the guy I'm thinking of, he's known to inspire creativity and high-spirited fun, as well as lust, which some people mistake for love. The point is, someone might have summoned him without knowing how to control him, and he could have wrested control from the conjurer."

"So how do we find this demon—what's his name?"

"I can't speak his name. Someone with my powers could summon him, just that easily, without even meaning to. I'm still not entirely sure, but if it *is* the same one, he's likely to find *us*. Or me, anyway. He knows me, and I'm the one who bound him last time. It's possible he's been drawing me out to Alcatraz on purpose."

"I don't like the sound of that," he said with a frown. "And you're saying my behavior was affected by this creature?"

"This particular demon is known for inspiring lust. It's not your fault. Nobody's immune to it."

"Still . . . I'm not sure what that says about my character."

"That you're human? I'd say that's a good thing."

He looked unconvinced.

"Carlos, it had the same effect on me—I was feeling things for you I shouldn't have been feeling. And I'm *engaged*."

Carlos raised an eyebrow. "Gave you the hots, did I?"

"Hotter than a stolen tamale, as my mother would say."

He laughed and relaxed. "I have an idea: Why don't we keep what happened between the two of us and never mention it again? It'll be our little secret."

"You're on." I sighed and laid on the accent. "Though I will always remember our brief jailhouse romance, a spark that burned brightly but not too well."

He chuckled softly. "So, not to turn the talk from demons and all, but . . . what's Patience's story?"

"I knew it!" I said, and we laughed.

"Sorry if all this chitchat seems inappropriate under the circumstances," Carlos said, hugging Elena closer. "I'm trying to distract myself while we're stuck here, waiting. I'm a man of action, not words."

"No explanation needed," I said. "What would you like to know about Patience?"

"Is she single?"

"She is, yes. She's also smart and talented and challenging and, I would imagine, never boring."

"I can't wait to tell her she was wrong to tell us we shouldn't come to Alcatraz." He hugged Elena closer. "True, we nearly died and apparently ran across a demon, but we found Elena, after all."

"Hey, I have an idea—why don't you stand up with

Sailor at the wedding and I'll match you two up? She's a bridesmaid, you'll be a groomsman. It's perfect. Everyone gets lucky at weddings."

He gave a wry chuckle. "Sounds like trouble."

"Oh, yes, I would imagine," I said. "But trouble can be fun."

Just ask Sitri.

Chapter 16

Alcatraz was soon swarming with police and emergency responders who had arrived in response to the fire alarm and Carlos's call for help. Elena was airlifted to the hospital for treatment, Carlos by her side, as was Forrest Caruthers, who had been hit over the head and knocked unconscious in the hallway, and was suffering from smoke inhalation. I eavesdropped as the fire captain on the scene puzzled over the origin of the mysterious fires. The consensus seemed to be that it was a fraternity prank.

That was no boyish prank, I thought, sipping a Coke and waiting for my turn to answer questions.

I limped home late that night after a lengthy debriefing and refusing the ministrations of the medics. What was troubling me wasn't something modern medicine could fix.

When I got there, Aunt Cora's Closet was dark. Maya and Bronwyn, Conrad, and the others had closed up shop and long since left for the evening.

I knew Sailor and Patience were attending a family dinner—really a family meeting—with Renna, so I couldn't (a) make up with Sailor, or (b) have Patience read for me—which, now that Elena had been found, was a moot point—or (c) meet with Renna to see if she was possessed by a demon—and given what I had seen and felt on Alcatraz, I now feared that such a demon might carry the name of Sitri. On the other hand, maybe the extended family would be able to deal with whatever was bothering their aunt. Maybe it wasn't demonic at all.

I tried not to think about the damage that could be inflicted by a practitioner as powerful as Renna if her talents were exploited by, or somehow combined with, a demon's.

Ugh.

Upstairs, I checked Oscar's cubby over the refrigerator but his nest of blankets was gobgoyle-free. I had gifted him a travel cloak a while back, which enabled him to go pretty much anywhere he wanted in time and space. Not that he necessarily needed it, I thought. Oscar seemed able to get around on his own, anyway, in some mysterious fashion. I wondered whether he had snuck into Beijing's Forbidden City yet, or whether, as I suspected, he really wanted Sailor and me to be at his side when and if he found his mother.

I showered off the grime from our adventure in Alcatraz's dungeon and ancient ventilation shafts, then checked to see how the wax was dripping on the black five-day candle, then performed the second day of the MoonWish spell. Now that I knew I was dealing with Sitri, I carved *Twelfth Prince* into the candle, to call on him directly. As tonight's sacrifice I left out a beer, a shot of whiskey, and a cheese and chili tamale that had miraculously escaped Oscar's notice.

The offering on the final day was supposed to be a blood sacrifice. Given that it was Sitri, a demon that I had already battled, that seemed more necessary than ever. I pushed that from my mind for the moment.

Sitting at my little pine breakfast table, I flipped through my massive Book of Shadows to find the section I had added when I went up against Sitri the first time, in the third-floor closet of the School of Fine Arts.

I had written down a quote from the *Ars Goetia*:

The Twelfth Spirit is Sitri. He is a Great Prince and appeareth at first with a Leopard's head and the Wings of a Gryphon, but after the command of the Master of the Exorcism he putteth on Human shape, and that very beautiful. He enflameth men with Women's love, and Women with Men's love; and causeth them also to show themselves naked if it be desired. He governeth 60 Legions of Spirits. His Seal is this, to be worn as a Lamen before thee, etc.

Sitri's sigil, or seal, was a large *U* cut by a bar and topped by three Gothic crosses.

I remembered it well.

I read on: *Also known by the names of Bitru, or Sytry, perhaps the same or related to the Egyptian deity Set, a god of chaos and darkness. Sitri is a day spirit, his element is water, his tarot suit is Cups. This Prince is known for inspiring chaos, trickery, darkness, lust, and love. He is also connected to the creative arts and passion for life.*

In my Book of Shadows I had included the recipe for the brew I had made, the salts for the circle, as well as a list of the items I brought with me: my athame, or magical knife; sprigs of sorcerer's violet; a segment of sacred rope; and three horizontal slices of an apple cut to display the hidden pentacle, or stars, at its core.

Looking at it now, it struck me as a rather meager

magical toolbox with which to go up against any demon, much less Sitri. But of course what really mattered was my inner strength, the ability to focus my intent and subsume my conscious mind to channel the strength of my ancestors—the chain of powerful witches who had led to my walking this earthly plane.

Still, I had been overly confident. Quite arrogant, really. I could see that now. But isn't that the gift of youth? To tumble into things without thought, throwing caution to the wind?

Unless, of course, I had screwed up.

I had also written down the script for the exorcism, including calling Sitri by name and repeating the words, over and over, despite everything he threw at me:

With the strength of my ancestors, I am the power. I command you to show yourself. . . . I do hereby license thee to return to thy proper place, without causing harm or danger unto man or beast, I compel thee.

I closed my eyes for a moment, remembering the gruesome scene. The flies and wasps that stung me, the seductive visions that promised the love of my father. Sitri had tried his best, but I had, indeed, triumphed. I had trapped him in Solomon's Triangle and helped to save the school—and perhaps the city. I may have been young and naive, but I was strong even then.

But as I had told Carlos, that didn't mean that someone couldn't have opened a portal elsewhere. Anyone with the know-how—and enough foolishness—might have conjured Sitri.

So where did that leave me?

Yes, Elena had been found, and she was alive, and apparently not badly hurt. And that was huge. But I still didn't have a clue why she had been kidnapped or how all of this related to Sitri. Much less what to do about it, without making things worse.

Snap out of it, Lily.

I needed some company. Maya deserved a night to herself, though, and Bronwyn was spending the evening with the coven at Calypso's house. So I called Selena to ask if she would like to spend the night with me.

"I guess," she said, sounding neither interested nor uninterested. With her grandmother's permission, I drove to the busy Mission District to pick Selena up.

"What's for dinner?" she asked as soon as she climbed into the car, a bright blue nylon backpack slung over her shoulder.

"Um . . ." I should have thought about that before picking her up. Selena liked to eat almost as much as a certain gobgoyle of my acquaintance. "Today's your lucky day! We need to stop at the grocery store, anyway, so you can choose whatever you'd like."

She frowned, thinking. "Pad thai."

I laughed. "I can cook Cajun and Mexican and a fair amount of regular old American, but I'm no expert in Thai food. But if you look up the recipe, I'll give it a go."

Selena used her phone to find a fairly simple-sounding recipe, and we had fun in the grocery store's extensive Asian foods section, picking out wide rice noodles, chili sauce, and a jar of pad thai paste, which promised to make the dish that much easier. Then I stocked up on other basics, such as bread and eggs and fruit and—in deference to Oscar—potato chips, Cheez Doodles, and a jumbo bag of Tater Tots.

We lingered in the frozen food section while Selena debated which flavor of ice cream to choose for dessert. I made a silly joke about a box of chocolate-dipped frozen bananas called "monkey tails," and when she laughed, lights bounced off the metal edges of the freezer doors and played across her face, a kaleidoscope of disco lights revealing her special metal magic.

When we got back to my apartment over the store, Oscar was watching an old movie on my ancient DVD player. I imagined he had intuited, somehow, that I was going to make dinner and hadn't wanted to miss out.

"I figured the tamale you left out was for a spell," said Oscar, seeking praise for not having given in to the temptation to scarf it down. "Not to mention the booze."

"Thank you, Oscar. Never let it be said virtue goes unrewarded in this household," I said, tossing him the bag of potato chips. "You and Selena can chop the veggies for dinner."

"We're making pad thai tonight," said Selena. It did my heart good to hear her excitement in the words. The teenager used to be so somber that now every smile, every laugh, felt like a gift.

They chopped and I cleaned the shrimp and prepped the chicken for the pad thai, then started the brew for Conrad's morning tonic. While we worked I gave them an abbreviated account of what had happened on Alcatraz.

"You shoulda brought me with you," said Oscar, shaking his big head.

"You're right, I should have," I said, putting on a pot of water for the rice noodles. "It's just that pet pigs are a little tough to explain, at times."

"You should have brought some *silver* with you," added Selena, shaking her head just as Oscar had.

"Do you think that would have helped?" I asked. Selena was still young, but she was growing in confidence, control, and knowledge when it came to magic.

"Couldn't hurt," she said with a shrug, offering no further explanation.

The meal ready, we took our seats at the kitchen table. The pad thai was pronounced a resounding success, and we finished the feast with ice cream while practicing making conjure balls from soft red wax. Talking and laughing together around the table, we made a homey scene: Just a witch with her protégée and gobgoyle. Practically a scene out of Currier and Ives, if it hadn't been for the cauldron full of brew and the ongoing spell to battle a demon.

I served Oscar and Selena seconds on ice cream, then ran to the bedroom when I heard the landline ringing. It was Carlos.

"How's Elena?" I asked.

"Officially her condition is 'serious but stable,'" he answered, sounding weary but relieved. "There's no sign of assault, thank God, but she is suffering from exposure and was given some kind of drugs. As yet she hasn't been able to tell us what happened."

"I'm just glad she's safe now."

"As am I. Lily . . . I owe you one. A *big* one. And Elena's wife wants to give you a medal, or their first-born, your choice."

I smiled. "If Elena recuperates and is able to shed some light on everything that's been going on, that will be more than enough thanks for me."

"I have to warn you: Given the trauma of her experiences and the drugs, it's possible she won't remember much, if anything."

"Her recovery, mental and physical, is the most important thing," I said. "Why don't I ask my grandmother's coven to cast for her? They can use Elena's hat that you brought."

"Should I tell the nurses on her ward to expect a coven of Texas witches to drop by?"

I smiled at the visual of a witch invasion at the

hospital. "I don't think that'll be necessary. My grand-mother is usually able to help from a distance. I'll give them Elena's hat and her picture on the 'Missing' post-ers; they should be able to work from where they're stay-ing. It might help, and couldn't hurt."

"Like I said, I'm not proud. We'll take all the help we can get. Anyway, just wanted to let you know what's what. I'd better get back."

"Of course. And get some sleep yourself, Carlos."

"Lily?"

"Yes?"

"Again, thank you. *Gracias, de verdad.*"

"You're welcome. *De verdad.*"

I hung up, thankful that Elena was on the road to recovery, but frustrated that we still didn't know what was going on.

While Selena and Oscar watched a movie, I went out to my terrace garden and started gathering roots and herbs. A far-off siren wailed, and the sounds of people laughing and yelling drifted up from Haight Street. Part of me yearned to be with Graciela's coven at Calypso's enchanting house, ensconced in a forest clearing, the warm energy of wise women wrapping itself around me like the warmest, softest, hand-sewn quilt.

Instead, I was here, in my little urban oasis with Os-car and Selena.

As in Calypso's greenhouse, my Solomon's seal plants were growing—and flowering—in a location I hadn't planted them, which just happened to be di-rectly over bits of broken glass that I had buried here, long ago. The shards came from the full-length mirror in Sitri's closet at the School of Fine Arts, which I had shattered during my first encounter with the demon.

Interesting.

I dug up the shards, nicking myself a couple of times in the process, and placed the pieces, still encrusted with garden dirt, in a silver bowl Selena had polished— and imbued with some of her power—last week. I covered the bowl with a woven Mayan cloth and set it in a salt circle. I wasn't sure what I would do with the shards, but because they were connected to Sitri—he used to manifest in that mirror—they might well come in handy.

Their movie having ended, Oscar and Selena joined me on the terrace, following me around as I gathered my herbs. Oscar nattered on about one place or another that he wanted to check out on our honeymoon trip.

"Could *I* come, too?" asked Selena.

"Not this time, Selena. A honeymoon is really more of a couples' thing."

"Oscar's going."

"Yes, but it's·. . . different."

"Different how?"

"It's hard to explain," I said. "I made Oscar a promise and to fulfill that promise he needs to come along."

She didn't look convinced.

"Besides, your grandmother needs you," I added. "How would she cope with her store without your help?"

"That's true," she said, again showing a new maturity.

"Mistress, can I go with you and Maya tomorrow?" Oscar asked. "I read that the famous East Bay architects, Julia Morgan and Bernard Maybeck, were medievalists, and the medieval folks love putting gargoyles on their buildings."

"How did you know we were going to Oakland tomorrow?"

He shrugged. "Also, I like the East Bay. That's 'beast' in pig Latin. Get it? Cuz I'm a pig?"

"What's pig Latin?" Selena asked.

"Stick with me, kid, I'll learn ya."

As I puttered about, weeding and watering the plants, Oscar taught Selena how to say "I eak-spay ig-pay atin-lay." He was being so nice to her that I caved.

"I suppose you may come with us tomorrow," I said. "But you'll have to remain in your piggy guise."

He made a rude sound. It wasn't as if I needed to remind him of such things.

"And wear a leash."

Selena covered her mouth with her hands and snorted in laughter. So much for their détente.

Oscar narrowed his eyes. "It's humiliating."

"I know, Oscar, but it's hard enough explaining to people why I have a pig with me. An unleashed pig is even harder." I turned to Selena. "Would you like to come, too?"

"Can't. I have to go to class in the afternoon, remember?" Selena attended summer school a couple of days a week to make up for a bad grade in algebra. I felt her pain.

I made a simple salve out of mugwort and honey for my assorted scratches—the ones Noctemus had given me, the ones from the Spanish dungeon, plus the nicks from the mirror shards—and then another small jar of salve to speed the healing of black eyes while Oscar and Selena played a few hands of go fish at the kitchen table. Then Oscar crawled into his nest over the fridge and I tucked Selena into the bed I'd made up for her on the couch.

Before heading off to bed myself, I checked the wax of the spell candle one more time. It was flowing and pooling freely, as it should.

Although it was only the second day of the spell, I could feel its strength building, the conduits aligning.

I just hoped Sitri held off for another three days.

The next morning I checked in with Carlos, who reported that Elena was about the same, resting comfortably, but had been unable to tell them anything about her ordeal. He also spoke with the FBI, who said that a forensic archaeologist was going to analyze the skeleton we had stumbled over. Unfortunately, results would take a while.

"Unlike on TV, this sort of thing takes a long time in real life," said Carlos.

"I wonder: Could I look at the letters from Ray Perry's cell?"

"I don't see how. They're part of a historical exhibit."

"I'll be careful with them. Surely it's not a violation of privacy if he's been dead for decades."

"Probably not. Otherwise, your average historian would be in deep water. But what difference could they make?"

"I was wondering if they could tell us something about what was going on in the prison when Perry was there."

"Okay. I ask again: What difference could they make?"

"Hear me out: Suppose Perry never escaped? Suppose he was killed the same way Albright was?"

"You like him for the skeleton we found?"

"It's possible."

"A lot of things are possible."

"Listen: I don't usually see spirits, but Perry has shown himself to me twice now. Once in the attic where his shirt was found and then again yesterday, in the cell right before we were trapped inside."

"You're thinking there's a connection."

"I'm thinking there must be a reason I encountered two unprecedented events in two separate locations."

"You think he wants you to unmask his murderer?"

Is that what I thought? My witchy unconscious often reached conclusions before deciding to let my conscious self in on it.

"It's possible," I said. "I mean, the guards themselves would be dead at this point, surely. But maybe Perry wants me to solve his murder. His letters might describe some of the guards, or his treatment at their hands. Maybe they were hidden or never noticed, and squirreled away until the archivist found them."

"Seems to me you're grasping at straws, Lily."

"Isn't that what I do best?"

"Fair point. I'll see what I can do. Oh, by the way, I've got the wool coat you left at the crime scene. It's a little dirty and smells like smoke, but I figured you might want it back."

"*Thank you.*" I had awakened last night at three in the morning, wondering whether I needed to worry about that coat. I knew only too well that our clothes carried traces of us, and could be used against us by those of ill intent.

Besides, it was my favorite coat, and perfect for San Francisco's foggy mornings.

When Maya and Bronwyn arrived for the day at Aunt Cora's Closet, I told them the good news about Elena. I skipped over the details but reported that she was relatively unscathed.

"And what about you?" Bronwyn asked, noting the scratches on my arms.

I examined them, surprised. The mugwort salve should have resolved them already. "I'm fine, nothing a few days of healing won't fix. I put some salve on it that should help. Maya, would you be willing to print out a few things from the Internet for me?"

"Of course," she said, opening up the shop laptop. I wasn't able to speak Sitri's name aloud without risking calling him, so I pointed to his name in a reference book listing all known demons, and asked her to download a drawing of him, along with his sigil. She gave me a questioning glance, but didn't say anything.

"Oh! Lily, look at what I found!" Bronwyn showed me the 1970s pantsuit she had picked out for the wedding. "Patience decided on the emerald green silk—a wee bit formal for a handfasting but there's no denying it will add a touch of glamour! Lucille has already pinned the dress for the alterations. So: Three down, one to go!"

I glanced at Maya.

"Yeah, I'm still looking," she said. "I'll find something eventually, don't worry. I think I'm overwhelmed with choices. Would you pick out, like, four or five dresses, using your 'special abilities'? I'll try them on in the next day or two."

"I'd be happy to!" I said, pleased. Maya generally preferred jeans and rarely got into the spirit of trying on dresses just for the fun of it. "I'll take some time to pick something tomorrow morning. For the moment, I have to run a few errands before our noon appointment. Are you two okay holding down the fort this morning?"

They both agreed.

First things first: I really needed to consult with Aidan. Usually I went by his office at the wax museum because I'm not a fan of talking on the phone. But time was short, so I went into the workroom and called. No answer.

Was he avoiding me? I rarely had this much trouble getting in touch with him.

Determined, I loaded my backpack down with supplies and headed out.

In theory, I had agreed to meet with Renee only with Aidan at my side. But since he was AWOL, I went by the cupcake shop only to find it still closed. I left a note for Renee saying I wanted to speak with her, along with a jar of salve for the black eyes she'd gotten from her head injury. She probably wouldn't trust it, but it was a peace offering of sorts, an invitation to speak. It seemed ridiculous to communicate in this way, but then everything about Renee seemed ridiculous, starting with her cupcakes and cheery face and the fact that she kept potent lachrymatories alongside her collection of silver spoons.

Next, I drove to the Transamerica Pyramid Center at 600 Montgomery Street. The elongated, pyramid-shaped skyscraper took up an entire city block and for years had dominated the San Francisco skyline, until the bullet-shaped Salesforce Tower arose to dwarf it. The Transamerica building always made me think of *The Towering Inferno*—a cheesy disaster flick from the 1970s that was one of Oscar's favorites. My familiar was a major Steve McQueen fan. Supposedly the pyramidal design had been inspired by nothing more sinister than a desire to allow more sunshine to reach the street level. But if Oscar was correct, the building sat at the point of a truncated pyramid made up of streets—though I'm not sure what that might or might not mean.

Still, it seemed interesting that Kyle Cheney had his offices here in this building. On the other hand, there were dozens of renters here: lots of fancy corporate clients, banks, investment companies. Cheney's offices sat among many moneyed, powerful peers.

I marched into the lobby and approached the reception desk, asking if I could go on up to Cheney's offices.

"Sorry, there's no public access to the building. Was there someone in particular you were looking for?"

"Could you call up to Seth Barbagelata?" I said. "He works with Kyle Cheney's company. I don't have an appointment but maybe he has a few minutes to talk. Do you happen to know him?"

"Do I know him?" The guard's eyebrows rose as she picked up the phone and tapped an extension. "That is one *fine*-looking man. I'm happily married and all, but it's hard not to notice."

The guard had a brief discussion on the phone and said Seth would be down shortly.

"Sorry I can't let you go up," said the security guard, a tall woman in her forties. "There used to be a viewing platform, but it closed a long time ago."

"That's too bad," I said, thinking that the least the skyscraper's owners could do would be to allow folks upstairs to see the view. I'd always wanted to go to the top of the Empire State Building; I wondered if there were any gargoyles on it. That reminded me . . . "There aren't any secret gargoyles on this building, are there?"

The guard looked amused. "Secret gargoyles?"

"I just wondered. Sometimes they pop up where one least expects."

"I don't think the early '70s were a big era for gargoyles," the woman said. "But it's a nice thought. You know, they coulda hid one, like the Bay Bridge Troll. There's a live feed of the view over there, in the visitor's center, if you're interested."

I watched the screen for a few minutes, checking out the Oakland skyline and the traffic on the Bay Bridge, until Seth arrived.

"Well, hello there!" Seth was immaculately dressed in a bespoke Kingsman double-breasted suit. Once again he struck me more as a model than an executive assistant, but I supposed there was no reason he couldn't be both.

"Such a pleasant surprise! How nice to see you again, Lily."

"I'm sorry to make you come downstairs," I said. "I would have come up, but apparently it's not allowed. Do you have time for a cup of coffee?"

As he glanced at the expensive-looking platinum timepiece on his wrist, a discrete diamond ring on one slender hand sparkled.

Kyle Cheney must pay extremely well, I thought.

"Sure," Seth said. "I don't have to be anywhere for an hour. And it's no bother at all, honestly. I've been here since dawn; it would do me good to get out of the building for a few minutes and get some fresh air. There's a café on the next block, why don't we go there?"

We walked out into a cool gray morning. The streets of the city's busy financial district were hopping, pedestrians crowding the sidewalks and cars, lined up bumper-to-bumper, honking.

"Did you notice the plaque?" Seth asked, gesturing to a bronze marker in the small redwood grove next to the Transamerica building. "It's dedicated to Bummer and Lazarus, two stray dogs from the 1860s, back when Emperor Norton roamed these streets."

According to the plaque, the dogs "belonged to no one person. They belonged to San Francisco. . . . Two dogs with but a single bark, two tails that wagged as one."

"You have to love a city that would commemorate two stray dogs that lived more than a century ago," I said. "And who's Emperor Norton?"

"A very eccentric—some say crazy—man from the city's wild and woolly days, who claimed he was emperor of San Francisco. He even had his own money printed up, and local shopkeepers accepted it as currency. San Francisco's always been full of interesting characters."

"So I've been learning."

"Here's another interesting factoid," Seth said. "Remnants of an old gold rush–era ship were found when excavating for the foundation of the Transamerica building. Once upon a time, this whole area was waterfront, until landfill gradually expanded the city further into the bay."

"I didn't know that."

"San Francisco isn't a very old city, but it has a marvelous history." He paused and flashed a brilliant white smile. "I guess I'm becoming a bit of a history buff. Kyle must be rubbing off on me. Almost there," Seth said as we passed several nationally known coffee chains. The Transamerica Pyramid sat at the edge of Chinatown and North Beach and the Financial District. We passed Chinese and Italian eateries and finally stopped in at a small café where Seth was greeted by name.

"I try to avoid the chains," he said. "These little holes-in-the-wall are what makes the city special, don't you think?"

We ordered our coffees and took a seat at a small table.

"How's the planning for the Festival of Felons going?" I asked.

"I'll tell you what, this little shindig of Kyle's is keeping me up to my ears in work. We've been planning it for months, obviously, but now we're dealing with all the last-minute details."

"So it's still happening as scheduled? I mean, considering everything going on . . . ?"

"Oh, yes. Hard to stop a speeding train, you know. Besides, Kyle said you found the missing woman in the dungeon yesterday, is that true?" He lifted his shoulders and shivered. "That must have been quite an ordeal. I'm so glad she's all right."

I nodded. I still hadn't quite processed everything that had happened.

"Seth, I was looking at the list of festival sponsors—"

"Happy to add your name to our website!" he said. "I'm sorry we haven't done it yet; I'll get right on it."

"Thank you, but I was wondering: I noticed Renee Baker, the cupcake lady, was listed as one of the sponsors."

"Yes, she's been quite generous and has offered to donate ten dozen cupcakes and meat pies to the event. I'm getting hungry just thinking about it."

"How did she come to be involved with the festival, do you know?"

"Kyle's one of her investors."

I blinked. "Excuse me?"

"Kyle invested in her cupcake business. Renee Baker wanted to expand into an empty shopfront next to her existing store but needed capital. Kyle makes a point of helping small companies, especially those owned by women and minorities. Feels it's part of his civic duty."

"That's admirable," I said.

Kyle shrugged. "It's good karma, and good business. If the investment takes off, he makes money. If it doesn't, he has a tax write-off. He wins, the small business owner wins, the city wins, everybody wins. Are you looking for investors to expand your own business?"

"Oh, I . . . I don't think so, thanks. I like things the way they are. So, Seth, you mentioned you had a relative who was a guard on Alcatraz."

"My great-uncle," he said with a nod. "I never knew him, but his daughter used to tell us stories about it. She lived out there as a little girl, though she was an old woman when I knew her."

"Did he have a Polish last name, by any chance?" No, that wouldn't make sense, I told myself as soon as I asked it. Ned Przybyszewski, the former owner of Emmy Lou's house, didn't have any children.

"No. He was a Krewson. George Krewson."

A pair of customers gave Seth the once-over, and I wasn't surprised. He was a pleasure to look at, with blue eyes that reminded me of a deep pool of cool water.

"He died long before I was born, but his daughter was still alive when I was a kid. At family gatherings she would tell stories about growing up on the island."

"What kind of stories?"

"How she and the other children had to get up early to catch a boat to school in the city. She said she hated that part, because it was always so cold and damp in the early morning. The boat ride home, though, she said was lots of fun. Also, she remembered how the families would gather in the prison chapel on family movie night. At Christmas the warden arranged for a Christmas tree and held a party, where trustees—prisoners whom the warden trusted—served cookies and punch. In some ways life was very unusual; for example, the prisoners did the laundry for the guards and their families, except for their underwear, and the children weren't allowed to wear shorts or anything too revealing. But in other ways it was surprisingly normal. Kids played ball, ran around, and jumped rope, fished. Even went bowling."

"I noticed a photo of that in the museum."

Seth nodded. "The facility had a small bowling alley in the old officers' quarters, as well as a soda fountain and a store, for the guards and their families."

"Did they have any interaction with the prisoners?"

He shook his head. "They weren't supposed to talk with the prisoners, under any circumstances. In fact the prisoners weren't allowed to talk to each other, either. They lived under the rule of silence."

I thought about the ghostly whispers that had reverberated through the halls and tunnels of Alcatraz.

"Some got around it by emptying the water from the toilets in their cells and communicating via the pipes. Hard to imagine that would work, but apparently it did. Human ingenuity is really something, right?"

"So true."

"Like I said, I wish now that I had paid more attention to my cousin's stories. I remember her saying that most of the prisoners weren't as scary as everyone made them out to be, and that her dad actually became friends with a few."

"Friends?"

"Well, friendly. There was one guard for every three prisoners at Alcatraz, so I guess they got to know each other pretty well."

"Did she ever mention any of the prisoners by name?"

"I don't think so. Or maybe she did but I wasn't paying that much attention. You could probably ask one of the park rangers about all this, I'm sure they'd know better than I do."

I stared into my cappuccino, at a loss.

"What is it, Lily?"

I looked up to see sympathy and concern in his eyes. He put out one hand and laid it on my arm.

"It must have been very traumatic for you, finding Elena like that. Are you sure you're all right?"

His vibrations were open and friendly, which explained his easy charm. But they were also guarded. I wondered if he had experienced abuse in his past, had endured something that made him compassionate to others, while maintaining his guard. One never knew what others had suffered, no matter how beautiful or serene their external persona.

"A friend of mine mentioned that Mr. Cheney had hired some of his friends as security guards. Is that another good cause your boss believes in?"

He gave me a crooked grin. "He's got something of an employment agency going, it's true. Kyle wanted to add extra security for the party, but it's tricky because it's a national park, so it's a federal case—literally. But yeah, Kyle's got an army of helpers."

"Conrad said it was called Co-Opp Industries? What does that refer to? It's not a cooperative, is it?"

He shook his head. "No, to tell you the truth I'm not sure where the name comes from. Kyle has dozens of smaller concerns and investments under his umbrella company. But I do know he employs a lot of people and often tries to give folks a second chance."

The barista came out from behind the counter to ask if Seth wanted anything else.

"No, but thank you for asking," Seth said, holding her gaze. "That's so kind."

"No problem," she said. She looked at me like an afterthought: "You?"

"I'm fine, thank you," I said.

She left, and Seth gave me a smile and a slight shrug.

"Anyway, I wish I could tell you more about my great-uncle. The only thing that really sticks with me is that early in his career there was an escape while he was on duty. He was written up for that because he was friendly with one of the escapees; it was the first attempt where the prisoners actually made it into the water. But there was no sign they survived. They were probably swept out to sea."

"Was one of the men Ray Perry, by any chance?"

"Sorry, I don't remember the names. I mostly remember the bowling alley. And I remember thinking it would be cool to take a boat to school."

"When did he work at Alcatraz?"

"I'm not sure, exactly, but I know they lived out there from the opening of the prison up until World War Two."

Ray Perry escaped in 1937.

"Like I said, you'd probably find out more from the curators on the island. Some of those oldsters were guards themselves, or knew someone firsthand."

That was a good idea, but the thought of going back to that island was not exactly enticing. Maybe I could spend some time on the phone. Ralph Gordon appeared eager to talk.

"My great-uncle always wanted to write a book about his experiences, but never got around to it. He must have been something of an intellectual, though. According to his daughter, he spoke Latin and some other languages, and knew a lot of history. But he didn't live that long, actually . . . they say he got sick and wasted away, right after he left the island."

I searched my mind for what else to ask Seth, but couldn't think of anything in particular. I didn't know what I was hoping to learn.

Seth glanced down at his watch.

"I should let you go," I said. "I really appreciate you taking the time to talk to me."

"Anytime. Like I was saying, this city certainly does have an interesting history."

Not to mention, an interesting present day.

Chapter 17

Next on this morning's list of errands was the one I was least looking forward to: the San Francisco School of Fine Arts. As I approached my car, I spied the distinctive silhouette of batlike ears in the rear window.

One of Oscar's more disconcerting traits was the way he popped up without warning. I had no idea how he managed to get around town without attracting attention—neither a pig nor a gobgoyle could stroll down a city street unnoticed—nor how he was able to track me down so easily. On that latter point, I could only assume he used a gobgoyle GPS device of some kind. But since Oscar also had a knack for showing up whenever I was in grave danger, I wasn't about to complain.

"Heard you might need some backup," said Oscar as I climbed in.

"And just where did you hear that?"

Oscar said nothing but his eyes widened in an attempt to convey innocence.

"Well, I'm glad to see you," I said. "I'm headed to the School of Fine Arts."

"Cool! I love students."

"We're not going to visit the students. This is serious business."

An oversized goblin hand waved away my concern. "Road trip! We should stop for snacks."

"It's only a few blocks away," I said, amused by his enthusiasm.

He ignored this. "Road trip!"

The San Francisco School of Fine Arts was located off Chestnut Street, near the vibrant North Beach neighborhood. Originally an Italian immigrant enclave, North Beach was host to a bevy of Italian (and Italian-ish) restaurants as well as numerous bars, cafés, nightclubs, strip clubs, and jazz joints. Finding parking on Columbus Avenue was never an easy feat, so I used my parking charm to encourage the owner of a gas-guzzling Escalade to make way, and pulled my car into a space near the corner of Chestnut.

As we approached the doors of the School of Fine Arts' Spanish-revival facade, I glanced down at my porcine companion trotting along by my side. Bringing a pig into the school would likely cause a bit of a commotion, but there was no way Oscar would wait in the car.

If I left him there, he'd join me, anyway. I decided to brazen it out.

Luckily, the school was on summer recess. The front hall was empty, and as we proceeded along, past the school's administrative offices, no one appeared to notice us. As we walked down the hallway we passed a few people and I searched for signs of unusual strife or discord, which I knew from my previous encounter with Sitri had been one of the first indications that the demon had been conjured. But the students seemed calm, with only the usual marks of creative young people: multicolored hair and plenty of piercings, bright paint splotches on clothing and hands.

A few students noticed Oscar and pointed him out to friends or asked to pet him. I just smiled and barged on through to the rear stairway at the end of the hall, avoiding the central staircase that led to the haunted bell tower.

Today's business wasn't ghosts, but a demon.

The stone stairs had grooves in the centers of the treads, worn down by the feet of legions of nuns, and now students, traipsing up and down this staircase for more than a century.

As I mounted the steps, I thought back to when I was last here. It had been only the second murder I was involved in solving. It seemed like ages ago; I had been a different person then. I felt so much older now, definitely more experienced, and hopefully a tad wiser. I was a lot more confident in my abilities, but . . . also more jaded. Encountering death and violence took a toll, no doubt about that.

We reached the top floor, under the eaves, where the former nuns' rooms had been converted into faculty offices and storage closets. I used to know one faculty member here, Luc Carmichael, but his office door now sported a different nameplate. Perhaps Luc had changed offices, or perhaps he had moved on. I had dated Luc's brother, Max, for a while, but it hadn't worked out, and we hadn't kept in touch.

Jiminy Crickets, that felt like a long time ago.

At the end of the hall was a heavy cabinet, behind which used to be the door to a large storage closet. After battling Sitri, we had sealed the doorway with concrete blocks and covered the blockade with an enchanted plaster mixed with my magical brew. As a last step to sealing the portal, I had sketched protective symbols into the wet stucco, and then we had moved the heavy cabinet back in front of the doorway so that only a few people knew of the closet's existence.

"Oscar, would you please help me to push the cabinet out of the way?"

"You didn't tell me there would be heavy lifting involved," Oscar groused, even though in his natural form he was quite capable of lifting a grown man over his head. "I'm here to supply brains, not brawn."

I gave him a look.

He sighed and effortlessly shoved the cabinet aside, then jumped back and swore.

The signs I had etched into the then-fresh stucco had been altered—burn marks elaborated upon my designs, incorporating them into a large U topped by gothic crosses.

Sitri's sigil.

Several of the cement blocks had been sledgehammered, and the stucco around the edges gouged out, creating an opening big enough for someone to pass through.

Dangitall.

"Mistress!" Oscar said, starting to back down the hallway. "Time to go."

"Aren't you the one who says he's not scared of anything?" I asked.

"I'm not scared. But I'm not stupid, either."

"Does this mean you're not going in with me?" I asked as I whipped my woven pack off my back and started taking out supplies.

"You're going *in?*"

"Of course. Why did you think we were here?"

"Not to confront a demon," he replied. "You didn't say *anything* about confronting a demon. I would have remembered that."

"You insisted on coming, remember?"

"I thought we could go to the Russ Building to check out the gargoyles. Besides, I told you, I like students."

"Well, if you like students then we need to take care of this particular demon before he starts screwing around with them. Remember what happened last time?"

Demons are fascinating creatures—frightening as all get-out and to be avoided at all costs unless absolutely necessary, but intriguing nonetheless. Though they could slaughter puny humans without much effort, they preferred to hang around and mess with us, to make us think we're losing our minds—or help us to do so. They enjoyed watching us ruin our own lives—and kill ourselves, and others—instead of doing it themselves. It amused them.

The last time we had encountered Sitri, he had incited all sorts of mayhem among the students and the faculty. On one memorable occasion, a professor's face seemed to melt off and he flung himself out a window.

I tried to shake off the ghastly image.

"Oscar," I said, lighting some incense and candles, slipping protective stones and crystals—amethyst, lapis, black obsidian, citrine, and rose quartz—into my pocket, and stroking my medicine bag to center myself. "I'm going to see if I can figure out what's up. Stay out here if you want, but come to my rescue if things take a turn for the worse?"

He nodded and mumbled something under his breath.

"What did you say?"

"No-thing, mis-tress," he responded in a long-suffering, sullen singsong.

I knelt down. Ignoring the grit digging into my knees, I peeked through the gaping hole.

Rays of orangey late-afternoon sunlight sifted through cracks in the boarded-up windows, illuminating the large storage closet. The chamber appeared as I remembered: a full-length standing mirror with broken glass; a large chest of drawers; and a steamer trunk that once held the frilly Victorian underthings belonging to the long-ago nuns who had been involved in conjuring Sitri. In exchange, he had spurred on the great quake of 1906.

But the salt circle and binding triangle that I had used to contain him had been broken open.

I glanced over my shoulder. Oscar had retreated down the hall and was poised near the top of the stairs, as though ready to make his escape.

Turning back to the hole in the wall, I hesitated. Maybe Oscar was right. Maybe it would be the height of stupidity to enter this cursed closet. It might also be unnecessary. The last time I'd dealt with Sitri he had been conjured by accident and hadn't yet gained his full strength. If someone had summoned him intentionally this time, and had offered him a sacrifice, Sitri would have quickly gained power and control and could go anywhere he wanted.

It was enough to determine that I was correct. The vibrations I'd felt in that cursed dungeon on Alcatraz did, indeed, belong to Sitri. So at least I knew for sure this was the demon we were up against.

Stucco shards crumbled under my knees as I started to back away from the hole. Suddenly, I felt something pulling at my arms, sucking me into the closet. As I fought against it, the closet fell away, becoming a deep dark hole, a dank and musty chasm into which I was about to tumble.

A terrible screeching hurt my ears. I recognized it from the last time I was here. It was the sound of wind whistling through Sitri's wings.

If I fell I would be lost. Not dead, but something far worse: *lost*. Forever.

"Mistress!"

I felt Oscar grabbing my ankles, anchoring me as he tried to pull me back. For a moment I was lifted off the ground, the ghastly tug-of-war threatening to tear me apart.

I found my voice and began chanting and repeating a protection spell.

Finally, with a mocking tone, I heard:

"Liiiily, ssssso good to sssseeee youuu . . . I hear congratulations are in order, but to whom are you marrying? And why are you naked?"

I remembered what the *Ars Goetia* said about Sitri: *He mocks women's secrets and causes them to become naked.* I heard a grunt as Oscar gave a mighty heave and yanked me backward, sending us both tumbling onto the hard tile of the hallway.

We took a moment to catch our breath, staring at each other.

"Are you all right?" I asked Oscar.

"*What* did I tell you?" he said, sounding decidedly grumpy. "Didn't you learn your lesson the first time? And what happened to your clothes?"

I was clad only in my undergarments and my shoes—my medicine bundle was still tied to my waist, thank heavens—and I spied my sweet little yellow sundress lying in a heap on the floor inside the closet. There was no way I was going in there to retrieve it. *Dangitall.* I really liked that dress.

"*You might like this, witch,*" came Sitri's horrifying voice.

A frilly chemise, a dress-length Victorian petticoat, came sailing through the hole in the wall, accompanied by demonic laughter.

"*Well, hardy har har,*" I shouted back, my Texas twang showing. "You are one downright sorry, egg-sucking dog! I'll be back!"

Oscar picked up the chemise and held it out to me, averting his gaze in an exaggerated fashion. "Really, mistress? You're calling a demon names?"

"He's treading on my last nerve," I grumbled. "What was all *that* about?"

"He's playing."

I took the chemise, though I didn't like the thought of wearing it, not one little bit. Not only had Sitri given it to me, but it had originally belonged to one of the sacrificed nuns. But I didn't have much choice, since my only other option was to stride through the school, and down the street, in my underwear. Besides, although the petticoat's vibrations were negative they were not very strong; I would be able to resist them. I hoped. I caressed my medicine bag, sprinkled a little brew on the fabric as I mumbled a protective spell, and pulled the chemise over my head.

Oscar gave a low whistle. "Very pretty, mistress. Why is it that a garment like that makes you look more naked than when you're naked?"

"This will have to do, for the moment," I muttered, fastening the last shell button on the bodice. Despite my bold words, I was more than a little chastened—and very worried. Sitri had grown in strength. And the feelings he inspired were tangible: lust aimed at no one in particular, uncertainty and doubt, mockery and ridicule.

But I was stronger now, too. I just hoped I was strong enough to summon and control him.

Because Sitri was definitely on the loose in the City by the Bay.

Dangitall.

Chapter 18

"Wow," said Bronwyn as I entered the store in my frilly Victorian getup. "You look—wow! You were walking the streets in that?"

"We're on Haight Street," said Maya. "I'll bet no one batted an eye. But you might want to change before our appointment at Laney College."

"True, but . . . what happened?" asked Bronwyn. "Where did the pretty little sundress go?"

"It's a long story," I muttered, flipping through a rack and selecting a sky blue knit dress, with a tank top and a dropped waist, that I had bought for a buck at a yard sale in Santa Cruz hosted by a commune of retired hippies. I stepped into the dressing room, took off the Victorian chemise, and slipped on the cool, clean knit, whose vibrations were joyful, even comical. I needed a little levity at the moment.

Then I packed my backpack with more salts, all-purpose brew, stones, and herbs. I also included the image of Sitri that Maya had downloaded from the

Internet for me. It was from a medieval woodcut and portrayed Sitri as part feline, part bird, and very beautiful.

Maya watched my ministrations and raised an eyebrow. "We're going to see a professor at a community college in Oakland, right? Not a nest of vampires. I mean . . . unless you know something I don't?"

"No, no," I said, feeling myself blushing. "But after what happened yesterday at Alcatraz I just want to be prepared."

Half an hour later we were headed east on the Bay Bridge: Maya, Oscar, and I.

Laney is a community college in downtown Oakland, near Lake Merritt. It was an urban campus whose clutch of modern buildings looked more like an industrial park than a college to me, but then again, what did I know? I had never finished high school, much less gone to an institution of higher learning. We parked and left an unhappy Oscar to wait in the car, then walked across a wide concrete plaza to find Dr. Guzmán's office. Students in shorts and T-shirts milled about, carrying backpacks, on their way to class or just enjoying the beautiful day. Through the center of campus ran a pretty little channel that connected Lake Merritt to the estuary and eventually to the bay.

We found Gabriel Guzmán's office down a nondescript beige hallway. His door was decorated with scholarly articles and colorful artwork, political cartoons, and a clipboard with a sign-up sheet for office hours.

Maya tapped on the door. A muffled "Come in" was the response.

Inside, jammed bookcases dominated two walls. In addition to books of all shapes and size, the bookcases held decorative objects, such as abalone shells that gleamed bright pink and green in the light from the window. But it was the woven baskets that grabbed my attention. Made of reeds and grasses, they incorporated intricate designs in shades of near-black against the buff color of the dried reeds. I wondered if the designs had meaning or were simply meant to be pretty.

Dr. Guzmán stood up and reached across his desk to shake our hands. He was just beginning to gray at the temples, with a round, unsmiling, but friendly face and sloping dark eyes. He gestured to us to have a seat.

"What can I do for you?" he asked.

"We appreciate your taking the time to meet with us," I said. I didn't want to ask any leading questions about a curse and hoped he might volunteer the information. "We were wondering what you could tell us about the history of Alcatraz, especially what it meant to your tribe, that sort of thing."

His dark eyes rested on me for a long moment. "You're doing a research paper?"

"Not exactly. I'm . . . there have been some strange things happening on the island, and a national park ranger friend was kidnapped, and—"

"Kidnapped?" he demanded.

I nodded. "We don't know if it has anything to do with Alcatraz per se, but we're asking questions to see if there might be any connections. . . ."

Sensing I was losing focus, Maya jumped in. "Really, anything you can tell us would be helpful. We're especially interested in what the indigenous peoples thought of the island of Alcatraz, historically, if there's any mythology, that sort of thing, surrounding the island."

"As you may know, the Miwok and Ohlone were dominant in the San Francisco Bay Area, though there are a lot of different groups within those tribal classifications," said Guzmán. "I'm Chochenyo, but even so,

I would never pretend to speak for all Chochenyo. But I can tell you that Alcatraz resonates with meaning for a lot of native peoples, for a variety of reasons."

"Historically Alcatraz was under Ohlone sovereignty, right?" Maya asked.

He nodded. "It was. But even in antiquity, it was a complicated place. There were never any settlements or villages there; my ancestors sometimes went to collect bird eggs, but primarily the island was reserved for outcasts, or people who did wrong and needed to be separated from society."

"Someone else mentioned that—bad guys were essentially marooned out there?"

He smiled. "Most of them probably could have swum to shore or constructed a raft, if they managed to read the tides right. But they had plenty of food out there if they worked for it, and this was a long time ago. My point is that the island was not considered suitable for living. For living a good life, that is."

"Have you ever been there?" I asked.

He shook his head.

"Not even for the sunrise ceremony?" Maya asked.

"Sorry to sound so ignorant, but what's the sunrise ceremony?" I asked.

"The Indigenous People's Sunrise Gathering is a commemoration of the 1969 to '71 occupation of Alcatraz by the 'Indians of all tribes,'" said Guzmán. "It's a one-day event, on the National Day of Mourning. Otherwise known as Thanksgiving."

"But you've never gone?"

"My grandmother told me not to go, and that's good enough for me. Alcatraz lives on in the imagination as a scene of a fairly successful political action—the occupation of the island drew attention for the plight of the Native American in a way that little else had. And there's no denying the symbolism: This was once native land that was turned into an island prison for native peoples deemed to be 'hostiles.' Did you know Hopi prisoners were kept there in the late 1800s, when it was still a military prison?"

"I read about that," said Maya. "They had refused to hand their children over to authorities?"

The professor nodded. "They were declared to be standing in the way of their children being educated. It wasn't mentioned that the children were taken away from their families and villages and that this forced 'education' resulted in Hopi children being forbidden from reading their own language, wearing their own clothes, much less worshipping their own Hopi deities."

"That's dreadful," I said.

He shrugged. "History is full of dreadful things. In the case of my ancestors, they dealt with the impositions of the Spanish missionaries and then the Union-led massacres against villages in the mid-1800s. You don't have to look very far to find historical atrocities against native peoples in this country."

I was at a loss for words.

"I want people to understand our complicated history," Guzmán continued, "to recognize the role we played in the development and history of the United States that we experience today. But then again . . ." he added with a smile, "a few scholarship programs wouldn't hurt by way of reparations."

"We should mention it to Kyle Cheney," I said. "He seems eager to invest in the community."

"You know Kyle Cheney?"

"Just barely. He's sponsoring the Festival of Felons, a charitable fund-raiser being held on Alcatraz in a few days."

"A festival on Alcatraz seems like a really bad idea," Guzmán said, shaking his head.

"Could you tell us more about what happened with the occupation?" Maya asked.

"The leaders weren't Ohlone, I can tell you that. They called themselves 'Indians of all tribes' and the original leaders came from several different nations: Mohawk, Cherokee, Eskimo, Ho-Chunk. They set off in a boat from Sausalito, offered to buy the island from the US government for some glass beads and cloth, and claimed the island for 'as long as the rivers run and the sun shall shine.' They kept the occupation going for almost two years, which was impressive given what a struggle it is to get enough water and food out there for such a large group. The cause was recognized by some celebrities like Jane Fonda, which popularized the cause."

"You're right, that is impressive," I agreed. "So what happened?"

"Over time, the idealism wasn't enough to sustain them. The group started to split into different factions, and then the daughter of one of the leaders, Richard Oakes, fell from a stairwell and died. Oakes left the island. Fires broke out in a number of buildings—some say the authorities set them to drive the occupiers out; others say it was vandalism carried out by the occupiers. But I'm no expert on Alcatraz. There's a curator out on the island, a former guard, and his father was a guard there before him. Seems to know his history; I'll bet he could be more helpful to you than I can. His name's Ralph Gordon, here's his number."

"Thank you," I said, taking the piece of paper with the number from him. "As it happens, I met him the other day."

"I've thought about joining the sunrise ceremony one of these days, just to acknowledge what it represents," said the professor. "But I don't know. It's hard to go up against a grandmother's warning. She always believed the island was cursed."

"Really," I said.

He nodded, watching our reactions. "That doesn't surprise you."

"Not exactly, no." I let out a humorless laugh. It was strangely comforting to know that I wasn't the only one who felt the island was cursed; it was an ancient acknowledgment.

"My grandmother told me stories of creatures that lived out there, sort of half-human, half-bird. Some called them Feather People, while others described them as feline, but with wings."

I rummaged through my backpack for the page Maya had printed out, which showed a medieval conception of the demon Sitri.

"Similar to this?" I passed him the page.

"Could be," Guzmán said. "The depictions I've seen are much more stylized. This is European, though, obviously."

As I knew too well, demons recognized no national boundaries.

Oscar was snoozing when we returned to the car, which I had parked in a shady spot on a side street a few blocks from campus.

His piggy eyes blinked at me, the message clear: Next stop, gargoyles. Oscar had already searched for gargoyles near Oakland's Paramount Theatre, but there were still several other spots in Oakland left to check out.

I hadn't thought through what to say to Maya about why we needed to hunt for gargoyles in downtown Oakland. I could simply claim I wanted to take a quick tour of the older buildings in this historic East Bay city, but how would I explain Oscar's frequent comings and goings? Should I brazen it out, say I did this all the time, and my pig was just fine roaming the streets of Oakland all alone? If I were Maya, I wouldn't buy that for a second.

I glanced at little piggy Oscar in the backseat, and then at Maya, the intelligent young woman who had accepted with equanimity everything I'd thrown at her so far, from spellcasting to demon exorcisms. I gave an inner sigh. The weight of keeping secrets was starting to press down on me at the very time I needed to reserve my energy to confront one pesky demon. I wanted to come clean with Maya about who, and what, Oscar was.

According to Bronwyn, friends placed trust in one another. It was time I lived that philosophy.

I drove to Old Oakland, a pretty section of town full of Victorian-era town houses that had been repurposed to house businesses and art galleries. On 9th Street, between Washington Street and Broadway, lionlike creatures with golden rings in their mouths gazed down upon the street from their positions under the eaves. These weren't the gargoyles Oscar was looking for, but the lions made me think of what Professor Guzmán had said: There was a legend about half-cat, half-bird creatures on Alcatraz. Could they be Sitri himself or his minions? A powerful demon could hold thousands of underlings in thrall. *He commanded sixty legions*. . . .

I found a parking space in front of Bluebottle Café.

"Oh, excellent idea," said Maya. "Coffee, chai, or something else?"

"Maya, if I treat, will you go in for us? I'll stay with Oscar."

"Happy to, but this time it's my treat. Your usual?"

I nodded, and Maya climbed out of the car and disappeared into the café. I turned to Oscar. "Oscar, how would you feel if I told Maya and Bronwyn about you?"

"What about me?"

"That you're a shape-shifter."

"They don't already know?"

"How would they know? You always stay in your piggy guise around them."

"They're your best friends, and you have such a soft spot for cowans." He shrugged, his big eyes gleaming like green glass. "I just assumed you told them."

"I would never 'out' you without your consent."

"Thanks, mistress. That's real classy of you."

I smiled. "You know I'm not your mistress anymore, Oscar. Not technically."

"I like to call myself your familiar so it seems only fair to call you mistress. I know we don't have a traditional relationship, or anything like that. But still."

My heart swelled. "It works for us, doesn't it?"

Oscar nodded.

"So you really don't mind if I tell Maya?" I said as she emerged from the café, coffees in to-go cups.

"Nope," he said, and shifted back into his porcine form. I opened the car door for him, and he trotted off down the block, glancing up at the lionesque faces high above.

"Is Oscar going to be okay on his own?" Maya asked as she climbed back into the car.

"Yes, actually. As a matter of fact, I wanted to talk to you about him," I began, accepting the proffered cup of French roast black coffee with gratitude. I needed the jolt of caffeine. "What I'm about to tell you is going to sound a little . . . strange."

"Stranger than witchcraft in general and cursed shirts in particular?"

"I guess when you put it like that, it's not all that strange. All things considered." I sipped my coffee. "This is *really* good."

"Bluebottle. They're a bit of a phenomenon around here." Her dark eyes were worried. "Lily? What did you want to tell me?"

"I'm sorry, it's nothing bad. It's—"

"And where did Oscar go? Are you sure that's wise? This is a big city, after all."

"He'll be fine. This is what I want to tell you: Oscar's not . . ." I paused, searching for the right words.

"Not what?"

"Not a regular pig."

She cocked her head. "I know that. He's a miniature Vietnamese potbellied pig, right?"

"Yes, but besides that . . ."

"He's a very special little guy, Lily. I know I wasn't wild about having livestock in the store at first, but I've been won over."

I smiled. "I've always really appreciated that."

"Good."

"Okay, I'm going to stop beating around the bush, here. The thing is, Oscar's a . . ."

She leaned in. "Lily?"

"A shape-shifter."

She leaned back. "I'm sorry?"

"He's not a pig—that's just a guise he assumes around normal people."

She paused and took a sip of her latte, as though pondering my words. "You're saying he's usually something . . . else?"

I nodded.

"What is he?"

"It's hard to explain. He's an unusual cross between

a goblin and a gargoyle," I said, the words finally flowing. "Oscar's been searching for his mother, who suffers
under a curse that turns her into stone most of the time.
That's why we're forever looking at gargoyles."

"He thinks she's here, in downtown Oakland?"

"Could be."

"Huh. I always wondered what was up with him. I
know pigs are smart, but he seemed a little *too* smart.
That's really . . . that's really something. But aren't
goblins usually considered, I don't know—evil?"

"They get a bad rap. Some goblins can be, uh, difficult for humans to deal with, but others aren't. They're
really not all that different from fairies, though usually
not as pretty."

"And Oscar is one of the good ones, I take it."

I nodded.

She was quiet for a few moments. "Could I see him
in his natural form?"

"I'll leave that up to him," I said.

"Does he speak English?"

"Oh, yes. He speaks many languages."

"*Geesh*, I feel bad now for all the other-white-meat
jokes I used to make right in front of him."

"Don't worry about it. Oscar doesn't take offense
easily."

"Is this . . . is this a common thing?" she asked.

"How do you mean?"

"I mean, are there a lot of shape-shifters around?"

"I don't think it's all that common, no. But I've met
a few over the years. You just never know, really."

"That's a thought that's going to fester."

"Tell me about it."

"You said Oscar's searching for his mother? But has
no idea where she might be? That's so sad."

Just then I saw Oscar trotting along the sidewalk, heading back to the car. He saw Maya staring at him, stopped in his tracks, and returned her stare.

"Try to act casual," I whispered.

"Sorry," she replied. "Still processing."

Maya opened the door and Oscar jumped into the backseat.

"Hello, handsome," I said to break the tension. "So, where to next? Oakland's Chinatown?"

"Sure," said Maya, game as usual. "Let's go check it out."

The Asian Resource Center on 8th Street had a few architectural oddities, including several human-ish heads and monkeys eating berries of some kind. They were fun, but not gargoyles, or even chimera, for that matter. Just carved figures.

Oscar circled the building, then trotted back up to us, shaking his piggy head.

Maya checked her phone. "It says here that there are lion-head gargoyles on the entablature on the Bank of America Building on Broadway. Worth a try?"

After a quick tour, we scratched that building off the list and headed north to the Berkeley Women's City Club, which had been designed by the renowned architect Julia Morgan. According to Maya, it was characterized as "Mediterranean Gothic" and boasted Corinthian columns, banister trefoils, a vaulted ceiling over the staircase, and a line of funny little guys holding shields, but no genuine grotesques or chimera. From there we headed back to Oakland and stopped at another Morgan design, the Chapel of the Chimes, where we took in the beautiful mosaics and painted murals, arches and fountains, and more concrete tracery. But no gargoyles.

"We could check out the Mountain View Cemetery next door," said Maya.

"Oscar and I looked around the cemetery already," I said. "A while back."

"I don't get it," Oscar growled in the backseat. "Julia Morgan and Bernard Maybeck have the gall to call themselves medievalists but don't put gargoyles on their buildings? What's up with that?"

"I know, can you believe it?" I laughed, then noticed that Maya froze, her eyes wide. She slowly turned around.

"Wow," Maya whispered. "He's . . . talking. And . . . he looks different."

I glanced in the rearview mirror. Oscar's eyes went even wider than Maya's.

"Wow," he echoed. "I've never let a mortal see me before. Unless I was trying to kill them."

"You're not going to try to kill *me*, are you?" Maya asked.

"Didn't even cross my mind."

"Glad to hear that," said Maya. "Wait a minute: Isn't Lily mortal?"

"I mean a cowan mortal," Oscar said. "No offense."

"I don't really know what that means, so I won't take offense."

"Cowans are nonmagical folk," I said. "It can be a slightly derogatory term, coming from certain quarters, but I'm sure Oscar doesn't mean it that way in your case. Right, Oscar?"

"I'm feeling a mite peckish," Oscar said, turning the conversation to one of his favorite subjects. "Who's up for lunch? I hear the New Gold Medal has great noodles."

"I could eat," Maya said.

"Let's do it," I said, relieved at how well the great

reveal had gone. "But since Oscar can't go inside, we'll have to get the food to go. We can eat at Lake Merritt, unless Bronwyn needs us back at the store."

Maya called Bronwyn to confirm that everything was fine at Aunt Cora's Closet, then placed an order at the New Gold Medal.

It occurred to me that Sailor's aunt Renna lived nearby, in the Oakland hills. It would be better to approach her in the company of Patience, but yesterday's experience in the bowels of Alcatraz had lent an urgency to the matter. I feared that Sitri was ratcheting up, gaining strength, and collecting minions; in light of that, I wasn't sure I would be able to take the full five days for the MoonWish separation and binding spell. But at the very least I could try to make sure Renna was safe—and that she wouldn't become an unwitting pawn of Sitri's.

Sailor would not approve of my going there, especially alone, but so be it. I would try to explain it when I saw him tonight. I hoped I had enough energy for our Talk.

Maya agreed to get the food and have a picnic with Oscar while I went to figure out what was going on with Sailor's aunt. We drove to the Oakland Hills.

Renna's house was bubblegum pink and surrounded by a wrought iron fence. A large hand-painted sign, decorated with curlicues and flourishes, declared: FORTUNES READ, DESIRES FULFILLED. I pulled up in front of the gates and reached out to hit the buzzer.

Renna's husband, Eric, answered the intercom. After a brief pause, he told me to come on in, and the automatic gates swung open.

"You sure you'll be okay?" Maya asked as she took my place behind the wheel. I slung my backpack full of supplies over my shoulder.

"Of course. Enjoy lunch and pick me up in an hour?" I said, thinking that if Renna, never my biggest fan, threw me out I might not even need thirty seconds.

"If you had a cell phone, you could just call me when you're done."

"I'll use the house phone if it looks like I'll be done a lot earlier or later."

"Just saying. You might be overcoming your fear of cell phones, Lily. You're starting to use mine a lot, you know. Don't get me wrong—you're welcome to use mine anytime. But maybe you're not as scared of them as you used to be. Give it some thought."

For years I had avoided computers and cell phones because I didn't trust the ghosts in the machines: all those electrons bouncing around, scattering energy, sapping strength. But Maya had a point: Perhaps I was strong enough now to embrace modern technology.

I was a modern-day witch, after all. Maybe I should start acting like one.

Maya waved as she and Oscar drove off, and I watched with mixed feelings as the cherry red Mustang disappeared around a corner. I did not have great memories of Renna and Eric's house. I stroked my medicine bag, straightened my shoulders, and marched up to the big pink door, noting the line of salt across the threshold and the loops of rowan along the porch railing. Charms to keep evil at bay. They didn't always work.

Sailor's people were Cale Rom, originally from Spain. Many Rom—but certainly not all—dealt in magic and divination, which had helped them to survive centuries of harsh mistreatment and attempted genocides. I didn't know enough about Rom culture to understand the subtleties in differences among the groups, but I knew one thing: Many in Sailor's extended family were powerful psychics.

The last time I was here, Eric and Renna had been assaulted and left to die, and their house had been set on fire. I had arrived in the nick of time and been instrumental in rescuing them both, but I got the distinct impression Renna held me partially responsible for what had befallen them. There was no denying that life in the magical community had been calmer before I came to town.

And previous to that, I had failed to keep a promise to Renna, though I sort of came through in the end in a different way. But that didn't count.

Anyway, suffice it to say I wasn't Renna's favorite person. Happily, Eric was the one who answered the door.

He was dark, short, and stocky but athletic-looking, dressed in jeans and a sweatshirt with the logo of UC Berkeley Bears.

"Lily," he said. "It's been a while."

"Eric. It's good to see you."

"Patience mentioned you might be stopping by. And Renna just saw your arrival in the cards."

"May I come in?"

He nodded and stood back, waving me in.

"Something to drink?" Eric offered as we walked into the kitchen. A large accordion sat atop a tall stool; it featured ornate scrollwork and gold leaf, the beautiful details of an antique instrument.

"No, thank you. I'm afraid this isn't a social visit. I'm concerned about Renna. Was someone able to help her last night at the family meeting?"

He shook his head. "She's been a little . . . difficult."

"More than usual, I gather."

He gave me a wry smile. "She's a handful at the best of times, true, but nothing like this. She's always been stubborn and impatient, but never . . . cruel. That's new."

"What else?"

"She occasionally speaks in tongues and has started swearing—a *lot*. Then there are the night terrors . . . but mostly she's just not herself. For instance, her altar's a mess. That's the first thing I noticed, as a matter of fact. She never neglects her devotions."

An aversion to sacred things was common among those in thrall to a demon. Within the Christian church that often meant desecrating religious icons. For Renna, it would be her altar.

"When did this start?"

"A few days ago."

"Patience said it began after she did a reading for two men?"

He nodded and handed me a thick, leather-bound appointment book.

"I was just leaving when they arrived, so I barely saw them, but it's written here in her agenda: She noted it was a 'DR,' a discovery reading. Usually that means someone is searching for something, a misplaced heirloom, for example. That sort of thing."

Renna's handwriting was distinctive, with a backward slant and looping letters. She had written the names *Smith* and *Jones* at the appointment time, followed by the letters *DR-ALCSHRT*, as well as a phone number. I recognized that number—it was the same one the man calling himself Jones had left with Emmy Lou Archer.

"I have no idea what the abbreviation *ALCSHRT* refers to," he said. "I'm just guessing whatever is happening is somehow connected to that appointment. She was her old self before the reading, but when I came home later that day she called me a series of filthy names and locked herself in her room."

"Did you try calling the men?"

He nodded. "Number's disconnected. Patience had someone trace it; it belonged to a burner phone."

"What did they look like?"

"Coupla white guys, midtwenties, maybe. Nothing special."

"Height? Hair color? Anything?"

"I've been racking my brain. They didn't really register, to tell you the truth. They were casually dressed . . . seemed like average height. One had medium brown hair, the other was taller and sort of reddish hair. . . . One might have had some piercings. . . . I'm sorry, I truly didn't take note."

"What about the camera by the gate? Do you have photos of them?"

"I'm embarrassed to admit it, but that camera's not connected to anything. It's just for show, keeps the nosy neighbors at bay and makes clients more respectful."

"And I take it Renna hasn't been able to tell you anything more about what happened during the reading?"

"She won't talk about it." He shook his head, picked up the accordion, and slipped the strap over his head. He began to play a soft, slow tune. "The only thing that calms her down is the music. She doesn't want to talk, barely wants to eat, and hardly sleeps at all. She just stays in her room. It's clear she's struggling with something, and I have no idea how to help her."

"Is it all right if I go speak with her?"

He searched my face for a moment, and I could have sworn he was trying to read my aura. Finally, he nodded. "If you wish. But be prepared."

I held up my backpack. "I came with supplies."

"I hope those are some powerful supplies," he said softly as I headed down the hallway to Renna's room, where she had read for me, what seemed like a long time ago.

Pausing outside the door to ground myself, I stroked the medicine bundle tied to my waist and breathed deeply. I knocked softly and opened the door.

Chapter 19

The first time I met Sailor's aunt I had been shocked that she did her readings in the sanctity of her bedchamber. I have always kept my personal space separate—and safe—from strangers. But Renna's talents were very different from mine, and she gleaned some of her psychic faculties from the intimacy.

When I'd been here before, the room had been carefully staged for readings, with a table in the center, covered in a thick woven brocade, a shallow bowl of water atop which floated rose petals, beside a live toad and a human skull. A stack of oversized tarot cards, soft and dog-eared from use. Her private altar had been set up in a large corner cabinet, with candles and incense, offerings and mementos of loved ones.

The deck of tarot cards still sat neatly on the table. But otherwise the room was a shambles: Papers, herbs, books, and clothing were strewn willy-nilly about the floor and atop the chests of drawers. The sheets had been ripped off the bed and lay in a heap on a crumpled throw rug, and words in a foreign language had been scrawled on the bedroom walls in what looked like dark red lipstick.

Renna was a large, curvy woman easily ten years Eric's senior. Power had emanated from her before, and even more so now. But at present her power, like the state of her room, was scattered and chaotic.

"Lily Ivory," Renna said with a smile, her voice hoarse. "It's been a long time."

"Good to see you, Renna. I wanted to stop by to say hello and, should you be so inclined, offer you a dress of your choosing from my shop for the wedding—"

She started giggling and dancing around me, throwing rose petals and chanting:

I've seen you where you never were
And where you never will be
And yet within that very place
You can be seen by me
For to tell what they do not know
Is the art of the Romani.

She had chanted that song the first time we met, but then it had been part of her act, a way to set the stage for the reading. Now it had a decidedly creepy edge. Renna wasn't possessed in the classic sense—her head wasn't spinning or anything like what happened in Hollywood movies. But she was definitely not herself.

I could tell she was fighting it. Her forearms were covered in scratches, and as she stared at me she yanked out strands of her hair.

I was guessing that Smith and Jones were two of the legion beholden to Sitri, and they had—maybe intentionally, maybe accidentally—passed the contamination on to her. Renna was too powerful, and too spiritual, for a creature like Sitri to easily hold in thrall. It was more like an infection, as though she'd fallen victim to a demonic cold.

On the other hand, someone like Renna would be quite a prize for a demon precisely because of her powers.

"Come, Lily Ivory, take a seat and let me read for you."

Watching her carefully, I sat at the table. Eric's accordion music wafted down the hallway, the sounds soothing and strengthening.

"You remember what to do?" she asked.

I nodded and made a sign upon the cards, coming down with a fist first, then a chopping motion. I repeated the motion three times.

In a practiced move she spread the cards out on the table in a smooth arc.

"Choose one," she said.

I did so, and she took it from me and smiled.

"Three of Cups. Cups Cups Cups! That's all there is these days! Love, sex, feelings, sex, relationships, sex."

"You said that last one already," I said.

"Oooh, but look: It's reversed." She shook her head and made a *tsk*ing sound. "Such a shame. It means the cancellation of celebration, and those around you going behind your back. How are Sailor and his lovely Amanda these days?"

I blinked. When dealing with demons—or those influenced by demons, to whatever extent—it was critical to maintain one's self-control, to not allow them to get into your head, to push your buttons.

But who in the Sam Hill was *Amanda*?

I stroked my medicine bag and kept my voice steady. "Who is Amanda?"

She chuckled and winked. "A beautiful woman,

very sophisticated. Lovely auburn hair. Pretty, pretty Amanda. Plain little Lily."

I tried to ignore the insult.

"Pick another card."

I picked one, and Renna held it up and studied it.

"Who is she to Sailor?" I demanded.

Renna turned the card toward me with a flourish: the Queen of Cups, a beautiful redheaded woman sitting on a throne.

"Sailor's queen, of course. His wife."

A few items flew about the room before I gained control of my emotions. Given the state of Renna's chamber, I doubted anyone would care so I didn't bother to clean it up. Instead, I concentrated on my composure.

"You mean his *ex*-wife," I said.

"Hmmm, maybe, maybe not." Renna gave me a cat-who-swallowed-the-canary smile. "Some can't see the forest for the trees. So sad. Pick another card."

This one was another Cups.

"Oooh," she cooed. The sound was getting on my nerves, though I tried to ignore it. "The Eight of Cups represents disappointment and sadness, walking away from a relationship."

"Which could mean Sailor is walking away from his ex-wife and toward me."

"I doubt you're the *Queen* of *Cups*," Renna said, a sudden edge to her voice. She started pulling cards out of the deck and flinging them down faceup on the tabletop, one after the other. "Look at this: The Five of Cups—dreams dashed, mourning over something lost. Four of Cups, ennui and boredom, dissatisfaction. Six of Cups—looking back to one's past with nostalgia. And the only major arcana is the Tower."

She threw it at me. The Tower card displays a scene

of destruction and violence, a tower on fire, stones tumbling, a man falling to his death.

"You chose those cards, not I," I said.

Renna glared at me. She seemed to choke as though something were stuck in her throat, and then her eyes rolled back in her head. She started making strange, guttural sounds, her tongue waving back and forth in her mouth. She held her arms straight out at both sides and began spouting something in Latin and other languages I didn't recognize.

It was undeniably freaky, but I'd encountered this sort of thing before, years ago. I felt confident that it was just for show, to put me off.

I stood up and studied some of the papers scattered about the room. I didn't see a sigil, but did find two drawings of a catlike face with wings, and many others of cups and water. All were symbols associated with Sitri.

Renna stood up suddenly and started raking her arms with her fingernails.

"Renna, stop that," I said. "You're hurting yourself."

"Get him out!" She grabbed me and whispered fiercely: "Listen, Lily: When Maya opened the box, she started the countdown. You must fuse your astral energy to physical combat! You can't see the forest for the trees! Use the salts!"

Then a change came over her face, she relaxed, her eyes closed halfway, and she leaned toward me with a seductive air. I had also been through this before; it was decidedly creepy to be kissed without one's consent, especially by someone possessed by a demon.

This time I was prepared. I slipped an *auribus teneo lupum* amulet over her head, holding her tight as she tried to pull away. Then I pressed my medicine bag hard against her skin, allowing the crystals and nails within it to make a temporary mark in her flesh, all the while chanting a protection charm. She screeched, an inhuman sound, then slumped, panting, in my arms. I lowered her to her bed.

I sprinkled saltwater on her, anointed her arms and forehead with ash and a salve made from olive oil and rosemary, and drew a pentacle in honey over her heart.

Renna's tension seemed to ease; her panting and twitching subsided, and she fell into slumber.

That was all I could do in the moment. I took a scarf from around her neck and tucked it into my backpack. When I got home I would cast a separation spell. Like the one I was doing in preparation to confront Sitri, the spell would take several days to come to fruition. But I was confident I would gain the upper hand; I wasn't alone in this battle, after all. Renna was fighting from her side as well, and she was not a woman to be gainsaid.

I turned to leave, then paused and removed all the Cups cards from her tarot deck.

Weary but relieved, I slipped out of the bedroom, shut the door behind me, and joined Eric in the kitchen. My eyes fell on something I had missed before: a pink bakery box from Renee's store.

Eric put his accordion down and looked at me hopefully. "How did it go?"

"I believe this was an accidental possession," I explained. "In fact, 'possession' is the wrong word for what's happening. One or both of the men who came to consult with Renna are in thrall to a demon, and because of her sensitivities she absorbed some of their vibrations. Sort of like when you sit by a fire and the smell of smoke lingers on your clothes for a while."

"Will she be all right?"

"I think so, yes. She's fighting it, too. I placed an

amulet around her neck, and I took one of her scarves and some of her cards, and when I get back to my place I'll use them to start a separation spell. It will take a few days to come to fruition, but then she should be back to normal."

"I really don't know how to thank you," said Eric.

"I'd like to take these cupcakes with me, if you don't mind."

Surprise registered on Eric's rugged face. "I, um . . . Sure, help yourself."

"Have you eaten any of them? Did Renna?"

"I didn't, but I'm not certain about Renna. I don't think so, though—she hasn't been eating, and there are still a dozen cupcakes in the box."

"Were there a dozen cupcakes originally, or was it a baker's dozen of thirteen?" I asked.

"I never looked," Eric said.

I opened the box. There were twelve beautifully decorated little cupcakes, but I couldn't tell if there had originally been one more.

"Where did they come from?" I asked, pretty sure I knew the answer.

"The guys who came to talk to Renna brought them. Smith and Jones."

Smith and Jones were treading on my last nerve. Who *were* those guys?

Chapter 20

I was relieved to find Maya and Oscar waiting in the car by the curb when I left the pink house. I was tired and fighting a headache, which I often experienced after dueling with spirits. I called it my "witchy hangover."

Maya, no doubt picking up on my mood, offered to drive us home. I accepted with pleasure and climbed into the backseat to keep an eye on the box of cupcakes. As we crossed the beautiful new Bay Bridge into San Francisco, Maya peppered Oscar with questions, interacting as easily as if she'd always known he was a gobgoyle. He was hunkered down in the footwell so people in other cars wouldn't be able to see him, and slurped the leftover Chinese noodles while chattering excitedly about where he came from, why his mother was suffering under a curse, possibilities for our honeymoon gargoyle-seeking expeditions, and plans for the upcoming wedding.

Oscar was sweet to Maya in a way he rarely was with me, I noticed.

Meanwhile, I was lost in thought. I could only hope that Renna hadn't eaten any of the "fairy cakes." Because if she had ingested an ensorcelled cupcake I might not have diagnosed her correctly, which would affect the separation spell. If the two men who came to speak with Renna were connected to Sitri—and I was convinced they were—did that mean that Renee-the-cupcake-lady was also working with Sitri?

The connection seemed irrefutable. Smith and Jones had gone to Renna for help. In her appointment book, Renna wrote *DR-ALCSHRT* next to their names. It seemed logical to assume that *DR* referred to "discovery reading." Did that mean *ALCSHRT* was an abbreviation for "Alcatraz shirt"? If so, then Smith and Jones had asked for Renna's help in locating Ray Perry's inmate shirt, and she must have sent them to Emmy Lou Archer—but Maya had gotten there first. Then Emmy Lou told Smith and Jones about Aunt Cora's Closet, and they were sitting in their white van outside waiting when Elena walked out.

But how did they know the shirt was in the bundle? And why would they kidnap Elena, too? Despite Carlos's protestations, I feared it was possible Elena was working with Sitri, was somehow in his thrall. If so, I would have to exorcise her as well. Maybe I should open a new business: vintage clothes and demonic exorcisms, at your disposal.

Renna said that Maya inadvertently kicked this whole thing off by opening the box that contained the shirt. There had been an attempt to safeguard the photographs with knot magic; maybe the shirt had been protected by magic that had faded as well. So maybe there were some guards on Alcatraz—and certain prisoners such as the Albright brothers—who had worked for Sitri many years ago. Przybyszewski might have changed his mind and tried to pull away—resulting in the feeling of bad juju in his house, and in his early death.

I had cast Sitri out of the School of Fine Arts a while ago, but he might well have enjoyed an eternal portal on the cursed island of Alcatraz. He and his Feather People, the legions of his lesser demons. They would have grown stronger over the years from the misery of the prisoners.

When we arrived at Aunt Cora's Closet we found Bronwyn alone in the store. She told us Duke had just run out to pick up some sandwiches.

"May I tell Bronwyn?" Maya asked me excitedly, then looked at Oscar.

"Tell me what? Oh, do tell!" urged Bronwyn. "I love secrets!"

I glanced at Oscar, who nodded as he trotted over to his pillow for a post–Chinese food nap.

"Oscar's not a regular Vietnamese potbellied pig," said Maya.

"Of course he's not!" Bronwyn gushed, her voice taking on the gentle tone she reserved for animals and small children. "He's our special itty-bitty Oscaroo, isn't he?"

"Well, yes. But he's also a whole different critter. He's a shape-shifter."

Bronwyn laughed.

"I'm serious. He can talk, and everything."

Bronwyn looked from Maya to me, then to Oscar, then back to me.

"No!"

"Yes."

"Really? No!"

"Yes!" Maya said again, starting to laugh.

Bronwyn looked at me. I nodded.

The bell over the door tinkled as Selena walked in.

"What about Selena?" Bronwyn whispered.

"She already knows," I said.

"About what?" Selena asked.

"Oscar's true self," I said.

Selena shrugged. "I don't see what the big deal is. We have a bunch of animals at the shelter way cuter than *him*, in either of his forms."

Selena had been volunteering with animals at the shelter, and the work had, by and large, improved her capacity for empathy and compassion. But not toward Oscar, apparently.

Bronwyn stared at Oscar, who was fast asleep and snoring on his pillow. "How does he . . . I mean, how does it happen?"

I smiled. "When he wakes up, I'm sure he'll oblige you."

"That's really something. Should I . . . could I tell Duke?"

This was the problem with spilling secrets, I supposed. It was hard to tell where to stop.

"I asked Oscar for permission to share his secret with you and Maya. Let's wait and ask him about Duke when he wakes up. Is that okay?"

"Of course it is," said Bronwyn. "There are plenty of coven matters that I keep to myself; Duke doesn't have to know *everything*. I'm a woman of mystery, after all. . . ."

The bell tinkled as Duke strode into the shop with a paper bag and a newspaper in hand. In his late fifties, he had salt-and-pepper hair and the physique of a man who had worked with his hands his whole life. He used to be a professional fisherman and still kept a small boat on the docks in China Basin.

After we all traded greetings, Duke set the newspaper on the counter and started to unpack the paper bag, handing Bronwyn her sandwich.

I tilted my head to read a bold headline: *Local Billionaire Kyle Cheney Pulls Disappearing Act*. I pulled the newspaper toward me to read the rest of the article.

"Did you hear about this?" I asked no one in particular.

"I heard it on the radio," Bronwyn said with a nod. "No one's seen him since yesterday afternoon. They don't know where he's got to."

"That's not long enough for him to be considered missing, is it?" I asked. The article didn't say much, only that unnamed sources had reported Cheney had missed a number of appointments, that he was on medication, and that he had been acting oddly lately.

"Probably went off for a little alone time on his own private island somewhere," said Duke.

"But he's putting on the huge shindig out on Alcatraz!" Bronwyn declared, as though Cheney disappearing was the height of rudeness.

"That's so strange," I said. "I met with Cheney's assistant this morning, and he didn't say anything about it."

"Why would he?" Duke asked. "A corporation would most likely try to keep this sort of thing quiet, so as not to spook the shareholders. Probably went into rehab. Or again, I vote for hiding on a private island."

"I suppose that makes sense," I said. "Speaking of islands, could I ask you a question about the tides in the bay?"

Duke's eyebrows rose. "Sure. What about them?"

"Are they consistent? I mean, could you figure them out by the phases of the moon or something like that?"

"I suppose you might be able to, if you knew enough about such things. We always kept a tide log on the boat. It's also published in the newspaper . . . or at least it used to be, back in the day. Not sure about these days. I know it's available on the Internet."

"Has Bronwyn mentioned to you that I've been out to Alcatraz recently?"

He nodded. "She's filled me in. Terrible. But Bronwyn tells me your friend has been found, and she's okay?"

"We hope so," I said, reminding myself to call Carlos and check in. "Thank you. I'm trying to figure out if the Alcatraz prisoners who escaped into the water could have gotten to shore."

"You and hundreds of others over the years, I imagine. There's a force in the bay called Dead Man's Current. If you get caught in it, it's almost impossible to overcome if you're in the water, or even if you're on a small craft. It'll pull a person out to the open sea, not slowly, but surely. There are periods of time when Dead Man's Current is not as strong, though, so from the island of Alcatraz you might be able to push north to the shores of Marin, or maybe to Angel Island."

"Wouldn't it be depressing to succeed in escaping Alcatraz, only to wash up on *another* island?" said Bronwyn.

"Angel Island's much bigger than Alcatraz," said Duke. "And it's separated from the mainland only by the relatively narrow Raccoon Strait. If you managed to navigate through the tides and currents from Alcatraz to Angel, you could walk around to the other side of Angel Island and have a straight shot over to Tiburon. That trip in the northern waters of the bay, from Marin County to any of the islands, is easier than any other approach, as a matter of fact."

"So you're saying a person could have escaped from Alcatraz that way? And lived?"

"It would be risky, but it's possible," he said. "Although, I don't mean to cast aspersions, and I certainly didn't know the guys, but the Albright brothers didn't seem like the sharpest tools in the shed. I always wondered if they had a little help."

Bronwyn beamed at Duke. "He knows so much about everything, even Alcatraz. Darling, are you sure you won't go on the ghost hunt with me?"

"History is one thing, ghost hunts quite another," he said with a smile and a shake of his head.

After we closed up shop, I hurried upstairs to my apartment. I was looking forward to seeing Sailor tonight. I wanted to apologize. I wanted to talk. I wanted to ask him what he thought about Sitri, and the cupcakes, and Alcatraz. I wanted to kiss him and feel his arms around me.

But then he called to cancel.

"I'm so sorry, Lily. Please believe me when I say it's unavoidable. Tomorrow night, for sure."

Oscar had disappeared again as well.

So Sailor had bowed out tonight, and Oscar had better things to do than to hang out with yours truly. I wandered around my empty apartment for a few minutes, straightening a few things and feeling sorry for myself. I had become so accustomed to being surrounded by others—friends, family, familiar—that I sometimes felt at loose ends when on my own.

Then I glanced at my Book of Shadows, the gift of my ancestors, a tangible reminder of my connection to others, and gave myself a stern talking-to. *You spent years as a solo act, Lily. Remember how long it took you to open up and accept friendship and to build a sense of community? Well, the flip side is that sometimes you will miss them when they're not around. But that's no reason to feel sorry for yourself—that's a reason to ap-preciate what you have. Buck up, witch, and make yourself useful.*

Fine. I certainly wasn't going to sit around waiting for boyfriends and gobgoyles to show up and amuse me. I had plenty to do.

Starting with those benighted cupcakes.

Bringing the pink box Smith and Jones had taken to Renna and Eric, I drove to Renee's bakery. Not only did I want to keep the cupcakes out of Oscar's hungry gullet, I wanted to use them as Exhibit A when I confronted Renee about them. But when I got there the shop was dark, the cheerful yellow CLOSED sign still hanging in the window. The note and little pot of salve I had left were gone, but otherwise there was no sign of her.

Where else might I find her? It dawned on me that I had no idea where Renee lived. I peered through the shop's front window. The display cases were still well stocked with brightly frosted cupcakes, and one shelf held savory meat pies. Renee had once dosed me with one of those meat pies.

My stomach growled at the memory; much as it pained me to admit it, the meat pie had been delicious.

It made me realize how long it had been since I'd eaten. I had skipped lunch in favor of dueling with Renna and should have taken Maya up on the offer of the Chinese food leftovers. My kitchen cupboards were bare despite my shopping trip with Selena. It was tough to make time for the routine parts of daily life, like grocery shopping, when chasing down demons.

And if a growly stomach weren't pedestrian enough, I needed to pee. Pretty badly.

I tried the doorknob, just in case. Locked, of course. But there might be a way around that. I wondered how many laws I would be violating if I entered Renee's cupcake shop and did a little snooping. I remembered seeing delicate bottles of lachrymatory salts on a display with her souvenir silver spoons. I'd like to take a closer look at those. But . . . getting into the shop wouldn't be that easy, would it? Renee was a powerful practitioner; surely she had cast some sort of supernatural protection over her store in case a nosy witch showed up in search of lachrymatories and a restroom.

Indecisive, I hunched over and peered through the window again, cupping my hands around my eyes to see better. The poster for the Festival of Felons hung proudly on her back wall.

"*Busted*," a voice behind me said.

I jumped, whirled around, and staggered back against the door. I nearly released a blast of power, stopping myself just in time.

Aidan Rhodes. Golden hair shimmering in the early evening sun, periwinkle blue eyes twinkling. It reminded me that I almost never saw him out and about in the daylight; he was more of a middle-of-the-night owl because it was harder for him to maintain his glamour before the sun went down.

"What are you doing here?" I demanded, trying to still my heart.

"What are *you* doing here?" he asked with a smile.

"Looking for Renee, obviously."

"I thought we agreed you wouldn't meet with Renee without me. I know she seems like an innocuous cupcake lady, but she's quite powerful, Lily. Don't underestimate her."

"Yeah, well, that's all well and good in theory, but you've been hard to pin down lately."

"Just for a couple of days."

"Those were a couple of very long and eventful days."

"You spilled a drop of your blood on my book."

"No, I didn't. Noctemus did. Tell her to keep her claws to herself, will you?" The salve had done its work; the scratches were still visible, but no longer inflamed.

"My point is, something's been started in motion."

"That sounds ominous."

"Could be. A witch like you has to be very careful about her blood. So, what are you doing here?"

I shrugged. "I'm not entirely certain, but we probably shouldn't talk about it right here. Suffice it to say, I wanted to talk with Renee and since she wasn't here, I thought I'd take a look around."

"You don't think Renee would have taken precautions against such things?"

"I imagine she has. But still. I need a bathroom."

He let out a silent chuckle.

"Well, in that case . . . after you."

We both felt the wall of protection, but like the spell I cast each day over Aunt Cora's Closet, it was gauged at stopping someone intent on vandalism or decimating the cupcake inventory, not a determined witch and her friend, a powerful warlock. Our combined powers could overcome it without much trouble.

But if Renee still kept the lachrymatories here, she would have set up a much stronger kind of protection. Something magical, and possibly violent.

Unfortunately, I had left my Hand of Glory at my apartment, so we might be bested by much more prosaic concerns, such as how to defeat the dead bolt on the front door.

Aidan and I were leaning over, examining the knob and the locks, discussing whether our combined magic could open them and whether this situation was worth taking the risk of combining our magic—the effects of which sometimes got out of hand—when the strong beam of a flashlight lit up the little alcove that had dimmed in the fading light of day.

"Hey, you two!" came a voice. "What's going on?"

Dangitall.

We turned to face two young men in security guard uniforms. One was slightly taller than the other, but otherwise they were both thin and nondescript. They were blinking and squinting, wavering a bit on their feet, as though they had just awakened from sleep, or were currently under the influence. Perhaps both. I mumbled a quick spell, hoping I would be able to influence them. It didn't always work, but given their condition I thought I might be able to sway them.

"Hi," I began. "Sorry about this. We—"

"Oh, hey, we know you, right?" said guy #1.

"Yeah," said guy #2. "From the Haight—you're the vintage dress chick."

"Yes. Yes, I am the vintage dress chick. Indeed I am." I snuck a glance at Aidan, who seemed amused by this turn of events. "It's nice to see you."

"Sorry if we scared you," said guy #1.

"Yeah, sorry," said #2. "We got a call about some suspicious characters lurking in the doorway."

"And we saw you on the security camera, see?" Guy #1 gestured to a camera tucked under an eave. "So, like, are you . . . looking for something, or whatever?"

"I've got a wicked hankering for a cupcake," I said. "Also, I need to use the bathroom."

"*Dude*," said #1.

"Um . . . can't help you with the cupcakes, I mean, Renee was pretty firm about not letting anyone in. But I guess you could use our bathroom," said #2. "The security desk is right next door here, in the construction zone. There's a bathroom in there."

"Thanks," I said. "That would be really great."

They led us into the neighboring shopfront. It had been gutted, the vintage clothing long since cleared out, and I was enough of a businesswoman to wonder what had become of the former owner's exquisite inventory. A glance at the rather clueless security guards numbers one and two, though, assured me it wasn't worth posing the question to them. They waved me into the small restroom down a short hallway.

When I emerged, Aidan and the security guards were hunched over a set of blueprints laid out on a large worktable. They were stamped with a line drawing of a cupcake, and in small print it read: *A division of Co-Opp Industries.*

Kyle Cheney hadn't just invested in Renee's Cupcakes, as Seth had told me. He had acquired it entirely.

"Yeah, Renee's hiring for the kitchen and counter help," #2 was saying.

"It's pretty awesome," said #1. "I haven't had a job in, like, forever. There's benefits and everything, if we last past the probation period."

"You were hired by Kyle Cheney?" I asked.

"Not, like, by him in person or anything. But he's got this company that hires people—sometimes they recruit at the soup kitchens and shelters. The dude's trying to give people a chance. It's pretty awesome."

"That's totally awesome," Aidan agreed.

"I heard Cheney's gone missing," I said. They both shrugged, blank looks on their faces.

"Has anyone asked you to do anything else?" I asked them.

"Like what?"

Like make a sacrifice to a demon?

"Oh, just anything. Maybe something that seems out of the ordinary . . . ?"

The young men exchanged a glance and shook their heads.

"Mostly it's just security," said #1. "We're not always here in this location, though. We're gonna be working out on Alcatraz in a coupla days for a big festival, which is pretty awesome."

"The Festival of Felons?"

They nodded.

"Do you know how we can get in touch with Renee?" I asked. "I'd really love to talk to her."

"Dude," said #2. "I've got her phone number, and she comes by occasionally, but since the shop's closed for the remodel she hasn't been around much."

"I noticed she still has cupcakes on her shelves," I said.

"Yeah." He didn't elaborate.

"Do you happen to know where she lives?" I asked.

They both shook their heads.

"I do," volunteered Aidan.

"You do?"

"Of course I do." He seemed amused that I was surprised. "I know everything, remember?"

"Duuuude," said one of the men. "That's awesome."

Chapter 21

"Shall I drive?" Aidan asked as we left the shop under construction.

"Yes please. I'm too hungry to drive. I wasn't kidding about hankering after a cupcake or one of those meat pies. Not that I would eat one, because: Renee. But still."

"We could always skip trying to track Renee down and go out to a nice dinner instead."

"You're acting awfully casual, given what's going on. Surely you've heard about what's been happening on Alcatraz and the signs of the demon—the one from the San Francisco School of Fine Arts?"

He gave me a Look. Of course he knew.

"What can you tell me about Kyle Cheney?" I asked.

"Rich guy, filthy rich. Tech money. Philanthropist."

"I don't trust him."

"You don't trust anyone with that much money," said Aidan.

"That's not true," I said, defensive. Then reconsidered. "I guess it's sort of true. Seems to me that too much money's a little like too much magical power: It leads to corruption."

Aidan just smiled.

"Cheney's offices are in the pyramid building, which, according to Oscar, sits at the top of a truncated triangle."

"Which means what, exactly?"

"I don't know, but it's an interesting factoid."

"Aren't there a lot of different businesses in the pyramid building?"

"Yes," I admitted grudgingly. "But Cheney also invested in Renee's Cupcakes."

"Indeed."

Cheney had invested through Co-Opp Industries, which was no co-op. Could it be referring to the *coincidentia oppositorum*? If Kyle Cheney and Renee Baker joined forces, they would make a powerful combo: With his money and philanthropic reputation he was trusted in the community, and no one ever suspected the friendly cupcake lady was capable of casting spells through her baked goods. With Kyle's money funding her store's expansion, Renee would be able to affect even more people.

And the timing of his—and Renee's—disappearance was interesting, right before the Festival of Felons. Maybe they were too busy trying to take over the world to attend to business as usual.

"Listen, Aidan. I'm worried that things are ratcheting up. . . . Is it possible Kyle Cheney's upcoming Festival of Felons out on Alcatraz might be the setting of some sort of mass demonic sacrifice?"

"Of course."

"*It is?*" I had been hoping I was wrong. Panic loomed. What was I going to do? How did I even begin to approach something like this? I wasn't prepared; it was too soon. I needed to touch base with all of our magical allies. . . . The MoonWish spell wasn't even complete. What would I—

My thoughts were interrupted when Aidan pulled his shiny Jaguar into an In-N-Out Burger drive-in. I ordered a cheeseburger—animal style—and extra-crispy fries.

"Better?" Aidan asked after I wolfed down the burger and finished off the last of the fries. By now we were in the East Bay, caught in the perpetual bumper-to-bumper traffic on Interstate 80.

"Mmm, much better. Thanks." I sighed, dabbing at a drop of ketchup that stained the bodice of my dress. "You know, the traffic around here is a nightmare." Continually congested freeways were the bane of the Bay Area, and of course the worst at rush hour. "Hey, as chief magical guy around here, can't you do something about that?"

He smiled. "I guess I have a few other things to attend to, first. I'll leave that up to the urban planners."

"Not sure there was a lot of urban planning with regard to these freeways," I groused, feeling like a local. Locals were forever talking about traffic.

Once we passed the heavily populated towns of Berkeley, El Cerrito, and San Pablo, the buildings started thinning out, leaving more empty fields and rolling hills covered in dried grasses, studded by an occasional California oak tree.

"Anyway, an upcoming battle is hardly a surprise," said Aidan. "Though the inclusion of a demonic power is, I'll admit, a new angle to deal with. But we've been seeing warnings of this on the horizon for some time now. Sailor's organizing his friends and relatives, and I've been working on solidifying the other alliances. A battle like this is no one's idea of fun, but we'll prevail. Or not, in which case it's doubtful we'd survive, so I don't suppose we'll care."

I stared at him. He wasn't kidding.

"As I've told you," Aidan continued, "your arrival was the tipping point."

"So, you're saying that I really am attracting all of this to San Francisco? I feel like a magical Typhoid Mary."

"I was thinking more like a magical hot spot."

"Hot spot?"

"It's a place people can get Internet."

"Or a place where fires start."

"True, but an Internet hot spot is sort of a conduit for things, was my point. So it's not that you're carrying the typhoid, you're just allowing it to pass."

"I'm not sure I like that interpretation any better. But . . . at least this would mean that the prophecy refers to me and not to my alleged brother."

"What alleged brother?"

"You don't know? I thought you knew everything."

"Are you serious?" Aidan looked beyond worried; "panicked" might be a better word. His knuckles went white, and I could see his glamour shift slightly to reveal the painful-looking scars he usually kept hidden. Aidan was *never* worried, much less panicked. What was going on?

"Aidan? Talk to me. Is he bad news?"

"I have no idea," he said. "But we've proceeded from the assumption that you're the one named in the prophecy. If that's wrong . . ." He trailed off and seemed to be thinking. Finally, he relaxed his grip on the wheel. "I suppose we'll just have to address that when, and if, said brother arrives in our fair city. What do you know about him?"

I shook my head. "Nothing. My grandmother's coven told me he existed, but even they don't seem to know much else."

We drove in silence for a stretch, passing huge oil tanks and more rolling hills. Aidan took an exit off the freeway with no signs of life other than the occasional oak tree and dry brush. After a few more minutes, we came to the entrance of a gated community. Aidan paused briefly to speak to the guard in the kiosk, and we rolled into something called Kinkade Village.

"It's named for the painter Thomas Kinkade—do you know his work?"

"He's the one on all the puzzles and calendars? The 'painter of light'?"

Aidan nodded.

"Isn't his art a little . . . cheesy?" I asked.

"That all depends on your point of view. Not for the residents here, obviously. They even have a slogan: 'Calm, not chaos. Peace, not pressure.' Nothing wrong with that, if you ask me."

The faux Victorian, pseudo French provincial, and pretend New England cottage-style homes were nestled close together; steeply gabled roofs were covered in faux-slate tile, the fronts decorated with gingerbread trim, sweet porches, and stone facades. Streetlights were made to look like old-fashioned gas lamps, and the concrete sidewalks were stamped to look like cobblestones. Most of the gardens consisted of small patches of verdant green lawns bordered by rosebushes and enclosed by white picket fences.

"It's kind of . . . odd, isn't it?" I asked.

"You don't find it charming? It's meant to be charming."

"Maybe it's just the association with Renee. Something made to look one way—sweet and charming—with something else entirely lurking just below the surface."

"And speaking of Renee," said Aidan as he pulled to the curb, "here we are."

Renee's cottage was pseudo New-England-cottage-by-the-sea, except that we were nowhere near New England, much less the sea. There were pansies in cute little pots on the porch, and I wondered whether she had always yearned for a place like Calypso's beautiful farmhouse. This seemed like such a pale imitation of that kind of genuinely calm, peaceful place.

"So now what?" I asked.

"Let's go see if she's home," he said, climbing out of the Jaguar. I did the same, and we mounted the porch steps. The place was lit up like a Christmas tree, but no one answered the tinkling sound of the doorbell.

I leaned over and tried to peek through the window, but my view was obscured by lace curtains. I couldn't make out much more than overstuffed furniture and plenty of tchotchkes—and several vases full of calla lilies. *Alcatraces*.

For the second time that evening I considered breaking in and searching Renee's place, but what exactly was I expecting to find? It was highly unlikely Renee would leave any obvious supernatural weapons or detailed plans for mystical dominance just lying around. What we really needed to do was to speak face-to-face, to see if we could come up with any sort of diplomatic solution to our conflict, some way to avoid the upcoming war.

"It was worth a try," Aidan said as he plucked a red rose from the vine encircling a porch column and held it out to me.

"I don't want anything of Renee's, thank you," I said.

He smiled and put it in his buttonhole. Not for the first time I wondered how such a beautiful man could still seem so masculine, even while sporting flowers. But then, as my San Francisco friends would remind me, no need to get hung up on the gender thing.

"Renee will know we've been looking for her," he said, leaning against the white-painted balustrade. "It might be a case of waiting until she gets in touch with us. Or the battle, whichever comes first."

"You're saying she won't be willing to talk?"

He shrugged. "She hasn't been particularly open to a diplomatic solution so far, unless you count asking you to throw in with her."

I snorted. "Yeah, like *that's* going to happen."

"I think once she realized she couldn't defeat you, she hoped to get you to join her, somehow. Be careful; I don't think she's given up on trying to lure you over to her side."

"Do you really think she and Kyle Cheney are linking to form the *coincidentia oppositorum*?"

"It would make sense."

"And that means . . . what *does* that mean, exactly?"

"That they'll be a force to be reckoned with. If you're right and the demon we knew from the School of Fine Arts is back, and the Festival of Felons is a celebration for him, then the showdown will take place then."

"I'm doing a five-day spell—it won't be ready until the full moon."

"Let me check in with a few people to be sure, but you may have to speed things up by one night. You can supercharge the spell with a blood sacrifice tomorrow night, if it's almost ready."

"What do you suggest?" I occasionally did blood

magic, but that was different than sacrifice—that was using my own blood. An actual blood sacrifice meant taking the life of a living creature. Even killing spiders made me shudder.

"My sacrifice wouldn't be the same as yours; this is a very personal thing. You should look it up in your Book of Shadows."

I gazed out over the faux-fairy-tale village. We were discussing blood sacrifice while standing on a porch overlooking a street out of a Thomas Kinkade painting, nestled in the dry golden hills of Northern California. It was surreal, and more than a little disconcerting.

"Where do *you* live?" I asked Aidan.

"Me?"

"Yes, you."

"Best bet for finding me is at my office."

"Surely you don't live at the wax museum, though. Where—"

A golf cart pulled up, and two security guards hopped out.

"Good evening," said one. These burly guys didn't look as if they would be as easily influenced as the guards at Renee's construction site. "We got a call about a disturbance."

"Our apologies," Aidan said smoothly. "We certainly did not intend to disturb anyone."

"No, of course not," I said. "Do you know if Renee's around?"

"Don't know, and wouldn't tell you if we did," said the guard. "Time for you to go."

"Fine," I said. "We were just leaving."

"See that you do," said the other guard.

We descended the three porch steps and got back into the car. The golf cart followed us until we passed through the gate, which closed behind us.

"Sheesh, a little overzealous, weren't they?" I said. "But I suppose I should be getting back home, anyway."

It was disappointing that I wouldn't see Sailor tonight, but I had plenty to do: I needed to charge the spell against Sitri, cast a separation spell for Renna, and brew for Conrad's morning tonic.

Also, I supposed I should spend some time with my Book of Shadows and ponder the possible blood sacrifice.

"Me too," Aidan said, checking his watch as he pulled onto the freeway. It was nearly eight o'clock, and the traffic had died down. "In fact, I have an appointment with Sailor and Amanda tonight."

"Sailor and *Amanda*? As in Sailor's ex-wife?" I demanded, my voice scaling up.

He nodded.

"What are you doing for him, or for her? Or for him *and* her?"

He gave me a scathing look. "You know very well I can't tell you that, Lily. Confidentiality and all that."

I pressed my lips together in irritation. "I'm about to marry the man, so I think I have a right to know why he and his ex-wife are meeting with you."

"I couldn't agree more," he said with a slight inclination of his head. "So ask him."

"Why didn't he tell me?" I said to myself as much as to Aidan.

"I imagine he didn't want you to feel jealous. But enough about your boyfriend."

"Fiancé."

"Whatever. Listen, I have to tell you something," he said, his voice serious. "It's no secret that I've been losing strength. I don't know whether it's related to the prophecy, the upcoming battle, or something more organic, but I will need to leave town for a while. I'll be leaving you in charge, like last time."

"I've gotta say, I didn't love being the boss."

"There isn't anyone else who can do the job, Lily. You know where I keep the Satchel—though to tell you the truth, I'll be calling in most of those markers for support in the battle. In any case, you're welcome to use my office while I'm gone for meetings and that sort of thing. Or feel free to borrow things, as you've done in the past."

"Oh, yeah, speaking of that, I've been meaning to tell you, I was in your office the other day—"

He waved off my excuse. "It's not a problem. We've got to work together at this point. Noctemus knows you'll be in and out; she won't scratch you again."

Wanna bet? I thought. "Does she talk?"

"Excuse me?"

"Does Noctemus talk?"

"Of course not."

"*My* familiar talks."

He smiled. "Oscar's not a typical familiar, as you well know."

"Then how do you and Noctemus communicate?"

"It's more by intuition, perhaps a little mind reading. Like the relationship between any human and pet, really, but more so."

"I've never had a pet. Anyway, back to you leaving me in charge: I'm not great with bureaucracy."

He cast me a quick grin. "That's the worst part of the job. There are other aspects that are more rewarding."

"Like what?"

"Like keeping San Francisco from falling into the wrong hands. Keeping magical folks safe, to provide them with a haven. This can be a cruel world for misfits, as you very well know. You think San Francisco's openness is an accident? It's not easy to remain welcoming to those who are different, who might disagree with your belief system. And yet that's what makes the City by the Bay so special."

I smiled. "You're waxing poetic tonight."

"Must be the gibbous moon," he said. "Only two more nights till it's full."

Two more nights. Did we *have* two more nights?

Chapter 22

Aidan dropped me off near Renee's cupcake shop, where I had parked my car. I considered going to Sailor's apartment in Chinatown and waiting for him to come home. But that felt like I was setting up a confrontation. Also, what if Amanda arrived at his apartment *with* him? Just the thought of it made my stomach clench; I didn't trust what might happen with my magic in the heat of the moment.

I had to have confidence in him. I *did* have confidence in him. In *us*.

So instead I stopped by the grocery store and stocked up on supplies, for real this time. Not only did I want to keep Oscar happy, but I needed items for the increasingly intricate offerings for the MoonWish spell against Sitri.

Back at my place, I found solace in the rote pleasure of putting away groceries and filling the larder. I prepped Conrad's brew for tomorrow morning and then switched on some music and took my time cooking a big pot of shrimp and okra gumbo to leave out as tonight's offering for Sitri. Oscar should know what it was and why it was out, and even *he* respected the sanctity of offerings such as this. But just in case, I penned a sign: DEMONIC SACRIFICE! DO NOT EAT!!!

Casting a spell is not as easy as simply uttering the words. It takes a lot of energy to focus one's intent sufficiently to alter reality, and lately I had been feeling depleted. So prior to spellcasting, I took a long shower, washed with lemon verbena soap, and dressed all in black. I knelt in front of the table, lowered my head, closed my eyes, and focused on the sound of my own breathing for a full five minutes.

That done, I started intoning the charm, concentrating on Sitri and our upcoming meeting. I took my time, allowing myself to linger on the words, pondering their meaning, their heritage. These spells had been passed down through generations along a line of powerful women, and had finally landed here, with me.

One last thing to do before retiring: I lit a red and yellow candle for Renna's separation spell, circling it with her scarf. I spread out the tarot cards in as smooth an arc as I could, which didn't come close to approximating the neat results of Renna's practiced hand.

I sighed.

As with most things in life, spellcasting wasn't as easy as it looked.

The next morning I cleansed Aunt Cora's Closet, cast my daily protection spell, and took advantage of the quiet and solitude to pick out five dresses for Maya, holding each in my arms to feel its vibrations. One—a sleeveless 1960s dress with a bright geometric pattern— would be perfect, but I would wait and see which one Maya felt best in after she tried them on.

Then I called Eric, who told me that Renna had slept well and that, although she was still holed up in her room, she wasn't shrieking like before and had even requested some chicken soup. He thanked me profusely and asked what I wanted for the handfasting. I suggested he bring his accordion and play for us. I couldn't imagine better music for the celebration.

As soon as I hung up, the phone rang again.

It was Carlos. "I've been trying to get in touch with you."

"Is everything all right? How's Elena?"

"She's doing better. Still hasn't been able to tell us anything helpful, though. Keeps repeating 'co-op.' Maybe she's thinking of selling her condo?"

"I don't think—," I began, but he cut me off.

"Lily, it's about your grandmother's coven—"

"*What?*" I demanded, fear surging through me. "Are they all right?"

"They're fine," Carlos said, a note of humor in his voice. "But they need someone to post bail."

"Graciela, *really*? I can't *believe* the thirteen of you," I said as I led the group out of the jailhouse. At least my mother and Calypso had had the good sense to sit this one out. "As if I don't have enough to deal with just now. You rented a boat and tried to land on *Alcatraz*?"

"Who knew it was off-limits? It's just sitting out there, undefended," said Viv.

"That's true, Lily," said Agatha.

"Setting aside the fact that simple common sense would suggest it's not a good idea to attempt a naval invasion of a national park," I replied, "there are, like, *twelve*-foot-tall signs posted all around the island saying no one's allowed to land there."

"Those signs are left over from when it was a prison," said Graciela, not cowed in the slightest. "They don't apply anymore."

The others nodded, as if that were perfectly obvious.

"How did y'all even get there? Where's the school bus?"

"In Sausalito," said Rosa. "We hired a very nice man to take us over in his boat. I do hope he doesn't get into trouble."

"Was he arrested, too?"

"Oh, no, we sent him away, before the feds nabbed us," Betty said. "It wouldn't do to have a stranger there. This was coven business."

"Then how were you planning on getting off the island?"

The women looked at one another. "We hadn't worked that part out yet," Agatha volunteered.

I shook my head and tried to calm down. At the corner where I had parked my Mustang, we found Conrad waiting with the shop van. A few minutes later, the Lyft that Conrad had ordered arrived. We spent the next fifteen minutes waiting while the coven decided who should ride with whom back to the school bus in Sausalito.

"That's enough!" I said as the coven bickered about who got to ride shotgun. "Graciela, Pepper, Caroline, and MariaGracia, you're with me. Everyone else—take a seat or get left behind. We're leaving."

Graciela, Pepper, Caroline, and MariaGracia joined me in the Mustang.

"Now that it's just us," I said as I headed to the Golden Gate Bridge, "please, explain why you felt compelled to hire a boat to go to Alcatraz."

"Ghosts," said Pepper.

"It's hardly surprising there would be ghosts on Alcatraz," I said. "In fact I'd be surprised if there *weren't* ghosts."

"Well, of course," said MariaGracia.

"That's not the problem," Pepper agreed.

"So what is the problem?" I asked.

"They're highly agitated," said Caroline. "I felt it last night with the pendulum."

"I'm not really a ghost gal." I thought back to the image of Ray Perry in the attic, and again in the dungeon, and added: "Normally."

Caroline nodded. "Showing themselves to those who haven't seen them before; they're definitely agitated."

"How does that work, exactly?"

"It takes a great deal of energy for them to manifest," said MariaGracia. "It's not a good sign."

"Also, all the birds have left," said Pepper.

"Is there . . . I was told there's an ancient curse on the island. And the woods folk want me to sink it."

"Are you the one who's been causing the earthquakes?" asked Caroline.

"Excuse me?"

"Those earthquakes lately," said Caroline. "They're unnatural."

"I feel like that, too," I said. "But according to the locals it's just something people in California live with."

"These aren't normal quakes," Caroline insisted. "They're centered on Alcatraz."

"That's why you were trying to get out to the island?"

"Among other reasons," said MariaGracia.

"How are you planning to destroy Alcatraz, *m'ija*?" Graciela asked me.

"I'm not. I can't just go around sinking islands. Even if I had a clue as to how."

Graciela directed me to the Sausalito yacht harbor,

where we found the school bus parked nearby. Our impromptu caravan came to a halt, and a coven's worth of witches poured out of the vehicles. After doing a quick head count to make sure all were accounted for, I thanked Conrad and the Lyft driver, who left to return to the city.

A grizzled elderly man wearing a captain's hat and tending a nearby boat hailed the coven like an old friend, clearly their partner in crime.

"Call me Captain Buddy," he said, coming over to shake my hand.

"I appreciate your kindness to my aunts, Captain Buddy," I said. "But for future reference it's actually against the law to land a boat on Alcatraz Island. You could have been arrested and charged with a federal offense."

"Well, now, that seems like a mighty silly law, if you ask me," he replied.

"It does, doesn't it?" Caroline said.

"I know a lot of boat pilots refuse to go out there," said Captain Buddy. "But I do it all the time."

"We didn't intend any harm," MariaGracia said.

"Be that as it may—," I continued.

"You're mighty welcome, young lady," Captain Buddy replied, beaming at Pepper, to whom he appeared to have taken a shine. "Always happy to help out lovely ladies in distress."

"But—"

"Any good restaurants around here?" Graciela asked.

"I'm starving. That jailhouse swill was awful," Pepper said.

"I could really go for some good Mexican food," MariaGracia said.

"Copita Tequileria has eighty-seven different kinds

of tequila," Captain Buddy said. "I'm partial to their fish tacos with pineapple pico de gallo. And it's walkable; just up the street there."

"Eighty-seven different kinds of tequila?" Iris said, a reverential tone in her voice.

"I surely could use a margarita," Graciela said.

"Well? What are we waiting for?" said Rosa. "Let's get this show on the road."

"*Vámanos*," said Winona.

I gave up. A shot of tequila might do me some good, after all.

It took us nearly half an hour to walk the two blocks from the Sausalito yacht harbor to the restaurant. Downtown Sausalito's main thoroughfare is chock-full of intriguing boutiques selling everything from antiques to souvenirs to dirty postcards to local artwork, and the women immediately scattered in thirteen different directions, exclaiming loudly over the cute items and the high prices. When everyone finally arrived we were seated at a large banquet table decorated with brightly colored paper flowers. The women spent another twenty minutes deciding what to order and bickering over which appetizers to share.

"Oh, before I forget," I said, "would the coven do some distance healing for a woman named Elena Romero? I have her hat in the car—it even has a strand of hair—and a photograph. She's a friend of mine who went through a terrible trauma."

"Of course we can," said Betty, squeezing my hand. "We'll cast for strength."

"Thank you," I said, downing my shot of tequila and biting into a slice of lime. Thus fortified, I said: "So listen, I need to tell you all what's been going on and what I fear you might have been sensing about Alcatraz."

As we snacked on chips and guacamole and quesa-dillas, I filled them in on what had transpired so far, about Renee and the *coincidentia oppositorum*, and what I feared would happen on the full moon. By the time I finished, all thirteen were exchanging significant glances around the table.

"Might as well tell her everything," said Graciela, her tone grim.

"What is it?" I asked. "Tell me."

Caroline took a deep breath: "My pendulum indi-cated a big earthquake, a devastating one. The Big One. And Alcatraz will be the only thing left intact."

"We're gonna need another round of margaritas over here," said Graciela, motioning to the waitress. "Every-body except Agatha, she's our designated driver."

Chapter 23

"Not that I doubt your abilities, Caroline, but couldn't your pendulum have been wrong?" I asked.

"Iris read the tea leaves, and Pepper triple-checked with her tarot, and MariaGracia consulted her crystal ball. All the indications are there."

Graciela set down her margarita. "We're going to need Selena's help."

"*No*. Absolutely not," I replied. "Selena's just a child."

"*Es una bruja*," Graciela said simply. "She's a witch, and she's not much younger than you were when you went off on your own. She's more capable than you know, Lily, especially in this sort of thing. She's still searching for her footing in the regular world, but in the magical one, she's well-grounded. You and Aidan have done a good job."

"I appreciate that, but that's not the issue. There might well be real-world murderers out on that island," I said, steeling myself against the nightmarish memory of Selena being held by the last homicidal maniac we went up against. "I don't want Selena caught up in that."

"You'll need her. It's in the cards," said Pepper. "Trust her, Lily."

"Also, you must reconnect with Sailor," said Darlene. "He'll need the strength of his connection to you on the astral plane."

"I'm . . ." I blushed to realize they knew Sailor and I weren't getting along. "I hope I'll see him tonight. We also have other magical allies as backup."

"Good," said Nan. "You'll need them all."

"Have y'all decided what kind of ceremony to perform on me?" I asked. "To reconcile my two guiding spirits?"

"About that," said Graciela. "We've decided it's best to wait."

"Why?"

"You're going to need the fierceness of the newer one," said Rosa. "She'll give you an edge, by helping to fuse the astral and physical planes."

"Betty divined it yesterday, and we confirmed it last night when we drew down the moon," said Caroline.

"But—"

"Look, Lily," said Iris, coming over to my chair with a garland made out of brightly colored paper flowers that had once graced the table. "I've made a garland for you. So pretty!"

"Um, thank you, Iris," I said, dutifully putting it on.

Darlene leaned over to me and whispered loudly: "Iris has no gift of sight, but her color magic is spot-on. That garland might come in useful."

"You honestly think Deliverance Corydon will be an asset?" I asked.

Around the table, thirteen heads nodded. These

were wisewomen, experienced in the natural and the supernatural. I would have to trust their assessment.

"So to recap: I have to conjure the demon I told you about," I said, "and try to wrest control away from Renee and Kyle, assuming they're the ones who have called on him."

"Alcatraz was one point on a triangle of defense made up of Fort Point in San Francisco and Lime Point here in Marin," said Viv. "Use that triangle power to piggyback on your Solomon's Triangle."

The table seemed to tilt, and for a brief second I wondered whether that second shot of tequila had been one shot too many. But then I realized that this was yet another "little temblor," as Bronwyn called them. Could Caroline be right, that the Big One was coming to San Francisco? If so, the death and destruction of the Festival of Felons wouldn't be confined to the island of Alcatraz. The city of San Francisco, the entire Bay Area, would be devastated.

"The only safe way to conjure is to ring the island with salt," Winona was saying.

"The entire island?" I asked.

She nodded.

"It's twenty-two acres," I said. "I just don't see how it's possible. And part of it is inaccessible, it's a bird sanctuary. . . ."

"There are no birds there now," Nan pointed out. "They've all flown away."

I returned to the Haight and spent the afternoon at Aunt Cora's Closet with Maya and Bronwyn. I helped a mother and daughter to find coordinated outfits for a baby shower they were attending this weekend, and then had fun picking out dresses for a college student who was petite enough to fit into some of our smallest ensembles. I pressed and hung up some new inventory, replaced the herbal sachets I hung on the rods to keep the garments fresh, and then went through the receipts from the past week. All felt normal and easy, even a bit tedious.

It was heaven.

That evening I caught a glimpse of myself in the mirror I had placed precisely opposite my apartment door to repel bad spirits. I still wore the bright paper flower garland Iris had given me, but otherwise I looked haggard. There were bags under my eyes, and I looked wan. No surprise there; I hadn't slept well lately. There had been no more vivid nightmares, thank the goddess, but I was burdened with worry about Renee and Sailor and Elena and now the Big One that threatened to destroy all of San Francisco.

What a mess. As they'd say back in Jarod: *I got my ox in a ditch this time.*

And it was one heck of a ditch. All the more reason to get to work. I squared my shoulders, lifted my chin, and focused on completing the second day of the separation spell for Sailor's aunt Renna.

On this fourth night of the MoonWish spell, I put out a small pumpkin, cinnamon bark, three lemons, a coconut, and Goldschläger liqueur, then burned two sticks of precious Japanese agarwood incense. Tomorrow would be the final night of the spell—the blood sacrifice night—and after that was the full moon. And the Festival of Felons.

There was no way to avoid it any longer. I sat at my kitchen table, opened my old red-leather-bound Book of Shadows, and looked up: *blood sacrifice.*

The list of popular sacrifices was long: a chicken, a dove, a pigeon, a quail—really any feathered creature.

No vermin, since the death of a rat or a mouse wasn't considered a sacrifice as such. *Tell that to those who kept them as pets*, I thought to myself. I read on: a bat, a squirrel, a dog or a cat; a sheep, a cow, a steer. Livestock was a big category.

Back in the day, sacrificing a farm animal might mean your own family would face hunger. That was a true sacrifice. But in today's day and age?

Aidan said a blood sacrifice was necessary, Graciela and her coven said it was necessary, and my Book of Shadows said it was necessary.

But . . . *was* it necessary?

I was a modern witch. Could I update some of the traditional ways? Could magic modernize and change with the times, just like everything else?

I cast an eye around my apartment, trying to imagine what would be hard to part with. The only valuable thing I owned—monetarily speaking—was the crystal ball Graciela had gifted to me when I left my hometown in Texas. The cloudy, gleaming crystal sat upon a base of gold filigree, encrusted with jewels.

But the truth was, offering the crystal ball wouldn't really be a sacrifice for me. I'd never learned how to "see" any visions with it and had often been tempted to throw it out the window when frustrated by my lack of success.

A true sacrifice meant giving up something you loved.

I didn't have a lot of things I loved other than my friends, the Haight, my life in San Francisco. I loved Oscar and Sailor and Selena, Bronwyn and Maya and Conrad, my mother and Graciela. But I wasn't about to give up any one of them. Not even for the promise of controlling a demon.

My eyes fell on the old oven mitt my mother had

sewn. It wouldn't be attractive to anyone except me, but it would be a sacrifice to give it up. Still, the oven mitt wouldn't be enough. What about the trousseau Maggie was sewing for me, with a little bit of well-intentioned knot magic and love in every stitch? The maternal love I had yearned for, for so long?

Could I bring myself to give up such a thing?

As I pondered, I heard the sound of heavy boots on wooden stairs.

Sailor.

I met him at the door.

"Hi," I said, feeling strangely shy.

"Hi," he responded. Our gaze held for a long moment. "May I come in?"

"Of *course* you can come in." I turned away, at my wit's end. "Land sakes."

"Come here." He pulled me into his arms. We hugged for a long moment; I closed my eyes, rested my head on his chest, and reveled in his scent.

"I like your garland," Sailor whispered. "You look like a fairy queen."

"I'm glad you're here," I said.

"Me, too," Sailor said as we moved into the kitchen. He set the bottle of wine he had brought on the counter. "Before we get into things, do you know where Aidan is? He seems to have gone missing."

"What do you mean, he's gone missing?"

"He's not here. He's gone. And no one knows where he is. Hence, he's gone missing."

"But that's not unusual for Aidan, is it? He's disappeared before," I said, taking wineglasses from the cupboard and a corkscrew from the drawer. "In fact, several times in my recent memory."

"He's always been careful about finishing business

before he leaves. He didn't do that this time. Something's wrong," Sailor said, looking worried.

"You don't even like Aidan."

"No, I don't, and I would be happy to see him leave town once and for all." Sailor opened the bottle to let the wine breathe. "But not like this. When's the last time you had contact with him?"

"Last night, as a matter of fact. Right before he left for an appointment with you and 'Amanda.'" I couldn't help putting a spin on his ex-wife's name.

"He never showed."

My heart sank, not because Aidan had missed a meeting—the man had a flaky side—but because Sailor had broken a date with me to be with Amanda. Could I have been so wrong about him? Did Sailor still have feelings for his ex-wife?

"Aidan's been getting weaker," Sailor continued. "I know you've felt it. I think a *vila* has been following him."

"I thought *you* had a *vila* following you."

"Who told you that?"

"Your aunt Renna."

"When was this? When did you see Renna?"

"A while back, remember? She wanted me to find the charm you used to remain independent from her and Aidan."

"I remember."

"But I also saw her yesterday."

"What? Why?"

"You know very well why."

A muscle worked in his jaw. Sailor's heavy five-o'clock shadow made me want to reach up and touch his face, feel his whiskers tickle my palm. Any other time, I would have done so. How had things become so strained between us?

"She's doing much better, by the way. I'm surprised Eric didn't mention it."

"I've been a little busy lately," Sailor said, not meeting my eyes. "What happened with Renna?"

"She told me Amanda is your 'queen.'"

He let out a harsh laugh. "That's overstating the case just a tad."

I didn't want to ask—but I had to know the truth. "What does that mean? Do you still love her?"

"Of course I do."

"You—what?" I felt my heart pounding and a sick despair in the pit of my stomach.

He ran a hand over his face in a gesture both exasperated and weary. "It's not what you think, Lily."

"Really? Seems pretty straightforward to me. You love her."

"No, no—not like that. I love her like a brother."

"Oh, *please*," I said, angry now. "How gullible do you think I am? If Amanda reminds you of a sister, then you have some very odd ideas about sisters."

"I'm not explaining this well," Sailor said, growing calm. "You've never been involved in a serious romantic relationship, Lily, so maybe it's hard to understand. I loved Amanda once, and I will always care for her. But at this point those feelings are . . . familial, for lack of a better word."

"What else?" I asked, trying to keep a rein on my emotions. "You're holding something back."

He gazed at me, then looked away. "You're right, there is something else. I haven't wanted to tell you this because I was hoping I could resolve it, make it go away so it wouldn't worry you. But . . ."

"Land sakes, Sailor! Just spit it out before I have a coronary."

"Amanda and I aren't divorced."

"Excuse me?"

"The legal papers weren't properly filed. Amanda told me she had taken care of everything, and at the time I was so anxious to get away that I didn't follow up."

"So . . . you're still married."

"Just technically."

"That's kind of a big technicality, don't you think?"

"It doesn't have to be. I had a lawyer draw up new papers, and Amanda and I have signed them. We were supposed to meet with Aidan last night in the hopes that he could expedite things—he has some pull in this town. But in any case, all the *i*'s have been dotted and all the *t*'s have been crossed this time, I made sure of it. Without Aidan's help the divorce won't be official for six months, but it will happen, and then you and I can officially be married."

Relief surged through me. "So you still want to marry me?"

"If you'll have me," he said, his voice quiet. "I realize I should have told you sooner, Lily, but I was . . ."

"What?"

He shrugged, ran a hand over his chin, and blew out a long breath. "To tell the truth, I was . . . afraid."

"Afraid of what?"

"That you wouldn't understand. That you wouldn't wait. After everything that's happened, what we've been through, I wouldn't have blamed you if you'd had enough. I wouldn't have been able to bear it if you didn't want me anymore."

"There's nothing I want more."

Relief washed over his face and my heart leapt.

"Besides," I said, "Bronwyn hasn't received her certification, either, so the handfasting won't be legal in the eyes of the state, anyway."

"But more than official in my eyes," he said softly.

"I'm yours, body and soul, Lily. May the goddess help you."

I laughed, Sailor smiled, and we held each other tight.

"Anyway, it could be worse," Sailor murmured. "Amanda remarried a couple of years ago, so she's officially a bigamist."

I turned into his chest to stifle my laugh. "Lord, what fools we mortals be."

Sailor kissed my hair and quoted: "'And I serve the fairy queen, To dew her orbs upon the green.'"

"That sounds a little bit dirty," I said, pulling back and looking at him askance.

Sailor reared back. "It's not *dirty*; it's also from *A Midsummer Night's Dream*. It's about the fairy circle. Anyway, you started it with the Shakespeare quotes."

I smiled. "I know, I know; that's one of Maya's favorite scenes. Doesn't it go on to say something about the fairy queen crowning him with flowers and making him all her joy?"

"I believe it does."

I placed my garland upon his head.

"You expect me to wear this?"

"You look fabulous. A true fairy prince." He smiled but looked uncertain. "I'm serious. It suits you. You should wear a garland for our handfasting. So just to be clear: This divorce—or more particularly, this *lack* of divorce—is why you've been sneaking around lately?"

"I haven't been 'sneaking around,'" he protested. "I've been dealing with clients and trying to solidify our alliances in case we have to confront whatever's on the horizon with Renee-the-cupcake-lady. All the omens point toward something ratcheting up in the astral plane."

I nodded. "I think the demon we first met at the School of Fine Arts has been summoned, perhaps to serve Renee's *coincidentia oppositorum*, so they can take over."

"Who has Renee found to be her opposite?"

"I'm not sure . . . but I think it might be Kyle Cheney."

"*The* Kyle Cheney? The rich computer guy?"

I nodded. "He invested in Renee's cupcake company, and he's employing a bunch of young and inexperienced people to work as 'security guards.' He's also disappeared recently. I think the Festival of Felons might turn into some sort of terrible demonic sacrifice."

"Have you told Carlos?"

"I intend to, but at the moment I'm not sure how to explain it, plus I'm still trying to figure it all out. Then, too, I have two more nights until the spell is complete and I'll be strong enough to go up against the demon without losing my soul."

"Good point. The festival is in two nights, isn't it?"

"It's also the full moon."

"Time to plan and prepare."

I nodded. "So, not to change the subject or anything, but did you invite Amanda to the handfasting?"

Sailor looked surprised. "Why would I do that?"

I shrugged. "If she's important to you . . ."

"She was important to me, of course she was," he said. "But I was a different person then, Lily. I could never be that man again. I'm *your* man now, lock, stock, and barrel."

"Well, then, my man, it's time we had that talk we keep talking about."

I filled our wineglasses, and we went out to the terrace to enjoy the fresh summer evening and the moonlight as we spoke about children, how we would share my small apartment without driving each other and

Oscar crazy, how we would mingle our finances. Some of it was hard, a lot of it was awkward, but all of it was necessary.

Two glasses of wine later, Sailor said: "So, have we covered everything?"

"I'm sure we've missed a few things, but I feel like we got to the important stuff. Oh! One more item."

"Shoot."

"What's your middle name?"

"Zeus."

"Zeus? Your parents named you 'Sailor Zeus'?"

"What can I say? Maybe they didn't like me very much."

I grinned. "I love it. I might have chosen Eros, the Greek god of love instead, but I'll take it."

"Not sure the name 'Eros' works well in the twenty-first century."

"Oh, right—unlike *Zeus*," I teased. "Actually, there's one more thing we need to discuss: I asked Carlos if he would stand up with you at the handfasting. I know I should have talked to you about it first, but—"

Sailor cut me off with a kiss. "I think it's a great idea. Invite whomever you want. Charles the Charlatan, Amanda the Bigamist and her current husband, all of Conrad's gutter punk friends, assorted gobgoyles of Oscar's acquaintance—I don't care." His voice dropped, husky with emotion. "As long as I'm marrying you, I'll be the happiest man alive."

I kissed him back, and there was no more talking.

Chapter 24

The next morning I awoke to a commotion in the shop and slipped downstairs to find the Victorian petticoat Sitri had tossed to me dancing to a ghostly tune emanating from a supposedly nonfunctioning music box. This had happened once before, the first time I brought clothes from the School of Fine Arts into Aunt Cora's Closet.

No doubt about it at this point, Sitri was at play.

Before opening the store later this morning, when I cast my usual spell over Aunt Cora's Closet for protection, I would cleanse widdershins thrice with saltwater. A little extra was called for in light of what was going on. And I would burn that petticoat.

But for now, I let the frilly chemise spin and twirl, not wanting to waste my energy.

Upstairs, I found that Sailor was up and had already put on coffee. After a good-morning kiss, I asked:

"So you think Aidan is truly missing?" I asked. "Not just out of town for a few days?"

"Like I said, he drops out of touch from time to time, but he always puts someone in charge or leaves word of how to reach him. He did neither this time."

"As a matter of fact, he mentioned to me last night that he would need to take a leave of absence, but he gave no indication his departure would be imminent. Last I heard he was on his way to meet with you and Amanda."

"I did have a vision last night, of a red rose."

"Isn't a red rose the symbol of romantic love?"

"It can be—so maybe it came to me because I was with you. But it's also related to blood, and sacrifice. Is Oscar around?"

"His nest is empty," I said. "I haven't seen him since . . . actually, not since night before last, now that I think of it. That's not unusual, though. He's been searching for his mother, so he's gone a lot these days— or nights, to be precise."

"When you see him, ask if he knows how to get in touch with Aidan."

"Of course. In the meantime, what can we do?"

"I've tried to divine him, and so has Patience. But Aidan's too well guarded—it's sort of like you. I can't read you, even when I try."

"You often seem to know if I'm in danger," I pointed out.

"In times of great stress I feel you calling for me, but even then not always. If I'm in a trance, for example, I won't feel it. I had no clue about what you and Carlos went through on Alcatraz the other day until you told me."

Guilt passed over his handsome features.

"You can hardly keep tabs on me twenty-four/seven, Sailor. I wouldn't want you to, even if you could. You and I will never be strangers to danger. I think that's part of what we'll have to get used to, both of us."

He nodded. "I know. You're right. I just . . . I don't like it."

I smiled. "I'm not wild about it, myself. I'm guessing that's part of the challenge of a relationship, to hold on to each other without holding each other back."

"Sounds like somebody's been reading self-help books on how to build a lasting marriage."

"Actually, I think I saw it on a T-shirt down by Fisherman's Wharf," I said with a laugh. "But who says great wisdom can't come from a T-shirt?"

Sailor went off to check on his aunt Renna and to discuss the family's part in the upcoming battle, and to continue his search for Aidan.

I dealt with the petticoat and cleansed the store, and when Bronwyn and Maya arrived I gave them a brief rundown of what I feared would happen the day after tomorrow, at the Festival of Felons.

"That sounds . . . really bad," said Maya.

"Lily, is there anything we can do?" asked Bronwyn.

"Maybe leave town, in case I fail?" I said. It was a feeble attempt at a joke, but as soon as I said it, I realized it contained a large dose of truth. I feared failing and letting down my friends, my community, my people. There was no way to evacuate the entire city, even if I could somehow convince the authorities of the looming threat. But I wanted the people I loved to be safe, at the very least. "Seriously, do you think you could take your families and get out of town?"

"Oh, my. Are you sure we can't be of help?" Bronwyn asked. "I could call the Welcome coven together. . . ."

"This is beyond the capabilities of the Welcome coven," I said. "Though I certainly appreciate the offer. It's going to be . . . bad. But I won't be alone, we have a lot of allies."

Just then the bell tinkled over the front door as Carlos strode in.

"How's Elena?" Maya asked.

"She's doing much better, thank you. She seemed to turn a corner last night and seems much more herself."

"I'm so glad," said Maya. "Please give her my best."

"I will, thanks," said Carlos. "Lily, do you have a moment?"

"Of course." I led the way into the back room and we took seats at the table.

"I couldn't get you copies of Perry's letters," Carlos said. "At least not yet. It took a while to get the full story, but the archivist who found the letters did, in fact, read them, and scanned them into the computer."

"And?"

"They're keeping them on the down-low for the moment. According to the letters, not only did Ray Perry allege abuse at the hands of some of the guards, but he claimed they were performing rites in the dungeon in an effort to call a demon."

I nodded.

"You don't seem surprised," Carlos said. "Is this what you suspected?"

"It's what I feared. Did the letters refer to any of the guards by name?"

He referred to the notebook he kept in his pocket. "Stephens, Krewson, Przybyszewski, Mylon, Gordon. Those names mean anything to you?"

I nodded. "Hold on a second."

I ran upstairs and brought down the framed photograph of Ned Przybyszewski in his guard uniform I had found in Emmy Lou Archer's attic, along with the bundle of photos that had been at the bottom of the box.

"This is Ned Przybyszewski," I said, handing Carlos the framed photo. "Maya found the inmate uniform—the shirt that started all of this—in the attic of his former home."

"So he was in on whatever this was. Ray Perry was killed—"

"Sacrificed."

"And the guards made up the story about him escaping to cover it up."

"I think so."

Carlos flipped through the photos. "Do these tell you anything?"

"That scrap of material they're wrapped in is made of the same chambray as the prisoners' uniforms. And the stains look like—and feel like—blood."

Carlos met my eyes. "I don't know if the DNA's still viable at this point, and even if it is, we don't have Perry's DNA to compare it to."

I nodded. Carlos turned his attention to the photos.

"These look like photos of the cellblocks and the prison grounds," I said. "I plan to give them to the Alcatraz archive; but thought you'd like to see them first. Maybe you'll spot a clue of some sort."

He paused and studied the photos, setting one aside. Then he flipped one toward me so I could see it. It showed several prison guards standing with a half-dozen prisoners.

"You suppose these are some of our alleged abusive guards?"

I took it from him. The faces were hard to make out, but I thought I recognized one of the men.

"Wait—did you say 'Gordon' was the name of one of the guards Ray Perry mentioned?"

"Yep."

"I wonder . . . do you remember a volunteer we spoke to out on Alcatraz, a man named Ralph Gordon? He was a guard at the prison right before it closed. He looks a lot like this guy, here—try to imagine this fellow with a big white mustache."

Carlos peered closely at the picture. "I do see a resemblance, but I don't see how that could be the same man. Perry was said to have 'escaped' in the '30s, right? And these photos are from that era. Unless Ralph Gordon's discovered the secret to eternal youth, this couldn't possibly be him."

"Maybe it's just a coincidence; it's hard to see these faces clearly. Except . . ."

"What?"

"Those in thrall to a demon often appear to be much younger than they are. And those that try to pull away from the demon tend to die unnaturally early."

I looked closer. There was one very good-looking man in the group, a real "historical hottie," to use Bronwyn's term. I almost pointed him out to Carlos, but what I was thinking seemed too far-fetched, even for me.

"So what does this tell us?" Carlos asked.

"I think Alcatraz has been a cursed island for a very long time. It would make sense that a demon might be drawn to it. It might even have been there since the beginning of creation." I thought of the Feather People Guzmán told me about. "Anyway, if the guards were linked to the demon and offered him a blood sacrifice, it would strengthen his presence greatly. What's more, I think Renee Baker, the cupcake lady, and Kyle Cheney have joined forces to stage a supernatural showdown on Alcatraz on the night of the Festival of Felons."

Carlos was silent for a long moment.

"I m-might be wrong," I stammered. "I *hope* I'm wrong."

"But you don't think you're wrong."

I shook my head.

"Why Kyle Cheney?" Carlos mused. "The man already has more money than God, and he has a reputation as a philanthropist. Why would he get involved with something like this?"

"Maybe that's how he became so rich in the first place? I don't know the answer. A lot of people seek money and power, and some are willing to do anything for it, even throwing in with a demon. Think about it— Cheney has access to all kinds of folks who trust him and who rely on him. They might well do a lot for him."

I thought about the security guards Aidan and I met at Renee's shop the other day. They were open and sweet and not fully in control of themselves. They would be easy prey for a demon's minions. Could they—or others like them—have been "Smith" and "Jones"? Did they carry out Cheney's dirty work?

"Is there any way you can shut down the Festival of Felons?" I asked.

"That's a pretty big order. It's sold out. And what am I supposed to say, that there's a demon on the rise on Alcatraz?"

"Could you say you received a terrorist threat or something like that?"

"I won't lie, Lily."

"I know, I'm sorry. Is there anything you can do?"

He blew out a long breath and stood. "Let me make some phone calls. I can say that I've heard unsubstantiated rumors of impending acts of violence, something along those lines. But the feds are still in charge out there, so I'm not sure how much pull I have."

"It's worth a try. Anyway, I'll be there, along with

some other allies, so with luck we'll be able to quash whatever's developing. I hope."

"I hope so, too." His dark gaze held mine for a long moment. "Be sure to stay safe, Lily. This whole thing sounds completely outlandish, but even *I* felt something out on that island, in that dungeon. Something unnatural. I didn't like it."

"You and me both. Also, you might want to get your family out of town for the weekend. Just in case. It's possible that . . . the city might be hit by an earthquake. A big one. Unless I can stop it."

He gazed at me for a long moment, then nodded. "Will you be okay?"

I smiled. "Of course I will. I've got this, no problem."

My words sounded surprisingly steady, but I wasn't fooling either of us.

After Carlos left, I made Maya and Bronwyn promise me that they would get out of town tomorrow night. They agreed to go stay with Calypso and started making calls to warn our other friends.

Tonight would be the final night of the preparatory MoonWish spell, and tomorrow night was the Festival of Felons.

I called my friend Hervé Le Mansec, who assured me that the voodoo practitioners were in the loop. They had already bought their tickets to the Festival of Felons and would have my back. I got the same response from Selena's grandmother Ursula about her *botánica* network, and the Feris and other magical communities. We had different skills, distinct spirit guides, disparate gods, sometimes clashing belief systems . . . and yet we would come together with one goal: to stop Sitri and those in his thrall from harming millions of innocents.

As I hung up the phone I realized: I hadn't bought a ticket for the festival, which was now sold out. How was I supposed to get to Alcatraz?

Well, I'd figure that out at some point. At the moment I had a more pressing concern: a proper sacrifice for the final night of the MoonWish spell. I headed to Calypso's house, to have a chat with my mother about the trousseau she had so lovingly made for me.

I hated to sacrifice it. I could only hope she would understand why.

Chapter 25

On the way back from Calypso's house, I stopped in Sausalito in search of Captain Buddy and found him mucking about his boat. He seemed pleased to see me.

"I have a favor to ask," I said. "A huge favor."

"Shoot," he replied.

"I need someone to ferry me and a few friends to Alcatraz Island tomorrow night. There will be about fifteen of us in all."

"It's against the law, you know," he said, sounding virtuous.

"I thought you said you do it all the time."

"Well, now, that's true enough," he said. "But that's before I knew I could get arrested for it."

He seemed to hesitate, so I waited.

"Will Pepper be coming, too?" he asked.

"Oh, yes. Pepper will be there. Wouldn't miss it for the world."

"In that case, I'm at your disposal," he said with a wink.

Something occurred to me. "Captain Buddy, you didn't happen to take a couple of men and a woman out there four days ago?"

"I wouldn't swear as to the day, exactly, but a couple of days ago I did take a trio out there. It was a little odd because it was only late morning, but the woman was drunk as a skunk, could hardly even stand. Her friends said they'd gone to a champagne brunch for her birthday."

"What did the men look like?"

He shrugged. "Young, in their twenties. Sort of non-descript, brown hair, nothing special."

"Did they say why they were going out to Alcatraz?"

"Let's see," Buddy said, scratching his whiskers. "Said something about the woman being a park service ranger who was stationed out there, so they were taking her back. Why they thought that would be a good idea, considering the state she was in, is beyond me, but people are strange."

"That they are." I sighed.

"Anyway, I'll be happy to take you and your friends tomorrow if you put in a good word for me with that lovely lady friend of yours, Miss Pepper."

I agreed, and we settled on a price and a time for our rendezvous.

My next stop was the wax museum. I needed my lachrymatory salts for tomorrow night. If demonic activity and the *coincidentia oppositorum* leading up to the Big One didn't call for the nuclear option, I didn't know what did.

As was her wont, Clarinda yelled as I sailed past the ticket booth. As was my wont, I ignored her.

Noctemus stared down at me from the ledge over her master's closed office door. I had been hoping to find Aidan there, both to be assured that he was all right and to ask him to undo the Etruscan spell safeguarding my lachrymatory salts. I should have asked him before, but Aidan had always seemed so much a part of things—and so in control—that I couldn't imagine him gone, as in *actually* gone.

Slowly, I reached out to open the door, hoping Noctemus didn't think it was her duty to keep me out.

Instead, she leapt gracefully to the floor and slipped inside as soon as the door was ajar.

Same office, same library, same late Victorian bordello furnishings. No Aidan.

Now what?

Noctemus was now perched on a bookshelf, delicately licking her little paw.

"I need help," I said, trying to convey what I needed through intuition. "Aidan said you would help me."

She stared at me with wide, unblinking blue eyes.

"Please," I continued. "I need my lachrymatory salts. They might help me save San Francisco, and, perhaps, your master."

The cat languidly moved to the middle of the shelf, which contained a series of grimoires of different cultures from across the globe. I came close and saw what looked like a bookmark of yellowed parchment stuck in one volume.

I pulled it out and read: "*Qui affecto protego, mixtisque iubas serpentibus.*"

Was this the first line of a spell?

Noctemus had leapt down and was now pacing back and forth in front of a wooden side table. I opened the table's small drawer and found yet another piece of parchment, with another line in Latin: *et posteris meis stirpiqu.*

The cat then pawed at a red velvet cushion on the

couch. I lifted it to find still another note. For the next several moments Noctemus led me on a scavenger hunt through Aidan's office, where I found notes hidden under the carpet, in a desk drawer, under the telephone, and behind the velvet drapes.

I was careful to keep the notes in the order in which Noctemus had showed them to me. For a spell to perform properly, the lines must be recited in the correct sequence. Get the order wrong and not only would the desired spell not work, but one ran the risk of conjuring something else entirely.

"Is that all?" I asked Noctemus, who sat in the precise middle of the office, staring at me.

She blinked.

"Because if there are more, now's the time to speak," I said.

I could have sworn Noctemus rolled her eyes at me.

"Then, thank you," I said, and the cat leapt onto a leather office chair and curled up to take a nap.

I entered Aidan's special octagon room and closed the door. I faced the sealed niche that contained my lachrymatory and read the spell from the notes as best I could, in the proper order. I stumbled over the words— I wasn't well versed in Latin—but my intent was clear, and I was focused.

There was yet another rumble as the room rocked.

I repeated the spell thrice. The niche in the wall sprung open, revealing the diminutive slender glass bottle, within which tinkled tiny salts, the residue of my teenage tears.

The last tears I had ever shed.

I wrapped the lachrymatory in a silk scarf I found on Aidan's chair and placed it carefully in my backpack.

Then I grabbed the Satchel, which contained the

names and contact information of everyone who owed
Aidan a favor. I sat at his desk, picked up his phone,
and started dialing.

An hour later, I'd called in several of Aidan's markers and asked each person to contact another five, like
in a phone tree. I hung up secure in the fact that I had
magical folks lined up for tomorrow night.

Finally, I sat back in his chair. It felt surprisingly
comfortable, easy to be here. Maybe Aidan was right.
Maybe I was ready to fill his shoes, to lead the local
magical community.

Unless, of course, everything came crashing down—
quite literally—tomorrow night. Was this all related to
an unleashing of negative power previously held in
check by Aidan?

More on point, where had Aidan gone? Sailor was
right—this was different from his usual disappear-
ances. I thought of the red rose Aidan had picked at
Renee's house and put in his buttonhole. Had it led
Renee's minions to him? The gesture had seemed at
the time very out of character for a warlock as knowl-
edgeable as Aidan to embrace something belonging to
an enemy. Had he done it on purpose?

I noticed the grimoire that still sat atop Aidan's
desk and flipped it open to the section on Sitri.

Sitri was known to *appeareth at first with a Leopard's head and the Wings of a Gryphon, but after the
command of the Master of the Exorcism he putteth on
Human shape, and that very beautiful.*

If Albright's death was a blood sacrifice to conjure
Sitri, then could the Master of Exorcism—whoever that
had been—have asked Sitri to assume a human form?
A beautiful human form?

*Some think Sitri and Egyptian deity Set, a god of
chaos and darkness, are one and the same.* Demons

respect no national boundaries. And they are able to take many forms and through their minions to be in many places at one time.

Maybe it wasn't Kyle at all.

When I returned to my apartment with my trousseau, Oscar was taking a baking sheet of Tater Tots out of the oven.

"Where have you been?" we asked each other in unison.

"You don't usually have trouble finding me," I said, placing the beloved trousseau on the coffee table.

"There's something wonky going on lately," said Oscar, setting the baking tray on the stove and taking off the oven mitt. "Astral plane is all screwed up. I've been looking for Aidan, and I *never* have a problem finding *him*. To be honest, mistress, I'm worried."

He sat at the kitchen table with a plate piled high with steaming Tater Tots and dipped one into a pool of ketchup.

"Not too worried to eat, I see," I said.

"Sorry?"

"Never mind." I took a seat opposite him and munched on a Tater Tot.

"Good?" he asked.

I nodded. "Oscar, let me ask you something. The other day, Renna said something that's been bothering me ever since."

"Ranch!" Oscar said, and hopped up to get the ranch dressing from the fridge. He added a dollop to his plate, next to the ketchup. "Best of both worlds. So what'd Renna say?"

"'You can't see the forest for the trees.' She said it twice."

"Huh. Maybe she was a philosophy major. You know,

like if a tree falls in the forest and nobody's there to hear it, does it make a sound?"

"Yeah, not at all like that. Here's what I'm thinking: It always bothered me how the kidnappers knew Elena had the bundle. What if Forrest leaving the store was a signal?"

"You mean Forrest was in on it?"

"Maybe, maybe not. But it would explain that part of what happened."

Oscar dipped one end of a Tater Tot in ketchup, and the other in the ranch dressing, and chewed it with a happy grunt.

"Here's something else I've been wondering about: If they wanted the shirt, why didn't they just snatch the bag. Why kidnap Elena?"

"To get you out to Alcatraz, probably."

"You think?" I dredged another Tater Tot through the ketchup and popped it in my mouth. "But then why dump their van near Pier 39? Because apparently they took a boat from Sausalito, not Pier 33."

"Again, to get *you* out to Alcatraz. They took a boat from Sausalito so they wouldn't get caught, but left a clue near Alcatraz Landing so you'd know to go out there. If they left the van in Sausalito you wouldn't make the connection to Alcatraz."

I thought about what he was suggesting and ate another Tater Tot, and then another. Then I got up and brought the package of photographs to the table and flipped through them.

One of the guards in a photograph, standing next to the man who looked like Ralph Gordon, looked a lot like Seth Barbagelata. Seth . . . as in Set? Which was another name for Sitri?

Seth was very beautiful. And charming. Was he also deadly?

"Is it possible that Kyle Cheney wasn't the master-mind, after all? That it was Kyle's assistant, Seth?" I asked aloud, while munching on another Tater Tot. As a trusted employee Seth would know how to access Cheney's resources without leaving any way to trace it back to him. And if Seth was Sitri come to human life, and the other half of Renee's *coincidentia opposito-rum*, he had to be stopped, no matter the sacrifice.

I looked at Oscar, who was gazing at me with a grave expression, as if sensing my concern.

"Mistress?"

"Yes, Oscar?"

"At this rate, we're gonna need some more Tater Tots."

Chapter 26

The day of the Festival of Felons arrived cloaked in a thick blanket of fog that never burned off.

Long ago, that parrot in a Hong Kong bar had advised me to go to San Francisco, but to be sure to "mark the fog." Normally we magical folks love the mystical-seeming mist; it evens out the light and highlights the extraordinary while obscuring the ordinary. But today the air was cold and soggy, the chill cutting through clothing and sinking into one's bones.

Carlos had not succeeded in convincing the feds to shut down the Festival of Felons, which had begun with great fanfare that morning, with a variety of events scheduled all day long. The daytime events didn't concern me. The showdown I was dreading would not begin until tonight's full moon rose over the island.

I had used the daylight hours to review the plan—such as it was—with my magical allies, and to gather the supplies I needed. The little map of Alcatraz which I had picked up a few days ago from Ralph Gordon was by now dog-eared and covered in notations, with arrows indicating who would be where and when, going in every direction, as if drawn by an insane general or football coach.

Last night's sacrifice of the trousseau had been exquisitely painful but also remarkably effective. After sprinkling several drops of my own blood on the beautiful embroidered linens, I burned them on my terrace while chanting, Oscar at my side. Almost immediately I felt the MoonWish spell come to fruition, the conduits opening, and a surge of strength I'd never experienced before.

When I approached my mother with my plan for the trousseau she had labored over, she had once again surprised me by waving off my concerns. "Oh, my dear girl. If any part of me can help to keep any part of you safe, don't you know I'd jump at the chance? There's plenty more where that came from, after all, and besides—I think I'm finally getting the hang of this knot magic." She even offered to accompany me to Alcatraz, but eventually agreed to stay in Bolinas with Calypso. Bronwyn, Maya, and their assorted loved ones would join them there, out of harm's way.

I begged Oscar to promise to stay with them, to protect them no matter what. If things didn't go well out on Alcatraz, I wouldn't put it past Renee to go after them—and Oscar—once she'd gotten rid of me.

Of course Oscar wanted to come with us to Alcatraz, but I played the mistress-familiar card, even though we really didn't have that kind of relationship. But if anything happened to Bronwyn and Maya, I wouldn't be able to live with myself. And if anything happened to Oscar . . . I couldn't even think about it.

"Anyway, you still need to finish negotiations with the woods folk," I told him. "If all goes as planned we'll meet you there after, and we can work out the honey-moon plans with Sailor."

"That's a big *if*, mistress," said Oscar. But he agreed, with reluctance.

I fought against taking Selena with us for the show-down, but the coven was adamant that we needed her powers to join with ours, so I had a long talk with Sele-na's grandmother. Ursula listened carefully, consulted her divining sticks, and agreed with the coven: Selena's magic was needed on Alcatraz. I bowed down to the wisdom of grandmothers and promptly weighed the poor girl down with so many protective amulets and talismans that she could barely move.

At the appointed hour, Selena, Graciela's coven, and I met Captain Buddy at the Sausalito yacht harbor for the trip to the island. He had spruced himself up and reeked of Old Spice aftershave, and showed a great deal of solicitousness while helping Pepper onto his boat.

The sun was going down, its last rays struggling to penetrate the wall of fog that encased us. My senses took in the chill in the air, the sound of water lapping at the boat, the steady churning of the engine. In the distance a foghorn blew intermittently, its doleful bellow high-lighting the danger awaiting us. As we got closer we heard the sounds of a raucous party—music, laughter, the occasional high-spirited shout—and gradually the shape of Alcatraz emerged from the fog, looming over us. Captain Buddy piloted the boat over to an old dock on a rocky stretch of the now-abandoned bird sanctu-ary. As Pepper had pointed out, the birds had flown away.

With a sudden, visceral jolt I remembered my night-mare, the harbinger of all that had happened.

Dead Man's Current, pulling at my legs.

We disembarked—which took a while given the rocky shore, the bobbing boat, and thirteen elderly passengers. If I'd had my way, the women would have stayed behind at Calypso's safe haven, but the coven had adamantly refused. "Why do you think we came all the way here, *m'ija*? *Que ridículo*," was Graciela's only reply.

Selena had spent most of today with the coven, casting and talking and learning, and though her usual quiet self, she was also uncharacteristically helpful. Like me, she wore Keds and carried a backpack full of magical supplies slung over one shoulder.

The island thrummed malevolently beneath our feet and the party sounds intensified as we made our way along the Agave Trail and up West Road toward the ruins of the warden's house. As I observed the throngs of partygoers, I spied Hervé and other voodoo practitioners setting up on the south shore. In the brush, away from the crowds, a coven of Feris was drawing down the moon. As the crowd shifted and parted, I spotted other familiar faces, members of magical groups with whom we were allied.

We weren't doing this alone.

Party tents had been pitched in front of the administration building and the main prison cellblocks, and women and men—and more than a few children— milled about, imbibing soft drinks and not-so-soft drinks, eating hot dogs, running in and out of the buildings and around the grounds. A band had set up not far from the warden's house, as if to provide a musical score for the rotating beam and periodic foghorn of the lighthouse just behind it. People were laughing, dancing, and more than a few were enjoying brightly frosted cupcakes.

Heavy fog obscured the Golden Gate Bridge, the

lights of San Francisco, and even the bay itself, making it easy to believe that this island, here and now, was all that existed in the world.

Suddenly there was a low bass vibration and a loud rumble as a small temblor shook the island. When it passed, the crowd cheered and yelled as though the earthquake were part of the evening's entertainment.

I led our group through the main cellblock and rendezvoused as planned with Patience and Sailor in the dining hall. Still wearing the crown of paper flowers I had given him, Sailor gave me a kiss and a long hug and then placed the garland upon my head. No words were necessary; his eyes said everything.

Patience lifted one eyebrow and looked away.

"Everybody ready?" I asked. Nods all around. "Let's go."

We headed to the recreation yard on the southern D-Block. The rusting water tower—with its red graffiti—loomed high above us. Partygoers were everywhere—in the old showers, the cells, the dining room. There were twenty or so in the recreation yard as well, where our view was blocked by tall cement walls, topped with a cyclone fence and razor wire.

Graciela's coven remained at the top of the stairs, mumbling a spell.

Patience and Sailor descended the steps to the yard and began to dance.

They started slowly, but soon their movements became exuberant, wild; they stomped and clapped with abandon. Around them, mingling with the crowd, their Rom cousins joined in, clapping and singing and ululating.

A long time ago, in Andalucía, I watched a group of weary agricultural workers dancing flamenco like this, moving not with the polished technique of professional dancers on stage, but with utter passion. I remembered sitting in that cobblestone square, watching the whirling and singing, and thinking the dance was almost magical. This time, it truly was.

Sparks began to fly as their feet pounded the concrete ground. A swirl of white butterflies appeared and whirled around them, a sign of the woods folk joining their strength to ours.

Graciela nodded to Selena, who was standing with us on the platform at the top of the stairs. She tossed her shiny coins and *milagros* down upon the dancers, and as the metal pieces flipped and turned in the air they emitted tiny pinpoints of light that filled the courtyard and joined the sparks thrown up by the pounding of Sailor's and Patience's dancing feet. The lights mixed and swirled and spun, swiftly forming a great, glittering cone that covered the entire courtyard.

"The salts," Graciela said to me. "*Now.*"

I opened the stopper on my lachrymatory, shook the precious salts into the palm of my hand, and tossed them into the air. They mingled with the brine of the sea air to form a canopy that rose high over the island, expanding and pulsating to the rhythm of the dancers, until it burst and the salts fell back to earth, forming a ring around the entire island.

The crowd, thinking they were seeing a fireworks display, cheered.

"Run, *m'ija*," said Graciela in a fierce whisper. "Run!"

I ran.

Chapter 27

I flew as fast as my feet would carry me, back into the building, through the dining hall and the display area, to the entrance to the Spanish dungeon. Several people in bright blue T-shirts were screaming, running up the stairs, and pouring out into the corridor, pushing one another in their haste.

The last one out was Charles Gosnold. He was pale as the proverbial ghost.

"Lily!" he exclaimed, grabbing my arm. "Don't go down there! I'm serious. . . . It's not spirits, it's much worse than spirits."

"What is it?"

"I—" He shook his head and tried to drag me away from the stairs. "It's . . . there are people down there, and they . . . I can't even say. But there was blood."

"I have to go down, Charles. Get outside and keep your people away from the buildings."

"But—"

"*Go.*"

He hesitated another moment as though unsure whether to leave me, but then turned and ran. I noticed on the back of his commemorative tour T-shirt was a large graphic of a cupcake.

I turned back to the stairs and started down.

Whispers followed me, incessant reminders of the ghosts who roamed these halls. But what I feared was not spirits, but, as Charles had warned, something much worse.

Down in the bowels of Alcatraz, it was pitch-black. I pulled my Hand of Glory from my backpack and slung it around my neck. It illuminated the broad arched hallway and I walked as quietly as I could, feeling the thrumming vibrations, listening to the whispers, trusting in my witchy intuition.

Ray Perry appeared in front of me, just as before. The dark voids of his eyes remained fixed on me. He put his index finger to his mouth as though to mime "*shhhhh!*"

And then I heard it: chanting. Men's voices, intoning together.

It grew louder as I progressed down the corridor to where it ended at a T. I smelled incense, and herbs, and something much worse. Slowly, I peeked around the corner.

Hundreds of candles illuminated a gruesome scene: A circle of robed men stood around someone on a gurney. It was a ritual sacrifice. A human sacrifice.

I tried not to fixate on the prone man. I had to concentrate on the imminent threat in front of me: the chanting men.

One by one they turned to face me, lowering their hoods.

I recognized several street "friends" of Conrad's; the tall skinny redhead and four other nondescript scruffy almost-men, a few with facial piercings, two of whom I assumed must be Smith and Jones. Riggs, the man who had taken Carlos and me over by boat. Even Captain Buddy, whose friendly face had become flat and devoid of emotion. All in thrall to Sitri.

Ralph Gordon, the hale old man with the white mustache I had first met when trying to buy a ticket to this cursed island, stepped forward.

"It's good you're here," he said. "At last. They said you'd come to join us."

I nodded. "Where are Renee and Seth?"

"Stay here with us," said one of the young men.

"Yes, stay," said another.

Their words were slurred, as though drugged. Or perhaps they were simply drunk with the demon's power. I focused on Gordon; he appeared to be the ringleader, and the most cogent of the group.

"Have you been here since the beginning, then?" I asked him, wondering how to help the man in the center of the circle, wondering if it were even possible. He had lost a lot of blood, but I didn't sense death. Not yet. In fact, I felt something else, something familiar. . . .

"No, of course not. My father was, though. He started here at Alcatraz when the prison opened."

"So it's a family tradition."

He nodded. "You know, as a young man I never saw eye to eye with my father—he had some strange ways of looking at the world. But he passed away too early, and then I came to work here on Alcatraz in his stead. Guess some things are in the blood."

"In Cole Albright's blood?" I asked.

"Albright used the demon's help to escape and lived a full life, then came back to sacrifice himself. Good man. It should have worked better, but there was something off about the shirt. Renee said you probably mucked with it so it didn't carry all the vibrations it should have."

The earth rumbled under our feet. I was trying to remain cool in the face of human sacrifice, but temblors still threw me off-balance.

Ralph Gordon smiled. "Just a little shake. The Big One's on its way."

"Yes, about that . . . I need to speak with Renee and Seth. They'll want to speak to me—as you know, they've been trying to draw me out here to Alcatraz for days. That's why you kidnapped Elena."

"Dude," said one of the young men. "We didn't hurt her, or anything."

Two men had circled around behind me, and another two were armed with pistols. I started chanting, mumbling under my breath.

"Stop that," said Gordon, his eyes squinting with suspicion. "What are you up to? I thought you were here to join us. . . ."

"*Dude*," said one of the young men.

Piggybacking on the power from the blood sacrifice, and building with my chanting, my strength was mounting. I could feel Deliverance within me—I knew her now, could feel her fierce power. Where the Ashen Witch's presence felt like the softest wool shawl, the warm embrace of a mother figure, Deliverance's was an obsidian knife, ready to cut. It was slick as glass but tough as stone. The MoonWish spell helped keep me grounded, tethered to this earth.

The astral and physical planes were fusing.

But I was distracted and for an instant my intent wavered. I realized . . . the vibrations of the blood at my feet were very particular and very familiar. I knew them from somewhere. . . .

Aidan.

The man at the center of this ritual, the human sacrifice, was Aidan Rhodes.

I looked at the man on the gurney for the first time. His glamour was gone. Under the blood and grime, thick burn scars showed, shiny and painful-looking, on one side of his face, head, and neck.

And then I understood: Aidan had taken Renee's rose on purpose, had put himself in the position of sacrifice, knowing that his blood had a very special power, a unique quality that would allow him to transfer the power to a magical ally. To me.

I placed my hands on Aidan's chest. He was barely there, not far from death.

His eyes flickered open and he attempted a smile.

"*Go*," he said. "Don't waste the sacrifice. Use it. Use Sitri."

I gasped as he spoke Sitri's name aloud.

Just that quickly, I could hear the terrible, shrieking sound of the wind passing through Sitri's wings.

In a rage, I yanked my head in the direction of first one man circling behind me, and then the other, sending them flying into the wall. I held my arm out, pointed, and cursed the other men one after another, lowering my head as I mumbled in a smattering of English, Spanish, and Nahuatl as my grandmother had taught me—but now in fluent Latin as well, even though I wasn't aware I knew it.

The gun-wielding men yelped and dropped their weapons, shaking their hands in pain. The pistols clattered to the stone floor, glowing red with heat.

One after another the men shrieked, fell to the filthy ground, writhed. The skinny redhead tried to run, but I yanked my head and fixed him with my gaze, and he froze, fell to his knees, and screamed along with his colleagues.

Let them scream, said a voice in my head.

Enough, came another voice.

I came out of my trance with a jolt.

I could feel another deep, primordial rumble of the earth. I had to finish the job before the bigger quake arrived.

"Where is he? Where is Seth?" I demanded, standing over a beefy man with a spiral tattoo who was lying prone on the floor.

"Please don't hurt me!" he cried. "Make it stop!"

I glanced again at Aidan. They hadn't set out to kill him immediately; instead, they were taking their time. Sitri loved fear and pain—it fed him. They had been using medical instruments to torture him. *Antique* medical instruments.

I remembered Forrest saying that the only place more haunted than the dungeon was the hospital wing.

I hesitated, making eye contact with Aidan briefly before his periwinkle blue eyes flickered closed. Was it . . . could it be for the last time? My heart lurched, but I forced myself to concentrate on what I knew I had to do.

"*Go*." I heard the voice. Was it the Ashen Witch, or Deliverance? Did it matter? I fled.

I ran back through the tunnels, my crown of flowers still in place and the Hand of Glory slung around my neck, blood on my hands, hair wild. I imagined I looked like one of those medieval woodcuts of a vicious, vengeful witch.

I *felt* like a vicious, vengeful witch.

I mounted the stairs two at a time and sprinted toward the hospital wing. Breathing hard, I stopped and listened, trying to feel. The rumbles were gaining strength, the "little temblors" leading up to the Big One.

I followed the hospital signs to a dark, spooky stairway. Mounting the steps slowly, I was on guard, careful as I entered the hospital wing. Institutional-green paint peeled off the walls and ceiling; there were bars on the windows and doors. From outside came faint music and party sounds, combined now with howling winds.

Beyond a set of small offices were a series of cells and examination rooms. Most were empty, but one was furnished as it would have been during the prison days: Old-fashioned metal cabinets lined the walls, an ancient wicker wheelchair sat in one corner, a claw-foot bathtub in another. A gurney and two cots were simply made with wool blankets.

And Seth and Renee, holding hands, sat on one of the hospital beds as though perched upon a wretched throne.

Renee was still the plump, fiftyish woman with a sweet smile, though she showed remnants of two black eyes from the concussion she had sustained not so long ago; Seth was still abnormally beautiful, with eyes that reminded me of a glacier bay. I could feel their combined power pulsating, joining in the dreadful thrum of Alcatraz Island itself.

Together, they were the *coincidentia oppositorum*.

They had set up an elaborate altar on the nearby gurney, including a pyramid of cupcakes vibrating with the energy of their cursed ingredients. I imagined they included the salts of the lachrymatories Renee had been collecting; those salts, like my own, throbbed with the power of concentrated grief. There were several offerings of noxious food and wine, alongside the remains of a few small animals and a multitude of insects. A pair of thick, blue-rimmed glasses, smeared with blood, looked like the ones Kyle Cheney had worn.

On the second cot lay Forrest, his park ranger hat on the floor beside him. He appeared to be sleeping. I imagined he was drugged or gravely injured.

"*Lily*," said Seth. "Excellent. So nice to have you here with us."

"Yes, it's, um, great to be here," I said, trying to calm my breathing. I was still panting from the run and the adrenaline. "You don't mind if I make myself at home, do you?"

I whipped the backpack off my back, set it down, and crouched to take out the sulfur incense. I lit it and started to make a line on the floor with the Solomon's seal that I had harvested from my terrace garden and dressed with my own blood. A small cloth bundle contained the shards of the mirror I had dug up in my garden, the glass in which Sitri used to appear. I could feel it hum in recognition of the demon. It would help with the connection to him.

"You know you are the conduit," Seth said, "and now that you're here, nothing will stop the next step."

He gestured with his head, and I realized there was now a half circle of men standing behind me, blocking the only escape from the barred space.

"Now that you've felt it, now that you know. Sitri recognized you, you know, right from the start," said Seth in a seductive tone. "You will join us, and nothing will stop us. Just imagine how it will be."

"You can't stop it, Lily," cooed Renee. "The agreements have been sealed with sacrifice; the Big One is going to reshape the Bay Area, and we will reap the rewards of the urban renewal. We will reshape this place in our image."

"Yeah, about that," I said. "I'm not really into threesomes."

Except for the three sides of a triangle, I thought to myself. I walked as casually as I could across the room, dragging my foot behind me to make a line in the dust. It wasn't the best way to create the second leg of the triangle, but with sufficient power vested by me, it would do. I just prayed I had sufficient power. Even with the support of the magical allies behind me and both spirits within me, I still doubted my abilities. The strength of the combined magic in Seth and Renee's *coincidentia oppositorum* was like nothing I'd ever felt before; it was like a soaring brick wall.

"With the strength of my ancestors . . ." I began, but I was cut off by the deafening sound of the winds through Sitri's wings.

"Lilyyyyy . . ." Seth stood. He had grown larger, somehow. He was immense and threatening, and yet seductive. He was Sitri and yet not Sitri. *"You and I could rule everything we could see! Imagine! No more violence, no more war, just peace and love and understanding. . . ."*

His words were enticing, and somehow I believed him. It took all my strength to remind myself that he was a liar. Even now, even given all that I knew, I wanted to believe what he was saying, I wanted to accept what he had to offer. To reign without fear or consequence. No more self-doubt, no more second-guessing.

No wonder regular, unassuming humans fell prey so easily to demonic forces.

Ignoring his words, I swatted away the gnats and wasps he sent to pester me. I started to intone: *"With the strength of my ancestors, I am the power. I command you to show yourself . . . I do hereby license thee to return to thy proper place, without causing harm or danger unto man or beast, I compel thee!"*

Forrest moaned, breaking my concentration.

I glanced over to see Renee standing over him, a bejeweled athame in hand.

"You can save your friend's life, Lily," she said. "Just take his place. It's entirely up to you."

"Fine, I'll take his place," I said. If Sitri could lie, so could I. Tipping a small vial behind my back, I drew a line of cemetery dirt as I walked toward Forrest. As I approached the cot, I realized there wasn't quite enough dirt to close the triangle.

"You're *cheating*," Renee seethed. She lunged toward Forrest with the knife, but I jumped at her and shoved her violently to the ground. The men blocking the doorway rushed toward me, but I lowered my head and mumbled an incantation, feeling Deliverance's rage move through me. One after another they fell to the floor, writhing.

"With the strength of my ancestors . . . *I compel thee!*" I repeated the command.

Seth jumped up and began his own intonation, casting against me. He was strong, exuding energy and vitality, dominance and mastery. I felt my strength waning.

"*I know you by the name, Sitri, Bitru, or Set,*" I continued, pointing at him. "Sitri, the Twelfth Prince. With the strength of my ancestors, I am the power!"

Seth's head whipped around, and his neck seemed to contort.

"No!" I heard Renee's voice, like a whisper.

I had called on Sitri, I had spoken his name aloud. I had done my preparations, and I was not defenseless. I had performed the MoonWish spell, making a sacrifice of my own time and energy, not to mention the precious trousseau my mother had sewn for me.

I had garnered magical allies. I had even embraced Deliverance Corydon.

Seth was strong, but I was stronger. I just had to close that last leg of the triangle, and—

"And what about *now*?" Renee said. "What about your precious Aidan? What will you do to save *his* life?"

I looked up to see an unconscious Aidan had been

rolled in on the same gurney from the dungeon. As I looked, his eyes fluttered open to give me a glimpse of that astonishing periwinkle blue, then closed again.

"He'll be fine," said Seth, his voice gentle, persuasive. "I promise you, Lily. All you have to do is work with us as our conduit, and Aidan will be safe. *Everyone* will be saved. We'll see to it. We can make it happen—just think, if you work with us, you can curb our less noble impulses. Be part of the solution! I promise you, everyone will be saved if you—"

I lunged toward Aidan and placed my forehead to his, smelling the metallic tang of his blood. I felt a surge of energy, of pure power. In this moment, Aidan and I were our own *coincidentia oppositorum*; the two of *us* would be the ones to rule this city, this region, this magical domain.

The third side of the Solomon's Triangle magically closed around Seth. I was deafened by the screaming sound of the wind through Sitri's wings as he arose within the triangle, surging up, appearing far too huge to remain within the triangle. And yet he was trapped there, along with a horrified-looking Renee, holding her hands over her ears as she writhed on the ground, screaming "*No*! No no no!"

I repeated the words of the exorcism, over and over.

Sitri started to cackle, a horrible grating noise that reached down to my gut, but I could feel his strength weakening, while mine grew. I sensed the magic of Graciela and the other allies I knew were here on the island with us, backing me up. I even felt Oscar—whom I prayed was still safe in Bolinas—helping me open the portals. A flock of white butterflies appeared and began to ward off the stinging insects.

"*I do hereby license thee to return to thy proper*

place, without causing harm or danger unto man or beast, I compel thee!"

And then, with one final surge of fury, I cast Sitri back to the astral plane.

Nothing was left in the triangle but a pile of smoking ash stinking of sulfur, and a bloodied Renee.

The rumbling started again, stronger this time. Renee lifted her head and gave me a smile of pure evil.

"You see? You can't stop it. It's already been put into play. You had a chance to save it, but now? Say good-bye to your precious San Francisco."

The earth began to shake, and this time it was no small temblor. Medical trays clattered to the floor, a glass-fronted cabinet fell over and shattered on the cement floor. The walls creaked and groaned around us.

Sailor rushed into the room, lifted Aidan onto his shoulders in a firefighter's carry, and we ran to escape the building. The ground shook so that we careened from one wall of the hallway to the other. My shoulder smashed painfully against a fire alarm, and I paused to pull it just in case people didn't realize they needed to evacuate, immediately.

As we were about to turn the corner I glanced back to see the ceiling of the hospital wing crash down onto Renee, the altar of cupcakes, and Solomon's Triangle.

Sailor managed to carry Aidan to safety in time. We stumbled out into the foggy night to see the salts still sparkling over the island like so many fireworks. The lights formed a shape that had broadened and taken a conical aspect over the entire island.

The earth quaked harder, and things began to tumble. The metal water tower creaked, tilted, and finally fell over in a deafening crash. An exterior wall of the warden's house fell onto the courtyard below, narrowly missing several partygoers who screamed and ran, falling to the ground with the force of the movement of the earth. I tried to move but careened into Sailor, who had already set Aidan on the ground. Sailor embraced me and eased me down to the ground in the open courtyard, sheltering me with his body, even though we were away from anything that could fall on us. Still, I clung to him as the earth repeatedly fell away and surged up, jerked this way and that, tossing us like toothpicks in the back of a truck with no suspension, heading down the ruttiest of roads.

There was nothing more to be done.

If the spell worked, the earthquake would be limited to Alcatraz Island. All we could do now was wait and see.

After what seemed like an eternity, the earth quieted. The fog miraculously lifted, giving us a view of San Francisco. The skyscrapers still stood, the lights still twinkled, the traffic still moved. The Golden Gate Bridge still spanned the mouth of the bay, connecting San Francisco to Marin. Sausalito appeared just as it was.

The earthquake had hit Alcatraz, but not beyond. We had prevailed.

Several new craters had opened, revealing sections of the Spanish dungeon, now caved in. I wondered whether the group of chanting men had made it out. Fire broke out in the administration building, and the partygoers were crying and yelling, but most seemed to have emerged relatively unscathed. Alarms screamed and national park police swarmed over the courtyard and were checking the public areas of the cellblocks, in triage mode. I wondered what they would make of what they found in the hospital wing.

I spotted members of Graciela's coven already tending to the injured. Graciela herself came to lay hands upon Aidan, who had fallen back into unconsciousness.

Suddenly a murmuration of birds appeared overhead, swirling and swooping, returning to the island. They reminded me of the white butterflies sent by the woods folk, which first had appeared when I battled against Deliverance Corydon. But this time Deliverance had worked *with* me. I had managed to maintain control of her, and her fierce, unforgiving edge had helped.

I glanced at Sailor, feeling the delicate tenderness that came after a battle won, after danger faced and survived. The unspoken acknowledgment of something precious which had come far too close to being lost. An acute awareness of profound luck, of being touched by grace.

"Sure you want to go through with the handfasting?" I asked Sailor. "According to Aidan—and Seth and Renee—I'm something of a magical hot spot. Last chance to get out of it."

Cupping my head in his hands, ignoring the grime and the blood, Sailor bent his head and kissed me.

Chapter 28

Bronwyn, Maya, Lucille, Selena, my mother, Graciela, and half of her coven were gathered in Calypso's big living room. We were resplendent in our vintage clothing. The coven sisters wore their sparkly best; Bronwyn looked chic in her early 1970s Yves Saint Laurent trouser suit; Maya was charming in a brightly colored dress from the late '60s; Selena looked adorable in her blush rose ensemble.

Even though we were all wearing outfits from different eras, they somehow worked together. We had already done a photo shoot at the store, and for the past two hours Susan Rogers and the newspaper photographer had been following us around Calypso's house, snapping up a storm.

The rest of the wisewomen were outside, hovering over the food tables. Other friends were assembled near the fairy circle of redwoods at the edge of Calypso's verdant garden, drinking sangria and chatting. I snuck a peek out the window and saw that Renna and

Bronwyn's granddaughter, Imogen, were absorbed in intense discussion, laughing. Wendy and Starr and Wind Spirit, all from Bronwyn's coven, were dancing to a lively tune Eric was playing on the accordion, and every once in a while Patience burst out in song, a mournful, beautiful sound. Carlos watched her, a small smile lighting up his usually carefully guarded face. Conrad joined in the dancing, his face alight not with a drug-induced high but with the joy of friendship and music. Elena and Bethany sat, arm in arm, in the shade, quietly watching the festivities. Two dozen others— including several other friends and relatives of Sailor's—were enjoying the day as well.

It was time for the handfasting.

After the events of the past few weeks, I could hardly believe it.

Oscar ran in and out excitedly, dividing his time between our gathering and the folks outside near the food tables. He sported white frosting on his snout, and I hoped he hadn't snuck a bite of the wedding cake Iris, Calypso, and Caroline had stayed up all night baking and decorating.

He had been preening ever since he managed to negotiate a settlement with the woods folk to allow Sailor and me to have our handfasting in the redwood fairy circle.

Alcatraz was more than a little worse for wear, but that wasn't my main concern at the moment. In fact, a big part of me hoped that cursed island would go ahead and sink into the bay, living only in the fading memories of locals and those unfortunate enough to have resided there against their will, like Ray Perry. According to Carlos, the forensic anthropologist had used dental records to determine that the skeletal remains had, indeed, belonged to Perry; along with the allegations of abuse in his letters, the curators with the National Park Service were deciding how to present this newly discovered bit of Alcatraz history. Professor Guzmán had called to invite me to the next Indigenous People's Sunrise Gathering—he had heard what happened and decided it was time for him to go. It would be good to replace my last images of the place with something more positive, with togetherness and solidarity and recognition of the painful past that had brought us all to the place where we are, right in this moment.

Speaking of this moment, I had more pressing concerns, such as fitting into my wedding dress, a '20s-era champagne-toned slippery silk satin with a sweetheart neckline and asymmetrical skirts. My mother had worn this gown for her own wedding, and her mother and grandmother before her. I was crowned with the tiara my mother had won as Miss Tecla County; Bronwyn had garnished it with wildflowers.

"It fit before," I said, trying to suck in my stomach, slightly mortified. I supposed my recent indulgences in burgers and Tater Tots weren't helping the situation. You would think all the stress would melt away those pesky extra pounds, but that didn't seem to be the case.

"No worries," said Lucille, already approaching with pins in her mouth, despite the pincushion strapped to her wrist.

A few extra pounds be damned. I was feeling good. Great, as a matter of fact. Powerful. Ready to step into Aidan's shoes, magical satchel in hand, to take on the foes and the challenges. I had gone up against a *demon*, once again, and had prevailed. And after all this time, I had been completing my training with Graciela's coven. I felt like I was coming into my own.

As a last act before being shipped off to one of Graciela's colleagues in Michoacán to heal, Aidan had once again secured my lachrymatory, which had miraculously remained unbroken and somehow refilled with salts. Renee had been pulled from the rubble and, at least for now, appeared to have acknowledged how close she had come to death and recognized me as being in charge. Forrest had survived the quake as well and was still hospitalized but on the road to recovery. Unfortunately, Kyle Cheney had not been so lucky; the wealthy man had been found dead in the Spanish dungeon, yet another demonic sacrifice. Sitri had been sent back to his primordial dimension, though like any demon he could again be conjured to this plane. There was no end to human foolishness. If he returned, I could only hope I was strong enough to go up against him for the third time.

At least I was reconciled with Deliverance Corydon, at peace with the role she was playing inside of me. I needed her strength, and I would use it, with the backing of Graciela's coven and all the witchy women who had gone before me to provide balance and keep me on the right path.

Enough with the self-doubt. I was about to marry a wonderful man who would stand beside me and—despite what Aidan had warned a while ago—would serve to make me stronger, rather than diminish me.

I was ready to be the witch I was destined to be. Nothing was going to stop me now.

With a jolt, I came back to the conversation swirling around me.

"Is she . . . ?" Miss Agatha asked.

Graciela's hands were on my belly, a faraway look in her eyes.

A murmur arose and spread through the assembled women like wildfire.

"Is she *what*?" asked Maya.

"Anticipating," whispered Pepper.

"Oh, Lily!" exclaimed my mother.

"Anticipating *what*?" I insisted.

"*Nope*," Graciela declared loudly, with a chuckle. "Just a food baby."

I let out a long, relieved breath. I knew I—*we*—wanted children, I just wasn't sure we wanted them *yet*. I wouldn't mind enjoying our honeymoon first, for example—after a great deal of discussion, Sailor, Oscar, and I had decided to begin in Barcelona and then head to Florence and Paris. If we couldn't find Oscar's mother in one of those beautiful cities, we'd come up with a new game plan. Also, I wanted time to settle into my role as the godmother of the San Francisco Bay Area magical community—at least until Aidan had fully healed. According to what Rosa had read in her cards, Aidan would recover from his recent injuries but had a more difficult challenge to overcome: He had been hounded by a *vila* since he had killed a rival that threatened Calypso, many years ago, which was why his strength had been waning.

As Aidan had once told me, we magical folks might heal well, but we scar like every other human.

"*¿Lista?*" asked Graciela. "Ready, Lily?"

"*Sí*," I said, and this time I knew I was telling the truth. "Yes. Absolutely."

The druzy in my antique engagement ring glittered as I walked out into the sunshine. Eric played an evocative tune on the accordion; its ancient beat measured our steps toward the altar. Friends and family and coven sisters gathered around the redwood circle, where wisps of mist lingered despite the sunny day. Half a dozen butterflies flitted this way and that, making me feel as though we were ensconced in Snow White's enchanted forest. Maya, Selena, and Patience stood to one

side, and Conrad and Carlos on the other, with Oscar
in his piggy guise at their feet. True friends. *Family.*

I never could have imagined this day when I first had
arrived, so very alone and lonely, in San Francisco.

Bronwyn welcomed everyone, thanked the woods
folk for having us, and beamed as she invited the Lord
and Lady to step into the circle.

My mother and Graciela hugged me as I passed.

"Lily and Sailor, may your paths come together,"
said Bronwyn, "today and forevermore."

"*Path of thy path*," intoned the crowd.

I entered from the left; Sailor—wearing a crown of
wildflowers—did so from the right. Here in this magical fairy circle, surrounded by redwoods and loved
ones, butterflies flitting about, I lifted my face to the
beautiful man who had captivated and frustrated, delighted and annoyed, but most of all had enthralled me
from the very start.

"Heart of my heart," Sailor said, his voice gruff with
emotion.

"Breath of my breath," I replied, my own voice surprisingly steady.

"*Power of thy power*," replied the crowd.

Bronwyn gave a short speech about love and connection, the stars and the earth and the Lord and the
Lady of the forest. I barely registered the words, but I
felt the strong, primordial thrum of the earth beneath
my feet, the whispers of fragrant air upon my cheeks.
Sensed the loving vibrations of the witnesses surrounding us, and even felt the shining presence of the fairies.

"And now," Bronwyn said, her cheeks wet with
tears, "Sailor and Lily, place your hands together, and
hold them fast."

We stacked our hands: his, mine, his, mine.

"It is time to declare to your friends and family, to

the woods and to the desert, to the sky and to the earth, to yourselves and to the ancestors: Do you accept this handfasting?"

I looked into Sailor's dark eyes. He gave me a very slight, crooked smile.

"Vow of my vow," Sailor and I said in unison, our voices mingling and resonating, echoing through the forest:

"We do."

Author's Note

Alcatraz is a fascinating rock of an island, sitting as it does in the middle of the San Francisco Bay. It was never inhabited by the indigenous peoples of the bay, but was used as a military fort and prison by the Spanish, and later by the United States. It was converted to a federal prison in 1934, and occupied by the Indians of All Tribes from 1969 to 1971. Today Alcatraz is one of the US Park Service's most popular tourist attractions.

Though there are plenty of stories alleging the presence of ghosts out on Alcatraz Island, any stories about demonic sacrifices (or a demonic presence!) are purely the result of my imagination.

The character of Ray Perry was modeled after the prisoner Theodore Cole, who escaped with Ralph Roe on a very foggy day in December 1937 by sawing through iron bars and jumping into the frigid bay. They were presumed drowned.

My story of Cole Albright, who escaped the island by fabricating papier-mâché heads and constructing a boat out of raincoats, was based on the true story of brothers John and Clarence Anglin and their associate Frank Morris, who escaped Alcatraz in 1962 but were also presumed lost at sea. To learn more about their story, see: "Alcatraz Escape," at fbi.gov.

For more information about the history of Alcatraz, check out: "Alcatraz History," at alcatrazhistory.com; and "History Culture—Alcatraz Island," at nps.gov.

For more about the 1969–71 occupation of Alcatraz by the Indians of All Tribes, see:

"We Hold the Rock—Alcatraz Island," at nps.gov; and "1969 Occupation of Alcatraz," and "Alcatraz Proclamation," at nativevillage.org.

Bewitched and Betrothed is entirely a work of fiction.

Continue reading for an excerpt from
the latest book in Juliet Blackwell's
bestselling Haunted Home Renovation
mystery series,

A GHOSTLY LIGHT

Available now!

The tower reached high into a gray sky. A faint glow—dare I say a ghostly light?—seemed to emanate from the lighthouse's narrow windows. Probably just a trick of the light, the afternoon sun reflecting off curved stone walls.

Just looking up at the tower through the cracked bay window made me dizzy.

"I'm thinking of calling the inn 'Spirit of the Lighthouse.' Or maybe 'the Bay Light,'" said Alicia Withers as she checked an item off the list on her clipboard. Alicia was big on lists. And clipboards. "What do you think, Mel? Too simple?"

"I think you need to figure out your plumbing issues before you worry about the name," I replied. That's me, Mel Turner. General contractor and head of Turner Construction.

Also known as Killjoy.

Alicia and I stood in the central hallway of the former lighthouse keeper's home, a charming but dilapidated four-bedroom Victorian adjacent to the lighthouse tower. The structures had been built in 1871 on the small, rather unimaginatively named Lighthouse Island, located in the strait connecting the San Francisco and San Pablo bays. Not far away, the Richmond–San Rafael Bridge loomed, and barely visible to the southwest was the elegant new span that linked Oakland to Treasure Island and on to San Francisco. The nearest shoreline was Richmond, with San Rafael—and San Quentin prison—situated across the normally placid, though occasionally tempestuous bay waters.

It was a view to die for.

Lighthouse Island's foghorn and lamp had been staffed by full-time keepers and their assistants and families for decades, the flashing light and thunderous horn warning sea captains of the bay's surprisingly treacherous shallows and rocky shoals. But the humans had long since been replaced by less costly electronics, and the island's structures had fallen into disrepair.

The house itself had once been a beauty, and still boasted gingerbread trim and a cupola painted an appealing (but now peeling) creamy white. Also in the compound were a supply shed, the original foghorn building, and a huge cistern that collected rainwater for the keeper and his family on this otherwise dry rock. The only other structures on the island were the docks and lavatory, located in a small natural harbor to the east, which were still used occasionally by pleasure boats seeking refuge from sudden squalls—and by those interested in exploring Lighthouse Island, of course.

"I'm just saying," I continued. "There's a lot of dry rot to contend with before you start inviting guests to your Lighthouse Inn."

"Oh, *you*," Alicia said with a slight smile, which I answered with a big one.

I had known Alicia for quite a while before spying an iota of good cheer in her. She was still a serious, hardworking person but had relaxed a lot since I first met her on a historic restoration in Marin. We had bonded late one night over a shared love of potato chips and home renovation television shows. And then we quite literally kicked the butt of a murderer, which had definitely improved her attitude.

"I'm sure you know I haven't lost sight of the all-important infrastructure," continued Alicia. "But I need to register my domain and business names, so no, it's *not* too early to think about such things."

She whipped out a thick sheaf of lists and flowcharts and handed them over. I flipped through the papers. There were preliminary schedules for demolition and foundation work, electrical and plumbing and Internet installation, Sheetrock and mudding, overhauls of baths and kitchen, and installations of moldings and flooring and painting and light fixtures.

I raised my eyebrows. "Thanks, Alicia, but I usually work up the schedules with Stan, my office manager."

"I know you do, but I was up late one night, thinking about everything that had to be done, and figured I might as well get the paperwork started. I based these on your schedules for the job in Marin, you see? I can e-mail everything to Stan so you can rearrange it as you need, and plug in the actual dates and the like. I hope you don't think it was too presumptuous—I couldn't help myself. Ever since Ellis agreed to back me on this project, I can hardly *sleep* I'm so excited!"

Several months ago Alicia's boss, Ellis Elrich, had asked me to evaluate "a property" he was considering. It wasn't until he told me to meet him at the Point Moro Marina that I realized this would be no ordinary renovation: It was Lighthouse Island, and the Bay Light.

I—along with much of the population of the Bay Area—had watched over the years as the historic Victorian-era lighthouse descended into greater and greater decrepitude. Every time my family drove over the Richmond–San Rafael Bridge, my father would shake his head and grumble, "It's a damned shame." Mom would shush Dad for swearing in front of the children—"Little pitchers have big ears, Bill"—but craning her neck to watch the sad little island as it receded from view, she would add, "You're right, though. Someone really ought to save that place."

Never did I imagine that, decades later, *I'd* be that person.

But historic renovation was my business, and Alicia's boss was filthy rich. Which was a very good thing, because this lighthouse was in need of a serious infusion of cash. I already had in hand the architect's detailed blueprints, as well as the necessary permits and variances from the city and county, which had also promised to fast-track the code inspections. The Bay Light's renovation would be a highly unusual public-private partnership that cash-strapped local officials had agreed to in the interest of saving the historical structures. I was impressed by the city's eager participation but didn't ask too many questions. Ellis Elrich had a way of making things happen.

"So, here's what we're thinking," Alicia said, making a sweeping gesture around the former front parlor. "We take down this wall, combine the space with the smaller drawing room next door, and make this whole area the bar and restaurant."

"It's not very large," I pointed out, comparing the blueprints in my hand to the existing floor plan.

"It doesn't have to be. There will be at most ten overnight guests, so only five small tables are required for their meals—or we might just do one big table and serve everything family-style, I haven't decided yet. And visitors won't be that frequent—there aren't that many people who stop in at the yacht harbor, and even with our boat ferrying people over from the mainland, it will still take some planning to come to the island. It's not as though we have to take into account foot traffic! So I'm thinking we'll be at capacity with about twenty guests for drinks and dinner. But for those that make it, we'll be a gorgeous little oasis in the bay."

Alicia sighed with happiness.

I was pleased for my friend, but experienced enough to be a wee bit jaded. At this point in a renovation, most clients couldn't see past the stars in their eyes and the longing in their hearts. Starting a historic renovation was a lot like falling in love: a blissful period of soaring romantic hope and infatuation that lasted until the grueling realities of sawdust and noise and confusion and delays—not to mention mounting cost overruns and unwelcome discoveries in the walls—brought a person back to earth with a resounding thud.

"We'll keep the bare bones of the kitchen, but include updated fixtures and some expansion, of course. But we'll make the study and part of the pantry into a first-floor suite for the live-in manager—"

"That would be you?"

"Oh, I dearly hope so, if I can find a replacement to serve as Ellis's assistant. I can't leave him high and dry."

"But he wants this for you, right? Isn't that why he's bankrolling the project?"

Alicia blushed. "Yes, he does. Ellis is very . . ."

"Sweet," I said when she trailed off.

She nodded but avoided my eyes. Now that she had loosened up a little and was no longer the tight-lipped martinet I had first met, Alicia was charming. The scar

on her upper lip and another by one eye—relics of difficult times at the hands of her abusive (now-ex) husband—
only served to make her pretty face more interesting.
The wounds on her psyche were another matter altogether, but through therapy and a whole lot of emotional
hard work, Alicia had made great strides toward healing.

And now, unless I was mistaken, she had developed
a serious crush on Ellis Elrich, her boss and savior.
Ellis was a good guy, surprisingly down-to-earth for a
billionaire. Still, the situation seemed . . . complicated.

Oh, what tangled webs we weave.

"Anyway, that will leave three guest suites upstairs,
each with an attached bath. And one in the attic, awaiting renovation. Oh! Did I tell you? The attic is full of
old furniture, and there's a trunk of old books. There
are even the original keeper's logs!"

"Still? No one took them after all this time?"

"I suppose that's the advantage of being on an isolated island. Can you imagine? We can put some on
display to add to the historic maritime ambience!"

I smiled. "Of course we can. I can't wait to look
through everything. You know me and old books." Me
and old everything, actually.

"We might be able to create one more bedroom in
the foghorn building, unless we decide to turn that into
a separate office. The problem, though, is the noise."

"What noise?"

"The foghorn still sounds on foggy days. It's not the
original horn; it's an electronic version. But still, it's
loud."

"How loud?"

"*Really* loud."

"That could be a problem. So, what do you want to
do with the tower itself? The architect hasn't specified
anything here."

"That—" She stopped midsentence and her face lost all color.

"Alicia?" I glanced behind me, but didn't notice anything out of place. "What's wrong?"

"I thought I saw . . ."

"What?"

"Nothing," she said with a shake of her auburn hair.

I turned back to scan the scene, paying careful attention to my peripheral vision. Fervently hoping not to see a ghost. Or a body. Or both.

Because I tend to see things. Things that would make many people scream, run, or faint dead away. Not all the time, but often enough for it to make an impression. Owing to my profession, I spend a lot of time in historic structures, so it probably isn't surprising—for the open-minded, anyway—that I've been exposed to more than a few wandering souls who aren't clear on the veil between our worlds.

The fact that I trip over dead bodies, on the other hand, is . . . disturbing.

For me most of all, I should add.

Happily, in this moment I saw only the debris-filled main parlor of the old Keeper's House. My mind's eye began to imagine the space filled with vivacious guests sharing meals and stories, children holding cold hands up to the fire in the raised stone hearth, perhaps a calico cat lounging on the windowsill. The visitors warm and happy, safe from the chill winds blowing off the bay, the occasional mournful blast of the foghorn or flash of the lamp atop the tower adding to the dreamy atmosphere, to the sense that they were a world away from a major metropolitan area, rather than minutes. Alicia was right; with Ellis's deep pockets and Turner Construction's building skills, the inn could be magical. *Would* be magical.

Who's the romantic now, Mel Turner?

"Let's . . . I think we should go, Mel," Alicia said, her voice tight.

"What's wrong, Alicia? Are you okay?"

"I'm fine. It's just . . ." She walked toward the front entry, its charming beadboard paneling buckling in the center, and led the way out to the deep wraparound porch. Thick wooden boards had been laid over rotten sections of the porch floor to allow safe passage to the steps. "I think I'm just spooked."

"Did you see something . . . ghostly?" I asked, surprised. Alicia had never mentioned being sensitive to the supernatural.

"No, it's nothing like that. It's— Well, I'm a little jumpy. I received a letter not long ago."

"And?"

"It was from Thorn."

"Thorn?"

"Thorn Walker. He's . . . he was my husband. Thorn's my *ex*-husband."

"How did he find you? I thought you changed your name, covered your tracks."

"I did," Alicia said with a humorless laugh. "Ellis hired a lawyer and a skip tracer, and they helped me to create a new identity. But . . . it's all my fault. I haven't been as careful as I needed to be, and have let my guard down lately. When Ellis bought this island and announced plans to renovate the buildings and open an inn, I was photographed next to him. The photo appeared in several news outlets—it seems everyone loves stories about historic lighthouses! What was I thinking? Thorn's not stupid. I should know better than anyone that when he puts his mind to something, he can be quite determined."

"What did Ellis's security team suggest?"

She didn't answer.

"Alicia? Did you show Ellis the letter?"

She remained silent, heading down the shored-up porch steps, past an old NO TRESPASSING sign, and into a cement courtyard that had been built on a slight incline to funnel rainwater into the underground cistern. Back when these buildings were constructed, access to freshwater would have been a priority. Living on a virtually barren rock wasn't easy, and similar challenges had ultimately closed down Alcatraz, the famous federal penitentiary that still held pride of place on another island in the bay, much closer to San Francisco. When everything had to be brought in by supply boat, priorities shifted.

There would be no pizza delivery while on *this* job.

In fact, any and all construction supplies—lumber and concrete, nails and screws, equipment and tools— would have to be brought to the dock by boat and hoisted up with a winch.

The prospect was daunting, but exciting. I had been running Turner Construction for a few years now, and while I still enjoyed bringing historic San Francisco homes back from the brink, I had been itching for a new challenge. For something different.

And this was a *lighthouse*.

Still, one aspect of this renovation gave me pause: The lighthouse tower was several stories high, and ever since an altercation on the roof of a mansion high atop Pacific Heights, I had found myself dreading heights. Where once I wouldn't have given a second thought to scrambling up a tall ladder or hopping out an attic window to repair loose shingles, now the very idea made me quail. I told myself I was being silly, and that these feelings would dissipate as the memory of the attack faded. I would *not* let fear stop me.

If only my vertigo were subject to my stern general's voice.

Because this was a *lighthouse*. What was it about lighthouses that evoked such an aura of romance and mystery? Was it simply the idea of the keeper out here all alone, polishing the old lamps by day, keeping the fires burning at night, responsible for the lives of the equally lonely sailors passing by on the dark, vast waters?

"Alicia, I—"

My words were cut short when I realized she had frozen, a stricken look on her face.

A man stood in the greenery just past the edge of the courtyard. Smiling a smile that did not reach his eyes.

At least it isn't a ghost, was my first thought. My second: *Aw, crap. Is this Alicia's ex? And he tracked her here, to a secluded island?*

A ghost would have been a better bet.